BOYS OF BRAYSHAW HIGH

MEAGAN BRANDY

Copyright © 2018 Meagan Brandy

All rights reserved. This book, or any portion thereof, may not be reproduced or used in any manner whatsoever without the express written permission of the publisher, except for the use of brief quotations in a book review. This is a work of fiction. Names, characters, businesses, places, events, and incidents are either the products of the author's imagination or used in a fictitious manner. Any resemblance to actual persons, living or dead, or actual events is purely coincidental.

No copyright infringement intended. No claims have been made over songs and/or lyrics written. All credit goes to original owner.

Edited by: Ellie McLove, My Brother's Editor

Proofread by: Virginia Tesi Carey

Cover Designer: Jay Aheer, Simply Defined Art

Dedication

*To the one waiting for your time to fly, be strong.
The sun will come.*

Synopsis

"Girls like you aren't exactly welcomed at a place like this, so keep your head down and look the other way."

Those were the exact words of my social worker when she dropped me in my newest hellhole, a place for "troubled teens."

I didn't listen, and now I'm on their radar.

They expect me to play along in their games of hierarchy, to fall in line in the social order they've deemed me fit.

Too bad for them, I don't follow rules.

Too bad for me, they're determined to make sure I do.

Inconceivably attractive and treated like kings…these are the boys of Brayshaw High.

And I'm the girl who got in their way.

Chapter 1

Raven

Walk away.

Move your feet, exit this piece of shit cafeteria, and go get high. Chill out.

Yeah, that's what I'll do.

I keep walking, and I'm almost free and clear, almost through the door and away from the trouble I surely don't need but can't seem to escape.

But of course, nothing in my life is simple and just before my left foot joins my right, the final step through the open door, the bitch decides she's not done and runs her mouth. Again.

"Maybe if she wasn't such a slut her whore mom wouldn't have kicked her out for sleeping with her new man."

The laughter echoes, growing louder until it wraps around my throat like my mother's hands when in a fit, choking me until I lose focus.

I stop where I stand.

My eyes haze, rage winning over the calm bravado I attempted to force myself into.

"Trailer trash, bitch."

More laughs.

And there it is, the push.

Why do they always push?

Before anyone can stop me, not that there's anyone who would give a shit, I snatch the closest tray off the nearest table and in one swift move, one hard, full swing, smash it across the side of her face.

The cheap red plastic breaks against her head and screams ring around me.

Blood pours from the big mouthed bitch's forehead and she shrieks, her horrified gaze flying to mine. I wait until our stares connect, then quickly kick her chair sideways. Panic grows in her eyes as she crashes to the floor.

There's no time to escape, not that I have anywhere to go.

People scream, but no one dares to step closer to me. The lunch lady calls for help and everyone rushes to the side of the asshole on the floor because she's 'the victim.' Sure, I got physical first, but she started it. What did she expect?

If you can't take it, don't dish it.

And, yeah, the spat wasn't a lie, my mother is a whore. The dirtiest of dirty. Straight trailer trash at its finest, I'll admit it all day.

But she doesn't get to say it.

And I sure as shit couldn't let her get away with disrespecting me the way she did, publicly.

Not sure how she managed it, but my mother, the failure she is, taught me one thing - to keep my pride above all else.

Apparently, that's all a girl like me can control.

So, disrespect me not.

"My office! Now!" Principal Folk screeches. He doesn't call me by name, doesn't look my way, but why would he? Here I stand, caught red-handed - literally still holding half of the tray in my hand - as always.

He probably knew it was me the second someone called for help, before even walking in here.

I toss the tray to the floor and head straight to my home away from home - the cheap wooden chair with a ripped-up burgundy center that sits directly across from the principal's desk.

Monday was, as he warned, my "last strike," but yesterday I got caught smoking behind the gym, and I'm still here. Today's Thursday.

Wonder if he's in another forgiving mood?

I'm guessing not when forty-five minutes later he charges in and slams himself into the seat, glaring at me through his little nerd glasses.

His anger probably has something to do with the loud-mouthed girl – who very well may still be bleeding all over the stark white cafeteria floor – being his niece.

My fucking bad.

His eyes narrow as he judges me and my too-tight top and ripped-up jeans.

So, I smirk, taunt him a bit.

Because there's nothing this guy could say or do that could possibly be as fucked as every other day in my reality.

I grab the edge of the chair and lean forward. "Give it to me, Mr. Folk."

His eyes widen a fraction of an inch and as if he can't help himself, quickly cut to my top.

Men, they have no self-control.

Well, look at that, another thing learned from my mother.

"Clearly you don't want to be here, Ms. Carver. Every time I issue a warning you come back twice as hard."

When a slow grin stretches across my face, he clears his throat and looks away.

"This is your third high school in eighteen months and honestly, you're lucky you lasted here so long."

"Am I... Mr. Folk?" I drop back against the seat. "You sure you're not—"

"Stop." He glares before sighing. "This is serious. You've got the entire school's attention now. I can't make this go away."

I roll my eyes. "Just get on with it already. Where to next?"

He eyes me a moment before folding his hands and leaning forward against the desk. "I made a call."

My eyes slice to his.

"Your social worker—"

"I don't have a social worker."

"Apparently you do. She contacted me a few months back and—"

"Months?"

"Raven, listen—"

Right then, the secretary ushers in some dark-haired lady wearing slacks and a button-down. She reaches over the desk to shake the principal's hand.

"Mr. Folk, I'm Maria Vega."

"Ms. Vega, I appreciate you coming so quickly." He turns to me as she does the same.

"Hey there." She gives a fake hello, her roaming eyes and tight-lipped smile more curious than anything. "Do you mind if we talk for a bit?"

I don't bother speaking. No matter what I do or don't say here, she's already got me figured out as far as she's concerned.

"Mr. Folk and I have been in contact over the last semester. He's briefed me on your home situation and past issues, and at this time, we think it's best you be removed from your mother's care."

A laugh bubbles out of me before I can stop it. 'My mother's care' she says. Please.

The woman stares at me for a moment before sighing. She's quick to lose the sweet, caring woman act. "Look, I get it. You don't care what I have to say, fine. But we are removing you from your home. I'll take you to grab your things and then it's a day's trip to your new housing. It's a bit different, you being as old as you are, but we have a safe place for you."

"Yeah? They make cookies and tuck you in at bedtime? Or is that job left to the man there who creeps into the little girls' rooms at night?"

The woman's eyes narrow and Mr. Folk sighs. "Is there something you need to tell me, Ms. Carver?"

"Nothing you'd care about."

Her eyes jump to the small, fading cut below my left eye. "Try me."

"Pass." I hop to my feet, stepping close to her. "I'll be waiting out front."

"You'll wait right here if you want to avoid that girl's parents who are standing a few feet outside this door."

"You're mistaking me for someone who gives a shit." With that, I shove past the woman and walk toward the front of the student office, toward the loving mother and father of the little bitch who ran her mouth. I look from the girl to her parents, finding all their glares on me, their body language showing exactly what they think of me.

Dirty.

Used.

Worthless.

And they're not wrong.

Chapter 2

RAVEN

"You have got to be fucking kidding me," I mumble to myself as I scan the yard.

Ms. Vega shifts toward me. "You'll get used to it."

"What the fuck is this place?"

"This is the Bray house."

"Looks like Michael Myer's house."

She laughs lightly, then looks again, a frown taking over her face. "Well shit, it does. I never noticed before."

The porch is dipping at the center, likely from wood rot, the white paint chipping like large splinters. It's a perfect square, two small windows on each side of the door mirroring the two on the upper story, a creepy awning beneath them.

"It seems small, but it widens toward the back."

Small is a trailer with only enough space for a personal size fridge, one-sided sink, and two outlets for hot plates or a toaster oven.

"Anyway, this is a home for kids getting ready to age out,

and a few younger ones who had issues with standard style parenting. It's for the kids who are more ... challenging."

"So, there's a bunch of punks living here?"

"No." She shakes her head. "There's a bunch of punks at the high school. This place is cake compared."

"Sounds fantastic," I deadpan.

With a resigned sigh, Ms. Vega says, "Let's go."

She drags the duffle bag she loaned me behind her as she walks up, and I force my feet to follow.

When we showed up at my trailer the day before yesterday, my mother laughed and welcomed us inside. She sat there smoking a joint – of my weed – in front of the social worker and offered to help me pack. I thought for sure she'd flip, try to beat my ass or let her flavor of the week do it, as she always has when I'd get suspended or kicked out of places. She knew if social services stepped in it meant no more welfare for her, and no more welfare meant no more "free" cocaine – she'd have to put in extra time on her back without it. And that was a problem because the prime prostitute from Gateway Trailer park has expensive taste in powder.

I knew it wasn't because the worker was there, she didn't give a shit about that. Shit, she talked with the lady like she'd known her all her life – shitty and hateful with a nasty smile on her face. The worst that would happen if she was reported would be a few days in jail, and that meant nothing to her, they already knew her well. According to my mom, it's almost easier to score a sack in county than it is out here – and there, her trades are welcomed. She doesn't discriminate against gender. A woman's money is worth just the same, she'd say.

No, I knew by her nonchalant attitude she'd gotten herself a new supplier, be it a new dealer willing to take a trick for a trade or client who stuck, who knows.

Who fucking cares.

"You must be Ms. Vega?" I follow the voice to find an older

woman with deep wrinkles and dark frizzy hair. Her tone isn't exactly welcoming toward Ms. Vega, more quizzical if anything.

"Yes, ma'am." Ms. Vega hesitates for a second before stepping forward to shake the woman's hand. "Ms. Maybell, this is Raven Carver, seventeen, out of Stockton California."

When the woman turns my way, the roughness framing her eyes smooths.

"You had a small journey, huh, Raven?" the woman asks.

"It's Rae."

The woman smiles and if I didn't know any better, I'd say it looked genuine. And hell, maybe it is, another bastard's kid means more green in her pocket.

I'm aware I could be judging unfairly, but ... are there still people who choose to house fucked up rejects for fun?

"Rae." She smiles a little. "You'll be in room seven. There are two bunks per room, but the last two who were in there were sisters, so both left together last week. You'll have it to yourself for a bit, but that don't mean funny business will be any easier for you. Not sure if you were told, but this is a girls only home, the boys are there." She points across the lot to another white house about two court spaces away. "There's no drugs, no sex, no stealing, and absolutely no fighting amongst the other girls. Other than those few things, it's a nice deal here. Hurry on, put your things away and we'll get you to the high school. They're expecting you."

With a sigh, I make my way to the door, pausing when she calls out again.

"Oh, and Rae?"

I glance over my shoulder with an eyebrow raised.

"Behind the house is off-limits. You can go as far as the swing set there but beyond that, the dirt road? It's not for walking down. This whole front part, though, is yours to roam."

"Sure," I respond and face forward, taking in the mental institution style housing. Plain white walls with random couches against them make up the room, a single TV hanging high in one corner and bolted into the wall – preventing it from being easily stolen, I'm guessing. A card game left mid-play lays on the coffee table and an ashtray sits beside it.

"What the hell is this place?" I mumble to myself, jumping slightly when an unexpected voice answers.

"It's four walls to stuff the runaways and problem children 'til nobody is forced to pretend to care anymore." When I lock eyes with the girl, she decides that means I want the full breakdown and keeps talking. "All the kids here are shipped to the local high school as part of some poor kid program. It's quite a place. Nothing but a bunch of ritzy privileged assholes with the exception of us few fuck-ups, and a handful of others from the low-income housing track down the road. But it's not divided like you'd think, more one big system. You either tuck your tail and go about your day without being seen or heard, they allow that, or you're in the middle of it all and your every move is measured. Step outside the unit and you're treated like the trash they already see."

"Sounds like a nightmare."

She pops a shoulder. "It can be. Ran by some real gems."

"Ran by?"

"You think they'd let us all walk on their marble floors without having a leg up on us?" She shakes her head. "They're smarter than that. They offer us something we don't have back home, we stay in line. Tit for tat all the way."

"And people buy into that shit?"

This time her eyes skim my unhealthily thin frame from head to toe. "You'll understand soon enough." And then she's gone.

"Okay." I frown, and turn to my things, making quick work

of tossing my clothes into the dresser labeled with my name and walk back out front.

I toss my social worker – who popped out of fucking nowhere - her bag and she frowns.

"I told you to keep this."

"I don't want your pity shit."

"I have no pity."

"Then I don't want your shit."

"Get in the car, Raven," she tells me with an exasperated sigh.

Maybell walks toward me with a smile. "Ms. Vega was nice enough to send over everything I needed yesterday, so I was able to pre-register you. Go straight to the office when you get there, it's the first door on the left when you walk in. They'll give you your schedule."

With a nod, I walk away, but Maybell calls out again before I step into the car.

"There'll be a group of kids walking this way after school. A good lot are headed here if you'd like to join 'em. It's a little over a mile down the road, city bus works just fine too if you can pay for it. Stops right here." She points to the stop sitting at the edge of the sidewalk just in front of what she pointed out as the boys' home.

I don't respond and slam the door behind me.

Ms. Vega gets behind the wheel with a huff. "Look, Raven—"

"It's Rae."

"You need to make this work. I've talked to a few girls here. Maybell lets them do what they want if they follow the rules. At least here, you can still pretty much do as you please, be your bitchy little self and get away with it." She half laughs as she says it and my eyes cut her way. "You might think I'm just the lady to deposit you, but I'd like to think it will be better for you here. I don't expect you to be happy, but maybe you can move past the anger your mom left you in."

"What, do you double as a shrink or something?"

She grins and pulls away from the curb, driving the several blocks down to the high school. "No, but someone helped me once, and I'd like to help you the same."

"Don't waste your time, focus on the little ones that don't understand the lives they're living." I turn to look out the windshield. "I'm already ruined."

"Hey!" she snaps, and I turn to glare at her. "You're not ruined. Believe it or not, it only takes one person to make you see that. Give it time, you'll heal."

"Not interested. All I want is a life away from anyone who has ever heard my name, fucked my mom, or read my file." With that, I exit the car and I stare at my new reality – a giant brick building with a cement sign dead in the center.

With a shake of my head, I make my way up the steps, stopping when Ms. Vega shouts from behind me.

"This place isn't like most high schools, Raven. Things are a bit different here than they are where you come from."

Tension lines my stomach. "What are you trying to say?"

She eyes me a moment. "Girls like you aren't exactly welcomed at a place like this, so … keep your head down and look the other way."

A chuckle bubbles out of me. "Have you met me?"

"I'm serious," she stresses, unease lining her forehead.

"So am I."

"Do you want me to come in with you?"

"Goodbye, Ms. Vega."

With her eyes on the building behind me, she nods, gets back in her car and drives away.

I pause where I stand for a moment.

I could just take off now, but it'll do no good. I can't get a job on my own unless I follow in my mother's footsteps and at least staying here helps pass the time. Eighteen isn't too far off.

"Fuck it," I mumble and go to push through the door, but it bursts open before I can, and three guys strut out … three girls following close behind.

The guys don't see me as I shift to the side to avoid being hit by the metal door, but when the girls shuffle out, one of them makes it a point to bump me and she really shouldn't have done that.

I guess right off the bat is the best time to show her I'm not the one.

After she shoulder checks me, I spin and dart forward, grabbing a good full grip of hair in my hand. I go to pull her back, but the moment I do, a large hand wraps around my wrist.

"Now, now," a deep, teasing voice warns and my glare snaps over my shoulder to find a brown-haired guy who's about to catch an elbow to the jaw. "No need to act out. We make time for all those ready and willing."

"Get your hand off me unless you're ready and willing to get kicked in the dick."

"Ooh, sounds like a good time." He steps closer. "Now, let go, and show me what else that grip could do."

I tighten my fist and the girl cries out more.

The guy's smirk deepens, and before I can maneuver away, his hand is gripping my ass. "You wanna come? I can pull your hair too…" he whispers.

My body grows stiff against his and he barks out a mocking laugh as he lazily steps back.

My hand falls from the girl's hair and she grunts before storming back into the school. Probably to fix herself up, superficial as shit.

"Not as hard as you want to be, are you the new girl?" the

guy speaks, a hard edge to his tone as he falls in line with his boys, forming a tight arrow.

But he's not the one in the center.

I offer a shitty smile when really, I want to ram a pipe down his throat. "Guess not."

"Don't worry, baby, you're forgiven. I've got it on good word she's got no gag reflex."

I nod lightly. "So, she was perfect for you then?"

The guy tips his chin at my snide tone, but his friends make no move.

They're wearing sunglasses, so when I do glance from one to the next – purposefully avoiding looking them over any further – I can't read the look in their eyes, something I've taught myself to do when it comes to the male species.

I stand there until one of them, the tallest of the three, turns and heads for the parking lot, noting the asshole who put his hands on me is the one to get behind the wheel of a big ass, black, chromed-out SUV, not unlike the other flashy cars in the parking lot but by far the most alluring. There's something to be said about a sleek SUV with blackout windows. It demands your attention – likely why this dumbass drives it.

In my neighborhood, though, such a ride tells you where to score or which way to run – always the opposite direction is the answer. Unless you're my mother, of course. To her and her friends it's looking a lion in the eyes hoping it takes the bait – the fancier the ride, the bigger the payout.

I shake off the thought but catalog the vehicle in my mind.

Lifting my backpack over one shoulder, I prepare to step through the door for the first time, glancing up at the cement sign above before I do.

Welcome to Brayshaw High.

Chapter 3

Raven

The school officials didn't allow me into my normal classes today, making me sit through some mandatory behavior and 'how to avoid confrontation' videos instead. They even arranged for a cafeteria plate to be brought in – guess they read my file, too. I did, however, manage to sneak off for a couple minutes, pretending to be using the bathroom when really, I had to make a point.

The second the bell rings, summing up an uneventful day one, I'm out the door and soon the building. I continue past the groups beginning to form outside the school and make my way toward the Bray house, but before I can hook left, loud grunts and gasps fill the air.

I can't help myself and glance over my shoulder.

The assholes from this morning stare at the SUV while others whisper beside them, wide eyes and all.

The groper slams his door shut. "Who the fuck did this?!" he shouts, stepping forward, and funny thing, the entire crowd moves back with his advance. He scans the masses, instantly halting when his eyes land on me, and he surges forward, his buddies hot on his heels.

I stand in the same place, not moving an inch, not changing my demeanor in any way.

And I think it ticks him off, all of them actually, because all at once their brows draw in above the rim of their dark shades.

Unlike this morning, I let my eyes travel the length of the three and I'm not disappointed. If I had to guess based on this moment alone, I'd say they're the elite – sitting top tier on the pathetic little food chain high school demands.

Proof is in the way everyone cowers around us – too afraid to face full-on but too starving for gossip to walk away.

It's funny though, it's usually the preppy jocks with gelled up hair and button-ups who run around believing their dicks are magic, who run shit. The ones with clean and clear paths to ivy leagues and legacies, those are the type most choose to follow, hoping for an arm in.

But these three ... they're the exact opposite of a pretty boy.

The way they walk, all tall and assertive, forceful and dripping in swag, a physical dominance so solid it commands your attention – there's nothing clean cut or classic about them. And if my intuition is as on point as usual, then the line they walk is a little more than crooked.

They're rough around the edges, boys of power in the streets with something to prove.

Things to hide.

I know the type.

I also know what it feels like to be wrongly judged, so ...

"You better start running," comes from my left and I glance over to find a curly-haired girl eyeing the guys as they make their way to me, but I make no move.

They're in front of me in the next second.

"You keyed my fucking truck."

"Did I?" I tilt my head and his brows jump slightly before he rights them.

He growls and steps closer, but his buddy clamps a hand down on his shoulder, and little pup takes the master's order in stride.

The guy tips his chin and the herd around us starts to scatter like mice on a threat.

I roll my eyes and make a move to turn, but I'm flanked by the three before I can.

"You made a mistake, girl." This comes from the dirty-blond.

"I don't disagree. I mean, I'm here after all."

The tall, dark-haired one, the big, boss man, I've decided, says nothing, but his intensity has the hairs on the back of my neck standing to attention.

"You'll learn quick," the groper warns. "We don't put up with this type of shit—"

A humorless laugh escapes before I can stop it and all three of their pretty little heads tug back. I take a step closer. "I'll learn?" I mock, popping a brow like a brat. "Touch me like you did again, and I'll burn your sweet ride to the ground, you might even be in it when I do. Maybe then you'll learn." I flutter my eyelashes like a floozy, pulling on a man's upper hand by deeming the one that hangs between his legs. "A girl needs a little lead-up."

"Bitch—"

The big man raises a hand to cut him off and I swear his stare burns through those blackout lenses and into mine. Adrenaline bursts with each passing second, but annoyance wins and has my anger flaring.

Not a word is spoken, but as if all inner connected, the three turn and stomp away simultaneously. Groper, though, makes sure to throw a few glares over his shoulder.

"You're so screwed."

I spin to find the same girl standing off to the side, hidden by the shadow of the overgrown trees. "And you're nosy." I walk past her, but she catches up.

"Well, yeah but that's beside the point. And you're crazy if you think I was the only one watching. They all were."

"Then maybe you all need to find something better to do." As soon as I step off the school grounds, I stop to lean against a tree, pulling apart the worn rubber of my tattered pleather boots and slide my pre-roll out.

"Did you just pull a joint from the side of your shoe?"

"I wasn't sure if they'd search me or not." I shrug then wink. "And a blunt wouldn't fit."

She laughs and grabs it when I pass it her way.

When she stays at my side past the first two blocks, I skim her over from the faded black cargos and old band T-shirt. Not that it couldn't be what she'd chose to wear on her own, but something tells me she's headed where I am.

"You're Raven Carver, aren't you?"

I face forward with a frown.

"Sorry, but Maybell told me you were coming today. I didn't think you'd be at school already, but usually the only new kids who come are people from the home."

"Yeah, well, I wasn't exactly given an option so, here I am."

"Are you gonna run?"

I laugh lightly, shifting my eyes to hers. "Nah. I've got nowhere to be. Now I'm stuck in the system 'til I'm eighteen anyway, so fuck it. May as well cruise through."

"Those guys back there, you need to be careful. They're… not like most high schoolers. People around here listen to them, follow their every move."

So those are the guys the chick was referring to this morning.

"What you did today? They won't allow that without getting you back. They can't." She shakes her head.

"I keyed his Denali." I shrug. "Big fucking deal."

The girl stops, her eyes widening. "Yeah, you got that part right. It is a 'big fucking deal.' If they let some nobody, new girl like you – no offense – openly disrespect them like that, it'll threaten their entire system."

"System."

"Yeah. System. They're a big deal around here, and not just at the school. You either kneel at their feet or get stomped under them. They'll make sure you're shamed, one way or another."

We make our way up the dirt driveway. "He disrespected me first. If there's one thing I know about guys, it's if you let them walk all over you, they'll take pleasure in doing it."

The girl steps ahead, pulling open the screen door as she looks back at me. "If there's one thing I know about the boys of Brayshaw, it's that they'll destroy anything that threatens to mess up their vision. Watch out, Raven. Your little stunt today may have gotten the guys you're used to off your back, but for these guys? All you did was paint the mark brighter."

I raise a black brow and she scowls at me.

"A target from them means a target from all their followers," she spits.

Right. "Let me guess… you're a follower?"

This time it's her who pops an eyebrow. "Welcome to Brayshaw High."

I drop onto my mattress, plugging my earphones into the old MP3 player I stole from one of my mom's nightly visitors, slip my pocket knife into the waist of my sweats, and crank the music up as loud as it will go. I turn on my flashlight and set it beside my head and I lie there, staring at the door, hearing no sound but the angry cries of Halsey as she sings to me about the demons that are fighting their way out. Hours pass before my eyes give up on me and force themselves closed.

Chapter 4

RAVEN

SHE WAS RIGHT. THEY'RE ANGRY. ALL OF THEM.

So far, every person I've passed has met me with a glare, one they got right back from my end. Maybe it's the fact that I'm fresh for their critical little eyes or how my shoes have holes like my jeans and theirs are crisp as fuck with no fading, but I got a feeling it's a bit more than that since they're used to poor kids coming in and out of their school from the Bray houses.

Either way, there's a difference between nasty and needy and these clowns are needy as fuck. They need everyone to know where they stand as far as the new trash in class goes.

And it's cool. I'm used to the judgment; it makes my role a lot easier. It's when you try to change people's minds that things get tricky.

"Raven Carver," the teacher announces as she shushes me toward the back of the class and that's that.

Several hours and a few more non-stimulating classes pass before lunch rolls around.

I'm not much of an eater when munchies or sugar isn't involved so I pass on the free lunch options, grabbing an apple off the cart without being seen and drop down at the nearest empty table. I've only started to people watch when I'm jolted and my ass slams to the floor.

Laughter echoes around and rage has my vision blurring. I grind my teeth together to help regain focus.

Fucking karma.

I'm quick to my feet, spinning to glare at the girl who brazenly stands tall.

I've seen her around, noticed the way the girls gawk in envy while the guys drool in interest. She's the 'it girl,' the one with the harem behind her. Pretty brown hair and a prettier face. Tiny clothes and a fancy bag. Physically speaking, she's top shelf.

"You better watch yourself, trash. Mess with one of us again and see what happens." She looks left and my gaze follows, finding the girl who bumped into me yesterday hiding a few feet back, mixed in with the rest of her minions.

We've got the attention of the entire room now, and unlike they did with the guys where they were channeling their inner mutes, this time they openly stare and talk shit in the background.

Seems she doesn't warrant the same level of respect as they do, but she knows what she's doing. Get me on my ass for all the circles to see, deliver a drop the mic performance. This is her open and intended show of power.

No.

A slight chuckle escapes and then I'm shoving her against the wall before she has time to squeal, my forearm pressing into her neck.

I step closer, throwing her words right back. "Mess with me again ... and see what happens. I don't play poker, princess, I lay it all out upfront. You've got a problem? Put it on the table or find another to play your little game."

"Touch me and Mad—"

A whistle sounds and all the commotion stops instantly. Literally, not a single fucking sound heard in the second that follows, none but the slight screech of leather against freshly polished flooring. It's easy to pan multiple bodies growing closer with each step, and then they're stopping right behind me.

The empress begins squirming against my hold, pretending she hadn't already given up against my grip. I push tighter and her eyes squeeze shut.

"Let her go."

"I don't think I will," I respond, half looking over my shoulder.

Instantly, a male presence surrounds me and my muscles lock.

He's close. So close his hot breath creates a sheath of sweat at the base of my neck, tension growing in the pit of my stomach from the guy's nearness.

I attempt to shift away, but he only presses harder, his entire chest now flush to my back.

I battle to keep my breathing steady, force my body still, but he doesn't let up like I expected, like I had hoped, and survival mode starts to kick in. I'm seconds away from losing my shit and causing real problems for myself – or them, whatever.

The bitch in front of me smirks, thinking she's somehow won since the king's come to the rescue.

Doesn't she know how kings work?

A rescue means a price, a price turns into a favor, a favor becomes your moment of shame.

Shame is what ruins you.

But if he's the king coming to her rescue ... maybe she's his queen.

A large hand slides past my face to grip my wrist lodged against her throat, and with little to no effort, he pulls me from the girl, spinning me around to take her place as she falls to the side, coughing.

He does let her ass hit the floor so her pedestal must not be too high.

I fight to keep my eyes glued to the solid chest in front of me, but the pull is too strong, and my stare is forced to his. I inhale deeply as I take in the sight. With him right in front of me, I can't help but appreciate the view.

Sexy. Straight up, no denying.

Dark hair with darker eyebrows and caramel colored skin. Strong and solid, with eyes like ancient jade and the sharp edges of a monarch, he's damn near close to rugged perfection.

He glares.

Of course, it adds to the sex appeal, because why wouldn't it.

I'd roll my eyes at myself if I didn't think it would give my thoughts away.

"I'm diggin' this no glasses thing," I tease. "You should ditch 'em more often."

He's not amused, and those full lips of his part to speak. "You better learn quick what's allowed here or you'll be begging for a transfer before we're done."

"Not my style." I keep my eyes steady. "If I want it, I take it. If I want it … consider it mine."

Somehow, his frown seems to intensify as he crowds my space more, his giant ass body dwarfing mine. "This is our school, Snow. Our town. You'll pay for the little stunt you pulled with Royce's ride. And you'll learn. Around here?" One strong brow jacks up. "We make the rules and you follow … like a good little girl," he whispers all dirty like.

It's sexy, I'll give him that, but he's patronizing me, the shithead. Even still as he pointedly drops an impassive gaze to my chest, my tight black tank doing nothing to hide the rack my mother cursed me with.

I remember she was so proud when I finally "grew a pair," said no man could resist a build like mine. Sick bitch.

'Course they became a problem when her men suddenly wanted her daughter more.

The vein in his jaw ticks and I snap back.

"I hear you, big man," I whisper, and his porcelain eyes glide back to mine in slow motion. "You're strong, I'm weak. You're the king, and I'm the peasant. Anything else?"

His muscles flex against me, his pupils dilating, and silly me, it's enticing.

I almost want to push him further.

"Yo, Maddoc," his handsy friend calls. "Perkins is on his way."

"Maddoc" as he was called, purposely waits until the principal steps around the corner before moving back.

Mr. Perkins looks from me to the guys and rushes my way.

"Ms. Carver," he draws out. "Everything all right?"

"Everything is grand." I give a big, bogus smile.

He doesn't believe me but accepts the lie and turns to the trio.

"Boys," he spits. "Why don't you ... go get yourselves some food. I'll make sure Raven here finds what she needs."

There's a bit of a stare-off happening between the four, but it's the big man who speaks up first. "Why don't you kiss my ass and go back to your office where you belong?"

My eyes widen and I fight a grin, but these boys aren't smiling.

It's clear, they don't respect the man.

"I need to speak with my new student," he growls their way.

With cocky smirks in place, they back away with heads held

high, letting him and everyone else around know who's in charge.

I'm guessing they're all already aware, but regularity and all that.

With a swallow, the principal turns back to me. "I may have neglected to mention the trouble here."

"I can handle it."

"But you shouldn't have to." He steps closer, a glaze I'm far too familiar with lighting up his eyes. Some call it compassion, I call it manipulation. He wants me to think he's a caring, open door for me to seek out should I need a helping hand. A perception confirmed when he speaks again. "If you need anything, anything at all, or if they bother you … just let me know."

Yeah, I bet you'd be all too willing to meet my every need.

I don't bother hiding my eye roll or disgust as I step around, completely ignoring his fake fretfulness. I head for the doors leading outside, but before I can step through, my eyes catch a pair of olive ones openly studying me in the wings.

He holds my gaze, his full of a burning curiosity that only breaks when someone yanks the door open from the other side.

I don't look back, finally making my exit into the crisp air.

I run through what just happened, knowing one thing for sure. The principal's a sleaze. His words were simple, but his eyes were gelled with want.

I'm not surprised, most males in a power position are. I swear, there's no such thing as an honest, flat out 'good' man.

So quickly roped in by desire, they're willing to throw all morals out the window, and in the end, take what they want. I, for one, won't roll over.

And as far as these boys go, if they think I'm at their disposal, they've got another thing coming.

Maddoc

Raven, that's her name.

Ripped jeans and a tank that wouldn't fit my bicep, her figure's on full display. A full grip of tits, a nice fat ass, naturally earned, and hair that about teases the curve of her hips. It's as black as her name, a deep dark raven in color.

Her skin's a pale, milky white, lips a deep pink but free of fake color. And with eyes a stormy grey, she's more than a fucking wet dream – she's a porn star come to life.

She's like a real-life Snow White, only better. More hair to pull on.

Fucking trouble.

Like we know everything that happens around here, we knew she was coming, but I sure as fuck didn't expect a temptress in Timberlands.

I look to the side finding both Royce and Captain staring after her, and it's confirmed. She'll be a problem.

We don't have room for problems. Especially not the kind involving pussy.

She'll need to be put in check, and quick.

Chapter 5

Raven

Cops. Awesome.

Three of them, a K-9 unit even, line the curb nearest the female Bray house.

I can tell the others walking toward the house are on edge, and I get it.

Like them, my stomach muscles used to tighten at the sight of every black and white patrol car, but not anymore. After a while, it was almost a sense of reprieve, knowing they were likely there for my mom's patrons if not her herself. Usually meant a solid forty-eight hours without dread, but never more than that.

More times than not, I thought about running off. Technically, I could have at any moment and dear mother never would have looked, but I don't have an ID, let alone a license, and I need it to find work anywhere other than a strip club or dive bar. And with a mother who doesn't hold on to shit, I have no birth certificate or social security card to even attempt to get my own.

But it's whatever. One day, I'll turn and never look back. Seems far, but it'll be so worth it when it comes.

I shake off the pathetic poor me thoughts as I reach the porch, but before I can step up, Maybell rushes out the screen door.

She holds it open for the male officer as he fights to get a girl, can't remember her name, out the door. She kicks and flings herself around, forcing him to grip her upper arms as she has a fit.

Nira, the girl I walked here with that first day, steps up beside me.

"Not surprised. Knew she wouldn't last," she mutters.

"How long's she been here?"

"Couple weeks, but she ditches school all the time and someone said they saw her stealing Maybell's smokes. But she put hands on Victoria today, so she's good as gone."

"Victoria?"

"Do you even try to fit in here?"

I glare at her. "No. I don't. Why would I?"

She shakes her head, both our gazes following the officer as he attempts to get the girl in the back seat. "Victoria's my bunkmate. The bitchy blonde that walks around the house with a chip on her shoulder? Been here longer than any of us, supposedly."

"Oh."

She scoffs as she walks away. "At least pretend to be interested, Rae. We're better your friends than your enemies."

Friends. Right.

'Cause befriending a handful of girls who have problems the rest of the world pretends don't exist sounds like a good fucking time.

No. I can't afford fake friends and I'm not shopping for real ones, should those exist.

The fact of the matter is, in the end, the only way to walk away ... is to make sure there's nothing you're reluctant to leave behind.

To feel is to follow.

And I'll pave my path along no one's steps but my own.

"Come on now, Rae. Time for chores." Maybell waves me inside, but I glance at the girl in the back seat of the car, wondering what her story is, where she came from and what haunts her at night.

Then she flips me off so I do the same, rubbing my middle finger across my tongue with a smile and she grins back but turns away to try and hide it.

I laugh lightly and head inside.

Fucked up kids understand each other, it's the ones who pretend all's good who don't mix.

I toss my sweater on the bed and head for the chore list, finding I've got trash today. I make my way through the house, collecting the garbage and head out the back to the small dump bin, finding one of the guys in front of the boys' Bray house also headed straight for it.

"'Sup, newbie." He grins.

I look him up and down. Cute, but too skinny and not naturally. Clearly, the house isn't drug testing, boy's on one.

"Not a damn thing, on dump duty, same as you, it seems."

He nods, looking back to the house where a guy with long hair, maybe early thirties and built like a lineman taps his wrist and nods his chin.

"That your version of Maybell?"

"Yup, that's Keefer. He's cool."

"He know you're dabbling?"

The guy's eyes narrow on mine before he allows himself a

look, finally meeting my gaze again. "Probably." He shrugs. "I don't steal, and I don't cause trouble, so maybe he ignores it."

Right then a tall, trim but fit guy comes into view. He hops off the porch and lights a cigarette, not caring that the man in charge is barking at him from behind.

He nods at the guy in front of me, not sparing me a glance, then walks off.

"Be seeing ya, newbie."

As they walk away, I decide that's the guy – the one that didn't care to look my way – the connection to anything I might need.

I catalog him to memory and head back, but before I step onto the porch a black SUV identical to the one from school but free of key marks, pulls into the lot. It slows to a complete stop five-feet from me and my skin prickles beneath my sweater. Slowly but surely, it rolls forward again, disappearing down the dirt path at the back of the property line.

I stare after it a moment before it vanishes, leaving nothing but a cloud of dust behind.

"Boys of Brayshaw."

I glance to my left to find the blonde Nira was talking about also watching the dust as it falls back to the ground.

She doesn't say anything else, doesn't look my way, and then walks off.

I head back inside and finish up my task by adding bags to all the trashcans. Once the chores are done, the house sits down to eat, cleaning up after ourselves as we finish, which is when we're allowed more free time.

I start down the long hallway right as a couple girls start arguing.

"Fuck you! I didn't steal your shit!"

"I know you did, I saw you come out of my room!"

"Girls! Enough!" Maybell shouts, sliding between the two.

I squeeze behind the arguing duo, and slip into my room, dropping onto the mattress.

A mattress that doesn't belong to me in a room that's not really mine and a house that means nothing.

With a dozen complete and total strangers.

But this place is clean, the hot water works, lights are on, and there's food on the table every night.

It's definitely not the worst place to be.

Chapter 6

RAVEN

BASTARD.

I growl, swiping my hand down my arm as I glare at those fucking blackout windows I'm getting real tired of seeing. Finally, the back one rolls down and the handsy fucker, Royce, shows his face.

"How you doin', RaeRae?" he smirks, tracing the mud splatters that now cover half my body with his taunting stare.

What? He thinks dirt bothers me? Please.

I slept on the ground with nothing more than an old blanket and pillow at the reservoir for a week once when my mom refused to let go of one of her more ... persistent men.

Guess Royce is used to the prim and proper type who'd fret with a little grime against their skin. Weird if that's true, since visibly speaking he's the one who puts off more of an edge with his appearance what with the tattoo sneaking up his neck beneath his T-shirt and running down to meet his wrist, not to mention the small gauges in his ears. His brown hair matches his eyes and is a little wilder on top than theirs, but he keeps the sides trimmed nice. He's that tempting kind of sexy, but he knows it which is annoying.

Captain, I decided is the least 'in your face' type as far as being seen goes. He's just as captivating as the other two, but his attitude seems to be more subtle. He's the light eyed, blond of the three, cleaner cut with the pouty, jaded, model look. Perfectly side swiped hair and silky light skin. He's that silent killer type, seems soft, but he'll pounce when pushed.

"Better run on back and change. Wouldn't want anyone to call you names," Royce jokes.

"Don't you worry about me. Worry about why Captain is always sitting shotgun instead of you."

Royce's brows dip so low they practically meet in the center, but before he can pop off again, Maddoc reverses, positioning the truck so when he peels out this time, my entire face gets covered in mud.

Asshole.

But I hit a nerve with that one.

I consider it a win for me.

When I get to the school, I rush into the girl's locker room to inspect the damage done and find it's a lost cause, so I toss my dirty shit in my locker and wear the frumpy, completely wrinkled, loner uniform meant for gym – these are extras from the school left out for kids who don't have or forget their own and don't want to be knocked points for not dressing out.

The jokes start instantly.

"What happened, Rae? All night deal with the janitor? No time to go home and change? I mean, if you had a home to go to."

Original.

I ignore everyone all through the day until I get to PE and a picture-perfect face plants itself in front of mine. The queen bee, always fucking hovering somewhere.

"Nice outfit." She pops a hip, chewing on her gum like an obnoxious brat, her friends crowding around in anticipation of what, for sure, is to be a roasting session of sorts. Probably even pre-planned insults.

"How is it living at the Bray house with no men to share a bed with at night?" Her light eyes trail over my body in these used clothes. 'Course she's wearing a sports bra and spandex shorts – something that would never be allowed at any other school, I'm sure.

I don't entertain her and move to step past; she slides with me.

"What slum did you come from anyway?"

I sigh internally. "Your daddy finally let me out of the basement so long as I promised to play nice with others. But not as nice as I played with him, if you know what I mean." I wink and her face scrunches.

"Whatever." Her hands find her hips. "Stay away from the Brayshaws', and out of my way, and we won't have problems."

"What makes you think I want anything to do with them?"

Laughter echoes around us. Apparently, every girl in here is intrigued by what this bitch has to say to the new girl.

Even the males who are tucked away in the weight room at the back of the gym pause for the show. They can't possibly hear from there, but apparently, they're content in watching.

"Every girl wants to be a Bray girl." She rolls her eyes, tightening her high ponytail. "If you don't yet, you will, but I'm here to tell you to stick to those on your level."

"You saying the Brayshaws are on yours?" I make sure skepticism is heard when really, I couldn't care less.

"You saw how he defended me when you showed your trash."

"Is that what that was?"

Her almond-shaped eyes narrow and she steps closer to me.

"Keep your path from crossing with theirs. There's no room for another Bray girl."

When I roll my eyes, she smirks.

"I don't know why I'm wasting my time." She laughs, glancing around to make sure she's got the full attention of her cronies and those who wish to be but haven't yet found their in. "It's not like they'd ever stoop so low."

When my lips purse her eyes light up.

"I know all about you. Girl from the trailer park who uses her body to get what she wants. Tell me," she tips her head, "how much does a happy ending cost? Maybe I can help you out, bring in some clients and all that."

I should beat her ass, right here, right now.

"Ladies." The teacher comes around the corner, but neither of us break eye contact. "Chloe! Raven!" she booms and it's Chloe – as she called her - who shifts first, a fake smile in place. "Yes?"

She looks between the two of us with a glare. "Let's go."

Chloe flips her hair over her shoulder and skips away, but my feet refuse to move as I glare after her.

Someone told her – maybe the entire school – about my mom.

And when my eyes are pulled right and met with an icy emerald stare that pointedly holds mine before looking away, I know exactly who's to blame.

I have to face the fact there's nothing I can do to erase everything I come from, at least not until I escape myself.

I need to let off some steam.

I'VE BEEN HANGING AROUND THE PORCH FOR A FEW DAYS WITH my eyes locked on the boys' home, waiting for the guy from the other day to show his face. Finally, two days later, the timing is right, and he appears.

He jumps off the porch, bringing a cigarette to his lips as he props himself against the side of the house.

His eyes meet mine right as I stand, and in the same damn second, the screen door opens and Maybell walks out pretending she's interested in conversation.

She not-so-casually steps right in my view with a smile. "How you doin', Rae?"

I suppress a smile. If it was anyone else, I'd walk away, but Maybell's proving to be all right. She's real chill and doesn't pry into shit, like the social worker did instantly.

"I'm good."

She nods, taking a drink of her coffee as she looks out across the road. "Waiting 'til the last second to head on out, I see. Any trouble at the school I should know about?" she asks, taking a moment to look my way. "Anybody bothering you?"

The curious tone used when she asks makes me think there's a specific person – or three – in mind. But if she wants to know something, she'll need to be bold enough to ask.

"Nope," I answer, and she scoffs, but a small smile plays at her lips.

"You know..." She trails off. "I think you could fit in a place like this."

"Not like I have a choice, but even if I did, I don't care to fit."

"I'm not talking about the group home, child." She speaks low like she doesn't want anyone else to hear. She finally looks my way again. "I'm talking about here, in this town."

She doesn't wait for a response but walks back inside. I have a feeling she knows I'd do the opposite of whatever it is she might have said next. Not that I had a response for her randomness.

And, gee look at that, right when she does, the guy I was waiting for is hopping into a busted ass car at the curb.

With a resigned sigh, I step off the porch and head for school, deciding to track the guy down there instead.

I spend the better part of lunch hour roaming the outskirts of the campus, trying to figure out where the outsiders – the students who make it a point to separate themselves from the democracy that overtakes the school – hide out.

I finally spot him, though, posted under the bleachers against a cement beam. He's got dark circles under his eyes, a cut over his lip with a nice little lip ring through it, smoking a cigarette without a damn care.

"Hey."

He lazily spares me a glance. "Don't ask. I don't got shit for you to bum. This is my last one."

"No it's not, but good thing for you, I'm not the bumming type, and I prefer the green."

His bored stare comes back to mine.

"I'm looking for some trouble."

He scoffs and shakes his head.

"Check it out." I level him with a glower. "I know a solid punk when I see one. I don't need anything from you but a number or an in. Whichever you got and I know you've got at least one."

He looks me over.

Yeah, I'm skinny, but I'm not scrawny. I've got natural muscles made from natural things like pull-ups on broken metal fences and tire flipping in the junkyards.

What can I say, anything to keep from having to hear the moans coming from the room my mom and I once shared as I slept on the couch ten feet away in our single wide.

"Heard you caused trouble for the Brays."

"No more than they caused me, if we're being real."

"They don't like being challenged."

"You sure?" I tease.

He cracks a small grin before it disappears. "All right, maybe they do."

"I think they thrive on it."

"Still. They can make surviving real hard for people like us if we push and you're the focus lately."

"How would you know? You spend your days hiding out here."

"I don't hide anywhere." He glares. "And I have eyes and ears all around. The guys are pissed, girls are panicked. It's bad for business."

I shrug. "Yeah well, seems my being dropped here was real inconvenient to them and theirs. Not my problem and nothing I can do about it."

He scoffs with a nod, taking a long drag before facing me as he blows it out.

"What's your name?" I ask him.

"Bass."

"Well, Bass." No way that's his real name, but I don't care. "Will you hook me up or not?"

"Tell me, Raven Carver." He pulls a fresh pack of smokes from his jacket and offers me one. "What kind of trouble you lookin' for?"

I can't help but grin.

I knew it.

Chapter 7

RAVEN

THEY'RE BALLERS.

I should have known they were. All the rough and rugged, swagged out guys are - at least the ones from my neighborhood.

My eyes trail over the big man, Maddoc, with those seriously badass eyes as he dribbles like a pro, then makes a quick crossover, cutting past his buddy with ease. He jumps, making the basket with ease.

"Oooo. That footwork, son," Royce shouts with a laugh.

Maddoc throws the ball at Royce's head and turns to the other one.

"Why you keep letting me cross you?"

Captain shakes his head. "That's all you, man. I wish I could stop your ass."

"Don't bullshit me, Cap."

"I'm not. Maybe if I could guard you, I wouldn't have to

trip on coach benchin' me to start Clemmons when season begins. My focus is off lately and I don't see it coming back anytime soon."

"You got a lot of shit going on, man, but you'll be good when season hits, like always. And he won't," Maddoc tells him.

Captain shakes his head unbelieving and Maddoc rushes him. Gripping the back of his neck, he pulls his forehead to his in a brotherly way. "He will not fucking bench you. You're starting."

My gaze flicks to Royce as he makes his way to them. He clamps a hand on Captain's shoulder. "We got you, bro. We're taking state this year."

Captain nods.

And I'm a little taken back as I witness the silent promise made to one another that they'll reach their goals, whatever they are, together.

It's pretty fuckin' rad.

Three boys choosing to play ball at this ghetto ass, run down park when I know they can play somewhere nicer if they wanted, like in the school gym or on the outside courts there. Parentless punks if the rumors they live alone are true, finding their own little tribe in each other. Something worth fighting for.

I bet it feels good.

Turning away, I slink back against the tree and pull out my last official joint, light it and put it between my lips. Dropping my head onto the old Sycamore, I get one good hit, and then it's snatched from my hands and dropped before me.

"What the—"

"Don't talk," Maddoc's growl cuts me off, his face a blank bill, giving me nothing. "What the hell do you think you're doing?"

My brows lift and I gesture to the joint under his foot, fucking ruined. "Smoking." Obviously.

"This court is off-limits to you."

A laugh bubbles out of me and his frown deepens, his buddies sauntering over to join our little party. "This is a public park."

"Do you see anyone else out here?" His glare drops to the cut under my eye before snapping back to mine.

Now that I glance around, I don't. Not a soul but the four of us.

"Look, I couldn't care less about your little game. I can't smoke at the Bray house, I can't smoke at the school. Every fucking time I try to walk around the back of the property the staff lady flips out and says I can't go back there. That or some scavenger tries to come with me. I don't like people. I don't like sharing, and I don't want to be bothered, so go back to your game and I'll reroll what's still smokable. How's that sound?"

Royce lets out a quick chuckle but covers it by clearing his throat and turning away when, big man here, cuts him a glare. Captain, however, frowns my way and of course, Maddoc isn't impressed.

He bends until his pretty little face is level with mine. He moves his foot and looks to the joint then me.

I eye him for a moment, then when it's clear he's about to snatch it up I make a grab for it, but he's quicker and my hand hits nothing but dirt.

I push to my feet, shoving at his chest before stepping against him, and his features tighten. He stands stiff as a statue, peering down at the girl from the gutter much dirtier than him.

"You want in rotation, big man? Cool. But you're not walking off with that."

He closes his fist around it, those light eyes of his daring me to make a move.

And I would have already, if I thought there was one that

would work on a guy like him. Big and bold, fearless by nature and loyal by choice. A man undeterred by a female's body.

Rare as fuck.

Behind us, a car door slams and our attention is pulled.

"Fuck man, here we go," Royce whispers and Maddoc's muscles go stiff.

As the officer approaches, Maddoc's jaw clenches tighter and tighter, his hand twitching slightly.

My joint.

Wait, he's worried about being caught with it?

I quickly glance at all three boys, finding the same thunderous expressions etched across their faces, and my brows pull in. They're not concerned, they're maddened.

But why?

A low rumble leaves Maddoc and I refocus.

Sliding to the left, I tuck my body behind his large one. Not sure why, but I lightly tap the edge of his knuckle and his eyes flash to mine. There's no time for him to decide, but still, he holds his fist tight.

"Open," I hiss. A small pinch develops between his brows, but finally, his grip relaxes enough for me to grab the smashed up joint right as the officer steps up and we're all forced to face him.

"Well, well. If it isn't the last standing Brayshaws. Maddoc, Captain, Royce, staying out of trouble I hope?" he asks before his eyes slide to mine. "And a new little friend." The man steps closer, the curiosity he doesn't hide putting me on edge. "Don't believe I've seen you around yet Miss…"

He shakes his head when I only stare.

He turns to Maddoc and Maddoc's eyes cut to mine as he steps back. Spreading his arms out wide, his fists open so his fingers are pointing straight out. He licks his lips and drops his head back a bit in a lazy, carefree motion.

Clearly, this happens all the time. It's bullshit, but it tells me they must be on probation or something– searchable at any time. Guy's technically just doing his job.

The officer laughs at my frown as he searches Maddoc. "Soon as I learn who you are, I might need to search you just the same."

"She's ours to worry about, Graven. Nothing for you to learn," Royce grits and the officer chuckles, patting Maddoc in the back to let him know he's done.

Maddoc shakes him off and shifts to stand beside Royce, which happens to leave me on the other side of him.

"Take care boys. Be seeing ya." He eyes me a moment then turns for his car, gets in and drives away.

Captain lets out a low whistle while Maddoc's flashes on me.

"You almost got me caught up!"

My head pulls back.

Is he for real?

"No ... you almost got you caught up. Had you not tried to steal my shit; I wouldn't have had to get it back."

"Maybe you should stay out of our damn way."

"Maybe you should stop acting like I'm in your way!"

A deep growl fights its way up his throat, but he swallows it, the corded muscles of his neck throbbing as he does.

The three turn back to the courts, picking up their belongings before heading back to Captain's truck – seems they have three identical Denali's. They slide in, but Royce pauses, glancing my way briefly before he too climbs inside.

And then it's just me. Like always.

But that's how I like it.

Being by myself means I don't have to worry about other people, don't have to stop and think about how what I do will affect anyone else. It makes things a helluva lot easier.

Those guys are lucky I wanted my stuff back or their lovely leader would have earned himself a shiny new set of bracelets.

Now they probably think I was trying to help them out, 'fall in line' as they say, but that's not why I did it.

I did it for me.

I mean, why else would I?

Maddoc

"What do we do about the girl?" Cap questions and I grit my teeth, moving the icepack from one knee to the next.

"Her name's Raven," Royce tosses over his shoulder.

"I know her fucking name. And I don't know yet," I answer and Captain nods, falling beside me on the old sofa.

"There's something about her. She's not like the others." Royce pulls up a chair, flipping it around to sit in front of us. "She's—"

"Fine," Captain cuts him, making him laugh.

"Damn fine and feisty and—"

"A problem." I look between the two. "She's a fucking problem."

Royce glances off while Captain licks his lips. "What kind of problem, brother?"

"The kind you need to stay away from." I glare.

They fight it hard, then both start laughing like dicks.

I pop up, tossing my icepack at Royce who tosses it at Captain, then head for my room, done with this fucking day.

The assholes laugh harder.

But Royce is right, and I think Captain knew what he was getting at before they started fucking with me.

Other than the obvious banging body, Raven's got that 'fuck you and your world' attitude - something we're not used to. It only adds to her appeal.

She's sexy, likes to argue, and breaks the mold we've set.

But it's more than that. There's something about her that screams at something deep inside me, only I have no idea what. She's almost a mystery, one I need to unravel ... with my teeth.

Like I said, she's trouble.

Problem is, I like the taste of trouble.

Chapter 8

Raven

"Get up, let's go."

I lift my eyes to the girl in front of me. I forget her damn name again but don't bother asking. "And where is it you think I'll be going?"

"Maybell goes to bingo and has a few the first Saturday of the month, you know, after payday. She won't check beds tonight."

"So lemme guess ... you're going out?"

She sneers. "We are going out. No way are we letting you stay here to snitch us out. Let's go."

I slowly stand, dusting off the back of my sweats. "First of all, don't imply I'm a snitch – if it doesn't affect me, I don't give a shit. And second, I do what the fuck I want, not what I'm told."

The girl takes a half a step toward me but pauses when Nira calls out behind her.

"Back off, Victoria."

Oh right, that was her name.

Nira walks over. "Just come to the party, Rae. You don't have a damn thing better to do."

"True, but now I wanna stay to spite Victoria, here."

When Victoria's eyes narrow farther, my mouth tips up in a grin.

"You're gonna need someone to buy from when your stash runs out, right?"

My eyes cut back to Nira and she smirks. Little does she know, Bass could help me out with that. Not directly, but still.

"Come on, girl. There'll be plenty of wannabe dealers there happy to skimp you on a sack. Weed's not as good here as you're probably used to, but it'll serve its purpose."

I laugh lightly, knowing she's right about that. The Valley grows the good shit.

I look to Victoria. "Guess you'll be getting your way tonight."

Her eyes rake over my outfit and her pointy nose scrunches. "Maybe you should change."

"Maybe you should fuck off."

With a huff, she stomps toward the curb and looks down the street.

I turn back to Nira.

"Victoria's boyfriend is driving us tonight, so don't start shit by flirting with him, we don't need added problems and he won't cheat on her."

Suspicion has me frowning.

When Nira glances off, I let out a humorless laugh. "You read my file."

She considers lying but stands taller instead. "We read all the new girls' files. We deserve to know about people we're forced to live with."

"So you gathered I'm a whore?"

"You're the daughter of one," she throws out unapologetically. "I know firsthand our parents' problems are quick to become ours."

I don't say anything because there's no point. Nothing I say would matter.

If she lived half the life I did, the only thing we can trust is what we see with our own eyes.

The words of others mean jack.

Promises are a way of ending an unwanted conversation.

And lies make our world go round.

"You good in what you have on? 'Cause her guy will be here in a few minutes."

I look down at my joggers and black long sleeve. "Kinda party we talkin'?"

She grins. "House party for spoiled assholes. Huge, flaunty house and hoes galore. You think the jerks at our school come off privileged? These people are so flaunty they could give Beverly Hills a run for their money."

"Yeah, I'll be right back," I tell her and head for the house.

Last thing I want is to draw attention to myself and if these people are as flashy as she's letting on, then they'll pick me and my baggy sweats out in the crowd in an instant. At least with pants, I can shoot for invisible.

I walk past the girls playing around in the living room and make my way to my room, pulling out a pair of jeans and a white tank that hits just above my stomach. I grab my grey and black flannel and throw it over, stuff some cash in my back pocket, my pocket knife in my front, and head out the door.

And speaking of cash, I'm gonna need to talk with Bass again before I get too low.

Right when I reach the girls, Victoria's boyfriend pulls up – a guy I recognize from school.

"Hey, baby," he greets her and gives us a small wave.

She pulls the seat forward in his ancient, two-door and we silently climb into the back.

I ignore the conversation on the way over, quietly considering what I'm willing to spend on what's probably shitty weed in the first place while I note the street names the entire way over – never know when you might need to find your own way back. Before I realize it, we're pulling behind a pile of cars on a huge court.

"Damn."

Nira nods and climbs out ahead of me.

I look from the group of people on the lawn to the ones walking up a driveway the size of two basketball courts.

We get halfway up the driveway when Victoria turns to me with her freaky, narrowed stink eyes. "Don't mention being from Brayshaw."

"Why not?"

"Because I said," she snaps before stomping off, her man trailing behind her and I can't help but laugh.

Nira shakes her head, at Victoria or me, I don't know or care, and veers left.

I look over to see the other girls from the group home gathered near the porch, beers in hand, but I don't join. Instead, I make my way through the open garage and into the giant ass house.

Music blares from all around. Clearly, there's some badass sound system set up in the walls – the bass surrounds you.

Dozens upon dozens of teenagers are scattered around, dancing, drinking, and laughing with their friends.

I'm knocked to the side as I squeeze past a dancing couple, and the girl spins to glare as if she didn't just bump into me, but before she can pop off, the guy pulls her back in.

I make my way around the corner to the open kitchen where a group of guys are playing a card game at the table, cigars hanging from most of their mouths.

The blond one in the center catches my eye and winks before dropping his cards on the table, apparently winning his hand if the others' groans tell me anything. He must consider me impressed because a smirk is thrown my way next.

I offer a wink and continue past, taking it upon myself to grab a water bottle from the ice bucket on the counter.

As I spin back around, blondie steps in front of me. "And who might you be, sweetness?"

"A figment of your imagination." I grin, attempting to side-step him, but he slides with me.

"My imagination has always been damn good to me," he teases.

"I bet." I laugh lightly. "I'd also bet you don't have to use it all too often." I purposely let my eyes graze over his physique – he's firm in all the right places. "Or do the girls not fall at the man of the house's feet?" I throw out my guess and he smiles, telling me without words I'm right.

"Well, sweetness, you're still standing so I must be off my game tonight." He crosses his arms, smirking down at me. "Or maybe your ball's in the other court." His eyes drop to my chest, pausing for a slight second before quickly traveling over my outfit.

I pop a careless shoulder and step around him, spinning to walk backward as he turns to face me. "Maybe. Guess you'll never know."

"Never say never, new girl."

A crease lines my forehead, and his chin lifts an inch.

When I say nothing, taking another step away, he takes one closer.

"You a Bray girl?"

"I'm a temporary fixture."

"You all are."

Now he's pissing me off. "If you're asking whether I go to Brayshaw, the answer is an unfortunate yes."

He eyes me a moment. "That's not at all what I'm asking."

"You should work on being more direct, you know, having

some balls. I'm out." I spin and walk away and surprisingly, he lets me.

I decide to be a loner and witness the shenanigans from afar, so I take up shop against the cast iron fence lining the outer left edges of the backyard.

It's chilly out so I'm guessing the pool must be heated, that or the people swimming in it are too buzzed to notice.

"Are you poppin' a squat?"

I whip my head to the left, finding another girl from the group home making her way toward me with slow steps. "Am I pissing right here on the grass with all these people around?"

"Hey, whatever works," she jokes. "There's likely a couple fucking in the shower by now, so I can get why someone would rather piss in the grass."

I laugh, turning my focus back to the partiers, and the girl drops down beside me.

"This place is ridiculous," she mutters, shooting for annoyed but the envy is easily heard.

I glance around, and it's easy to understand why she'd feel that way. Shit, the ugly ass stone statues scattered across the yard must cost more than every unit in my mom's trailer park put together.

I turn to her. "Have you never been here?"

"Not this exact house, no, but plenty others just like it. Seeing how these assholes live and knowing where I'm sleeping at the end of the night, makes me kinda sick."

I scoff. "What's your story?"

"Mom left when I was two, Daddy liked his beer better than his baby."

I nod. "So, you a drunk too then?"

Her head jerks back and she gets a little loud. "Excuse me?"

"Clearly you don't like being judged." I raise an eyebrow.

"So why are you summing up these people because they have money and you don't? Don't be a hypocrite."

"You're a real bitch, you know that?" She glares, but it quickly turns into a grin.

"So I'm told." I laugh lightly. "And I'm guilty of it too most of the time."

"We all are," she responds, and I nod.

"I saw you talking to that guy in the house."

When I turn to look at her, she squints.

"You know the Brayshaws hate them, right?"

"No, but he acted weird, like he knew I was from the other side of town, and Victoria had a fit telling me not to talk about going to school there, so I figured there was bad blood there or something."

"Oh, there is. The Brayshaws would flip if they knew we were here, but these guys never seem to care when people like us, the ones on the outside of the inner circle, hang around as long as we lay low. Honestly, I think the one you were talking to likes when we come to these things, even though he ignores us completely."

"Why do you say that?"

She shrugs. "You know how people work. Gives him a bigger sense of power to know Brays are 'defying' their masters." She mocks with a laugh. "Anyway, yeah. They're rivals, have been for years I guess, schools and families. I heard every year the Brayshaws beat them out by a mile in basketball, but for some reason, they never bring home the championship title."

"They choke in the finals?" I draw out unbelieving.

There's no fucking way, not these boys.

"I don't know. There are rumors Graven sabotaged them each year, but the Brays don't speak about it. If something was done to ruin things, they handle that shit quietly. I heard after losing Sophomore season finals, they even disappeared for a few weeks. Nobody knows why, and nobody dared to ask."

My eyes drop to the grass in thought. Graven. That was what Royce called the cop who searched Maddoc on the courts.

"So wait ... this is a Graven party?"

"Yep, Graven Prep."

Huh.

I decide to keep the questions running through my mind to myself because what business is it of mine? And who the hell knows if what she's saying holds any truth.

"What's your name again?"

She opens her mouth to tell me, but we're cut off.

"Vienna, Raven!" We both jerk our heads toward Nira when she whisper-yells from the side fence, her eyes wide. "Hurry! We gotta go!"

"Shit," the girl beside me, Vienna I guess it is, hisses in a panic and hops up, jogging Nira's way. "Come on!"

I'm slower to stand, and right as I do, shouting begins, crowds of people forming a thick cluster beside the pool.

I walk toward the fence, my eyes flicking between the girls waiting at the back gate for me and the partiers who have turned to stone where they stand.

"What the fuck do you think you're doing in my house?" someone barks, but I'm not close enough to see who he's talking to.

"Caught one of your girls at our spot tonight, Collins. The second she realized we knew who she was, she booked it but not before admitting you sent her there."

I freeze.

I recognize that voice.

I move toward the chaos.

"Raven!" Nira hisses and Victoria growls. "What are you doing?!"

Still, I step farther into the darkness of the yard, but closer to the scene, seeing perfectly where the line is drawn.

The partygoers have all moved to stand behind the guy that lives here, Collins as they called him - the one I was talking to in the house - and directly in front of them, maybe two steps away… the kings of Brayshaw.

Maddoc, Captain, and Royce stand tall and wide, blank expressions worn by each as they face the thirty or so of the others.

I'm guessing the five who inch closer to Collins are his main men.

A red-headed girl catches my attention when she slinks toward the front, positioning herself at the edge of the group. She's trying to appear strong, attempting to show she's standing in a united line, but from where I am her fear is clear. She has one shoulder tucked behind the guy at her side, too afraid to fully stand against them.

Royce laughs, but it's a menacing sound that sends a chill running up my spine. "What's the matter, baby? Why'd you have to come out and play tonight?" He tilts his head mockingly, eyes traveling over her tiny skirt and jean jacket. "Bet your job was only to get inside … not let me inside you." He smirks and she shrinks into her shoulders, her gaze falling to the grass a moment. "Which one of these pussies thinks yours belongs to him? Let me tell him what you like—"

"Enough," Collins growls, and like a damn movie, all three Brayshaw step closer. "I hear your pops is asking for a parole hearing. Interesting timing, don't you think?"

My brows draw in and I look to the boys, but Maddoc doesn't even acknowledge he's spoken.

"Tell me why you sent her, and I won't break your point guard's arm tonight," Maddoc tells him, his voice unnervingly calm and focused.

"Fuck you," the guy I'm assuming is just that, the point

guard, spits.

I glance at the boys again.

Captain has somehow sneakily slipped a pair of brass knuckles over what I'm only now noticing are tatted fingers and Royce's are balled into fists. I look back to Maddoc and while he gives nothing away to the naked eye, there's an eerie air surrounding him. He's too calm, too poised. He's ready.

Fuck me, they're about to throw down.

I look to the other side, the Graven side.

Most of the partygoers have backed up a few steps, but Collins' numbers doubled in an instant, now a good dozen standing off against the tripod, as I've named them.

And then I see the girl step back and slightly to the side, slowly edging away from them ... but closer to me.

I cut a quick glance at Nira and the others who all start waving me toward them, none saying a word as they hide in the darkness of the yard, cowering away from the scene, but I turn back toward it.

They showed up here, three strong, expecting a fight knowing they'd be outnumbered.

I grin.

Silly boys, so cocky.

But the way I see it, the only way to get the upper hand is to have the element of surprise.

I slowly step forward, and before I'm even seen, I push the chick a few feet over, until I can fully shove her into the pool. Because why the fuck not, it was too easy not to.

Plus, seems she signed up to play the rat tonight. I've got no love for her kind.

A loud gasp leaves her as she emerges, and she spins to me ... along with every other head in the yard.

She shrieks, swiping her hair from her face as she pushes up on the side of the cement. "Who the hell are you?" she shouts.

The Brays' eyes are on me, I see it in my peripheral, but I

don't look their way. It would defeat the whole purpose, as every other person is looking my way too, meaning their heads are turned away from the three looking for trouble.

I don't acknowledge the girl, just laugh lightly as I back away, stepping into the darkness the shadow of the house provides.

I head for the girls waiting for me. The second I hit the fence line, there's a loud crack followed by a deep grunt – the first punch thrown.

Then the screaming and shouts start as they brawl in the backyard.

We run and jump in Victoria's man's car and head back for the group home.

"Are you fucking insane?!" Victoria sits forward in her seat, spinning to glare at me. "You better hope they don't figure out we were there with you or I swear to fucking God I'll—"

"You'll what?" I cut her off, leaning forward just the same. "What are you gonna do?"

"You better watch it, Rae." Her lip curls. "You can't walk around here like you run shit. There's an order you need to follow."

"That's your problem, Victoria. You want so bad to fit somewhere when you don't. None of us do. Not in this world. We have to wait for our time, create our own fucking life after we let go of everything in the one we were forced into. Stop trying to blend in and maybe you won't be such a stiff bitch."

"Don't pretend you know me, whore."

Juvenile.

When I roll my eyes and plop back against the seat, she spins around in hers.

I look to Nira who's frowning, then Vienna. Her eyes are narrowed, but she fights a grin.

I turn to look out of the tiny back side window.

Typical fucking night, I guess.

Chapter 9

RAVEN

"Skank," someone mumbles as they pass behind me and I slam my locker shut, spinning to see who it is this time, but there are too many people walking by to know for sure.

All fucking day this has been happening.

I mean, I'm used to it – comes with the territory when your mom's been the thorn in more marriages than not.

But this is different.

These people seem to think I've become a plaything. Word around campus is I'm fucking their king. And his brothers.

Doesn't help that every time one of them walks by, they say something along the lines of "be at my house earlier tonight" or "next time bring more than three condoms."

I snap back, but it only heightens the flame.

I shoved the first few who started in this morning, but it quickly became every other person who passed, and I got tired of talking.

"You're the first Bray girl without a trust fund."

I lift my head to Vienna with a scowl. "I'm not a fucking 'Bray' anything."

She laughs lightly. "Try telling the put out, uptown girls that."

I shake my head and look back to my paper.

"You know they're all acting stupid because they're jealous right?" she whispers, dropping into the free seat at my table.

We have study hall together – where those of us who need to make up credits spend our elective period.

"They've either fucked Royce and Captain and not Maddoc or vice versa and are pissed you've had all three. Or they haven't had their shot yet and now you're another body in the way of the prize."

"Brothers known to share? Twisted shit."

She leans in, scanning the room before speaking, "They're not blood brothers. It's not a secret or anything, but you didn't hear that from me. And don't even mention it. But that's totally irrelevant right now." She smiles, but little does she know she's colored me curious. "So, Royce and Captain share. Maddoc doesn't. He picks one and fucks them 'til he's bored or ditches them if they fuck someone else and then picks another."

"So he keeps a girlfriend?"

She scoffs. "Uh, no. Not girlfriends. Just fuck buddies with rules. And never PDA. You only know 'cause they trail him everywhere he goes or you'll hear him tell her when and where, things like that. But again, he doesn't pass his between the others while he's indulging, and if they try to jump ship, they're kicked to the curb by all three and basically hit nomad status. Nobody in the in-crowd will get at 'em after the Brays release them."

"Pretty sure all that's worse than if they were already known to share."

"It is."

"Well, I'm over this shit. It has to have something to do

with the party Saturday." I turn to look at her. "Which means they started the fucking rumor themselves."

Her jaw drops open, her mouth morphing into a smile just as quick. "They want people to think you're fucking them!"

"Ladies!" The teacher lowers her glasses down her face, glaring at the two of us. "Get to work."

We glance at each other, both laughing lightly before turning back to our papers.

So, they want people to think I'm merry-go-rounding, fine. Like I said, nothing new – assholes claim they've screwed me all the time. Somehow, my turning down guys gives them a complex, like how dare I, the dirty girl I am, deny them. It always turns into a story of how easy it was to get me on my back.

This time though, at this place with these guys, it'll bring even more problems to my feet, just like they want, but I don't roll over for anyone.

They think all the threats and so-called bullying will set me straight then they've got another thing coming.

Everyone already thinks me a slut, but I can twist this on them by not pushing back, like they must want.

They wanna play, we'll play.

When lunch rolls around I'm on my own – the group home girls don't owe me shit and technically we aren't friends, so I get they don't want to be guilty by association, so to speak. And unfortunately, that's how high school works. You are who you hang with.

So, I choose a deserted table, nothing but leftover food at the other end from a crowd who was too lazy to carry their trays to the trash.

I'm only seated for a solid five minutes when Royce plants

his ass on the table in front of me, swinging his large leg over so I'm now between his, my face just about level with his crotch.

He props his forearms on his knees, leaning close. "This position's familiar, ain't it, RaeRae?"

I don't have to look to know all eyes are now on us.

Royce waits for me to snap back so I say nothing, just tilt my head a little.

Captain is next to step up. He drops to one knee, his hand grabbing onto the table top, the other on the back of my chair. "Yeah, I remember it. Didn't take her long before it was my turn." Captain looks to Royce. "Bet she can take us deeper next time around. That is…" He looks back to me. "If your jaw's not too tired."

Laughter and more mutters start around me. These kings have trained their people well. They know when to shut their mouths and when to play into the mockery.

I glance up right as Maddoc appears, towering over all of us as he stands tall and broad, all alluring with that arrogant tip of his chin. He's on the opposite side of the table, his focused stare making my mouth run dry. I'm guessing this is his game, look at me like he wants to eat me alive – make them think he already has.

His gaze cuts to Royce as he shifts closer and the creases between his brows deepen. His eyes slice back to mine.

"Tell me, baby," Royce regains my attention, whispering loud enough for others to hear. Reaching out, he tries to touch my hair, but I jerk away. "You think you could go longer tonight, hmm?"

I should slap the fuck outta him for attempting to touch me, for getting into my space like this, but I don't.

Everyone is listening, it's dead fucking silent around us now that big man is standing here, so I lean in, enjoying how his eyes widen before he can stop them when my palm swipes across the zipper of his True Religions. "You want me to go longer?" I drag out each word, sounding every bit the breathy whore I'm thought to be because of them, my left hand moving to rub along Captain's bicep without bothering to look his way. "I tell you what, let me play with the big man first tonight."

I slowly lift my eyes to Maddoc and as if sensing my stare, his glare jerks from where I'm touching his buddy to mine and I swear, he stands even taller than his six-foot-four frame, a tiny, almost unnoticeable tip at the left side of his mouth.

I keep my gaze locked on his. "We'll call it a warm-up, and then I'm all yours." When Maddoc's nostrils flare, it's my lips now fighting a smirk. I lazily lower my eyes back to Royce. "You know, since he can't satisfy me like you can."

At my dig at their boy, both Royce and Captain's muscles tense for a split second before they pretend to laugh it off, and imagine that … suddenly they're done here and get up to leave.

I slowly drop against the chair and meet Maddoc's stare once more.

His lips are in a tight line, and the vein at his temple is protruding. I think it's safe to say he's pissed.

Good.

When they exit the building, the principal catches my eye from the corner of the room he's apparently been lurking in. He quickly looks from the boys to me, his forehead creasing but before he can come over and ask me stupid questions, I shoot from my chair and hustle out the back door.

It makes me sick when I have to act like that, but it's also the only power I have if any at all.

That alone is sickening.

My mother would be proud.

Chapter 10

Raven

"Um ... Raven?" I look up from my textbook when one of the youngest girls in the home sticks her head inside my door.

"Yeah?"

Her eyes are slightly wide as she speaks. "There's someone out front who wants to see you."

My brows dip. "Do you know who it is?"

She nods.

"Are you gonna tell me?"

She shakes her head and then the little shit runs off.

With a sigh, I pull my left earbud out and toss the MP3 player under my pillow before making my way to the door.

Victoria glares from her spot on the couch, but I ignore her and walk out front, only to meet that first step and turn back around.

"Now hang on a minute, you don't wanna be rude," Royce jokes and I spin back to look at him.

"What do you want?" I sigh.

"Come down here, Raven." He leans back against his SUV, folding his arms over his chest. "Or I'll follow you back inside."

"Like I care."

"You will when I tell Maybell I fucked you in her bed Saturday night. You know, when she was out at Bingo."

My brows crease. So they know Maybell's schedule, interesting.

He scowls at my curious expression. "Come down here. I even have a party favor."

He lifts up a decent size joint and leisurely steps into his ride, jerking his head for me to follow.

I frown, contemplating what to do here, but only for a second before my feet decide for me, carrying me closer to the shithead waiting. With a deep sigh, I slide in his front seat, just like he wanted.

He pulls around the house and heads a short way down the dirt road behind the property and parks off to the side. When he steps out, I follow.

He opens the back of the SUV and moves to sit on the ledge, patting the space beside him.

Rolling my eyes, I pull myself up and take the joint after he lights it.

"Thought you didn't smoke?"

"I don't," he snaps with narrowed eyes.

When I laugh, he grins and looks away.

"Gotcha." I take a hit and hold it in, looking out across the orchard. "Maybell doesn't let us come back here."

Royce nods.

"I've tried to sneak off this way to smoke a few times and before I can even hit the tree line, there she is, yelling from the back porch for me to head back to the house. She's got some telepathic shit going on, always popping up the second I make a move she might not like."

"She's got that predator intuition," he agrees, and my eyes widen slightly. Before I can ask any questions, like how he would know, he keeps going. "Surprised you listen."

"I'm surprised you're here."

Royce drops his head to the side to look at me.

"You got something to say, say it." I pass the joint back to him.

"You need to watch yourself," he warns, a dull look taking over his eyes.

And I'm out.

I hop down and move toward the house, but Royce snatches me by my arm and yanks me back.

I spin around, my hand held up to slap him, but he catches it.

"Knock your shit off, I'm not trying to be a dick here. Sit the fuck down, finish smoking at least, then you can storm off like a fucking child."

My eyes harden, and I yank myself from his hold. "Fine. And only because it's a free high."

He gives me a side glance when I drop back beside him. "For real though, RaeRae. You can't cause a power struggle at the school."

"Fuck you and your boys."

"Everyone already thinks you are," he throws back at me.

"Yeah, thanks to you guys. Now I'm not only the newest school slut, but I'm the only girl ever known to have a pass to fuck all three of you whenever I want."

"Yeah," he winces. "I think that might have backfired on Maddoc a bit."

"Yeah?" I study him. "And how's that?"

He shrugs. "What was supposed to cause you problems, gave you power."

"How do you figure?"

He tosses a perfectly good roach in the dirt. "There's been

plenty of Bray girls, but like you said, you're the only one to get to fuck all three of us on no timeline … and we appear to want more. That makes you the dominant female." He stares at me. "There's never been one of those before."

I lick my lips and look off. Fucking great.

So much for lying low.

"Let's pretend you'll tell me." I look back to him. "What happens now?"

"Nice try."

I pop a shoulder. "Worth a shot."

"Look, it's complicated now." He shifts toward me. "First you pushed us in front of everyone, we had to make sure the lines were clear. We run shit around here because we have to, for shit that don't concern you. Period. Yet you took it in stride. Then you showed up at the party, helped us get the upper hand back over the Graven douchebags. No Brayshaw students should have been there for any fucking reason, but since you were, we have to cover our tracks in case it gets back to the school. Better to pull you in than make us look weak by not being able to control one fucking female. Now, if it comes out that you were at that party, it'll be because we allowed it, because we brought you along. Not because you went off on your own."

I scoff, shaking my head and he shrugs unapologetically.

I watch him closely, deciding it's fine to fish just a little since he came to me and started talking. "You called the cop from the courts a Graven."

He opens his mouth to say something, but an engine is heard in the orchards behind us and Royce hangs his head instead.

"Fuck." He gives a blank stare and I shift to look behind us. A black SUV, identical to this one, is rolling up beside us.

It stops once we're in view of the driver window and slowly, the tinted window rolls down and Maddoc is revealed, Cap in the passenger seat. Both their eyes hidden behind those dark sunglasses they like so much.

I glance back to Royce and he winks before hopping down and offering to help me, but I move on my own and he hides a grin.

As he closes the back, I peek over at Maddoc, finding his jaw locked tight. I'm not positive, what with his glasses on and all, but it looks like his eyes are on Royce.

Guess his boy has stepped outta line by fraternizing with the enemy.

"I think you're in trouble," I whisper to Royce with a slight grin and he glares, moving to get into the back seat.

"Head back for the house, Raven," Captain tells me from his seat.

I bend to get a better look at him. "Whatever you say, packman."

He looks away, not entertaining me at all.

Maddoc's grip on the wheel tightens and he jerks his head to me before slowly creeping forward and down the small path to the roadway.

I step around Royce's now abandoned vehicle and glance the way they came from, seeing nothing but almond trees and a thin dirt road as far as you can see.

I head back for the house, high as hell and craving ice cream.

I HAND THE GIRL A FIVE AND SHE SNEERS WHEN I WAIT FOR MY change. Yes, it's only ninety-five cents, but I've been down to that with no food before. Ninety-five cents can buy four packs of noodles or an entire loaf of bread at the right store.

She's got an Apple watch on her wrist – my change will serve me better than it'll do her as a tip. Yes, I'm judging, but

I've been forced to latch onto the tiniest of details in my life. Sometimes it's the things others don't pay mind to that ends up being the key to keeping my head above water another day.

I exit the little shop and head the opposite way of the house, just cruising the street. When I pass a small sports supply store, a voice calls out.

"Hey, sweetness."

I turn, finding the guy from the house party this weekend, Collins, and a couple other guys chillin' at a small table.

"Oh, there's nothing sweet about me," I tell him.

"Bet that pussy's sweet." He smirks and his buddies chuckle to themselves.

When I laugh with them, Collins' eyes tighten.

"You'll never find out." I let him know with a slow shake of my head, but he's undeterred. His smirk only deepens.

"What I tell you, baby?" He stands and walks toward me. "Never say nev—"

"Raven," an even tone calls from my left and we both turn.

Maddoc is parked the wrong way against the curb. "Get the fuck in."

My head pulls back, and beside me, Collins growls under his breath.

"Fuck right off."

"Now," he calmly demands which pisses me off more.

"No."

The refusal has only made it past my lips when Cap hops out of the front and rounds the hood as Royce steps out of the back. Collins steps forward, his friends moving to stand as he does.

But they're completely ignored as Cap bends slightly and with no effort at all, tosses me over his shoulder. I'm thrown in the back seat, the door closed and locked before I can even protest.

I jerk away from Captain only to bump into Royce on the other side of me.

"Are you fucking kidding me right now?" I shriek, and they laugh.

I go to leap over the center console to the front, but Maddoc shoots a hand out, blocking me from climbing over. I fly back and hit the seat.

When I continue to try and escape, Royce sighs and pulls me on his lap, locking his arms around my middle to hold me down, my back against his chest.

I growl, glancing over my shoulder. "I swear to fucking God ponyboy—"

"Re-damn-lax and I'll think about letting you up."

At that, Maddoc glances back doing a double take.

"Put her on the fucking seat!"

"You wanna come back here?" Royce shoots back. "She keeps elbowing, she's gonna hit my nuts."

"What nuts?"

"Baby." With his arms still locked around me, his fingers move to dance against the jeans covering my inner thigh and I jerk. "You felt 'em real good when you rubbed—"

Suddenly, we're knocked against the window when the car jerks to a stop.

Cap and Royce start laughing when Maddoc hops out and rounds the front of the SUV, but cuts it off quick when the back, passenger door flies open.

Royce slides out without a word, wearing a huge grin, but Maddoc's only move is lifting his head to look at Cap, who then also hops out.

Once Royce is behind the wheel and Captain is seated beside him, Maddoc slides in next to me.

I shoot across the seat and reach for the handle but just before I can grip it, a large hand slips between my legs to grip my thigh and I'm yanked back.

With a shriek, I spin and shove my elbow into his neck, but just as quick, I'm maneuvered so I'm forced to straddle him, my hands now locked behind my back and the car starts moving again.

"Chill the fuck out," he tells me, his voice sounding bored while I'm heated.

"Let me the fuck out."

"No."

"What in the hell is your issue?"

"Quit fucking talking."

His uninterested tone is pissing me off. Especially since his actions tell me he's pissed or annoyed or something.

"And if I don't?" I question, popping a brow like a brat, trying to wiggle free from his hold.

His forearms quickly press down on my thighs to keep me from squirming around and I freeze realizing what I was doing.

And now, with his little move to keep himself from enjoying my ass moving against him, his mouth is damn close to my heaving chest.

He licks his lips, eyes forever hidden behind dark frames, and whispers, "I said stop fucking moving. That means, your hands, your ass, your mouth." He pauses a moment. "I'd tell you to stop breathing just to keep your tits outta my face if I thought you could control it."

I bow my back outta spite. "Better, big man?"

"You better watch it, Snow."

"Or what?"

The guys in the front start to chuckle and when I attempt to glare their way one of Maddoc's hands shoots up to keep my eyes on him alone, before clasping my arm again.

The car comes to a stop and both boys jump out, closing their doors behind them, leaving me and Maddoc alone in the back.

With a groan, I shake my head.

This is beyond ridiculous.

"What do you want? Let go of me." I attempt yanking free again.

"No."

"This 'no' shit is getting real old real fucking quick."

"You're testing my patience."

"As if I care."

Suddenly, he shifts us, pushing off the seat some, he brings my chest flush to his, locking his arms in place around me so I can't lean away.

I pull my lips between my teeth, watching as his pulse hits against the tan skin of his neck.

"I don't trust you," he spits.

A laugh bubbles out of me. "I don't need you to."

He ignores me. "Why were you at that Graven Prep party?"

"I was bored."

"And today, why were you with Collins?"

"How is any of this your business?" I struggle against him and his grip tightens.

"People think you're with us. We can't allow you to be seen with Graven assholes."

"Allow."

"Yeah, allow. This is Brayshaw's town, our fucking town. You live at a Bray house, go to our school. You belong to us. Stay away from them." His chest raises rapidly against me and I grow curious.

He licks his lips, his mouth taking on a firm line.

I lift my chin, quickly snatching his sunglasses between my teeth, yank them off and spit them to the side before he has a chance to grab them.

I lock my stare with his.

Caged and covered by a sheet of armor his green eyes turn the color of a night's jungle right in front of me.

That's when I notice the cut under his left eye. "The fight," I remember, my eyes shifting back to his.

He says nothing, but when I slowly twist my hand, he lets it slip from his grip.

I bring the pad of my thumb up to swipe across the broken, purpled skin and the hand that still holds onto my other tightens. "Why'd you fight in the first place?"

"Because he sent the girl."

"Why?"

"I said I don't trust you."

My lips twitch at that. "Right."

He stares a moment before releasing my other hand and sitting back. "Get out."

With a roll of my eyes, I move to push open the door as I awkwardly climb off of him. I glance around, finding we're back at the group home, but before I can take a step out of the vehicle, Maddoc grabs my arm and whispers one last thing, "Stay away from Royce."

A taunting smirk slowly finds my lips and I wink, earning a menacing scowl. "Sure thing, big man."

With a peace sign thrown over my head, I walk toward the house.

Chapter 11

Raven

I drop into the old wooden chair and pull out my binder. Maybell enforces this bogus ass group homework rule where we're all required to sit around each other and get our work done. And lucky me, I'm stuck at the card table with Victoria this week.

She side-eyes me several times before she turns her head to gain my attention fully.

"What?" I ask, not bothering to look at her.

"Do you even know the history with the Brayshaw boys or is that not necessary to push your thighs open?"

"Not necessary at all," I respond, uninterested in her gossip session. Rumors are close to never true.

"If you don't like people assuming you're easy, maybe you should stop responding to things like you do."

I slap my pencil on the table and look up at her. "I could swear up and down I wasn't, argue with every person who accused and still get nowhere. I'm not going to waste my breath on judgy assholes. People are gonna believe what they want, period. No point in trying to change a perception that's engraved already."

"So, you let everyone else win?"

"No. They lose, like you did just now."

When her forehead creases, I keep going.

"Your entire purpose with all that was to try and get a rise out of me. You wanted me to push or fight back and you didn't get it. Therefore, I win."

She rolls her eyes, going back to her work.

And just like I expected, she starts rambling not five minutes later.

"The boys aren't actually brothers, but they might as well be. Were raised together since they were infants, by Maybell herself, on this property even."

I try to keep writing but she hooked me, and her sneer tells me she knows it.

She glances around to make sure nobody is listening before turning back to me. "Their dads were all best friends, grew up together, same society and power bullshit – the Brays of their time. The moms, though, they were nomads. Not from any of the elite families. Money hungry whores maybe, who knows." She gives a nasty grin. "You know all about that."

"Fuck you. And what do you mean elite families?"

She gawks at me. "The Gravens and the Brayshaws, the founding families of this town." Her brows lift and when I give a small shrug, she shakes her head. "Do you pay attention to anything around here?"

"I guess not. I just thought they hated each other. Fucked each other's girls or something." No need to mention what Vienna told me. She likely already knows.

"They do hate each other, but the Gravens and Brayshaws were partners, in the beginning. But then the Brayshaws brought in another family."

She holds my stare and I guess.

"Maddoc's family?"

"Yep, none of the boys are Brayshaw by blood, but his family was the first to be pulled in. Then, over time, followed the other two boys' families, 'course it was before any of them were born. Anyway, after adding the three, suddenly the Brayshaws had a four-tier empire. The families were pinned against each other and the town was divided, people took sides."

"Sounds a little out there..." I trail off, unsure if she's feeding me garbage for fun.

"You have no idea. Here's where it gets twisted. Supposedly, they all were out on some backend job together where things went wrong, and they were shot at. One guy was killed instantly, but Maddoc's dad was able to get Royce and Captain's dads out before they were killed, too, only for them to die at the hospital later."

"Damn."

Victoria nods.

I eye her. "How do you know this?"

"Maybell has a book, a journal-like thing, and some files, from Rolland – that's Maddoc's dad's name. He explains it all in there, some newspaper articles and stuff. He gave it to her when the last blood Brayshaw died and he took over. That's when this property became his and he moved Maybell and the boys in. Supposedly, he was with them every day the first couple of years with her help, but I guess it was too much and his thug life won out over the daddy role. He became a sporadic parent after that. Anyway, guess he thought she might need to give them answers one day and probably didn't expect to be alive long enough to give them himself."

"You've read it?"

"No, but others who are gone now did and passed on the

information. I don't ever want to see it. If I do, I'm involved if they ever find out we snooped."

"Do they know?"

"According to Maybell's notes, she told them when they were twelve. Nobody talks about it. I doubt anyone outside of the few of us here know, and none of us are dumb enough to spread rumors outside these walls. It's just something we share with the older girls here since they live on the property."

"They live on the property?" My head pulls back.

"God, you are dumb." She eyes me. "Behind the house, the dirt road they're always on? That leads to their place. Soon as they hit high school, Maybell moved up here, left them back there on their own. Doubt it's legal, but nobody here is gonna question or exploit them. This is the safest place many of us have ever been. All I know is Maybell gets a monthly check on top of all the state funding for us."

"Why Maybell?" I ask despite myself.

"Guess she worked for Brayshaws, was Maddoc's dad's nanny even."

My brows pull in. "So where's the dad?"

"Prison." She leans forward to whisper again. "He got caught up with some crackhead chick in a stolen car full of goods, and they took them both in. And you know the deal, she cried rape, ratted on him and went home the same night. He got fifteen years." She sits back. "The boys were in elementary school when it happened."

I fall back into my chair. "So, she wasn't raped?"

"He swears no, but who knows. Men will say anything when their back's against the wall, just like the woman did."

"If they're so powerful, how'd he get convicted? Money always talks."

"A Graven talked quicker."

"What do you mean?" I draw out slowly.

"The prosecuting lawyer was a Graven."

I fly forward in my seat, my stomach suddenly turning. "No..."

"Yup." She smirks. "Fucked up shit, right?"

"How the hell could that even be allowed?"

She shrugs. "Like you said, money talks. Who knows the real deal?"

Fuck, man. No wonder big man flipped his shit. The Gravens had a helping hand, if not the only hand, in taking away the boys' only parent.

"And what about the moms, where'd they go?"

"Murdered by the maid. Guess Rolland was fucking them all not long after he moved them and the babies in and she wanted him to herself, got life instead." She closes her book and shrugs a shoulder. "Anyway. I can only handle so much of you. I'm out."

And she walks away, leaving me with a mess of fucking thoughts I have no business mulling over.

AT SCHOOL THE NEXT DAY, THE ONLY THING I CAN THINK about is the story Victoria told me and whether or not it's true. I thought about asking Vienna, but I don't wanna stir up shit if she's clueless. And I think she might be one of those chasing the popular train. The last thing she needs, if she is, is a form of blackmail that will only backfire.

Which is exactly why I hid in the trees this morning and waited for all the girls to leave, knowing Maybell and her helper had to hit the grocery store today.

I slip in through my window and head straight for Maybell's room, making quick work of picking the lock – she has to know half of us here could get in if we wanted, maybe the county requires it.

I check the basic hiding places like under the bed, top of

the closet, bottom of the drawers, already knowing I'd come up empty, and I do. Then I move on to the drug house hiding places I've seen firsthand – the underside of the bathroom counter, the floor air vents and possible secret compartments under the throw rug, but I come up empty. I stand and spin around slowly, letting my eyes scan over every inch of the room. A knitting kit sitting in the corner of the desk with an old magazine and Bible perfectly on top of it catches my eye.

I pull it out and lift the lid, smirking when I find a binder inside.

I flip it open, and right there in the first clear sleeve is a hand-written letter addressed to "my boys." I close it, place the empty box, magazine and Bible back where they were, lock her door and head back for my assigned room.

I pull out my mattress and make quick work of jamming the binder under the cheap headboard and then put everything back in place, sneak back out my window and head for school.

I don't know what's in there. All I know is nobody has a right to it but the guys.

I make my way to class, ignoring everyone all morning until Royce saunters over at lunch.

"What's on your mind, RaeRae?" Royce leans forward to whisper in my ear. "You're looking a bit tense."

Captain drops down on the other side of me. "I can help with that."

"We can help with that," Royce adds and they both grin.

I roll my eyes.

Maddoc walks up right then, his face blank as he looks between us. He holds my gaze a moment before purposely letting his float across the room. When it pauses, mine decides to follow, finding his on Chloe as she leans over a cafeteria table with a smirk.

A ping that feels a lot like jealousy hits in my ribs, and I look away, but not before he catches me watching.

Maddoc goes to step away and Captain stands to join him. They both look to Royce, who hesitates, but of course he too stands and the three of them walk away, not one glancing back.

Not sure why it bothers me when I never wanted to be interrupted in the first place.

For the rest of the day, not one of them gets in my way. There are no habitual stares or inappropriate comments. There isn't a single word actually, a fact that doesn't go unnoticed from every other person in this place.

From them, I get stares and whispers and side glances, but I don't acknowledge their presence – I'm good at avoiding eye contact.

By lunch the next day, I've figured it out.

Yesterday, was the start of their public show of release – I've finally been "let go" as the groupie.

It's almost laughable really, how every person picks up on their wordless show.

But it's whatever, I'm more of a loner type as it is. I didn't ask for their attention, they forced it on me. I'm happy to be the sideshow.

"Rae!" Bass calls from a few tables over, his feet thrown on the one in front of it.

I tip my chin and he tips his back with a grin, so I slip from my seat and walk his way, feeling several curious eyes on me as I do.

"What can I do for you, Mr. Bishop?"

"Come to the spot tonight, just to kick it. I'm not running the bets, so I get to chill." He grins. "Chill with me, Rae."

I laugh lightly, tapping my knuckles on the table. "I might."

"You might, means you won't."

"How do you know?"

He grins. "I speak Raven."

I laugh and step backward toward the door. "How about a 'we'll see?'"

He tosses a piece of a napkin at me. "I'll take it."

With a shake of my head, I turn for the exit for some fresh air before the bell rings.

When I look up, my stare locks with Maddoc's, finding his brows slanted in heavy disapproval. Yet he says nothing.

I leave the cafeteria, annoyed how a single look from the stranger behind me has me feeling fickle.

I brush it off and make my way down the short pathway to the courts where a few younger guys are shooting hoops. I doubt they're on the team, they're not all that, but they seem to be having fun.

I laugh when they get excited over a shot made from a few feet in front of the basket with no one around to give them a little run for their money.

The ball bounces and rolls to my feet so I pick it up and toss it back.

The cute guy with shaggy bangs nods his head with a large smile. "Thanks."

I shrug, grinning back and he takes that as an invitation to walk over.

I push off the fence to stand straight.

"It's Rae, right?"

I nod.

"I'm Jeremy." He reaches out if as he's going to shake my hand but sees how dirty his is from the ball and pulls it back with a laugh. "Sorry."

"You're fine."

"Right." He looks behind him, nervously, then back to me and I laugh lightly.

He's cute, clearly not full of himself, but confident enough to come over here. That's cool.

"Hey, so now that you're—"

"Go."

His eyes fly over my shoulder and my muscles lock, but I don't look.

I already fucking know who it is.

The guy lifts the ball in the air, then spins around with a tight smile, joining his friends again.

I shake my head with a sigh. "You got a lot of nerve, big man."

"You make a lot of stupid decisions, Snow. You think that guy or Bass Bishop wants anything from you other than a chance to slip inside you? Because they don't. All they know is you were handling three men last week, and now were set free. They want their shot."

"You should help me out," I deadpan. "Tell them how good it was, big man. You know, put in a solid word in the locker room?"

I turn to face him when he doesn't respond, and it seems that's exactly what he wanted.

He crowds my space instantly, forcing me to look up the closer he gets.

"You think you're worth the time and energy for anything other than a quick fuck in the back seat?" he growls. "Because you're not. You're the one they settle for when the worthy pussy is tied-up somewhere else. Not the one they'd work for."

His eyes rake over me with pure disdain. That, combined with the way his words are delivered with such disgust, is almost enough to wake the weak girl buried deep down inside me.

Almost.

He continues to stare, frustration growing more evident with each passing second. His nostrils flare as his brows push closer. He dips down, bringing his eyes level with mine.

Angry emerald.

He's mad and he's mad about it.

Fuck him.

"Get out of my face," I hiss.

"Get out of my head."

My brows jump before I can stop them and he jerks away.

He licks his lips, his frown as present as ever, and then he's gone.

Chapter 12

Raven

"Well, that didn't last long."

I roll my eyes, closing my PE locker, and turn to the pain in the ass behind me.

Chloe smirks. "For a girl who didn't want them, you sure came in quick and fell out fast."

"You're welcome." I step around her and head for the gym.

"For?"

"For freeing up your man, Clo. That's what you were worried about, right?" I turn, pushing the door I open with my back. "Him getting tied down before you had your shot."

"Maddoc doesn't get tied down."

"Then why you trying so hard?" I pop a brow. "What's the point if you can't keep him all to your bitchy little self?"

"You wouldn't understand, skank." Her eyes skim over me in repulsion. "Stay out of my way. It's my time now."

"Yeah, it is," I praise mockingly.

She rolls her eyes and when she pushes past me, I spot the hickey on her neck and my brows snap together.

Then I remind myself I don't care, forcing a fixed expression as I hit the free mats, but before I can drop down, a guy calls out.

"Hey, Rae, now that your nights are free again, maybe you can show me some tricks your mama taught you."

I tense a minute, then turn to face him, giving a fake smile. "You wanna feel something my mama taught me, huh?"

The guy, no fucking clue who he is, licks his lips and nods, his filthy gaze dragging over me as I approach him where he leans against the wall of the weight room.

My lip twitches as I reach him, and I trail my hand down his chest, feeling his abs flex beneath the cotton when my hand passes his abdomen. I pause at his waistband and his hips involuntarily push forward, his shoulders flat against the wall. My fingers float lower, and just before I grasp him through his track pants, a tight grip encloses over my wrist and yanks my hand away.

I shoot my glare left to find Maddoc at my side, his eyes hard.

I lift a brow and his frown deepens, so I lift my knee, jamming it right into the douche in front of me's dick.

"Fuck," he cries out. "Dumb, bitch."

I lean toward him, but Maddoc pulls me backward. "Learned that from my mama, piece of shit. How'd she do on the lesson?"

In the next instant, I'm lifted in the air and carried through a door that leads to the hall where the entrance to the locker rooms are.

Maddoc tosses me onto a pile of dirty ass gym towels.

I hop up, shaking the shit off, then glare at the asshole in front of me. "What the fuck?"

"What the fuck is right, what the fuck was that?" he roars.

"It's called, standing up for myself."

"You were about to put your hands on his junk."

"Did you not see me knee him in the nuts?" I shriek. "It's not like I was about to grip him and have a playdate for all the class to see. He was being a dick, so I was gonna hurt his. Still did, in fact. And why the fuck do you care?!"

"I don't!"

I cross my arms. "Really?"

"You callin' me a liar?" He steps closer and the hairs on my neck stand.

"If the jock strap fits."

He slides closer, his eyes cutting to my lips before hitting mine again. "Why are you so much trouble?"

"I'm not," I tell him, my eyes zeroed in on where his tongue sneaks out to lick the corner of his lips. "I'm silent 'til pushed."

"And why do I wanna push you?"

My gaze snaps back to his. He's even closer now. "Because I push back."

"You kiss back?"

"Try it and find out."

He moves in, gripping me by my ribs so he can put me where he wants me, with my back against the lockers. His dark eyes study me, trying to dig beneath the surface. Not sure what he hopes to find, but there's not much on the inside.

I'm jaded, trailer park trash with nothing to lose. My life, minus a detail or two, is in a ten-page file in a group home down the street, a file he's read.

"You fuckin' Bishop?"

"No."

"Plan to?"

"I'm not one for planning. I'm not known to stay in one place long enough for that."

"That's not a good enough answer."

I pop a shoulder.

"You piss me off."

"You piss yourself off. Stop butting into my business and everything would be fine."

He growls, his head dropping as his grip tightens, his fingertips pressing into my back.

Heat stirs in my abdomen and my chest inflates.

A light chuckle leaves him, and the sound, low and dirty, has my skin burning. But then something shifts in his eyes, like the heat and playfulness was detected by what plagues him on the inside and he switches gears, eyes now hollow and hard.

"You're predictable, Raven."

"Yeah." I drop my head back. "How so?"

"You come in here without a fight, let me put my hands on you without shoving me off – like you've done to every other motherfucker in this school when they've touched you." His lips move to my ear. "I knew you'd let me, though. Just like I know, under this silk skin you wear like armor, you pretend what others think rolls right off you, but that's an act, isn't it? There's one thing that gets to you. One thing you can't stand."

"Yeah, big man, and what's that?" My heart rate spikes in annoyance as he attempts to psychoanalyze me.

"Everyone thinking you're your mother's daughter." Before I can respond, he spins us, so I'm falling against him, his back now on the lockers. His eyes harden, his voice now brasher. "How many times do I have to tell you, Raven? I don't need to pay for sex, especially not when you already gave it up so easily. Proposition me again, and I'll have your ass sent straight back where you came from. We don't want trash in our school."

My forehead creases but before I can say anything laughter rings in my ear.

My stare is slow to shift.

A half dozen gym students have filed into the hall.

Their laughter rebounds off the walls, hitting like a wave down the long hall only to ricochet right back.

Blood pumps fiercely against my temples, taking over my vision for a short moment before I blink long and hard, forcing it away, bringing myself back to right now.

They open when Maddoc shoves me away, and I stumble, falling back onto the pile of shit on the floor. His eyes are full of spite. "Let me catch you trying to pick up clients at our school, Snow." He makes it a point to look at my feet, deeming me worth less than the dirty floor beneath them, a deep frown on his face as he shakes his head.

And I can't breathe.

I start to sweat, my skin begins to itch and I can't feel my hands. My gaze travels from person to person, finding each stare more ruling than the last.

When my eyes snap back to Maddoc, it's not just him I find, but the other two now at his side.

The tripod.

The boys of Brayshaw High, three strong.

They felt threatened by my actions, actions that helped them more than hurt them, but regardless, were out of line as far as they were concerned.

Here, you're not allowed to have your own moves if it messes with theirs.

They pulled me in, brought eyes on me, made sure everyone knew good and well who I was and where I came from. All so the bomb would hit that much harder when it fell.

The lead-up, all of it, was set to put me in my place, right here for the assholes around to see.

Now it's not speculation but confirmed fact as far as they're concerned.

Words straight from their leader's mouth.

I'm an apple plucked from the same tree.

A whore.

It's one thing for me to play into it, to act like the slut they see, make them think I fuck because I feel like it, but that's on my terms. My choice.

And he took it away in two point five seconds with two dozen witnesses.

He's right with what he said. I can't stand everyone seeing her when they look at me.

I bite into my tongue to keep from lashing out. Chances are the rage and disgrace will blend, ending in waterworks I can't control, and they don't deserve – that would be a nightmare.

They want my tears, but they won't get them this easy.

I force my feet to move, block out the snide remarks and instant offers that hit my ears and shove through the door with my head held high. It's fake, the vigor I show.

Truth is, these boys got me on my knees, where whores are most comfortable.

But I swear to shit, it'll take a lot more than three parentless punks to keep me here.

Chapter 13

Raven

I dab at my lip with the hydrogen peroxide one last time then set the little timer glued to the wall to keep us regulated on the hot water and step into the shower to let the dirt and grime run off the rest of me.

How I managed to sneak back into the house before Maybell woke is beyond me, but I made it with only minutes to spare, then slid into the bathroom before she could see I was a hot, bloody mess.

The timer goes off too soon, followed by a prompt bang on the other side of the door letting me know it's someone else's turn and time for me to get the fuck out.

I dress as quickly as possible and slip back into my room, flopping onto my assigned bed. The mattress is ancient and has a dip in the center from years of overuse, but it's got clean sheets and a soft blanket. Beats the hell out of the drop-down sofa I slept on in the trailer living room the past ten years.

The second I let my eyes close, Maybell pops in.

"Come on now, Rae. Breakfast with the others, chores, then the rest of the day is yours."

"I'm not hungry."

"And I'm not asking. Come on now, you need to put some meat on those bones."

Ugh. Kill me now.

Like the maintenance chores, each week we're assigned cooking duties. So far I've only had to set the table and wash vegetables. Turns out today, I'm on pancake duty with Victoria. Fucking yay.

She starts mixing as I pull out the large portable skillet thing they use to cook on.

I've seen them but have never used one before. It kind of reminds me of the hot plate we used at home, assuming there was something worth making.

When I get stuck staring at the dials, Victoria sighs and reaches over, showing me how annoyed she is with the flick of her wrist as she helps me out.

"Thanks."

"Whatever."

Okay then.

About fifteen pancakes later, and she starts talking.

"So." She adds more water to the batter. "What happened with you and the Brays?"

"Not sure what you're referring to."

"Rumor has it, last week someone saw you riding Maddoc in the back seat while the other two drove you around."

"Bet that was a sight to see, through the tinted ass windows and all."

She scoffs, turning to me. "You trying to deny it? Chances are someone took a picture. And the front window isn't as dark."

"I'm not trying to do shit. Think what you want, I don't really give a damn."

"Wouldn't matter if you did anyway, they seemed to have already passed you on." She goes mute on me after that, just the way I like her.

A little over an hour passes before I'm able to start on my outside chores. Thankfully, all I have left for today is watering the plants out back and spraying down the swing set.

Soon as I stand from wrapping up the hose a whistle sounds and I turn, squinting down the dirt road I'm not allowed on.

Royce jerks his chin, lifting a joint in the air in offering.

I glance at the house, finding the only girls outside busy with their own jobs, so I head his way.

"Wanna burn?"

"Why not, got nothing else to do."

He scoffs and points to a few logs laying at the edge of the dirt and together we move to it.

"So, what brings you to my neck of the woods?"

He squints at the trees. "Not sure." He shrugs. "Got bored. Had a joint and ended up here."

"Your boy won't like this," I sing-song and he glances my way. "He told me to stay away from you."

His eyes narrow a moment before dropping his head with a light laugh. "I knew I was right, but I half didn't wanna be."

"I'm sorry, Riddler, did you say something?" I snatch the joint from his fingers.

"Nah. Nothing." He glances my way. "But you should watch out. Maddoc don't play."

"Seems to like to."

Royce considers that a moment before a grin splits his mouth. "He does, don't he?"

I laugh lightly.

He stares at me, a crease forming at the center of his eyes before he speaks. "Come to a party tonight. A Bray party."

I shake my head. "Hard pass. I'm not interested in being

your punching bag, and your little game of 'sharing is caring' is over so no need to flaunt an old toy."

"All right. I'll rephrase." He shifts to glare my way. "Be at the party, or – same drill, slightly changed – Maybell finds your bed empty, since you like to sneak out after your curfew when you think no one's around."

I look away, but he continues to stare at my profile.

"Where do you go?"

I leap to my feet. "None of your fucking business."

"I'll see you tonight then."

"What is with you guys, surely you don't always get your way?"

"'Course we do. Sometimes it takes a little forced effort such as this to make it happen, but in the end, we win." He grins, and for a second, he seems almost innocent, until the joint hits his lips and he walks away with more swag than should be allowed for a single human.

With a roll of my eyes, I head back for the house.

Soon as I walk inside, Victoria is leaning against the frame to the room I currently live in, her arms folded over her chest.

"Thought you weren't fucking them?"

I tell her what she wants to hear to get her to go away. "Guess I'm a liar."

I drop onto the bed and lie there a moment before plugging in my earbuds. I pull my pocket knife from my bra, slide my hand under my pillow and pass out.

Maybell wakes me up for dinner and evening clean up. As soon as all is said and done, I'm antsy from sitting around all day – it's hard to let myself relax indoors when I'm so used to needing an escape. Not sure I'll ever convince myself there's a soft place to land when a roof is involved. I throw on my knock-off Vans and head out the door with nowhere to go in mind.

"Can I tag along?"

I glance over my shoulder at Vienna. "I'm just going for a walk."

"I could use a walk." She falls in line beside me, and together we head down the road, passing the park the boys play ball in.

Vienna looks over the broken-down court. "You know our school was built by a Brayshaw back in the day?"

I cut a glance her way. "I figured, yeah. Brayshaw High..." I trail off, curious where she's going with this.

"It was. Before, students below poverty weren't even allowed to attend, they'd actually bus them to the town over. It was only for the power families and their spawns. But then one day, all of a sudden, they were bringing in people like us."

"Strange change of heart."

She scoffs. "I heard it was because kids who had nothing, had nothing to lose. I mean, think about it ... if all the kids at the school were meant for greatness, who did that leave to do the dirty work when dirty is needed?" She trails off, effectively planting a damn seed.

I don't comment and now I can't shut my brain off. It sort of makes sense what she's saying. Power trickles down.

It's like in my neighborhood. Every dope dealer has a dealer who has a dealer, and so on. There's the piss on selling dime bags to kids on the corner, but that bag traveled from a bigger hand somewhere else at some point.

"Speaking of the Brayshaws," she mumbles, bringing me back to now. "Looks like they're having a party tonight."

"What makes you say that?" I give her a side glance.

She motions to the school parking lot that has just come into view. There are at least two dozen cars there, students all around, laughing and acting like fools, having fun.

"This is how it goes. The Brays plan a party once or twice a month, set a time for everyone to meet here and together they all head over, sometimes there's even a theme to keep it fresh and fun. If you don't make it here before Leo, one of the guys on their team, you can't go." She glances my way briefly before returning her eyes to the scene. "They don't give out the location and everyone has to check their phones at the door. It's like some super-secret shit."

"You ever been?"

"Nah." She shakes her head, pretending she's not interested but her next comment tells me she wishes she has. "Heard it's invite-only."

I spot Chloe sitting against the hood of some red little sports car and roll my eyes.

"Surprised you didn't get invited."

I scoff before I can stop it and she spins to look at me.

When I glare at her and look away, she starts laughing.

"You did! Why the hell are you not going?"

"Why would I?"

"Better question... why not? It's not like you've got somewhere else to be. Shit, I don't know about you, but this is the first time in a while I've had a spot to go back at the end of the night. My mind's not on how to get my next meal or where I can sneak a shower. We're fucking teenagers for a while longer. Why not act like one every once and a while?"

I stop and turn to her, watching to see any sign of a liar or a con. And not the kind we poor kids have to be from time to time but the shitty kind we can choose to be better than.

She stares right back, even lifts her chin a little, so I nod and start walking toward the herd of cars.

"Holy shit, wait," she whispers. "Are we really just gonna walk up in there and expect one of them to give us a ride?"

"I've learned not to expect anything." I turn to her with a

smirk. "We'll either catch a ride or have some fun stirring up shit for the in-crowd."

She pauses, shrugs and then laughs as we continue forward.

By the time we hit the parking lot, all the partygoers are hopping in the cars and a few kids are hitting each window with a little white card.

"What is that?"

"Directions maybe?"

"I don't think we'll be finding a ride."

Right then, a familiar black SUV pulls around the row of cars, and all eyes trail it as it pulls over…right beside me.

The window rolls down and some guy I don't know leans out.

"That's Leo," she whispers, and I roll my eyes.

The corner of his mouth lifts and he swings his eyes her way a minute, licking his lips before he looks back to me.

"And he can hear you." I tilt my head and he then glances to the back as the window rolls down, revealing a couple girls I recognize from gym. High and mighty smirks on their faces.

"Royce didn't think you'd show. I told him you would." He eyes me.

"You don't even know me."

"Don't need to know you to know you'd be here. Now get in."

That's when I notice the blonde in the front seat. She leans over Leo, running her hand up his arm.

I raise my hands and shrug in mock disappointment. "Looks like you're all full. Guess I missed my chance."

His smirk grows, but there's an edge to it he can't quite cover. "Get out," he says without even sparing the girls a glance.

All their glares whip from him to me.

Vienna chuckles beside me.

"We could squeeze—"

"I said out."

With low grunts, they do as they're told, slamming the doors as they quickly run to the back of the line of cars.

Leo's eye follows them. "We write the number of people in the car to make sure nobody gets picked up on the way. All the cards were already given out." He glances back to me. "I was their only shot for tonight."

"You can still change your mind. Bet they're a guaranteed lay."

He assesses Vienna. "I'm good."

"I'll be the judge of that," Vienna jokes, making him laugh. "Get in."

I look to Vienna and together we shrug and step forward.

When we both get in the back, Leo scowls out his window, then peels out.

This better be fun.

Chapter 14

RAVEN

IT TAKES A SOLID TWENTY MINUTES TO GET TO THE PARTY place, an old ranch house on a deserted piece of land. Nothing but the house lights seen for miles.

It's one of the creepy looking places that murderers buy so they can torture and kill their prey without perked ears and prying eyes.

And we've just got locked inside.

Leo fist bumps a guy on the way through the narrow hall and we get frown after frown as we bypass a huge ass line of students.

"Bathroom line?" Vienna whispers, and then we reach the end, seeing a big dude scanning each person and confiscating their cell phones.

My hand instantly hits my chest.

Leo sees it and frowns, looking from the metal detector to me. "You got a phone in there?" He pops a brow and I shake my head.

"Nope. No phone."

He's slow to accept my answer and then looks to Vienna. "You?"

"Dude. We live in a group home. Like we could pay a cell phone bill."

He nods and then we're through the dark curtain.

The other side is no majestic place. Nothing special or over the top.

An old house, clean but not kept up with lights and a few sofas against the wall. Some music coming from somewhere and a few kegs in the kitchen as well as a long table people are playing dice on.

Vienna spots a few girls she must know because they wave her over, but she doesn't budge.

"You can go," I tell her.

"I came here with you, that's messed up."

"For real, go. I'm not very social as it is. I like to roam around and check shit out. You'll have more fun with them."

She hesitates a moment, smashing her lips to the side. "You sure? I don't want you to think I used you or whatever."

"I'll see you later," I laugh lightly, pushing her along and as soon as she walks away, I can breathe a little better.

It's true what I told her. I'm better by myself.

I make my way to the keg, but stand back and watch several other people fill up their cups before I decide it's likely not poisoned and grab my own.

When I step through the living room to what I'm thinking served as a den when the house was occupied, I spot Captain leaning against the wall, a brunette between his legs.

He's pulling her shirt down, kissing on her shoulder, but his eyes meet mine when I walk by.

I step out back, spotting Bass sitting at a table in the yard.

"Raven Carver." He grins, calling me over with a nod of his head. "The fuck you doin' here?"

"Bass Bishop." I walk closer, bringing my cup to my mouth for a long drink. "I could ask you the same thing."

"Free beer," he jokes. "So how'd you end up here?"

"Lucky, I guess." I shrug.

He stands and walks toward me. "You get that all cleaned up?" he asks, reaching out to pull my lip down a bit.

I dab at the blood spot, showing him it's all dried.

He chuckles lightly and nips at my fingertip before stepping back to take his seat. He grabs a cigarette, offering one to me.

"I'm good."

With a nod, he turns back to his buddies and I move along.

I walk across the yard to the opposite side of the house, propping my hip against the old wooden panels that line the edges. Nothing but empty field for miles.

Not five seconds later a firm grip locks my hip in place and hot breath hits my neck making me jump.

"You shouldn't be here."

Maddoc.

"I was invited." I roll my eyes.

He pushes me forward two steps, the yard light no longer shining against my back. He whispers, "I'm not talking about the party. I'm talking about where you're standing."

"Why not?"

"Listen."

My brows draw in, but after a moment I hear it.

Soft giggles and quiet laughter, followed by the clear sound of a sultry kiss.

Deep breaths, soft mews, and airy moans.

There's a rustle of leaves followed by a whispered "yes" and my skin grows warm.

Maddoc pushes closer.

And then the zip of jeans is heard, and my core tightens.

There's no sound for a moment and I find myself inching closer to the darkness of the trees.

"Oh God," is breathed into the air and I pull in a lungful of cold air.

A deep raspy groan, a shuttered cry.

Maddoc's grip on my hips tightens and my pussy walls clench.

"She's almost there ..." he rasps against the back of my ear and I shiver against him. "Right at the edge, ready to come for him ... for us without even knowing it."

I squeeze my eyes closed, licking my lips as I focus on their sounds.

I inch closer, slowly peeking in time to see the shadow of the girl's head fall back as the guy's drops to her chest.

"They're there, Raven..." he breathes right as they cry out in release.

My body starts to ache with need.

Maddoc feathers his fingers across my skin and I'm ready to do something real stupid right here, right now.

But he's a devious dickhead who knew exactly what he was doing, and he shifts the mood quick. "Royce says you're sneaking out at night."

Bastard.

"'Course he did."

"Who you fucking?"

"Wow." I roll my eyes, willing my pulse under control.

"Tell me." He tips his head slightly, the scuff of his chin scraping against my neck causing me to shudder despite myself.

He chuckles against me and my head tilts - to avoid or to open up farther, fuck if I know right now.

"It's not your concern."

"The fuck if it isn't. You're mine to play with."

"According to who, you?"

"Damn straight."

"But I was 'released' from your little threesome, remember?" I glance over my shoulder, batting my lashes and his nostrils flare.

He pushes into me and I hold my breath. "You're mine if I say you are, you're trash when I decide I'm done. And I'm standing here telling you I changed my mind. I'm not ready to throw you out just yet."

He doesn't elaborate so I sure as shit don't ask for his reasoning.

His grip on my hip tightens a moment before a burst of wind hits my back.

I spin slowly to face him.

He licks his lips, drops his head back lazily as he stares.

He's too damn appealing to the eye. And he's wearing a backward fucking hat tonight.

That right there ... good fucking god.

I must show my appreciation for the ruler in front of me, because the corner of his mouth lifts slowly.

Captain saunters up right then, whispering in Maddoc's ear and instantly, his mask is back in place. Maddoc nods, gaze still locked on mine.

"I have eyes on you, Raven. Don't do anything stupid," he tells me.

"The fuck ever that means."

He walks closer and my spine straightens, a tingling sensation spreading across my ribs. He brushes his chest against me. "It means keep your legs closed to our guests."

"I'll do my best, big man," I deadpan, and he walks off with Captain, Royce meeting them at the edge of the lawn, and together they push through the side gate.

Stupid me, I follow.

Out front is a repeat of last weekend at Graven, only these people I recognize. They're the nomads from school, the one the girl told me about the first day, they are supposed to lay low, stay out of the way. Yet here they are.

"You really think this is smart?" Maddoc asks eerily calm.

The chick beside them holds her cell up, and Royce moves to take a half a step closer but stops when Maddoc speaks.

"I want that phone. Now."

The guy stands taller and the girl laughs, tauntingly shaking her phone as she hides a step farther away like a little bitch. "That's not going to happen," she spits.

"If you wanted a sex tape, I'd have been happy to be the star of the show," Royce quips, but his tone tells me he's being an ass, though I'm almost positive it's true.

She tilts her head, and from the side view I have of all of them, I can see the small smirk on her face. "This is a two for one, he screwed her, now we screw you all."

"You're about to cause a problem you won't be able to fix," Captain tells her.

She scoffs, glancing at the guys beside her. "Like I care. You can kiss your little basketball season goodbye."

"You send that, you'll regret it."

The girl smirks and the guys are brave enough to laugh – it's fearful but heard nonetheless. "You can't control us anymore. With this, we get our district transfers approved. We'll be at Graven by Monday."

Kiss the season goodbye?

What the fuck are they trying to pull? The one thing I've seen light a fire in these boys' eyes that's not driven by rage or hatred is when a basketball is in their hands. From what I can tell, it's the only thing they even give two shits about other than each other.

I owe them nothing, have no loyalties to honor. Nothing at all ties me to these boys and the stupid shit they do.

Yet something has my feet creeping along the house until the hose is in my hands. I use my knife to slice through it at a little bigger than arm's length. And again, something has me tiptoeing out wide to round the cars lining the left of the driveway so I can come up behind the party crashers.

With my hands on the ends, I create a loop and quickly and easily slip the rubber around the girl's neck and pull.

She yelps, but it's cut short when I kick her legs from under her and she falls on her ass, the phone flying from her hand.

The guys she's with spin quickly, but I haul her back a few steps and they pause.

After that first moment of shock, one decides to charge me, but Maddoc catches him by the collar, tossing him backward with little effort.

I tighten my hold as the girl flails around, widening my eyes at the guys. "Uh, hello. Grab her phone!"

Royce darts for it as Captain steps in the center with his brass knuckles on and ready, daring them to make a move for his boy who has his back turned.

Royce snatches the phone from the girl's feet and demands the password.

When she hesitates, I yank tighter, and she cries out the code.

Royce pushes some buttons on the screen and then glares, before snapping it in half and stuffing it in his pocket. "Hope you weren't attached to anything in your cloud. It's all gone now."

When she starts to kick, I tighten my hold even more. Adrenaline pumps through my veins, creating a natural – dangerous – high that grows stronger the more she gags. Her hands coming up to claw at my forearms, and I look down, following the small beads of blood running down my wrist, having felt nothing.

"Let her go now, Raven," Maddoc tells me.

There's a gentle, almost hesitance to his tone that has my ribs compressing.

I don't want to let her go...

Blood drips onto my shoe.

"Raven."

My head snaps up at the rough command and I freeze.

The party has come to the lawn for the show.

Shit.

I let her go and slowly push to stand.

Wide eyes and whispers surround me, and I take a half a step back.

I spin on my heels, speed walking down the dirt path.

I ignore their yells when they call me back and keep moving forward.

I spin my arms around, taking deep breaths to try and settle my erratic heart.

This is the least I've fought in the last two years and shit's building up inside me. Anger and resentment I hide until I can't, a numbness I crave but can't find without rage to kick start it. And they just saw it.

Fuck.

I groan and glance around.

There's fucking nothing this way, and thankfully the stars light up the road, but no way in hell will I go back to the party so all those people can look at me like some wannabee groupie fighting for their attention or forgiveness or what-the-fuck-ever.

That's not what this was.

I was there, those people were playing foul, and it irritated me.

There's nothing that gets me going worse than a vindictive piece of shit willing to sell someone out, ruin shit for someone else, for personal gain.

It's weak and pathetic.

Even if these boys are from some privileged family like I'm hearing, if half of what Victoria said was true, they've got to have mad underlying issues, and for them to want something for themselves, even if it's just to win some high school basketball games, is dope. I can get behind that.

Do they go about it wrong? Fuck yeah, they do. But still, they work hard, fight for what they want and no way in hell was some social climbing serpent going to ruin it for the fuck of it. Not without a solid reason or need for revenge – not that that's the best way to handle things, but in a world like mine, that's how it works.

If they lose what they're working toward, it needs to be because they stole it from themselves. Not at the hands of anyone else.

It doesn't take long for one of those familiar SUVs to pull up beside me.

The door is pushed open, revealing Vienna sitting there with wide eyes, so I slip in.

All three boys are inside as well, but nobody says a damn word. The drive is dead silent.

A little while later, when they park in front of the group home, Captain speaks.

"Go through the front door, don't worry about being seen."

I don't question him and neither does Vienna. We simply do what he says.

And it works.

Chapter 15

Raven

I'm in the land of Oz right now, I swear to God.

As I step around the corner, I'm stopped yet again by another damn stranger. Each one has some bogus ass compliment or faux interest question about how my weekend was or something else as equally lame. Too bad for this chick, I've braved through a solid hundred phonies and I just can't right now.

She smiles and bounces over, but I lift a hand and walk away.

I keep my eyes forward and shoot straight for English, practically sprinting inside when I reach the door. I drop into the seat and lean against my elbows, my hands shielding my face as I take a damn breath.

What in the hell is happening?

"I'll tell you what's happening."

I jerk, spinning to glare at the fool who must have just now dropped his ass behind me ... who isn't even in this class.

"Why are you here?" I frown.

He grins. "Not happy to see me, RaeRae?"

"Don't you have a class to be in or somethin'?"

"I'm in it."

"No," I drawl out slowly. "You're not."

He winks then waves a pink slip of paper over his head. "Mr. Bell, got something for ya." His eyes meet mine again. "Transfer form."

I spin in my chair, fighting the urge to cross my arms over my chest like a child.

The class starts a few minutes later and I don't miss the curious and not at all discreet stares sliding from our new classmate to me.

A few minutes pass and then Royce's hot breath hits my neck. "You wanna know what's going on?" he whispers.

Not sure if the sultry tone he gives is on purpose or if he simply can't help himself. It's full of heat and dirty promises I have no doubt he can keep.

"You had our backs. Again. And not because you had to, RaeRae."

My forehead creases.

"Guess what that means?" he asks but doesn't give me time to answer – not that I planned to. "It means you'll be under our watch, constantly. Every move you make, we'll know about. Every word spoke, we'll likely hear. You'll show your cards soon enough. And we'll be around when you do. Know what us being up your ass'll look like?"

I roll my eyes, still facing forward and wait for him to answer himself, knowing damn well he can't not.

"It makes everyone here think we've claimed you, that we've stamped our names on what I'm sure is a pretty pink puss. It'll be different from when they thought you were our toy, that was basically like a test drive – can she work a stick or can't she. Every guy here has been primed for you since, but if they want to play, they'll have to ask our permission first. You know, 'cause you'll be seen as our property now. You're suddenly the girl everyone will pretend to like when all they really wanna do is take your place." He chuckles darkly. "They'll all love to hate you."

When I spin to glare at him, he sits back in his chair with a vile smirk.

"Trust no one now, RaeRae. This is when the fakes come out to play."

I face forward again, scowling at nothing.

Shouldn't be too hard.

I trust no one as it is.

But really, I went from being their groupie to the whore they couldn't stand and now... what?

With a sigh, I pick up my pen.

I doodle in my notebook the rest of the period, escaping as quickly as possible once the bell rings, but Royce's maniacal little chuckle when I do should have been my warning, because as soon as I'm seated in my next class, tool number two saunters in, glasses still on and all.

I stare Captain down, knowing he's watching me behind his dark lenses.

"Is this necessary?"

He nods, his gaze roaming around the room before he turns my way. He drops into the seat beside me.

He seems the most sensible of the three, or at least the one more likely to let me speak even if it does go in one ear and out the other.

I lean toward him, speaking low. "So, people saw me rope up that girl, who cares. I'm sure people do stupid shit to get on your buddy list all the time."

"Not why you did it."

"You don't know shit! Pretend it was your idea. Tell them

... I don't know, that you used me to get what you needed and then broke my poor little heart."

Captain scoffs, tilting his head as he pushes his glasses up. His light eyes stare me down a moment before he shakes his head and looks away.

"Oh, spit it out, packman. Your boss ain't here to tie your tongue."

His eyes snap to mine. "Fuck you."

"Not a chance." I grin and look at that, he thaws a bit.

He sits back in his chair, his eyes lazily scanning over me before locking with mine. "You think anyone who spends ten seconds in your presence would believe that we broke your little heart?" he mocks.

"What's that supposed to mean?"

"It means your wires are crossed."

"You don't even know me."

"Yeah, well," he sighs, sitting back. "Guess we're changing that."

"And what's Maddoc think about all this?"

He eyes me, trying to read me but can't. I'm good at giving nothing to those who don't deserve it.

"You really wanna know?"

"Pretty sure I already do, just want you to be the one to say it."

"Nah, now this I've got to hear." He shifts in his seat as if he's looking forward to what I've come up with.

I laugh at his usual dry self, and right then, the teacher cuts the lights – apparently, it's movie day.

We're forced to stay quiet for a few minutes, but eventually, there are enough soft whispers going around that every ear won't be on us, so when he leans my way, I meet him in the middle.

"I'm betting, your boss" —he scowls which makes me laugh again and then I continue— "sorry. I bet Maddoc is pissed. This cramps his style, bad, and now he feels like the puppet when he's used to being the master. Now, to cover your own asses and keep others from fucking up your pathetic little order, you guys have no choice but to pretend all this is what you want, 'cause how dare anyone step off that thin white line you've drawn."

"Your bitch is showing."

I shrug and lean a little closer, bringing us inches apart, completely eye to eye and get serious.

"No for real, though, I'm not stupid. He's looking to play the part, to make sure every punk in this school sees me in your circle, at least once. The switching classes helps a good amount. Right now, you sitting here entertaining me instead of scowling like normal." I narrow my eyes and his harden. "It's all part of the process. You boys are ballers and you've set your game plan. But know something, packman… I may have a vagina, but I'm no pussy."

His jaw ticks and we're stuck in a stare off, neither of us moving for a moment when the lights flick on.

Finally, he lowers his glasses back in place and exits the room.

When I gather my shit and move to stand, I see Maddoc settled in the doorway. He cuts a quick glance to Captain as he steps in front of him and then his green eyes are back on me.

I walk right to him, forcing my classmates to squeeze past me.

"Your turn to play, big man?" I taunt, and he lifts his chin.

Oh okay, so that's his move telling me to start walking.

With a roll of my eye, I do a little prissy bow, crossing my foot behind the other and bending before flipping him off and shouldering past.

I'd swear a teeny chuckle fought its way out before he strangled it.

Sure as shit, when I step into class his chest hits my back, and two large hands land on my hips. I freeze, right there in the door with every fucking eye on me, Chloe's included.

Maddoc's whisper hits my ear. "Walk, Raven." His fingers skim across the waist of my jeans and my skin heats in unapproved excitement.

Yeah, it's been a while.

I step into the class and he keeps himself plastered against me until I quickly drop into my usual chair.

Of course, when he looks at the poor kid behind me, the dude moves without a sound and Maddoc lowers himself into the seat.

Right then, Bass walks in.

He nods his chin my way as he moves to his seat across the room and I give a small salute.

Cool ass cat and the only one in here who didn't notice Maddoc the second he entered.

Oh, but boss man noticed him.

He leans over me, his big ass body practically caving mine in.

"Why is Bass Bishop looking at you like he knows you better than anyone else in this room?"

I smirk to myself. "Maybe he does."

"Don't play, Raven."

"Don't worry, big man," I whisper teasingly, covering his fist with my palm, frowning when his fingers open to welcome mine. "I'm sure everyone staring thinks you're my number one."

He growls a bit but sits back, and for the rest of class I'm ultra-aware of the testosterone enveloping me from behind.

I could use a joint right about now.

I'M SITTING ON THE GRASS IN THE QUAD AREA WHEN A COLD splash hits my back, making me gasp.

My nostrils flare, the burn taking over and causing my eyes to water.

Bleach.

Fuck.

I rush to my feet, turning to the laughing figures behind me.

Chloe and her cultists.

"Hope you didn't think the Bray's little step backward meant we'd back off. They haven't announced you're off-limits to me, which means you're still on the edge."

My back starts to burn from the chemical searing my skin, but I don't show it.

"Careful, Raven. The fall is much harder the higher you are." With that, she tosses the ice bucket at my feet and strolls off.

I wait, making no move until she's around the corner, then yank my shirt over my head as I rush for the gym.

I ignore the whistles and stares and push forward, careful to at least keep my chest covered.

Right when I go to shove through the door, an arm latches around my elbow and I spin, letting my fist fly, but of course he catches it, his eyes narrowing.

The sting is too much at this point and moisture prickles behind my eyes, making his tighten.

"What the f—" Royce cuts off when the smell hits and he grips my hair bringing it to his nose.

He curses and pushes forward, dragging me to the girl's shower ... that he seems to have no problem finding.

He turns on the water and tries to grab ahold of my shirt, but I press it tighter against my chest.

"Let go of the fucking shirt, Raven. I've seen more tits than you can count, and you're wearing a bra."

"No."

He rolls his eyes. "Fine, get under the cold water. Your back's all red. It won't take it away, but you gotta wash the shit off." His frown curves into a grin in the next second. "Wanna take off your pants?"

I shove him back and step under the cool spray, wincing lightly when it hits my back. I let it run down my body a few minutes before gripping my hair and looking it over.

Shit. Ugly yellow and gold spots shine back at me toward the ends where the bleach ruined my black, never before dyed hair.

Bitch.

"Shit, RaeRae." Royce pulls my hair over my shoulder and runs his fingers through it. "Maybe you can cut it?"

Then she wins.

His fingertips run across my skin making me jump.

It's not like a heat burn, more irritating, but that fire feeling is still there.

I bend my back, and my bra scrapes against it making me wince.

"Son of a bitch."

"You need to unclip this thing, it's rubbing on you and it's soaked in bleach."

I huff, knowing he's right. "Fine, unclip it."

I pull my hair completely to one side and he steps under the spray with me, grabbing the clasp in his hand. Right when he goes to undo it, footsteps knock against the cement flooring behind us and we both turn to look over our shoulders.

Maddoc stands there, his face completely blank, but his hands are fists at his side, eyes not on me, but his boy.

It's a sight to see, I'm sure. Me and Royce dripping wet under water, my shirt off as he helps undo my bra.

Royce finishes undoing the clasp without looking and slowly lowers his hands.

The boys stare at each other a moment before Royce turns back to look over my skin, but my stare stays on Maddoc as he tracks Royce's every move.

Royce backs away after a minute and steps from the shower.

I reach out and turn off the spray, taking the towel he holds out for me.

I wrap it around my front, letting my bra and shirt drop to the ground.

That catches Maddoc's attention and his stare cuts to my discarded items.

Maddoc strides forward, his tension-filled eyes bouncing between mine before dropping to my shoulder, and for some reason I slowly spin, showing him what he's asking to see.

He doesn't touch me, but his eyes create a burn far deeper than the chemical that's only marred my skin's surface.

Captain comes around the corner in the next second, his eyes slow as they take in the scene, landing on mine last.

Maddoc doesn't move out of the way like Royce did, so Captain leans to the side to look past him, but he doesn't get too close.

And suddenly I feel like a helpless child again.

I'm not.

"All of you feel the need to be in the girl's locker room?"

They ignore me.

"Get Chloe and the others in the courtyard." Maddoc looks to his brothers.

"On it." Royce heads out.

"No," I argue and again, I'm ignored.

"I'll round the team." Captain starts to leave also.

"I said no!"

"I'll meet you guys out there," Maddoc tells them and fuck this shit.

I whip off a soiled shoe and toss it at their retreating bodies, hitting Captain square in the head.

They spin around with glares.

"I said. No." I step forward. "It's one thing to crowd my space, but I'm not a helpless little bitch who needs you to put yours in place. She wants to play, fine. It'll be on my terms."

"No. She made a move on you after she saw we had you in our hold."

"Not in your hold."

"Say what you want, it's what they should see and how they should understand."

"Okay." I nod, stepping back. "Okay, yeah. Go for it. Go run your little game, let her know you won't stand for it, make me your damsel."

All three stand taller, waiting for me to make my point but I wait.

Royce gives in first.

"Talk Raven, why would we not?" he snaps.

"You want them to think I fit in your world – still don't get that but whatever – yet you wanna step in to save the day after one little incident with the campus queen? All that'll do is make you look weak. 'Cause how could a nobody, dirty little whore – as you painted me before – like me, get under your skin to this point. A girl who, if you do this, can't even hold her own against a spoiled brat with a hard-on for three jackasses in Jordans?"

Three pairs of eyes narrow in thought and they look between each other.

"Weak links are holes in your armor. Back off and leave me be, nothing for you to worry about if you do, but if you insist on pretending we like each other, then let me handle this. I'm not weak. Don't make it seem like I am to feed your own egos." I shrug. "It'll only backfire."

"She's right," Captain agrees, and Royce swings a glare his way.

Maddoc, however, keeps his eyes on me.

He says nothing and goes to leave, a cussing Royce and silent Captain behind him.

Good.

This bitch needs to see ... I can handle anything she's got with a grin.

She's not used to girls like me.

She'll learn.

I quickly dress in some PE clothes, throw my hair up and leave the school.

When I get to the house, I've got it all planned on what to say to Maybell, but as I hit the steps, she opens the screen for me, a small smile on her lips.

"School nurse called, said you were headed home." She grasps my shoulders and helps me inside. "I warmed some soup for you, it's only from a can, but it'll do. Go on and get changed, it'll be on the table for ya."

I nod, and head for my room to put on some sweats and a T-shirt.

Thanks, boys.

Chapter 16

Maddoc

"Where is she?" Royce hums.

"Maybe she chickened out, took off," Captain says.

"What, like back where she came from?" Royce shakes his head. "Maybell would have told us."

Captain shrugs.

"No." I keep my eyes locked on the door. "She's coming."

"How can you be so sure? The rest of the girls already took off."

"Because she's convinced she's got pride. She couldn't walk away after yesterday if she wanted to."

Right then, the door opens and out she steps.

Royce laughs, smacking the back of the seat. "Hell yeah."

Captain grins and looks to me, but I keep my eyes locked on the lioness who has yet to spot us.

She lifts her backpack onto one shoulder and bends to tie the laces of her black combat boots, and when she stands, my dick thinks about going with her, 'cause fuck. Me.

Those boots make her little legs appear longer, her strong, thick thighs testing the stretch of her cut-off shorts, small enough to show her ass cheeks if she bends the wrong way.

She's wearing a white hoodie with bleeding roses in the center. The neck has been cut out so it hangs off the shoulder, showing the straps of her black bra, long, dark hair hanging down her back, silky straight and shining, a deep, dark blue now taking over the tips.

She looks like a project princess.

"She fuckin' spun that shit good, brothers. Damn." Royce grins then rolls his window down. "Get your ass in, Raven Carver."

She freezes and swings her head our way, scowling as she does.

A laugh bubbles out of her and she shakes her head. "Yeah, I'm not riding with you."

"Yeah, you are."

"No way in hell, that's all I need."

"Get in or we throw you in."

She flips us off and heads across the yard, so we roll beside her, stopping when she does.

At the fucking dude's house.

She leans against the porch, pretending we're not watching, and Royce drops back against his seat.

"The fuck's she doin'?"

Me and Cap say nothing, but watch as Bass fucking Bishop strolls out, looking like the other part to her duo, black, slick-backed hair, piercings, and shit.

He hops off the porch and they start walking, completely fucking ignoring the fact that we're trailing her ass.

Fuck this.

I hit the brakes. "Go get her."

With a laugh, Royce jumps and runs for her, tossing her over his shoulder as he salutes the fucker beside her.

She growls and runs that mouth of hers, but drops against the seat when he tosses her in.

We're silent on the short drive and then I'm whipping in the school parking lot, my tires screeching to a halt in the first open spot.

She jumps out, flipping us all off, and instead of going into the building she turns and heads back the fucking way we came, where that fucker is still walking.

I slam my door shut and Captain laughs.

"You all right there, brother?"

I ignore him and together we head for the entrance.

"Think she's fucking Bishop?"

Royce gives me a side eye and Captain raises a brow.

"Would it bother you if she was?"

When I don't respond, they laugh and shove me forward through the door.

Fuck her and fuck him too.

If I wanted her, I could have her.

I'd bet on that.

Raven

Bass says nothing about the boys' little show, so neither do I. Once we get to the school, the bell rings, but neither of us are in a hurry to learn.

"You sure you don't want to back out on tonight after yesterday? It's cool if—"

"I'm fine."

He grins and I roll my eyes.

"Don't be cheesy, Bass."

He laughs and grabs the door when I don't hold it open for him. "Hey, I was only gonna agree with you."

"Go to class."

"On it, Rae!" he shouts.

With a grin, I shake my head and round the corner, instantly slamming into a familiar body as I do. I stumble back, but not before he catches me in his arms.

I'm spun around until my ass hits the lockers, but he keeps a hand in the way of the metal, careful not to touch my burn against it.

"I want the truth from you."

"Be more specific, big man." I eye him and his hand moves to grip my hip.

"Bishop. That's who you sneak out to see at night."

"You're sounding like a broken record."

"Don't play."

"Fine. Maybe." Technically, the answer is yes. Not that he's earned it.

His nostrils flare and I raise a dark brow.

Oh, he doesn't like that answer.

"Whatever you're doing, it stops now."

I cluck my tongue, shaking my head. "That's not gonna work for me, big man. See I need Bishop." I hold in my smirk.

His fingertips dig into my skin, and want has me holding my breath.

He knows it, his smirk now coming out to play.

"I'll do anything he thinks he can, better."

"Is that an offer?"

"A guarantee," he growls.

"Well." I push off into him. "I'll remember that for when I get bored."

"You better watch yourself, Raven. You're Bray property now, and I'm done waiting for these fuckers to figure it out on their own.

By the end of the day, every-fucking-body will know it well. No bitch will challenge you and no guy will touch you unless we say go, so you better trim them nails, Snow, wouldn't want you to cut up your insides when you're stuck finger-fucking yourself each night."

"Fuck you."

His smirk turns venomous. "If you're lucky."

He pulls back and then he's gone.

And color me stupid, I think I'm hot for the bossy bastard.

It's been four days since Chloe's bullshit, and I'd swear she hates me more now than she did then.

That first day, she smirked and did a little swish with her head like victory was hers, that is until she let her eyes roll over me and saw I didn't chop my hair like she clearly hoped I would but covered the mess she made instead.

I had to pull out the bleach myself to make it even, then used a Kool-Aid packet I snuck from the cupboard at the home to add the color over it. It's not perfect and I'll have to touch it up, but it works for a temporary fix.

I'm assuming she thought I was as superficial as her, and my hair was my all. While I can admit, I like it, it's hair for fuck's sake – it grows back.

Still, eye for an eye.

And Maddoc didn't lie when he said he'd spread the word.

I've officially been deemed a "Bray girl" to the outside norms, but it's all a lie, a way for them to keep eyes on me and hands off – not sure why it matters. Probably because they don't want others to know I made impulsive decisions without their permission.

Chloe and her little crew are the bravest it seems. When the guys or their followers aren't around, they'll bump me or do their best to nail me in the head with a volleyball, nothing extraordinarily clever.

The door bursts open and laughter fills the locker room.

"Did you see her face?" Chloe laughs. "Priceless."

"I can't believe you forwarded that nude to her parents!" A minion laughs.

"She needs to understand she can't just date whoever she wants. We have standards and he's...poor. And grungy and likely to be the guy changing the oil not the one buying the car."

Bitch.

"How'd you get the picture anyway?"

"Had his locker broken into when he was in gym, and the message was forwarded to me. Best thing, she thinks he sent it to me to make fun of her!"

They all laugh like hyenas.

"He keeps trying to get her to talk to him, apologizing without even knowing why she's mad like a pathetic puppy, and she won't even look at him." She sighs happily. "Too easy."

I peek around the corner and when each girl is occupied changing out of their gym gear, I slip over and grab a handful of Chloe's hair.

She yelps, and jerks in my hold, but I let her go pretty quick.

She spins to glare and then her eyes shoot wide, her mouth dropping open.

I toss her pretty ponytail in her face and walk away before the shock can wear off.

Time for her to learn.

The boys may step in with unwanted orders, but don't try to cross someone on the court when their footwork's better.

You'll find yourself on your ass.

Chapter 17

Maddoc

"Let's hear it, D." Jason, one of my shooting guards, and the last fucking person I'd ever want on my team if we picked based on anything other than skill level, looks over at me. "Which one of yous got heavy hands?"

I frown, wiping the sweat from my face as I take the water Royce passes me, his expression matching mine.

"Fuck you talking about, man?" Captain comes up, his hands on his hips as he tries to catch his breath.

We worked a lot of cardio today, gearing up for week three of our season.

"Your new girl." He looks pointedly at each of us individually. "She spend too much time with one or another and you got mad?"

Something has me stepping forward, but Cap shifts in front of me with ease, giving me a warning glance to keep my shit together before I make a stupid fucking move by showing possessives over a fucking toy.

He steps away before Jason's eyes even hit mine again.

"You talking about Raven's face?" Our boy, Leo, drops onto the bench, switching out his old LeBron's for some slides. "Yeah, I saw that shit, too. She was walking back to the Bray house early this morning when I was out doing my route."

Leo is piss poor and delivers newspapers for a bit of cash at the crack of fucking dawn to the last few neighborhoods around here that still read the actual paper. Makes for a good second eye, sees what we can't and reports back when necessary.

"Yeah, that girl." Royce chuckles, only Cap and me can tell it's forced. "She's feisty."

And it's left at that.

Everyone parts ways and as soon as they're gone, I turn to my brothers.

"You guys see her yet today?"

"Nope." Cap shrugs and Royce shakes his head.

"What do you think happened?" Royce asks.

"Catty chicks?" Cap guesses.

Royce snorts. "Yeah right, none of them would get a hit on her."

"None are brave enough to try." I look between them. "We gotta find out. We already made it clear no one's to touch her after that bleach shit. Someone's not listening."

RAVEN

I SPIT, THEN WITH ALL THE ENERGY I HAVE LEFT, I THROW myself forward, hitting her square across the jaw. She stumbles into the crowd, her feet sliding from under her, ass hitting the ground.

The onlookers whistle and beer flies through the air, splashing onto me.

Fuck, I'll need to rinse these clothes before laundry goes in.

People try to get my attention, but I squeeze from the circle and move over to the crates.

Bass slips from the crowd with a grin as I'm jumping up. He flicks his lip ring with his tongue, shaking his head.

"Dayum, Rae. You only get better out here. You're a fucking beast."

I shrug, grinning to myself, sticking both hands out. He slaps money into one, then helps cut the tape off the other.

"Where the fuck you learn to box like that?"

"Mom's not much of a mom. Brought trouble."

"Ah." He nods. "You taught yourself, then?"

I inspect my knuckles on my left hand, squeezing my fists shut then opening them again. "When there's nobody else to keep hands off you, you learn to fight 'em off yourself."

He pauses, his eyes shifting between mine. "That bad where you came from?"

"I know others who had it worse."

He grabs my elbows and helps me down. "You always downplay your problems?"

I chuckle, shaking my head. "What do you know about my problems, Bass?"

"Not enough." He smirks and steps forward. "Change that, Rae."

I drop my grin to my feet before looking back up ... and then I'm pulled back.

"What the fu—"

I glance over my shoulder, and my blood boils as not one, but all three of my latest pain in the asses stand behind me. I try to jerk free of Maddoc's hold, but I'm only shoved down the line until Royce is gripping my forearms.

"That was some badass shit there, RaeRae," he whispers, laughing when I try and elbow him.

Bass shifts so he can meet my eyes through the three and Maddoc moves to block him.

"Rae—"

"You can go now, Bishop," Maddoc cuts him off. "And stay away from Raven."

He scoffs. "It's my job to bring in the—"

"I didn't ask you any questions," Maddoc cuts him off.

"Go, Bass, it's fine." I give him his out, no need for trouble to fall at his feet because of me. His eyes find mine again and he nods, glares at all three boys, then makes the smart choice by backing away. The last thing I want is for his side hustle to be blown up at the hands of these assholes.

They cage me in, all wearing familiar glares that have zero effect on me. I yank from Royce's hold, grab my sweater off the box and pull it over my head, snatch my backpack and place it over my shoulder and weave my way through the crates. And, of fucking course, they follow.

"This where you been sneaking off to late at night, to beat bitches' faces in?" Royce jokes. "And here I thought someone was keeping that pussy wet for—"

Royce grunts and I glance back, finding his glare on Maddoc.

"Why you fighting?" This comes from Maddoc.

"Because it's just so much fun." I roll my eyes, glancing from left to right to make sure there's no one watching, then slip through the broken fence and start through the parking lot.

"Money," Cap guesses as if there would be any other reason.

I cut my eyes toward him and he nods like he understands.

He doesn't understand shit.

I thought these boys were like me, but they're not. I don't know for sure what conditions they were raised in, how hard or easy they had it when push came to shove, but one thing's for sure, they were never poor boys from my kind of ghetto where you had to beg or steal to eat. I'm no thief and I refused to beg. It didn't take me long to find another way.

"Stop fucking walking," Maddoc complains and I stop all right, spinning to face him with a glare.

"Back the fuck off. Why are you guys even here? Shouldn't you be at your little party making sure no peasants make it through the door in the kings' absence?"

Royce grins at that and I roll my eyes. Idiot.

"Thanks to your bullshit, the school thinks you're one of ours. You—"

"No, big man," I cut him off with a mocking laugh and his jaw ticks. "They think I'm 'one of yours,' because you let them. Not my problem."

He gets in my face and I hold my breath. "Our boys are questioning us. You show up to school with random cuts and bruises and it's making people talk. We may be a lot of things, bastards in every way, but putting our hands on a woman when it's not part of fucking her, isn't our forte."

"Is that supposed to make me cream?" I whisper like a slut. "Listening to you talk about how strong you are, how bad you are, how your hands are meant for pleasure, not pain?"

His eyes harden.

"'Cause guess what, you're not the first boy to promise a prize at the end of the night who delivered a punch instead."

His brows snap at the center and he grabs my upper arm, but before he can open his mouth, voices float from the other side of the parking lot.

I jerk from his hold and start forward, but he yanks me back.

They drop down to hide between the cars and I frown.

"This is private property," Captain tells me as Maddoc yanks me down beside them.

I gape at them. "There's literally like three dozen people not fifty feet away, yelling and screaming, and duh ... illegally fighting." I widen my eyes like a brat. "It's no fucking secret there are people walking all around here."

The voice grows closer and Maddoc's head snaps toward the sound, his forehead wrinkling.

He recognizes the voices.

He meets Captain's stare before sliding it to Royce, who curses and props his head against the car door beside us, and it hits me.

They don't want to be seen out here. But why?

Maddoc glances around, but I can tell he already knows – there's no other way out of here.

Cap glares at me.

"What?"

"This is your fault."

My mouth drops open. "My fault?" I hiss. "You fuckers pretend to play nice, insert yourself in everything I do, tracked my ass down, and this is my fucking fault? Like the joint being in Maddoc's hand was 'my fault' or your followers thinking I'm with you because I noosed a girl for five seconds? You guys need to wake up and realize how weak you really are and fix it before someone who wants what you have comes in ready to take it. Can't even own up to your own bullshit 'cause it's just so much easier to lay blame on everyone else, huh?"

"Enough." Maddoc's voice booms in a hush.

I shift my glare to his. "It's enough when I say it's enough!"

The voices trail closer and all three of the boys' features tighten.

This, being here and being seen by these men, whoever the hell they are, is a problem for them.

Cap slips on his brass knuckles, Royce pops his and big man tips his chin.

Fuck.

I look down at my outfit – track pants, ripped up tennies, and a baggy sweater.

I squeeze my eyes shut.

This isn't my problem.

But I mean, if I'm seen, oh fucking well. I was on the cards tonight, meaning if I were questioned by security or who the fuck ever questions people at an underground fighting ring, I'd have reason to be here.

But what happens if they're seen?

Ugh, not your problem, Rae...

I bob my knee a minute before I shift to stand but bend so my height isn't over the car beside us. "Fuck it."

I start pulling off my battered shoes and socks and stuff them in my bag.

"The fuck..." Royce trails off.

My sweater is yanked off next and the boys' necks pull back.

I shove my shoes in my bag, pulling out a pair of dollar store flip-flops, not ideal for this, but better than the muddy sneakers.

My hand finds my waistband next and I start to slide my bottoms down.

"What's she doing?" comes from Cap, followed up with a, "Fuck if I know," from Royce.

"Stop fucking looking," growls Maddoc and then his hands hit my upper thighs, forcing my bottoms to stay where they are, halfway off my ass.

"I'm wearing Spanx under. Let go."

"What are you doing?"

"Distracting."

His eyes flare. "I don't fucking think so."

"I'm not asking," I force through clenched teeth and his fingertips dig into my skin, making my blood boil for two very different reasons. I downplay my reasoning. "I don't know about you, but I gotta get back."

Obnoxious laughter hits our ears and Maddoc glances over, giving me enough leeway to shift away from him.

I slide behind Captain, who boldly doesn't move when Maddoc tries to reach for me.

Their glares hit each other.

"Can't get caught, brother. Not here."

"You expect me to let her—" He cuts himself off before finishing his sentence.

Left in nothing but flip-flops, Spanx and my sports bra, I tap Cap's shoulder. "Give me your wife beater."

He doesn't hesitate to slip it off, leaving him shirtless.

Not a bad view at all – strong, solid back.

Maddoc growls as I pull it over my head, the black cotton hitting just at my thighs.

It's a little loose, obviously, but my ass cheeks are out and my legs look long and lean, so it does the job.

I pull my hair from the bun braid I'd thrown it up in and fluff it out so the waves fall along my shoulders and back. I lift my sweater and wipe away any dirt and blood that might linger near my lips and stuff it in my bag.

"Damn, Rae." Royce licks his lips and Maddoc steps for me again, but he's too late, I'm already rounding the back of the car.

I lick my lips and walk out as far right as I can before I hit the edge of the parking lot and head right for the men.

They spot me almost instantly and stand to attention.

I take a deep breath, lift my chin and sway my hips as I walk, just like mother showed me.

Draw them in with the twist of your body, lock them with your stare, and tease them with your mouth – it's the only way to fish, she'd say.

"Well, hello," one of the guys calls out, shining his flashlight in my face. "Can't say I'm mad to see you, but this is a private ground, sweetheart."

I can't simply say I was on the card for tonight, because then they'll dismiss me quick, telling me to get lost and I need to keep their attention longer than that.

I don't flinch or squint. I keep my eyes open. "And I just got done with a private party for two. I'd offer services, but my carriage is waiting up the street."

The light lowers to my body, so I can finally see to quickly count the men.

Four, all grown and if their beady eyes, twitchy movements, and sweat sheathed skin when it's pushing sixty degrees tells me anything, no one's clean. They've all got something running in their veins.

This is so stupid of me.

And for what? So the assholes that followed me here can slip out? To keep them from being seen or heard?

Stupid.

I would have hung back and waited for Bass to be done and walked back with him, now look.

"A private party, huh?" The flashlight lowers to their feet as I plant mine in front of theirs.

I shift with a smirk, purposefully moving to stand two feet to their left, forcing them to have to turn in order to look. And they want to look.

I'll have to scrub my skin extra hard with overheated water to rid myself of the things they're showing they want to do to me.

"Who was this little party with?"

"Can't tell. If his wife finds out, I'll lose him as a client. And he's too good to me for that." I spin my hair around my fingers, slowly licking my lips.

God this shit's exhausting.

The boys sneak past us at the rear of the vehicles,

Maddoc's eyes hitting mine for a brief moment as they silently pass.

The men, clueless as ever, chuckle lightly, one thumping the other with his elbow as if he knows who I'm talking about.

There's always a married sleaze mixed in a group of trashy men.

I give a sultry laugh on purpose and cringe internally at the way I sound.

I place my foot on the bumper, pretending to dust something off my ankle in order to get them to shift one more time so the boys can exit the yard.

One of them inches closer so I spin, quickly planting myself against the hood. They move in and my pulse spikes as I start to feel crowded.

The boys have to be at their truck now.

Time to get out of here.

I go to slip right, but one steps closer blocking my move, his slimy body brushing me, his excitement disgustingly present through his dirty jeans.

I laugh, but it comes out choked and then it's them who's laughing.

"Think you can handle a party of four, baby? We'll treat you good. Might not be able to walk tomorrow, but you hookers get off on that sort of thing, right?"

I grin, but it's tight and so is the grip that wraps around my wrist.

"Yeah, I think you'll like it. Why don't you—"

My free hand flies up, the heel of my palm cracking against his nose and instantly it starts gushing blood. The guy staggers back, his eyes wild, and one more moves in.

I swing my bag to hit him, but another wraps around my back. I relax every muscle, forcing him to hold my dead weight and the little bitch isn't strong enough.

My feet hit the ground again and I use that as leverage to kick the one coming at me from the front in the nuts.

It works for a second, but in the next, my throat is in bloody hands and I'm lifted off the gravel.

My hands move to grip his, but his lock is tight and not going anywhere, so I pull my legs up, forcing him to hold me there until I can get a good, flat-footed kidney shot.

He wheezes but keeps his fucking grip and I'm damn near out of options, especially if the others decide to move in.

He starts shaking me, growling in my face and then both our bodies hit the dirt with a loud thud.

I start coughing, scurrying back a few feet to try and gain a breath while he rolls around in pain. Pretty sure his head slammed real good.

When I look up, I find Maddoc.

And Royce.

And Captain.

What the fuck?

Movement to my right has me bouncing to my feet. I quickly knee one of the guys as he throws himself at me while each boy lays out another.

Royce grabs my shirt and starts pulling me away when more voices and more footsteps grow closer, so I grab my backpack and run with him, but when I glance back, I see Maddoc is still laying it on the guy who had me by the neck.

I slow my steps and Royce pulls harder.

"Let's fucking go!" he shouts, but I yank free, drop my bag and run back.

I catch Maddoc's arm in the air and pull.

He spins, ready to throw a punch but when he sees it's me, he freezes. His face travels over mine, inspecting for damage it looks like, before meeting my eyes.

I nod. "We gotta go."

His face tightens, his jaw clenching so I nod again.

"Now!" Cap hollers in from behind me and an engine roars.

Maddoc hops to his feet, gripping my hand to pull me with him, but I free myself and am one step ahead of him.

Royce holds open the back door and the three of us jump inside. Cap puts the pedal to the metal, and we're gone.

I go to climb over the console to hit the front seat and make more room, but Maddoc pulls me back down.

And yet again nobody says a goddamn word during the ten-minute drive back.

We pull up in front of the girls' Bray house and Cap screeches to a halt. Simultaneously, all their glares fly to me.

"What?"

They say nothing.

With a roll of my eyes, I go to hop out, but Captain hits a button, and gee look at that, child fucking lock.

"What you did tonight was reckless." Captain's eyes narrow.

"You basically summed me up in with one word. That's what I do, that's who I am."

"You could have gotten yourself hurt."

"Newsflash lost boys, this life isn't new to me. I get my hands sticky and I figure it out. Sometimes it's just more complicated."

"You did all that so we could sneak off," Royce says, sitting forward like he wants me to see him better.

I look off instead. "I did it so I could get back before Maybell found out I was gone."

"Bullshit," Maddoc drags out and I glare his way.

"Why else would I?"

"Don't be a pussy, Raven," he calls me out. "Say it."

I look between the three, all waiting for the obvious answer.

With a growl, I throw my hands up. "Fine. You guys were trippin' on those men. You knew them or of them, something.

Either way, you recognized the voices and didn't want to be found for a reason. I, on the other hand, don't fucking care so I figured I'd distract them for you." I glare at them. "You were supposed to leave ... unseen."

They eye me, but no one says a word. I haven't decided yet if quiet Brayshaws are worse than rowdy Brayshaws.

It's kind of annoying when you're the one they're staring at, but you're not privy to what's happening on the inside.

They have the same look on their faces – a look that gives you nothing. But there's something rolling around in their minds, a thought not spoken but understood among the three.

I will admit, it's hella cool how they're connected on a deeper level than what outside eyes can see, they seem to know exactly what the other is thinking.

This must be a part of why they're loved and feared. Or secretly hated, but respected nonetheless. Because in the company of others, they work as one.

They'll speak, mull over how to move forward from here.

But not in my presence.

Because who am I?

Just the latest trash dropped on a rickety doorstep with not a soul's back to lean against. Forever the unwanted outsider, something I've always told myself I was okay with.

A click sounds, so I try the door again and it opens.

I grab my bag and don't look back, headed for my bedroom window.

I slip inside undetected and change my clothes. I hit the bathroom and rinse what I can with the sink water turned on low so it doesn't wake the entire house – showers aren't allowed after lights out or I'd hop right in.

When I exit the bathroom, Maybell is standing there with her little nightlight in hand and I freeze, but she only nods.

"Go on to bed now, child."

I don't bother making up a lie. I have a feeling she knows more than she leads on.

I step around her, heading back to my room, and slip into bed. I turn on my flashlight, plug my headphones in and blast the music. I reach for my knife, place it in the hem of my shorts and stare at the door, waiting for sleep to force my hand.

My eyes just start to close when a figure flashes at my side. I quickly flip open my switchblade, my arm lifting to block the person's hand when it reaches for me.

The blade makes contact with skin and the figure jolts back.

I scurry across my sheet to grab my flashlight and point it on the person.

Maddoc is in front of me, glaring down at his shirt, a red spot forming just above his hip.

His eyes fly to mine. "You fucking cut me."

"What the hell are you doing here?!" I hiss.

He ignores me and lifts his shirt over his head to inspect the wound.

And fuck the wound ... hello abs, and son of a shit, those hip bones. Thick rooted veins offering the perfect path to follow with my tongue, starting a few inches past his belly button and disappearing into grey joggers. Joggers that do nothing to hide the size of his package as it fights against the smooth cotton.

He's thick.

I bet with the tiniest of tugs, his drawstring bottoms would slide right down, granting better access to the prize he's clearly packing.

When a deep rumble leaves him, my eyes fly back to his.

Oh right, I kinda cut him.

I scoot across the mattress on my knees before standing in front of him. I lick my finger and swipe across the wound to remove the blood and he twitches.

"Chill. I hardly broke the skin, can't hurt that bad."

He shoves my hand away when I dab at it. "It doesn't hurt at all."

My hands fly in the air and I drop back on my bed. "I'd say my bad, but it's yours 'cause you snuck up on me."

He licks his lips, staring at me, his shirt hanging in his hand.

"Why you here?"

"Making sure you are."

"You dropped me off, did you not?"

"That don't mean shit." He shrugs.

"So you wanted to know if I was really here or if I snuck into someone else's bed for the night?"

He doesn't deny it. Doesn't confirm it either.

"Well I'm here, guess you can go now."

He ignores me and moves to grab my knife, but I yank it back.

His eyes flash. "Why do you have that?"

"Habit." Not a lie.

His fixated stare makes me nervous and I force myself not to fidget.

That's definitely new and not at all okay.

"Why do you sleep with it?" he asks.

"Don't worry about it."

"Your mom's boyfriends?" he guesses and my nostrils flare.

"Don't pretend to care."

"I'm not."

"Then don't pretend interested in the answer," I snap, a hollowness taking over my stomach. "Get the fuck out."

He makes no move, trying to keep his frown in place, and while he's sly, I'm observant – he's looking me over, inspecting the damage done. Not that my scrapes and bruises would cause him pause but still.

"Fine. But hear me, Raven, you will not fight for Bishop again." He hops out the window.

I lean against the frame. "You gonna tell me to stay away from him too?"

He glances at me over his shoulder, those eyes as unrelenting as ever. "Don't ask stupid questions you already know the answer to." My eyes fall to his mouth when his tongue pokes out to skim across his lips.

Maddoc takes a step back and my eyes lift to meet his once more.

He shakes his head, disappearing into the darkness.

I grin to myself as I make sure to lock the window behind him. Asshole.

Twisting the knife around, I run my fingers across the fading engraving on the handle: family runs deeper than blood.

I don't know what it means, but the knife itself gives me comfort.

There was only one man who ever positively acknowledged my mom had a kid and remained that way all through his time around her. He was a piece of shit just the same, would show up and disappear into her room to be with her just like the rest, but he always brought me ice cream and a portable DVD player with a new movie each time. He'd tell me to turn it up and usually by the time it was over, so was his paid session. He'd grab the movie and go.

The last time I saw him, though, he didn't stay long. He dropped down beside me, looking a little solemn as he gave me this knife. He told me to hide it on me at all times and use it whenever I felt I needed to. He had said the words inscribed were true, that I didn't have to accept my life just because I was born into it.

He told me family was choice, not a burden of birth. He said it was up to me to find the feeling and never to settle for less than what I wanted.

I'm pretty sure he'd just realized my mom brought almost all her "work" home with her and he felt like crap about it, but at the time I took his words and held onto them. And since that day my knife grants me sleep at night.

Maddoc's blood is only the second person's to touch the blade.

Doubt his'll be the last.

I lay back down, flashlight on, earbuds in and knife tucked away once more.

Sleep never comes.

Chapter 18

Raven

It rained all night and shows no sign of letting up anytime soon, so everyone who could scrounge a buck-fifty jumped on the city bus for the short drive to school – a mile and a half in the rain on foot is not fun.

Lifting the sleeve of my sweater to cover my yawn, I drop my back on the bus bench and close my eyes. The ride is only five minutes down the road, but any extra seconds of rest will do me good right now.

After Maddoc left last night, I couldn't sleep. Adrenaline was too high as always after a fight, and I knew nothing short of a Xanax would work. Of course, I didn't have any of those around here.

Back home, though not always paid, I fought more often so the balance was better. All it would take is a couple of cheap beers or shots, if I had the money, to calm myself. I didn't have all this extra built-up energy inside me with nowhere to put it.

On a regular day, I only ever got maybe three to four hours of sleep, so I knew when I hit my pillow last night I was screwed.

The squeaky brakes jerk us to a stop and my back shakes against the seat, making my headache that much worse.

Bass's elbow hits me in the ribs, so I elbow him back. When he smacks my thigh, my eyes fly open and I roll my head to glare at him.

His face is blank as he tips his chin to the front of the bus, not bothering to move his DJ size headphones from his ears.

I ignore him and close my eyes.

"Son, you paying or not?" the bus driver asks in her scratchy smoker's voice.

"That'd be a negative, bus driver lady. Just looking for—" My eyes snap forward and Royce answers my glare with a grin. "There she is! Let's go, RaeRae."

"What are you doing?" I call from my seat about four rows back and he leans against the driver's holding bar.

"Waiting for you."

Every damn eye on this piece of shit bus is on me, and there are not just students from the Bray houses on here, but common workers and stragglers from the surrounding areas.

"Go away, Royce," I force through clenched teeth.

"Can't."

"Look, people have places to be—"

Royce's fierce chuckle has the lady's mouth clamping shut, and a vindictive smile forms on his lips. "This is Brayshaw business." He drops his name like a dick and the poor chick visibly pales. "The bus can move when I say it can move. And it doesn't until she gets off." He moves his eyes back to mine, all signs of playfulness gone.

The driver shifts to look my way. "I need you to get off now, dear."

"No," I snap.

Her features tighten, and I feel kind of bad but fuck, dude.

No.

Royce shakes his head like he's disappointed but expected my answer. He glances out the open door and shrugs.

And of fucking course Captain is now stepping on. He and Royce head down the aisle, and right before they reach me, a whisper hits my ear, causing me to jump.

"Move that ass, Raven. Now."

I turn to face him, but his eyes aren't on me. They're on my seat companion.

So, big man snuck on through the back door. Awesome.

"Get off already, Rae. Or we'll all be late." That comes from Victoria.

When I flip her off, Captain turns toward her, but she quickly averts her gaze.

With a light growl, I push to my feet, but I don't go out the back with Maddoc, I head forward and shove past the other two clowns who laugh and turn to follow.

I stop as I go to exit and glance to Bass, but he and Maddoc are stuck in a stare off, neither looking away before I step off the bus and into the rain.

Royce tosses his jacket on my head and I toss it in a puddle on the ground.

He glares, snatches it up and grips my arm, pulling me toward the stupid SUV. He opens the door and sweeps a hand, so I slide inside like the puppet they seem to love to play.

"This is bullshit."

"Not worth the fight, girl."

"Fuck off."

Captain grins and slides behind the wheel as Royce makes his way to the passenger seat.

Finally, Maddoc opens the door and eases himself in.

He doesn't say a word, doesn't even look my way, but for some reason, the boys laugh and then the car is moving.

Unreadable asshole.

I don't bother questioning them when we pass the school – it'll do me no damn good – but I'm not too mad about it when we pull up at a donut shop a few blocks down.

Cap steps out but pokes his head back in.

"Chocolate sprinkles and hot chocolate," Royce tells him, and I fight a grin.

"Coffee," Maddoc tells him and then Captain looks to me.

"Don't be difficult—"

"Two maple bars and a coffee, half cream/half coffee."

He frowns.

"What?" I ask straight-faced. "Thought I'd turn down sugar pretending to be a rabbit eater?"

Captain nods. "Yeah, for some reason I did." He heads inside.

I sit back, letting out a little sigh, excited about my treat.

Maddoc's lip tips up the tiniest bit and I jerk my stare forward.

"You don't have to pretend not to enjoy us, RaeRae." Royce grins in the mirror at me. "We're quite awesome to be around. You'll see."

"Will I now?"

"Yep. You will. 'Cause you're on lockdown, baby. Where we go, you go."

"Why?" I ask, but I'm looking at Maddoc now.

"Because that's where we want you."

"Again. Why?"

His eyes roam over my features before he faces forward again. "Not sure yet."

Right.

Captain comes back and passes out everyone's stuff, and when I open my bag, I find a third maple bar staring back at me.

I smile at the sugary goodness and pull some cash out of my pocket.

His grin disappears and a hardened glare takes its place. He shoves my hand away. "Do not try to hand me money again. If I offer you something, I'm fucking paying for it, do you understand?"

My pride screams to argue, but the look in his eyes tells me this is more than pride to him. He has a natural need to care for someone and my not allowing it will tear at what I'm gonna guess he's worked hard – or is working hard – to achieve. It'll tear at the type of man he wants to be.

I thank him, and his easy smile has something in my chest thawing a bit.

I bury my face in my food a moment to hide the confusing feeling.

So, Captain is the nurturer.

I look to Royce who grins like a little boy at his candy covered treat then turn to Maddoc who quietly bobs his head to the music, sipping on his black coffee as he watches the rainfall from his side window.

From where I'm sitting, they seem so simple. Just three teenage boys headed to school.

I wonder what Royce and Maddoc's roles are in their threesome?

What would mine be?

The thought has me jerking upright in my seat. The fact that I even stopped to wonder this tells me I need to get the hell out of this vehicle, which is why the second we pull up to the school, I reach for the handle but yay fucking me, child lock again.

Royce laughs and I turn his way.

"Precaution. Can't have you ditching us."

"You think forcing me off a bus and locking me in this bitch will help you in your incessant need to have me around?"

"Would you have come if we asked?" he challenges.

"No."

He tries to frown but grins and damn it, mine follows.

I laugh lightly and drop back in the seat. "So what's your guys' plan, for real? Why am I in this car with you right now? What purpose does this serve?"

"Nobody does a damn thing for us because they want to. They do it when they want something. You didn't hesitate. Didn't think twice, when you probably should have, so ... now we're curious," Captain says.

"About what?"

When both Captain and Royce look to Maddoc, I do the same.

He stares a moment before he says, "Everything."

The way he says it, combined with the frenzied look in his eyes tells me he ain't lying. He, for one, is curious about ... everything.

"Not that I'd believe you, but for the fuck of it, tell me ... do I need to watch my back when it comes to the three of you or is this a temporary treaty of sorts?"

"Treaty?" Maddoc raises a brow, a smirk on his thick ass lips.

"Yeah, your highness. Can I piss in peace or not?"

"Bad example, RaeRae, 'cause now we're all picturing you with your pants around your ankles."

My eyes snap to Royce's just in time to see him slapping at the air like he's smacking ass and I can't help it, I bust up laughing.

Captain reaches over and pops a chuckling Royce in the back of the head and Maddoc frowns at me.

I shake my head, licking my lips, ignoring how all three sets of eyes have zero self-control and each land on my mouth.

"Okay, you guys are way too dick-driven for a girl to be in your mix. Maybe you should rethink—"

"Out of the car, Raven. Time to put on a show."

A show.

Right.

I try the handle again and the damn thing opens.

I attempt to delay this little sighting they've clearly set up, but Maddoc is quick to tell me to hurry up.

All the boys, sexy and domineering in their own way stand at the front of the vehicle, tall and broad and untouchable, even by the rain it seems as the sky begins to clear. Gone are the easy smiles and teasing grins. Their eyes are empty, their stares blank.

This is who the world gets – cool, cold and calculated.

I hitch my backpack up over my shoulder and slowly move for them. I meet each one's stare, nodding as a silent message passes, and not just between them, but for me as well.

Here, they're not three boys who need more, they don't smile at donuts, or enjoy the rain.

Here, they're the Boys of Brayshaw and nothing else.

So why did I get to see a little from the inside?

An even better question, why does it make me feel ... I don't know how I feel.

Annoyed. Confused.

Optimistic...

I shake it off and together the four of us make our way up to the front. Once we hit the doors, Maddoc grabs my elbow and pulls me to the side.

I look to him with drawn in eyebrows, but he glances away.

We stand there a few moments and then the doors burst open, a man in a suit leading one of the teachers out, shining cuffs slapped across his wrists.

His head is down, but as he passes, it pops up. He spots the boys and pales, jerking his stare forward.

My eyes follow them down the steps and around the corner.

I didn't even spot a cop car.

I turn around right as a girl shuffles out, fear I recognize etched in her eyes as she cradles herself more with each step, a seemingly loving mother crying at her side.

The girl's eyes discreetly lift, quickly skating past the guys and instantly her tears fall. She grips her mother's hand, giving me a tight smile as she passes.

I cut my tense expression to Maddoc, but his eyes follow the mother and daughter to their car at the curb.

And then nothing else is said.

Royce pulls open the door, winking at me as I slide past him and again we fall in line. Every few feet more join, falling behind us. Leo, the guy who gave me a ride to the party, being one, but he doesn't acknowledge my presence, which is fine. The rest of the guys I recognize from gym – their teammates, I think.

No females walk over. But oh, do they stare.

When their feet stop moving mine do too.

Captain looks to the guys behind him and everyone scatters.

"She was abused," he tells me.

I nod, having gathered that, but it doesn't explain what just happened.

Cap nods and walks away, leaving me, Royce and Maddoc.

Maddoc gives knuckles to Royce then glances to me.

He pulls his bottom lip between his teeth as he walks backward, his head tipped back the slightest bit. It's sexy as shit, the bastard.

"See you in class, Snow."

I nod, unable to look away as he turns and walks off.

Girls call his name as he passes, but he pretends not to hear them and continues down the hall solo.

"Look away, RaeRae. Your nipples are getting hard and your bra has no padding." Royce eases the tension with his fuck boy ways.

I roll my eyes and head into class, not bothering to turn around when I say, "How would you know?"

"Baby, I know my tits, all right. And yours? Plump and high and perfect. Little jiggle, slight movement. At best you've got a scrap of lace or that thin satin."

I laugh lightly and he shouts, "Ha! Knew it."

Definitely not lace or satin, but some other stretchy material. It's cheap, simply put, so not much coverage.

"You're a horny bastard, aren't you?" I ask him as I slide into my seat.

He looks at me with a squished expression. "No shit, Rae. I'm a boy."

With a roll of my eyes, I pull open my bag, I take out my last maple bar. I tear it down the middle and offer him half.

He takes it with a wink and shoves the entire thing in his mouth.

"Look at us, RaeRae. Sharing sweets." He speaks with his mouth full, not bothering to swallow as he leans close and my eyes narrow. "Wanna share something else sweet with me?"

I snort and face forward.

The teacher comes in and class starts instantly.

Chapter 19

Raven

The boys have picked me up every day this week and it's starting to mess with my head. I don't know how to handle consistency at other people's hands. It makes me anxious. I go to bed wondering if they'll be there and wake up with the same question. It's annoying, but I can't help it. I've never known constant. Things, people, only ever come and go in my world so when something is repeated, I sit and wait for the reverse.

So today, to get rid of the knots in my stomach, I left before they could possibly arrive, just in case they didn't. An hour and fifteen minutes before school was even set to start, to be exact.

It's chilly, but fresh outside so I opt for the hill out back that overlooks the courts.

There are a few guys out there shooting hoops, I can't see who they are from here, but I can tell their game isn't as strong as the boys' is.

Okay, why is that the first thing I notice?

"Sup, Rae."

I look to the side to see Bass walking up. "Bishop."

"Saw you head this way pretty early this morning."

"Yeah." I look back to the courts. "I'm not a fan of regularity."

"I can get that." He drops down beside me, laying back on the grass so his face is even with mine. "Just another way our parents fucked us up, right?"

"You have parents, Bass?"

"Define parents?"

I scoff and look to the sky again. "Right."

"So what's up with you and the Brays?"

I shrug against the grass. "Nothing."

"You sure?"

"I am."

"Not sure they'd agree with you."

I sigh. "Yeah, me either."

This time it's him who scoffs.

We lay there, just chillin', until the first bell rings, warning us we have ten minutes to get to class, and then we make our way back inside.

The second we step through the door, the whispers start, and the dickheads in the hall purposely part ways, making sure the angry eyes at the end of the walkway have a perfect view of Bass and me.

And son of a bitch, why do I instantly get a sick twist in my stomach.

While Captain looks passive, Royce looks a little put out, and Maddoc .... well, Maddoc is fuming. I'm talking hellraiser ready.

Chills break across my skin at the possessiveness he's exuding. His gaze is greedy and I'm not sure he's aware of it.

"Sorry, Bishop," I whisper from where we stand. "Didn't think this one through."

"Don't worry about it," Bass speaks under his breath. "I came to you today."

"Yeah," I mumble, doubt easily heard and Bass turns to look at me. "But green runs the world, remember?" I shrug and walk away so he doesn't have to decide whether or not to.

The boys don't wait but meet me halfway, glares in full effect.

"Don't push us, Snow," Maddoc whispers, disapproval polished in his eyes.

He's the first to walk off, then Captain, but Royce hangs back.

He steps forward, eyes narrowing farther by the second. He pulls a bag from his backpack and shoves it in my chest before turning around and storming off. I don't need to open it to know it's half of his sprinkle donut.

I don't know these guys any better than the next, but for the first time in maybe, well ever, I feel like I let someone down.

I don't like it and unfortunately for me, I spend all morning stressing on it.

I drop into my seat for third period and wait for Maddoc to enter and take his.

Neither Royce or Captain said a word to me during our classes together and I found myself irritated over it.

And that only irritated me more.

I admit I like their banter. It's fun and easy. Natural like.

Whatever that means.

I lay my forearms against the desk, keeping my eyes on the door.

It takes a good fifteen minutes after the final bell before Maddoc finally rolls in, in no kind of hurry. His face is a perfect mask, hair mused, and collar stretched.

The sight has my mind racing. Thoughts of what, or who, sexed him up making me grind my teeth.

He licks his lips, those eyes of his, darker than normal, scanning my face as he moves past me for his seat at my back.

My leg starts bouncing as I fight not to turn around and inspect him closer, my need to know far too strong for my own liking.

Then Bass storms in with his shirt torn at the bottom, eye damn near as black as his hair, lip fat and swollen against the silver ring.

He doesn't look my way and my muscles grow stiff.

Son of a bitch.

I drop back against the seat, annoyed with my own damn self when a sense of relief floods knowing he wasn't held up at the hand of a female. I feel especially shitty about knowing Bass got the shit end of the stick, or rather, Maddoc's fist.

Maddoc's voice hits my ear in the next second, and I force myself still. "You asked me before if I'd tell you to stay away from him. I didn't do it, but I thought the answer you got was clear. This is what'll happen every time you don't listen." The hairs on my neck stand to attention, goose bumps rising on my arms beneath my long sleeve. "You ... are mine, Raven."

Because I have zero self-control at the moment, I turn to him.

'Course he's not sitting in his chair, like the rest of us. No, big man is braced against his desk. Like a true king, or dominant male making a point, he's raised taller than the rest of us, his chest strong and straight.

His expression doesn't change, his eyebrows hold stern, chin lifted so he can look down at me more. He's daring me to fight him on this, likely wishing I would so he can go caveman again.

Boy's got so much to learn.

I look from his eyes to his tight set mouth, and back.

And instead of arguing or pushing or anything else he clearly expected ... I wink, then face forward.

If it were possible, I'd swear I heard him smirk.

⏺

"We're going to the grove."

"Good for you." I drop my paper in the basket and shuffle out of class, Royce right behind me.

"Oh, sorry," he chuckles. "Guess that did sound a lot like a comment, huh?"

With a glare, I spin to face him, and he grins wide.

"Let me try that again. We are going to the grove. Meaning so are you."

"Right."

"Damn right." He flings an arm over my shoulder.

"Okay, I'll bite." I shift my grin to Royce while shrugging his arm off. "What the hell is 'the grove?'"

"Circle of cabins surrounding a man-made lake 'bout three hours north. Tons of sex, lotta alcohol, and more fun."

"Sounds like a blast."

"Fuck yeah it is. We go several times a year, party, get fucked up. It's a three-day weekend. Tradition."

"Because I'm privileged like you and yours and can take off for three days," I mock.

He glares and I pop a shoulder. It's true.

"Look, a three-day weekend with you guys isn't worth the trouble that being labeled a runaway would bring, and I'm not looking to trade the bed I've got for a cot worse than what I sleep on at home."

"Like that's... wait." Royce frowns. "What do you sleep on at home?"

"This isn't Q and A time!"

"Right." He nods. "What were we talking about again?"

"You guys leaving, me staying." I stop next to the girl's bathroom and he steps beside me.

"Nah, you're going. Let us worry about Maybell."

A laugh bubbles out of me. "Yeah, no. No way is that happening. Don't cause unnecessary issues."

"Don't worry, RaeRae."

I walk into the bathroom with an eye-roll. When I stop inside the door to pull off my backpack, Royce stumbles against me.

The girls in the bathroom shriek and I turn to glare at him.

"Royce. Go away."

"Nope." He crosses his arms, widening his stance. "Not 'til you agree."

I shake my head with a sigh. "You're gonna do whatever you want as it is. I don't know why I even talk or why you're pretending to care what I say."

"Aww," he coos, and I'd swear it's genuine, damn child. "You're catching on."

"And you're pissing me off." I cross my arms to match his. "Get out."

"Hey, Royce," comes from behind me and I turn to glare at the girl who just came out of the stall.

"Seriously? In the bathroom?"

The girl at least has the dignity to blush.

Idiot.

"Just do your business. I'll wait."

My fingers find my temple and I blow out a deep breath. "For fuck's sake, forget it."

I push past him, back out the door and he follows, but my feet slow when I spot Maddoc and Captain standing not three feet away, talking with each other.

Both their gazes snap to mine right as Royce's chest plows into my back again, causing me to stumble forward. His arm shoots out, quickly wrapping around my middle to keep me from face-planting onto the marble floors.

Maddoc's stare slices to Royce's hand fixed on my abdomen.

"Damn, RaeRae," Royce pretends to complain, but his natural flirty fire is easily heard. "Quit stopping right in front of me."

I pull away from him. "How about stay off my heels or maybe watch where you're going, or better yet, go away!"

Royce laughs and looks to his boys, nodding his chin their way.

"He tell you about this weekend, Raven?" Captain asks, an annoyingly cautious stare sliding between us.

I cross my arms and frown. "Did he tell me I don't get a say and have to allow you guys to convince Maybell to let me go, even though it'll cause problems for me at the house when all the girls see what they're sure to consider special treatment – because it is?"

"Yeah, all that." Captain nods and Royce grins, throwing his arm around my shoulder again.

"Sure did."

I look to Maddoc, but he doesn't say a word, his mask is in place, empty eyes and all as he studies me.

I hate how one look from him has me on edge.

"We're leaving now."

My eyes fly to Captain. "Now."

"Now."

"It's not even lunch."

"Quit fucking complaining," Royce chastises me. "And don't worry about Perkins busting you. It's handled. Maybell too."

When my eyes narrow, Captain looks away and Royce grins. "So—"

"Yes, fuck me, we did it behind your back, you were the last to know, you didn't get to choose, blah blah blah. Get used to it already."

"You boys are ... forget it. Fine, whatever." I sigh. "I hate school anyway."

"Our shit's ready. We'll give you ten minutes tops."

I glare at Maddoc. "I could pack everything I own in ten minutes. Think I can be ready for a weekend in two."

"Bring a swimsuit."

I frown. "It's November."

"And there are hot tub parties." Royce grins.

"Well, I don't have one."

Captain looks to Maddoc who nods his chin.

"Don't worry about it, let's go."

With a sigh, I throw my hands out, motioning for them to lead the fucking way.

Once we climb in Maddoc's truck, I tell them, "If I get kicked out, one of you bastards are driving me all the way back home. I'm not getting stuck in a juvenile hall where I won't know anyone."

Captain's lip twitches but it's Royce who says, "Deal." Big man says nothing and then we're off.

Chapter 20

Raven

"What is taking them so long?" I drop my head back on the seat.

"Stop whining, it's been ten minutes." Captain shakes his head.

"Ten minutes of sitting here. We've been in the car for two fucking hours."

"It's called a road trip."

I look out the window with a frown.

Captain turns in his seat. "Never been on a road trip?"

I roll my head across the seat to look back his way. "You'd have to have a car to go on a road trip."

He studies me. "Your mom never had a car?"

"Once. For about a week."

"What happened to it?"

"Clientele was low, she ran out of cash and needed a fix."

He nods, but no judgment shows in his light eyes. "None of your friends back home had cars either?"

Friends. Yeah, people never liked me much.

My face must giveaway my thought because Captain licks his lips and looks off.

"Dated a guy with a car once." I smirk and Captain's stare comes back to mine. He lifts an eyebrow. "Didn't take any trips, but we spent a lot of time in that car."

Captain laughs, making me laugh lightly with him.

The doors fly open then and in slides Maddoc and Royce.

Maddoc looks to me expectantly.

"Just telling Cap here about my extensive knowledge of a nineteen-ninety Honda Civic … hatchback."

Maddoc squints.

"Buckle up, big man. We're ready to get on the road." I grin and he lifts a dark brow.

With a laugh I sit back, snagging a bag of chips from his bag and pop them open.

"So, what's this place like anyway?"

"It's chill," Royce says. "Ours is the farthest in the back, up against the creek."

"Yours?"

"Yup."

When nothing else is said, unease circles in my stomach.

"Wait ... what?"

Royce spins in his seat, shooting for innocent, but looking like a damn problem child. "Half the senior class will be there."

"No."

"Yes."

"Royce." Fuck. "I don't wanna play with your friends," I snap.

"You'll play with nobody," Maddoc butts in with a scowl.

"Stop acting like you'd have a say."

"Stop pretending like I don't."

I shift in my seat to face him full on. "I'm not a fucking

whore, but if I wanted to act like one, I would. And there's not a damn thing you could do about it. I won't bend at your will."

"No, but you'll drop to your back at yours."

My mouth gapes, but I quickly close it, glancing off before my eyes give me away. Hate to admit it, but his floppy ass attitude delivered a small sting. I don't appreciate my mind and my emotions not being on the same page here.

He opens his mouth to say something else but, Royce beats him.

"Speaking of the female species and horizontal positions ... don't go around choking chicks or cutting off ponytails this weekend, a'ight? Pussy will be slim pickin', and I want a new rider every night. No cockblocking."

"Seriously?"

"Hell yeah."

"So ... you expect me, the ghetto girl from the group home, a literal fucking charity case, to step into some rich kid zone, and let them run all over me if they try?"

Royce pouts like a child and Captain clears his throat.

"I might be with Royce on this one. Maybe you can get yours when we get back?"

"The fuck?" Maddoc bites out, making Captain laugh.

"I only meant, if you feel the need to kick someone's ass, wait until we get back. Nobody will fuck with you, Raven."

"Exactly," Royce pipes up again. "So let's keep the legs loose for the weekend."

"For fuck's sake." I stuff the chips between the seats, cross my arms and look out my side window. They're trippin', hardcore.

Maddoc moves closer so he can whisper, "You really think we'd sit back and allow someone to fuck with you?"

"I have no idea what you'd do." I roll my head to meet his stare. "You're as hot as you are cold, big man."

"Stop making me crazy and I won't have to be."

I scoff, speaking low since he is. "Whatever you say. But don't act like I can't handle myself."

"I know you can," he says slowly, the green in his gaze almost unseen as black takes over.

Want. Confusion. Need. It's all there.

My body grows hot, and I fight the sudden urge to swallow. He's got me all wanton crazy with this whole 'fuck you while you fuck me' thing he's got going.

"We know you're as capable as we are, Snow. It's why you're here."

"Thought it was so you could keep an eye on me?"

The corner of his mouth tips up slowly. "That too." His fingers find my wrist and feather across, leaving an electric shock in their wake. "But let's be real, Raven. My eyes have been on you, haven't they?"

I search his eyes for intent but come up short.

What are you playing at, big man?

"If you think you're gonna catch me in some twisted shit, you're wasting my time," I whisper. "I told you before, I'm no planner."

He hums, a smirk now coming out to play. He leans in, his mouth now grazing my ear right as Royce's eyes find mine in the mirror.

"Those lips of yours will be on me soon." His tongue hits my earlobe and I dig my nails into my thigh to keep from reacting. "Plan on that."

He pulls back, moving over to retake his seat by the window and I close my eyes, forcing myself to repeat the national anthem in my head, over and over again until we're pulling onto a dirt road surrounded by large trees.

The boys roll the windows down and the smell of fresh, clean air hits my nostrils.

I sit forward, reaching over to roll my window down as well and take another deep breath.

"What is that?"

"What?" Captain asks.

"The smell."

He meets my stare in the rearview mirror. "Pine?"

When I shrug, he spins, looking over his shoulder at me. "Have you never been to the mountains?"

Suddenly I'm hit with a need to lie, but before I do, I look at the other two.

Again, no judgment stares back, so I go with honesty.

"No. Is it, I mean, is it always fresh like this? Like, clean air or whatever?"

Captain nods and continues to pull forward, swerving around a few large cabin homes.

"People live here?"

"Nah," Royce answers. "These are vacation spots. Nobody stays year-round."

Must be nice to have not one, but two homes.

"Is that?" I lean out my window and take another deep breath, ignoring the chuckles behind me. "Campfire?" I look over my shoulder. "Real campfire?"

"Is there such a thing as fake campfire?" Maddoc's brow lifts but amusement shines in his eyes.

"Yeah, there is. We had bonfires all the time, but that was, I don't know, a burnt, smoky smell. A fire kept going by beer boxes and trash. This is ... clean and" – I look out the window again – "intoxicating. Almost..." I can't find the word.

"Peaceful?" Captain offers, staring at me in the mirror again.

I nod but don't meet his eyes.

"Come on, Cap, move the car."

Captain licks his lips and continues down the path again until we're pulling up in front of a huge cabin.

It looks like a plain square, nothing fancy but with a porch that wraps all the way around.

When they get out, I do too, and the closer I move to the place, the more I see. It may be simple as far as the front goes, but there's a huge deck on the back, held up by thick wooden beams, it sits at what looks to be the second story of the cabin.

"The rooms are on the bottom, top floor's the party room, kitchen and deck. It's got a sick view of the creek."

"It's badass."

Maddoc passes me with my bag, so I try and take it from him, but he glares, yanks it away and keeps moving.

I raise my hands and trail behind him.

Right when you walk in the place, it's an empty entryway. To the right is a set of stairs and to the left a small hallway with several doors. Maddoc keeps moving until we reach the one farthest to the end.

"This is yours. You've got the bathroom, so you don't have to come out at night once you're done partying."

I nod, walking in to find the bathroom on the right of the room, not even a door to close it off from the small room. There's a dresser and bed with a mini fridge tucked beside it, and nothing else. But it's way more than enough.

"So, you guys don't have a bathroom in your rooms?"

"No, but that first door we passed was one, so we have our own." He turns to me with a glare. "Don't let Royce tell you different."

I laugh, dropping my jacket on the bed.

"This is cool, thanks."

He eyes me a moment but then his brows furrow and he walks out.

"Come on."

I follow behind him, stopping at the next door, the room right next to mine.

"This is me, across from me is Cap, then it's Royce, a spare for Leo, in case he needs it, and then the bathroom. You're the last room in the hall ... surrounded by us. Don't try to pull no shit."

Dick.

"RaeRae, Madman, let's go. Shots!"

I wiggle my eyebrows then follow the boys' voices up the stairs.

"Oh man." I look around the room, grabbing the shot Royce hands me. "This place is dope."

Wooden log futons act as couches on both sides of the room, a wide-open kitchen on the right and slider doors on the left.

Captain nods his chin, so I open the door and we all shuffle out on to the deck.

I lean over the edge and stare down at the ground then look out and over the creek that runs the back of the property, noticing a small bridge that leads to the other side.

"What's out there?"

"Bears."

When my eyes widen the boys laugh.

Whatever.

I go to lift my shot, but Maddoc stops me.

"Together." His eyes lock on mine before moving along each of us and my chest grows warm.

I'm really sick of that happening.

"Watch out for each other and don't act alone."

They nod then all eyes are on me.

I'm not part of this team, so I don't understand the sentiment or the seriousness that shines back at me in three separate sets of eyes, but I nod anyway and all at once we let the cinnamon flavored liquor run down our throats.

Right then, several sounds hit.

Music, laughter, slams of car doors.

Royce yelps and runs down the deck stairs, Captain heads inside for another drink and Maddoc's eyes lock on mine.

I go to follow, but Maddoc blocks my move.

"A lot happens out here, don't go disappearing."

"You mean don't follow a big bad wolf home?" I tease, using the Brayshaw mascot for fun.

But the way he grinds his jaw tells me he doesn't think it's funny.

He steps against me until I'm forced to lean back over the railing to meet his eyes. "You want a wolf?" he murmurs and that pulls in my abdomen. "I can make that happen."

I dig deep to force a steady breath. "I bet you can, big man..." I trail off and he steps back, disappearing the way Royce ran.

I need a drink.

Chapter 21

Raven

The party isn't really a party tonight, apparently most of the others will be here in the morning. Tonight, it's just the ones who ditched last period or prepacked and loaded their vehicles. Still, there are a solid thirty or forty people around.

Honestly, it's pretty chill. It's dark out except for the glow of the fire pits, and some string lights trailing down the pathways. I'm assuming they lead to more cabins. I'm kind of looking forward to seeing what this place looks like in the daylight.

"So, Raven."

I look to my right at the girl who spoke.

"Are you having fun?" she asks, her voice as peppy as she looks.

She couldn't care less – it's gossip she's after.

I lift my drink and wave it her way with a tight smile before turning my attention back to the boys who've got a little game of horse going with a trashcan. They've got a pile of pinecones someone rounded up they're using as the basketball so they don't have to dig out of the garbage every throw.

'Course, Royce had to make it more fun and instead of earning a letter to spell out the word horse with each basket made, they have to spell pussy. He made sure to let them know he wasn't referring to 'pussy' as afraid or an actual cat, but 'the place his dick was spending the night' kind of pussy – as if they didn't know what he meant.

They had a childish laugh over it.

"So, Raven, what cabin are you staying in?"

"Depends," I answer and all the females who have placed themselves near me, look my way.

The girl clears her throat and leans forward. "On what?"

When I smirk, the fluffy attitude falters and her claws show despite her best effort.

"You think you get top pick over all of us?" She sits back slowly, and her friends glare along with her. "Nobody even knew you'd be here. You don't get to ruin the plans the rest of us made because someone felt the need to drag you along."

"Janessa," a golden-haired girl warns quietly, her eyes wide in apology – she's clearly worried about the Bray's little "touch her not" rule.

But good ole Janessa, as she was called, is not deterred, she's got some liquid courage coursing through her and purses her perfect lips and fuck this bitch.

I was fucking around, but now she's insulting me.

No.

I see who she keeps eyeing when she thinks nobody's watching. She's not a sly as she assumes, but I do give her props for not going all out obvious.

Little miss blonde hair, blue eyes, prettier than me on my best day but more makeup on than my mom on cougar night at the bar, has her sights set on Captain.

"How 'bout a bet?"

Her eyes narrow. "Bet for what?"

"The commander, the skipper…" I goad her, but the confused look on her face tells me it's over her pretty little head. "You know, the Captain."

Her mouth forms a tight line.

"Wonder if he follows the code and … goes down with the ship."

She flies from her seat, ready to get in my face, but I meet her one step forward with three of my own.

"This has been in the works for the last two weeks. Back off."

"Bet."

She falters a bit. "Bet what?"

"Bet if we approach him, he'll walk away with you."

A weak little chortle leaves her, and she looks to her friends who wear tight expressions. They're as unsure as her, even though they pretend I'm talking crazy.

This is totally unnecessary, but now I want to ruin her fun since she got on my case for no reason.

"There's no point." She crosses her arms. "It's already set for later. Once he's done partying, he'll find me."

"I'm nothing for you to worry about then."

"As if you could take my place."

I shrug and step back.

She rolls her eyes and drops back in her chair. "Screw you and your bet, I already know for a fact he'll be mine tonight."

"Okay." I shrug and walk off before she can say a word.

Cap is standing off to the side with Leo and a couple girls from school when I approach.

"Wassup, Rae?" Leo holds his fist out, so I give him knuckles.

"Not a damn thing." I keep my eyes on Captain.

He studies me. "What'd you do?"

"Nothing."

"Nothing ... yet?"

I pop a shoulder. "You got plans with the bride of Chuckie over there?"

Leo spits beer, laughing and Captain grins.

"More like an open option, but uh..." He looks to the brunette beside Leo. "She's not needed now."

"I thought Royce was the slut?"

"I am." Royce moseys up, throwing his arm around me.

Maddoc slides over and pushes it off.

"What's going on?" Maddoc questions.

I look back to Cap. "Come on, packman. Let's cause trouble."

"Wait, I wanna cause trouble," Royce whines but I shove him away.

"Not your turn," I tell him, ignoring his pout. "She's acting like a bitch, and I wanna bitch slap her, but I'm too tired to deal with your guys' crap later. So, I'll settle for an ego hit instead."

"And how exactly do you plan to do that?" Maddoc snaps.

I grin and step toward Captain who puffs his chest out, a smile playing at his lips. "I'm tired, Cap." I run my fingers down the center of his chest, cutting a quick glance at Maddoc when he steps closer.

"The fuck's goin' on?" Royce whispers not so quietly.

"Put me to bed?" I ask Cap, unable to keep from smiling.

Bride of Chuckie is standing now, I see her in my periphery.

"Captain," Maddoc's voice rumbles.

Leo steps back at the sound, putting distance between himself and the four of us.

"Chill, brother." Captain doesn't take his eyes off me, but reassures his brother in a whisper, "Just having some fun."

He passes his drink to Royce, his other hand meeting my lower back and together we head for the cabin.

Yes, it's the one I was already staying in, but she doesn't know that.

At the door, Captain moves my hair over my shoulders and bends to whisper in my ear, his hands moving to grip my hips. He plays the part well. "It's no wonder the girls can't hang with you, Raven."

"Why do you say that?" I turn the knob, then cover his hands with mine as we shuffle in.

"Because you do what you want and don't let their shit get to you, at least not where they can tell."

When we get inside, he pushes the door closed and steps back.

I head up the stairs, Captain on my heels. We both move for the kitchen, grabbing some snacks from the cupboards.

I pull out some Wheat Thins, and he grabs a can of nasty spray cheese and a few waters.

"Anyway, thanks for that."

I laugh, stuffing a couple of crackers in my mouth. "Thank you."

"So what'd she say to you?"

I sigh. "Nothing that matters."

"Keep talking."

"People are assholes, especially when a girl like me is thrown in a world like yours. They feel the need to disrespect me to make themselves feel even more superior than they already believe they are. Like I get it, I have a stigma that follows me around, even hours away from where I grew up, it seems, but I don't know why people go out of the way to piss me off. I don't talk to people; I don't get in the way. I stick to my damn self when they let me."

"It's because they're jealous."

I look up to find both Royce and Maddoc at the top of the stairs having heard our conversation.

"You guys are not that cool, not sure why they're so

desperate to stand where I'm standing," I tease, motioning to Captain to squirt some nasty cheese in my mouth.

"They're not jealous of you being around us," Maddoc says as he moves to sit opposite of me, and Royce drops beside me.

"I don't get it."

"Of course, they want to be where you are, here with us, but that's not what ticks them off," Captain says.

"It's true, RaeRae. It's all about you." Royce steals my water, downing it in seconds, so I move to grab another. "You're new, sure, but you're feisty and free-spirited, fine as fuck with this sexy ass edge to you."

I scoff. "Okay."

"For real, you're like a biker princess or rock goddess, wrapped in a fat ass, shiny Do Not Touch tape that only makes everyone wanna touch it more. You're a little hood but still a Cali girl. They want to be you, imitate you, but they don't know how. They have fancy clothes and cars and Daddy's plastic, but no matter what they do or buy or who they pay, they can't reach your level, and they know it. You're this lethal ass combination of girl they never knew they wanted to be until now but couldn't match if they tried."

"Okay, no more." I pull my sleeves over my hands, and look over the boys, finding goofy little boy grins on each of their faces. Even Maddoc's.

It looks good on him. Little foreign but ... good.

"Holy shit, she gets embarrassed!" Royce hops to his feet, looking like he's seriously surprised.

"Dude. You're over here saying all this ... jazz while you three flawless fuckheads stare at me. Stop it."

They laugh lightly.

"For real, though." Captain tips his chin. "Want us to make her leave?"

"Nah." I shrug. "She's harmless. Your people just need to stop thinking they can control what I do by talking shit."

"They're not our people," Maddoc snaps and I roll my eyes.

"You know what I mean. They expect me to back off or keep quiet simply because they come from money or titles and I don't, but that's not the way I work."

"People act like that to you at your old schools, too?" Royce asks, bouncing his shoulder into mine.

"All the time. Eventually I started acting in spite, doing the opposite, or least expected, even if what someone assumed was right. I like to make sure they don't know it."

"Why?" Captain asks.

"If they don't know how to read me, they stay away. People don't like what they don't get, and if they don't get you, they can't get to you."

"That's ... kind of fucked up," Royce says, a little too gently for my liking.

I stand, not wanting to talk about me anymore. "Anyway, Cap. You're free to make your move on the brunette. I think this lovely ten minutes was enough for them all to think ... who the hell knows what they think now that you all came in."

"Aye," Royce teases, doing a little dance from his sitting position and I roll my eyes.

"Walked in," I laugh and Royce smiles.

"You really going to bed?" Maddoc's question comes out a little hoarse.

I don't look his way, I have a feeling his eyes hold a little more than I want to see after I ran my mouth just now. "I am."

"Look, RaeRae, lock your door. When the crowd dies down, some of the party will move up here. They'll have to come up the back, but still," Royce tells me.

"Sounds good."

I head down the stairs, but before I can shut myself inside, a foot is shoved between the door and the jamb.

Maddoc licks his lips and stands there quietly a moment.

"Big man..." I prompt with a grin.

"Check under the bed and in the bathroom before you lock yourself in here."

When I don't move, his gaze narrows.

"Do it, Raven."

I do as he says and then turn to him. "All clear."

He nods and turns to walk away.

"Wait, really?" I question. "That was what you wanted?"

"What else would I want?"

"I don't know, in?"

"In what?" His brow lifts and I tilt my head, narrowing my eyes.

"You wanna come in my room and chill with me, big man?"

"You asking me because you think that's what I was trying to do ... or because you want me to?"

"I wouldn't mind if you did."

"Not good enough." He shakes his head and walks a few feet back, so I pop a shoulder and shut the door.

When I start changing, I hear his room door open and then close and I smirk to myself.

I knew he didn't want to go back to the party.

My legs keep bouncing and I start drumming my fingers across my thighs. I close my eyes and lightly bob around to the music that flows from upstairs, but after a good four hours, it's no use.

I can't do it, especially not here with all these people around.

It's as quiet as it's been all night and the music has dropped to a lower level, slower more 'I'm fucked up and swaying" music comes on versus the "let's get wasted" party shit from before, so I stand up, pull my hoodie over my head and open my door.

I get a foot past the threshold when Maddoc's door is yanked open.

I jump, my hand flying to my chest. "Shit, don't do that."

"Where you going?" His tone is accusatory.

"Upstairs."

"Why?"

Shit. Uh... "Water?"

"That a question?"

"No." I cross my arms. "I'm going to get water."

"I filled your mini fridge with sodas and waters." He crosses his arms now.

He did?

"Well ... I want a snack."

"There's a bag of snacks on your dresser."

"Really?" comes out before I can stop it and he grows suspicious.

Oh, fuck this.

I shake my head, standing tall. "How about because I want to?"

I go to walk away, but he grabs my elbow pulling me back.

"Do you hear that?" he growls.

"What, the music?"

"Yeah, the music and zero talking."

"I don't care, I'll be quick."

"You are not going up there."

"I have to!"

"No, you don't."

"Why do you care?!"

"It's an orgy up there. Literally." His jaw clenches. "Every motherfucker up there is fucking with the person next to them, to the right, to the left, guy, girl, don't matter. It's a free for all, any and every person that's near." His brows jump mockingly. "You want in on that?"

"I ... fuck." My lips squeeze sideways.

"What?"

When I start pacing while biting on my fingernail, he sighs. "What, Raven?"

Fuck it.

I turn to him. "I forgot my knife."

"Your knife." His eyes narrow as he searches my face. "The one you cut me with?"

"Oh, please." My foot bounce against the carpet. "I barely grazed you."

"You forgot your knife. So, what."

I groan internally. "I need one. I ... can't sleep without it."

He freezes a second before gripping my wrist and pulling me into his room. He quickly shuts the door.

"What—"

"You're not going up there. You'll sleep in here."

"Oh, hell no!"

He crowds my space, his chest heaving against mine. "You will sleep in here with me, or in your room alone, with no knife."

"Fuck, okay. Fine."

I drop onto the bed and he moves to turn off the light, but when my features tighten, he pauses.

He doesn't say anything or ask questions, but he pulls out his cell phone and lights up the screen, setting it on the dresser before turning off the light.

The phone acts as a nightlight.

Maddoc climbs in the bed beside me but stays on his side.

After a few minutes, I flip over to face him, finding his eyes open and on me.

"Why didn't you go back to the party?"

"I thought you were tired?" he complains.

"I don't sleep without my knife."

"And the music and flashlight."

I shrug against the pillow, not acknowledging he remembered those little details from when he snuck in my room.

"If Maybell finds the knife, she'll take it."

"And if she takes it, I'll find it, take it back and leave."

His eyes shift between mine. "Just like that, huh?"

"Just like that. I'm already somewhere I didn't choose to be. If I feel like my ability to protect myself is gone, I will be too."

"You act like where you come from is better."

"You act like you know what my life was like when you have no clue. You may have read my files, big man, but those are the words of others put together by an educated man in the fanciest way possible to make it look like someone somewhere was doing their job. Reality can't be typed on letterhead and sealed with a stamp."

"So it was worse than—"

"Dirty trailer with an even dirtier mother, filthy men and fighting so I could eat or blow off steam when needed. Sleeping on the bleachers so I didn't have to listen to grown men accidentally moan my name instead of my mother's, then get my ass kicked because, you know, I shouldn't be so appealing."

Maddoc jerks to a sitting position, so I push up onto my elbow to mirror him. "Keep going."

"Waking up to men hovering over me, their hands in their pants as my mother made them coffee with yesterday's grinds."

"Your knife."

"That's a story for another day, big man."

"Tell me now," he demands.

"Nah." I lay back down, and he glares. "It's your turn to

share, but something tells me you're not the sharing type, so let's end this little therapy session."

He runs his hands through his hair and drops back on the pillow, staring up at the ceiling.

Not sure how much time passes, and I assume he fell asleep but then he talks.

"All that and you'd still go back."

"I don't have other options like you, so yeah. For now. Until I don't have to."

"You don't have to."

"I'm seventeen. I'm not gonna turn tricks to live and I don't have an ID to get a real job. I'll wait until I can hit the DMV on my own, and then I'll leave everything behind and start over. On my own. And I'll do it with nobody else's influence or help or opinion."

"So, that's your plan. Float until you can run."

"It's not running." My voice lowers to a whisper on its own accord. "It's survival."

"It's stupid."

"Maybe." I yawn. "But it's the best option I have."

He licks his lips. "Go to sleep, Raven. You're safe in here."

A tired chuckle escapes me. "No such thing, big man."

His green eyes bounce between mine, and a flicker of something I can't name passes quickly before it's gone. "Close your eyes."

I do as he says, not necessarily believing him, but I'm already in here now so fuck it. I've made stupider decisions than lying in bed with a half-stranger.

A WARM PALM RUNNING UP MY THIGH HAS MY EYES POPPING open and my muscles lock, but only for a second before I realize I'm in Maddoc's bed – not a dirty couch in a trailer park.

His hand stops at the apex of my thigh, his fingers pressing into my skin firmly, and then he sighs. Heat spreads through my abdomen as his warm breath fans across my cheek and throat.

Without so much as moving a muscle, I peek up at him.

He's fucking sleeping. Shit.

I squeeze my eyes closed as I try to work out the right move.

Everything I know tells me to run, that a man is touching me without permission, but my heart rate is stable and my breathing calm. I don't have that inner inkling telling me to get the hell out of dodge.

Which is the exact reason I decide it's necessary – no need in it getting comfortable, that's when the wool falls over your eyes.

I shift on the mattress, attempting to crawl from the bed and back to my own but his eyes pop open and find mine.

"What are you doing?"

"What are you doing?" I widen my eyes and his tighten in confusion.

I squeeze my thigh muscle and he drops his gaze to the contact.

But he doesn't move his hand.

He closes his damn eyes and tells me, "Go back to sleep."

"I wasn't sleeping," I lie.

"Yeah, Raven, you were."

Without moving the hand on my thigh, he uses his other to help flip me over, so my back is to him and he scoots forward. He's not against me but makes sure his large presence is felt.

It's felt all right.

But—

"Sleep, Raven."

Chapter 22

RAVEN

My eyes pop open the second the bed shifts, and I jolt upward.

Maddoc glances back at me with a frown, running a hand through his dark hair as he yawns. "I gotta take a piss, be right back."

I don't say anything, but I sure as hell watch the way his back muscles shift as he walks away. At first glance, I'd call it a cocky, intentional gait, but I'm learning that's not the case. He simply can't help himself, it's a natural swagger he couldn't dim down if he tried – not that he'd try. He likes it.

And it suits him.

With a groan, I glance around. I can't believe I slept in bed with Maddoc. And I mean I actually slept in his bed, as in without my knife, completely comfortable.

I groan.

So not good.

When the sound of a toilet flushing is heard down the hall, I jump up and hustle for my designated room.

I go to shut the door, but before I can, Royce pushes it open, effectively throwing himself in the center of the mattress.

"'Sup, RaeRae." He tucks his hands behind his head, and I move to drop beside him.

I pull the covers over my exposed legs, folding my hands under my pillow.

"Nothing—"

"Yo," Captain shuffles in wearing sweatpants and a T-shirt, rubbing at his eyes.

He drops on the foot of the bed, laying his head across my feet, his legs hanging halfway off the other side.

I look out the doorway when Maddoc's footsteps draw him closer.

When he glances inside, he pauses, glowering at me. He looks away a moment before he too walks in.

"We going for breakfast?"

"I'm too hungover for those twisty ass roads." Royce slides down the pillows and tucks himself beneath my blankets.

For some stupid reason, my eyes slice to Maddoc.

He stares but still gives expressive reaction.

"Well, I'm starving," Captain whines.

"I could always eat," Royce adds and they both look to Maddoc.

He scoffs. "Fine. I'll fucking cook, but if there's still people upstairs, I'm kicking them all out."

"Please do. That Bride of Chuckie, as RaeRae called her, is trying to stick around. Probably waiting to see Cap."

"Wait." I push to a sitting position and Royce reaches out with a grin, pretending to smooth my rat's nest from my face. I smack his hand away, leaving my crazy hair crazy. "You and that chick?"

"She was pissed off. Makes for some good hard head."

"She's still up there?" I grin and Royce laughs, looking to Captain.

Captain raises a brow and I smile.

With a laugh, he pushes to his feet and squeezes past Maddoc to get to me. He holds his hands out.

"Let's finish this, girl."

He spins around, so I latch on.

When his hands wrap my thighs to help hold me up, Maddoc storms out.

Captain and Royce both chuckle but nobody says a thing.

The second Maddoc's feet hit the top floor, he barks, "Get out."

And the handful of people scramble for their shit and go.

Of course, the chick takes her time slipping on her shoes.

Her eyes hit mine first, then move to Captain, who doesn't even acknowledge her but continues for the kitchen where he bends until my ass hits the table and I let go.

He spins around, gripping my chin in his fingers and I stare, waiting for his next move, laughing on the inside at the anger flying my way from the girl.

Captain leans forward, asking with his stare if he can go for it, but before I can give him a sign, Maddoc grips his shoulder and Cap pauses.

He chuckles and steps back.

I glance over my shoulder right as she stomps out the door, and Royce is quick to lock it behind her.

He pulls the sheets from the futons and rolls them up, tossing them in the garbage by the door. "Good as new, RaeRae, come sit with me." He plops his ass down.

I hop off the table, run down the stairs to grab the blanket off the bed and then back up. I drop beside Royce, tucking the blanket around me.

Royce flips through the channels, deciding on Red Riding Hood.

A few minutes pass and then Maddoc is standing in front of me, a hot cup of coffee in his hands.

I eye him as I slowly reach for it. "Thanks, big man."

He doesn't say a word, turning around to head back for the kitchen.

"Yo, where's my hot chocolate?!" Royce teases, jabbing me with his elbow.

Maddoc simply flips him off as he heads back into the kitchen, and not fifteen minutes later he's announcing breakfast is ready.

Royce doesn't hesitate to pop up and drags me with him. I move to sit at the cheap wooden table now topped with the fixings for chorizo and egg burritos as he joins them in the tiny kitchen.

I can't help but track their movements.

One gets the condiments, a different for each, one the drinks, again, different for each and the last has the plates and silverware. It's like they've done this a thousand times over.

So routine. Normal.

It makes me wonder if it's always been like this, just the three of them looking out for each other. Victoria said they've been together since babies but observing the three function as one is more than I expected. They come across as punks on a power high, but they're more than that.

I need to give them the journal I took from Maybell. It shouldn't be hidden in a house it doesn't belong in.

"You don't like it?"

My gaze snaps to Maddoc's and I frown, but when I glance around, I find they've all made their plates already while I was sitting here staring into space the last few minutes. I look back to him.

"I do." I don't say anything else, and the way he cocks his head just slightly tells me he knows something was on my mind.

Nothing else is voiced, and we spend the next few minutes eating in silence.

"Thanks, brother, good as always." Royce pushes to his feet. "I'll do the dishes in a bit. Imma head over to Mac's for a quick game. Catch you guys later."

"Hold up, I need a workout too." Captain follows after him and they both turn to look at Maddoc.

He pauses a moment before pushing to his feet. He looks to me. "We'll be back."

I nod, picking up my coffee to take a drink, and they walk out the back.

I take my time eating and then make quick work of cleaning the kitchen and collecting the few empty cups from around the living room from last night. Grabbing my blanket, I head back downstairs for a shower.

Dressing in my dark grey joggers, tennies, and white hoodie, I head down to the little creek and follow along the carved-out path, wrapping around the outskirts of the cabins.

This place is so much bigger than the dark night let on. With trees so high you can't see the top and miles upon miles of forestry, I can see why Captain used the word peaceful. It's just ... different out here. Quiet yet loud. There's a freedom in the air here you can't find on city streets.

As I come around the first corner, I run into a bunch of my new classmates jacking around outside their own cabins.

I keep going.

Eventually, I'm a solid mile away and at the farthest point of the circular area. I decide to cut through the center to head back, and wouldn't you know it, sitting around a morning fire is Collins.

What the hell would he and his people be doing here?

He's the first to spot me from his clan, and his eyes narrow, but when they shoot past my shoulder, finding me alone, he grins and waves me over.

"Raven Carver."

"In the flesh." I tuck my hands in my pockets and half sit on a large tree stump, nodding hello to the other guys who feel the need to stare.

"Thought I might find you here."

"Really?" I tilt my head. "'Cause I never would have thought I'd find me here."

He grins and I relax a little.

My hands form fists in my pockets when he stands and steps toward me.

He waits until he's right in front of me before whispering, "Anything change since our last conversation? You an official 'Bray Girl' now?"

"Don't act like you'd care either way." I don't bother whispering and at first, he glares. But it's true and he knows it, which is why he laughs in the next second.

"'Bout to play some air hockey." He steps back, looking me over with clear interest. "You in?"

I'm about to pass on the invitation to go inside what I'm assuming is his cabin – I'm not a dumbass – but then I glance left where his friends are unfolding a portable table and figure fuck it. Nothing else to do. "Sure. Why not."

He nods and heads for his cabin. "I'm getting another drink. You want something?"

"I'm good."

"I bet you are, Rae." He winks and walks away.

I roll my eyes and look back to his buddies.

A tall dark-haired guy with crazy grey eyes and a scar above his eyebrow hands me the puck and handle, but he doesn't say a word.

I make my way over to the table right as Collins is coming back out, suddenly shirtless.

I lift a brow because really? It's fucking cold out here, hence the need for the fire pits.

He only winks again, making it a point to brush against me as he passes.

I keep my eyes on him as he steps around the table, laughing when he grips the edges, purposely tightening his muscles.

"Don't be so extra." I scan his chest and abs and meet his eyes again. "You don't need to be."

"You saying I look good, Carver?"

"You really gonna stand there and pretend like you don't?"

He grins, waving a hand out for me to start us off.

We play three rounds and I whoop his ass each time.

"Damn it!" he shouts with a laugh, slamming his handle down on the table.

I smile to myself, setting mine down as well so I can push my sleeves up and tie my hair back in a high ponytail.

He makes his way around the table, stepping right in front of me. "Good game, Carver."

"Thanks, Collins." I squish my lips to the side to keep from laughing at his bull. "But maybe back up a few steps, huh?"

He's trying to appear harmless, and for the most part, he might be, but the slight gleam in his eyes gives him away. He's a stature driven, khaki-wearing, preppy bastard who craves a dirty victory.

He's only getting warmed up.

I should go.

His head snaps up in the next second, the sound of tires against gravel catching his attention. His brows dipping in the center. "What cabin did you say you're in again?" He looks back to me.

I lick my lips, staring at him head-on. "I didn't, but you didn't ask."

"What cabin you staying in, Rae?"

"Aspen."

Nobody says anything but based on how each head turns

toward Collins it's obvious they know who the largest cabin on the lot belongs to.

I move my eyes around the group.

Each sits up taller, a few stepping closer to their leader, closer to me.

And then Collins steps into me, quickly wrapping his arm around my middle as he pulls me against him.

I frown and go to shove him back, but his lips quickly fall on mine.

I'm about to knee him in the nuts when I'm yanked backward and basically tossed onto the dirt.

I look up just as Maddoc lands a nasty-ass punch across Collins' jaw. In the next second Royce jumps clear over the three-foot-high, two-foot-wide air hockey table, quickly moving forward to keep Collins' friends from jumping in to help their boy.

Maddoc's large, angry hand covers his throat, blocking off his airway, and he doesn't let up. He continues to squeeze his neck to the point where Collins' face starts changing shades and he frantically pulls at Maddoc's wrist.

But Maddoc gives him no leeway and my pulse spikes. Shit could get real bad, real quick.

But Captain comes around the table then and calmly lays a hand on his brother's shoulder. He whispers something in his ear and Maddoc's stare snaps to mine.

I swear he's fucking shaking, and I consider moving or speaking or something, but the manic look in his eyes has me thinking better of it.

With one more twitch of his wrist, he tosses Collins to the ground.

The boys back up a few steps until a solid line is formed in front of the others.

Outnumbered by a handful and still, they're dominant. Looked up to.

Feared.

I push off the ground, not bothering to dust the dirt off myself.

I step toward Collins who fights for a solid breath and Maddoc snatches my wrist, his lip curling up as he gets in my face.

"He just put his hands on me," I hiss.

I jerk my hand and at first, there's resistance, but then his frown deepens, and he loosens his grip enough for me to yank free.

Royce jolts toward me, attempting to grab me just the same, but I dodge him with a glare.

I step to Collins and when he looks up at me, I lift my foot and plant it in the center of his chest, knocking his ass back down to the ground while he's still feeling weak.

I drop down slowly, so my knee can take my foot's place and Maddoc takes a step closer.

My eyes bounce between Collins, my neck heating in anger the longer I stare.

"You little rich prick with a hard-on, how fucking dare you," I breathe, anger vibrating against my ribs. "I tell you to step back and you grab me, forcing your lips on me instead? That how you like to play?" I lift my other foot off the ground, forcing all my weight onto his sternum. "What you're feeling right now is nothing compared to what you will if you put your hands on me again."

He spits to the side, asking a question of his own. "Thought you said you weren't a Bray girl?"

"I'm not."

All three boys fire off at the same time.

"The fuck you aren't!"

"Watch your mouth."

"Don't be stupid."

I turn my scowl to them, ignoring the bitter laugh that leaves Collins.

"I'm—" I start to argue, but Maddoc cuts me off.

"Later."

Right then, Collins' hand darts up, ready to grab ahold of me, but before he can, Maddoc is stepping down on his wrist, his shooting hand – basketball player and all – and his eyes go wide.

I don't get to talk shit back, though, because in the same second, Royce's hand clamps over my mouth and I'm lifted, his arm around my waist as he carries me off … like a damn child.

He tosses me in the back of someone's Jeep. He waits until they skirt off before he lets go and when he does, he shoves away from me.

With a jerky movement and a pissy attitude, he faces forward, not saying a damn word to me the short drive back.

The second the Jeep skids to a stop I leap out over the side, Royce on my heels, and not a second later more dirt flies in the air as a second Jeep pulls to a stop and two more large bodies rush forward.

I run into the house, quickly spinning to shove the door closed and lock it.

Royce smacks the frame with a growl and dashes to the right, Maddoc to the left and Captain stays right outside the front.

I run up the stairs, rushing for the back door, but Royce is already there shoving it open when I hit the top of the stairs, so I run back down, making a dash for the room they put me in, but skid to a stop when I find Maddoc at the bottom of the stairs.

He clicks the lock without taking his eyes off me and Captain steps inside with his chin lifted.

Right then, Royce's chest hits my back and I jump.

"Nowhere to go now, RaeRae."

"Fuck off," I hiss, but I lift my head and stare down the two making their way up the steps.

"Start talking, Raven."

"About?"

"Don't play stupid."

"Don't be a little bitch. Ask what you wanna know."

Captain's brows jump slightly, but Maddoc's only narrow more. He looks over my shoulder at Royce.

Royce shifts behind me so I snap, "Put your hands on me right now, Royce, and get your balls bruised."

Maddoc's jaw clenches and he growls, stepping closer, but I don't back down or cower, and after what feels like forever, he backs up, spins around and storms out of the cabin. Captain follows.

"We ... brought you here," Royce trails off so I turn to face him. I'd swear I see worry in his eyes if I didn't know any better. "Don't make us regret it, Rae."

Rae.

Not Raven.

Not RaeRae.

Rae.

He walks out and suddenly I'm disappointed. But it makes no sense, because the acid on my tongue was poured by my own damn self and a direct hit, right at me.

And it pisses me off.

How could these boys bring me from fuming at them to mad at myself, and two of them with nothing but a look? And I don't even like that stupid nickname!

I drop my back against the wall and close my eyes.

Taking a deep breath, I allow myself a few rare seconds of uncertainty, and then I force all thoughts from my head and when my eyes open, I'm good. Ready to party.

I'm getting fucked up.

Chapter 23

Raven

They're fucked up.

Each fucking one, completely fucking wasted.

Royce has some brunette chick on his lap and another standing at his back, running her hands down his chest over his shirt while his tongue plays connect the dots with the freckles on the lap girl's chest.

Captain has the bride of Chuckie chick grinding against his dick as they dance under the stupid Christmas lights – he glares my way every few minutes like his fucking with her is somehow sticking it to me. He'll sure as shit be sticking it to her later.

Good for her, I guess. And he deserves all her crazy after if he wants to act like a dumbass.

And Maddoc. He hasn't glanced my way once.

Not that I've been waiting but still. Hasn't happened yet.

He's busy, though.

I haven't seen Chloe yet, but that is one of her minions with her paws all over him.

He drops on the edge of a wooden picnic table and she stands between his legs, her hand down his pants right there for anyone to see.

Sure, they're tucked away a little, a dark shadow cast over their table, but there are still people all around. At least fifty or sixty more than last night are scattered all around between the dozen or so cabins.

"Trade?"

I look over and Leo who collects my empty bottle, popping the top of a new one with his lighter.

"Thanks."

"Yup."

When he stands there and stares, I drop my legs from the chair. "What?"

"Boys are pissed."

"When are they not?"

He grabs a chair and drags it over, sitting in front of me.

"That was stupid, you going to the Graven side."

"I'd have had to have known there was a Graven side to know to stay away from it, right?"

He nods. "Right. But let's say you did. Would you have stayed away from it?"

"What do you think?"

"I don't know you."

"Yet here you are, an opinion sitting on the edge of your tongue."

He glares. "Fair enough."

I scoff, glancing away but look back. "If schools don't mix, why the hell are they here?"

"Nobody was willing to give this place up."

"What do you mean?"

"A good forty or fifty years back, Brayshaw was the only

high school in this town. All the families were tight, so they started buying these cabins. Eventually it became the party place for the kids – just another place for rich kids to run off to. But when the town divided, they built Graven Prep. Pulled half the students over there, which meant down the line –"

"They were forced to share this place."

He shrugs. "Either way, tradition remains the same and all teenagers end up here. As long as they stick to their own and us ours, all's good."

"Right." I nod, looking off.

I bring my beer to my lips, taking a long drink, but freeze when I hear a deep groan to my right.

I glance over to find Maddoc's head falling back as the girl jacks him off. His head rolls to the side and his hazy eyes open just barely, but when they do, they hit mine.

And with his eyes on me, he sets his drink down against the table top. It falls over he's so drunk, the beer running over the edge of the old wood but he ignores it.

His hands lift to the girl's shoulders.

He is not...

He does.

He pushes the girl to her knees, and she happily obliges. She bends and then her head starts bobbing in his lap.

He moans again, and this time his head tips back completely.

"Damn, he's fucked up."

"He knows what he's doing."

"He doesn't do PDA."

"This isn't PDA." I look to Leo who raises a brow. "It's not. She's sucking his dick. He's not touching or rubbing or kissing on her. No claim or mark is being made. He's simply receiving. PDA would be him showing everyone else what he's got." I look back to the two, fire growing inside me – not sure if it's the angry or horny kind – as I watch the free porn. "There's no pride in this."

I look to Royce, his mouth fused to both girls, one hand in one's shirt, the other under the second's skirt, then to Captain, who may or may not be finger-fucking blondie against a tree.

"No pride in any of this. It's using pleasure to pretend."

"Pretend?"

I nod.

"Pretend what?"

Pretend they're not worried and unsure. To pretend they're not confused why it bothers them what I do or who I talk to.

To pretend they don't hope I'm not like the rest.

For some reason, these boys think they need me.

Maybe it's to help them in some way, a pawn of sorts, or maybe they crave the presence of a female constant, one who doesn't require anything of them. One who doesn't judge.

Or maybe I'm completely trippin' and way off the mark. Who knows.

What I do know is, these boys in front of me, sure they act like sluts often, but this, right now, while not totally out of character for each is them acting out.

They're angry, maybe hurt, little boys who don't know how to process the emotion.

Damn it.

Running my hands down my face, I stand and pass my beer back to Leo, who sits back, eyeing me wearily.

He can't figure me out either, but he doesn't need to.

I go for Captain first. Yes, I look like the jealous girl, but oh well.

He puts up zero fight and allows me to pull him away by his hand, completely ignoring the girl when she whines from where we leave her.

I lead him into the house and deposit him on his bed. He

falls into the mattress with ease, kicks his shoes off and tucks his face into his pillow.

Next, I go for Royce.

He glares at first, but when I offer him a small shrug and smile, he smirks drunkenly and wobbles to his feet. He's a little harder to carry inside, but eventually, we make it to his room.

I push him onto the bed and when he makes no moves, I untie his shoes and pull them off for him. He grabs my hand before I can leave and pulls me in so he can kiss my cheek. I give him a wink on my way out, leaving him there to fall asleep.

And last, I go for Maddoc, who still has his dick down the chick's throat.

I mean ... clearly she's doing something real fucking wrong if he still hasn't—

No.

No. Not thinking about that.

I tap her on the shoulder, and she jolts, releasing him with a pop as she jumps to her feet.

Maddoc doesn't even flinch, not even a blink as he sluggishly drags his eyes to mine.

"You think you're allowed to get jealous?" he rasps, the alcohol making his tongue slip a bit. "You better reel that shit in quick, Snow. Not sure what role you think you play here, but pathetic girlfriend isn't it."

He glances at the girl, then looks pointedly at his dick.

And the chick actually takes a small step for him, ready to drop back to her knees, but when my feet take an involuntary step toward her, she freezes where she stands.

"I got you," I start, purposely waiting to the last second to pull my glare from hers to his. "You want me to let you entertain this bitch."

His lips part, ready to pop off, I'm sure, but his drunken state has him a step behind.

"And don't claim nobody lets you do anything because hear me, big man. I'd pull her and any other girl away from you by her neck, if I wanted." I look back to the girl whose eyes are wide and rattled. "But I'm thinking that won't be necessary."

Her cheeks heat under my stare and she tries to stand tall and proud, but her shoulders hunch instead. She ducks her head before hustling off, as she should.

I shift my eyes back to Maddoc.

He stares, his head still dropped back, dick out and all. But with the shadow of the cabin over him, he's not completely exposed.

When I make no move, suddenly a little uncertain of how to handle the big man, he shifts his legs and stands to his full height.

His pants slip a little, so he grasps a hold of the waist to keep them up, but he doesn't tuck himself back into his boxers.

There's a challenge in his eyes. He doesn't think I'll do it, and really there's no reason for me to, especially when it might still be wet from some bitch's spit, yet I step forward anyway.

I grab the edge of his shirt and lift it, my eyes locked on his as I grip the fabric of his boxers and pull it toward me.

My fingers only graze the silky skin of his dick when he jerks backward to tuck himself in, falling over slightly as he does.

I reach for him and at first, he tenses and I think he'll be stubborn and pull away, but in the next second, he welcomes me, hugging his body to mine. I spin around in his arms, and start for the cabin, keeping my hands on his around my waist to keep us steady, but every few feet he jolts to a stop and buries his head farther into my neck.

He's mumbling something against my skin, but I couldn't make it out if I tried.

When we make it in the door, I lock it behind me and head toward Maddoc's room.

Once in his doorway, he tugs away from me. He kicks his shoes off, falling against the wall with a hard thud as he does, then pushes off, throws his blanket down and angrily drops onto the mattress. He makes sure to face the wall away from where I stand.

With a roll of my eyes, I leave him there and run upstairs to lock the back door.

Fuck these partygoers – nobody's coming in tonight.

I decide on a warm shower, quickly washing, then just stand under the warm spray until my skin is wrinkled. I climb out, pull a T-shirt over my head and put on some pajama shorts.

I peek in on the boys who are all in the same spot I left them and then head for bed.

Unfortunately for me, I spend the next hour staring at the ceiling unable to erase the picture of Maddoc being touched and pleased by that girl. Pressure builds in my chest and I try to take a deep breath to rid myself of it, but it doesn't work. It's annoying.

With a groan, I smack my palms against my comforter right as a loud bang has me jumping.

My eyes dart to the doorway.

Maddoc stands there glaring as he stumbles into my room, but I don't move.

He loudly props his ass on the wall, using it as leverage to keep him standing as he yanks his shirt over his head, and I lay back, admiring the way his muscles tighten as he does. Next to go are his jeans.

He kicks them off and stands there frowning at me in nothing but boxers.

Then he shuts and locks my door.

"What do you think you're doing?" I ask.

His lips make a firm line.

"You think I'll let you come in here and climb in bed when

you only pulled your dick from some chick's mouth a bit ago and only after I made it happen?"

"Yeah, I do." His response is instant, and I almost want to laugh.

Always so sure. I kinda like that about him, the little prickhead.

He reaches for my lamp but then his glossy stare meets mine. Even in his drunken state, he remembers me and the dark don't get along and he leaves the little light alone.

Even though I'm irritated with him for reasons I don't care to play out, my damn body shakes anticipating his as he lowers himself onto the bed.

Maddoc slides under the covers until his skin is flush against mine.

His hand lands on my ass and he slowly slides it down until his fingers hit the apex of my thigh and he pulls, wrapping my leg around his hip, moving in until his dick is against me.

My muscles tighten against his hard-on, and a low, rumbly moan leaves him, but he makes no other move. He lays there, body pressed to mine, hands on my bare skin, and falls asleep.

And for some reason, with the sound of his steady breathing and warm skin heating mine, my body grows lax.

Sleep comes easier than it should.

Chapter 24

RAVEN

Quick, heavy footsteps sound behind me and then the board on the back deck creaks with a single foot planted.

I don't turn around but take another drink from my coffee cup. "Morning."

When there's no sound but retreating steps I grin and wait.

It only takes a few minutes before Royce meets me outside, instant hot chocolate I made with him in mind in hand.

He drops beside me with a grumbled, "Thanks."

I nod, still not looking his way. "You thought I was running around somewhere, didn't you?"

"Yup." He shrugs, and I appreciate his honesty. "The fuck was that yesterday?"

This time, I shrug. "I went for a walk, got asked to play a quick game, so I did."

"If you wanted to play a game, you should have come with us."

"And creep on your basketball game? No." I take another

drink. "You guys needed a legit practice or workout or whatever Captain said. And I'm fine doing my own thing."

"Well, your own thing was stupid."

"Hey. They're not my enemies, they're yours." I grow defensive and when his head snaps my way, mine follows.

"Our enemies are your enemies."

"Says fucking who?"

Before he can answer, Maddoc steps out on the deck, his shirt still off despite the chill, and I lose my train of thought.

His torso, God ... so long and strong. Deep cut ridges meet at the center and spread out across his ribs, but those damn hip bones are what have me stuck. Every damn time.

"Says you."

When he speaks my gaze flies to his, and a cocky gleam shines back.

I can't say I hate this playful side he's giving glimpses of.

"And us. You're Brayshaw whether you want to be or not, because we said. Your actions only solidify it to outside eyes."

There we go, that's more like the big man.

I roll my eyes.

Captain joins us then, lifting his coffee cup in thanks. "It's true, Raven. You publicly chose us on more than one occasion."

"I only did what anybody would do."

I look between the three and grow self-conscious as their facial expressions shift from angrily irritated to ... more. Frownless.

"What?" I snap, setting my mug down and jumping to my feet.

Captain, the nurturer, takes my vacated spot beside Royce and Maddoc steps forward. "That's where you're wrong. Nobody in our world helps because they want to. There's always a reason. We talked about this already."

"Well, I didn't have a reason."

This time when I look between the three, they're grinning. I mean, Maddoc more drops his stare to the old wood beneath him, but the other two definitely grin and I shift on my feet.

Royce sets his cup down and then hauls himself at me. Laughing, he wraps himself around my back and lifts me off the floor with a tight squeeze. "That's the point, RaeRae. You've got something we wanna figure out," he teases in a purposely dirty voice.

Maddoc smacks the back of Royce's head, and he releases me with a laugh.

I shove him farther away, but can't completely keep the smile at bay so I quickly grab my cup and dip back inside.

I'm pouring a refill when Maddoc's chest hits my back.

For a moment, he just stands there, his hot breath to my neck causing goose bumps on my skin and a heavy beating in my chest.

"What?" I ask, a little breathier than I wanted.

"You know what..." he whispers slowly. "You left me in bed today."

"I woke up. You didn't."

And I needed some air because my lungs were full of citrus and pine, full of Maddoc.

"Right," he murmurs. "And yesterday, you left my bed when I told you I'd be back. That meant stay put. You didn't."

I curl my toes to keep myself from fidgeting. "Maybe next time say what you mean instead?"

"I'm guessing it would have made no difference." His hand comes up and my eyes follow as he grips my hair, pulling it behind me. "Tell me I'm wrong."

"You're right." I clear my throat and reach for the creamer, but he snags it before I can, so I finally spin to face him.

He smirks and makes quick work of setting the creamer bottle beside us and lifts me onto the countertop.

My eyes widen.

Okay, we're doing this whole flirty thing. Not good since I can't quite think straight this early ... and having six-foot-something of solid man meat in front of me isn't helping. Even sitting here like this, I still have to tip my head back to fully look at him.

Pouty lips, high cheekbones and wild ass green eyes, emerald in color at the moment. Thick, dark lashes and darker brows.

He's a good-looking bastard.

There's that smirk again...

He hands me my steaming cup of coffee and lifts the plastic Coffee-mate jug, pouring it in until I tell him to stop.

He frowns at it. "Can you even call that coffee?"

"It's my version of half and half. Half coffee, half the goods. We can't all shoot shit straight like you, big man."

He stares at me, so I take a drink and look off before meeting his eyes again.

"What?"

"You slept."

When my brows pull in, he shifts closer, tipping his head back a bit.

"Without your knife, Raven. You slept, sound a-fucking-sleep, without your security."

"I was tired."

He smirks and steps back. "Right."

Right. Right?

"Stop looking at me like that," I snap when my stomach starts to feel knotted.

"Like what?"

"Like you know me. You don't, and you shouldn't try to." I slide down and make my way into the living room in hopes of settling the rattled feeling I've got going on right as the others come inside.

I don't want to be understood, just as much as I can't afford to let anyone in.

I want to be able to walk away when I'm ready.

I look back to Maddoc who now leans against the counter staring after me.

Yeah, he could be a problem.

"So tonight's heat night," Royce announces.

"Heat night?" I ask.

"Yup. Tonight is all outdoor, no cabins, no clothes. Only the hot tubs and campfires or fire pits to keep you warm." Royce does a little shimmy with his shoulders. "Or another body."

I scoff. "Yeah, pass. I'll chill in here."

"Can't."

I look to Captain. "Why not?"

"Cabins are off-limits all around. Anyone found indoors during the party has to sleep outside in a screw-you row."

"Do I even wanna know what you're talking about?"

"Anybody found indoors, has to sleep on the ground in a row of sleeping bags that have been fucked in at least once this weekend. All lights have to be turned out at dusk and if any lights are seen inside the cabins, people rush in and pull you out and then you're screwed."

"One, that's dumb. Two, I lose by default. No swimsuit, so unless I run around in a thong and bra ..."

"Not opposed to that but ..." Royce trails off and then runs off.

I look to the other two for answers, but they give me nothing, and just as quick as he went, Royce bounds back up the stairs tossing me a bag.

My head snaps back as it hits my face and chest. I look from it to him and he shakes his hand my way.

I peek inside and a laugh leaves me, my hand lifting to cover my mouth as I shake my head.

"You like it?" He grins, and I look to him, smiling.

I pull out a skimpy ass, blood red bikini.

"There is no fucking way, ever. Never." I laugh, setting it in my lap so I can grab my cup again.

"What?!" He hops to his feet, looking entirely too adorably clueless. "Why? You'd look bangin' in that."

"More like bangable ... as in easy."

The boys chuckle, but Royce frowns and moves to drop on the coffee table directly in front of me. "A swimsuit doesn't make someone look easy," he calls me out on my judgment.

I smile. Good for him. And he's right, but it's different when people think you're trashy already. The more skin you show, the more they're convinced you're everything they assumed, fighting for attention and whatnot.

"Is it sexy?" He raises a brown brow. "Hell yeah. Did I pick the smallest one I could find? Fuck yeah," he admits, and I laugh. "But for real, you can pull this shit off like no other, I know it."

"Thank you, but no."

"Man." He moves to sit beside me on the couch. "Fine." He pulls another bag from under his hoodie and tosses it in my face with a pout.

I knock him with my shoulder and open the second bag, pulling out a sexy but sleek black one piece with the sides cut out at the curve of the stomach. It's not far off from something I might choose for myself, not that I could ever afford it.

It must show, my approval for the sassy piece, because Royce scoffs playfully.

"Great." Royce hits his knees and pulls himself up. He walks over to Maddoc and shoves him on his way out the slider door. "'Course she likes the grandma suit you picked out."

I look to Maddoc who meets my stare a minute before following Royce outside.

Huh.

Captain's sigh has me looking his way right as he leans forward, placing his forearm on the little kitchen counter. "Careful, Raven. He's 'bout there, and when he hits that point, others better stay the fuck back. Don't feed into it if you're not ready for what'll follow."

"What are you trying to say?"

He eyes me a minute. "Maddoc doesn't get possessive. Ever."

"Bullshit. Everyone said from the get-go he was a bossy bastard."

"Bossy is different, and you know it. I'm talking the way he steps closer to you when you step closer to someone else, us included. Or how he doesn't like you and Bass hanging out, or how he gets crazed when someone puts hands on you. Or—"

"Okay, packman." I laugh mockingly. "Enough nonsense."

"I'm just saying his sights are set, and at this point, I'm not sure anything could keep him from getting what he wants."

"What, me?" My eyes widen jeeringly. "Big deal."

Captain frowns, his stare bouncing between mine. "You don't care?"

"That your boy wants to fuck me? Negative. It's natural, all part of how the male brain works. They see something they like, and everything goes triggery and a big fat neon sign blinks in their heads, flashing 'mine' 'mine' 'mine' over and over again." He laughs, but I'm not playing. "But what your boy and every other needs to learn is just because your mind is telling you something belongs to you ... doesn't make it true."

"You saying you wouldn't fuck him?"

A smile takes over instantly. "I'm not saying that at all."

Captain throws his head back laughing, and I laugh with him.

The other two pop their heads back in, deep frowns on their faces as they look between the two of us, Maddoc stepping in and disappearing down the stairs a moment later.

That only makes us laugh harder.

Royce scoffs and then steps back out when his phone rings.

Captain looks to me with a grin. "Shit's about to get real interesting."

"Only one more day, Cap, then it's all back to normal."

"Normal?"

"Well, back to your kind of normal. I'm still waiting for the tin man to show up."

"Why, so you can give him a heart?" he jokes.

"Nah." Leaving Royce's suit of choice on the couch, I hold on to the other as I stand. "I'm more one to disappoint, living proof some of us really were built without the love tick."

"Love tick?"

"Yup. Something beats in there, but it's incapable of giving, unworthy of receiving. Just a little off."

"That's some morbid shit, Raven."

"Yeah." I shrug. "But still true."

I leave him upstairs and head for my room, but when I find Maddoc lying across my comforter, I fold my arms and lean against the doorframe.

"Don't stand there and stare, Raven." He doesn't bother opening his eyes to confirm. "Get over here. Sleep."

"I just had two cups of coffee."

"So."

A laugh bubbles out of me. I glance behind me when the other two shuffle back this way, each disappearing into their rooms, neither caring to know what I'm standing here for. Two loud bangs sound, their headboards hitting the wall, indicating they've dropped onto the beds.

I look back to Maddoc finding him now studying me.

"We're hungover as fuck, it's a three-day weekend, and we have no plans 'til tonight." He stares. "Come back to bed."

I take a deep breath and figure 'fuck it.' I shut and lock the door and drop onto the bed.

He doesn't scoot closer like he did last night – if he even remembers doing so. This time he simply closes his eyes and falls fast asleep.

I lay there wishing away the confusion he's planted inside me.

Chapter 25

Raven

"Raven, let's go."

With a groan, I move back into my bathroom and stand on the toilet to look myself over.

The suit fits perfectly. Too perfectly.

It's tight on my ass and forms to my every curve, showing off the curl of my hips in the openings. I'm a little too skinny for my liking, but I never have been able to hold any weight. All the walking around and mere lack of food didn't help either.

Either way, not much is left to the imagination in this thing.

I turn to look over the back again and slip, falling against the wall.

I laugh, finding my footing as a loud bang hits the door.

"The fuck was that?" Royce shouts. "You good in there?"

"Yeah." I chuckle then frown at the mirror. I left my hair down, hoping to cover myself some – and keep me warm since it's fucking cold out – but now that I'm looking again, it almost makes me look more ... like her. Desperate. Willing.

I move to the bed and drop down, facing the ceiling.

It's not the suit or the way it looks or how much it shows. It's how every day when I look in the mirror, my mother stares back, mocking me with her nasty smirk. She's like the dirty devil glued to my shoulder, constantly hissing in my ear reminding me who we are and what we'll never be.

Some kids get pep talks of honesty and integrity, I get a prime hooker's playbook on how to seduce a married man for blackmail money.

And while I imagine a lot of daughters are told how much their beauty matches their mother's, I'm reminded how I'll never measure up to mine.

I can admit she's the far prettier version of me on any day. She's got the sleek hair and big blue eyes, heavy makeup and heavier tits. For a woman who has used drugs for as long as I can remember, she somehow keeps herself up.

I told her once that she'd look like a troll eventually and she simply laughed and disagreed. She claims cocaine is nicer on the appearance than other drugs, which is why she 'chose' that over meth. Idiot. She calls it the soccer mom drug, swearing half the women in the suburbs – the wives of her clients – are all on a line or two a day.

When I asked why, if that were true, she couldn't function the way they did, she gave me a black eye.

I had laughed and left for school.

I already knew the answer, I just wanted to piss her off.

A single line or two would never be enough for Ravina Carver. She needs an eight ball to keep her satisfied, and even then ... enough is never enough.

Sometimes though, say after a four-day binge with no sleep, she looks the part of the scavenger she is.

Those are usually the days she has heavy hands.

"Open the door," Captain calls.

With a sigh, I pull myself from the comforter and do as he asks.

His attention immediately drops to my body and damn if mine doesn't do the same to his.

I step back to have a better look at him standing there in nothing but a pair of grey and blue swim trunks.

Captain is ripped. Like ... ripped. Where Maddoc's got that hard-earned tall and tapered effect of the three, Captain is broader, so his muscles are fuller, but he doesn't have that hardened look. His body seems soft but strong, like he'd wrap you up tight and you'd involuntarily melt right there in his arms, beg him not to let go. He'll keep a girl real warm tonight.

"Raven."

I lift my eyes and he winks.

"You look good, too."

I roll my eyes and when Royce steps beside him, I look him over just the same.

He's the leaner of the three, but still has the definition of an athlete. He's tight in the right areas, with biceps that flex with each movement. It's the tattoos though that reel you in at the start. He screams bad bad bad and he knows it.

I laugh when I see his trunks of choice.

They're white – bad move number one – and have a hot dog image with wings printed right over his groin.

He sees me looking and thrusts his hips, making his dick bounce against the fabric.

"Oh my God!" I laugh covering my eyes. "Quit your shit!"

Clearly no boxers under there.

He laughs. "Don't act like you don't wanna look, we both know you're dying to feel me up again."

"Let's fucking go," the big man's voice booms over us.

With grins, the other two shuffle away and finally, big man is in sight.

Maddoc, the god he is, is wearing solid black trunks, and I'd expect no different. He doesn't need to be flashy to be seen. He's got the aesthetic that forces your fixation - you simply can't miss the man. Especially not right now with the way those trunks ride low on his hips. His happy trail is practically screaming to be played with.

I look to him, finding his stare stuck on my thighs.

Those fiery eyes lift to mine.

Yeah ... this is gonna happen eventually.

He takes a step toward me, but Royce clamps a hand on his shoulder.

"Lights out, brother."

Maddoc licks his lips and looks off, making me grin.

Captain collects all their phones and turns to me. "Putting these in the safe for the night, so stick close by us or Leo, 'cause you won't be able to call us if you need to."

"One, I don't have your numbers. Two, I don't have a phone," I laugh and shut my light off, meeting them at the end of the hall. "And three, I'm a big girl. I—"

"Just do what you're told, Raven."

I slink up next to Maddoc, slowly planting my hand on his bare chest, ignoring the way it gets my pulse kicking. His skin's as hot as he is. "Yes, boss."

He frowns, knowing I'll do whatever I please, just like I know he'll be waiting to step in should he not approve. I'm learning the ways of the bossy bastard.

"A'ight, let's have some fun!" Royce shouts as Maddoc pulls the door open.

A burst of cold air hits us and I shiver.

Royce pulls me in, brushing his fingers along my arm playfully. He drops his lips to my ear. "Told you, warm body'll work best for this."

I laugh and shove him off.

With a lungful of air, I step outside first and the boys follow.

THEY WEREN'T PLAYING.

Nothing but half-naked bodies everywhere.

Seems they've used the walking path to start lining up sleeping bags and I heard they've already got three people assigned to some - a couple who got caught fucking on the countertops in one cabin and a chick who forgot her lipstick got screwed as well. She tried to argue it, but apparently needing that perfect pout isn't reason enough for a free pass inside.

What the hell will happen when the girls start having to pee, who knows.

I glance around. The groups are spread out well so people can roam from one spot to another as they want. There are several different games going on around – dice, cards, beer pong, and quarters. I'm sitting next to the fools who suck at throwing disks.

"Rae!" Leo shouts. "Come on, girl, I need a teammate. Mine passed out." He motions toward a guy sleeping on top of a nearby picnic table.

"Didn't wanna risk getting caught headed for his bed?"

"Nope." Leo laughs. "But I'm not sure that table's any better than a screwed sleeping sack. First night, Cari Thomas fucked Mark Rogers on there, and last night, well you saw Madman gettin' his dick sucked. Probably wiped his cum on it."

"He didn't," flies out before I can stop it.

Questioning stares hit mine, so I get us back on track.

"Partner, you say?"

"Yeah." He eyes me. "You ever play Bottle Bash?"

"With actual bottles we dug out of recycle bins and a broken broomstick, yeah, not this fancy shit."

A guy on the other team grins and lifts the Frisbee. "All you gotta do is throw this thing and hit the target. We're too lazy to count technicalities."

"Aim wins the game." I toss the Frisbee in my hands.

Loud laughter catches my attention and I glance behind me.

About a court's length back, the Graven students party in front of what I'm assuming is one of their cabins.

"They won't come any closer," Leo says quietly.

Collins stares right at me, completely ignoring the chick sitting on his lap.

"Surprised they even come this way."

"They usually stay back by Collins' place, keep us separated by the trail, but after the fight yesterday..." He trails off and I meet his stare. "Seems they're making it a point to show their ground."

He's wrong. Collins wants to be seen. He wants the upper hand in whatever this is, and right now the only answer he sees ... is me.

He's gauging, watching for signs of possession from the boys to me.

He wants confirmation that to get to me is to get to them. But it won't work.

He doesn't realize I'm just an outsider with a closer view than others at the moment. But I'm not a part of them.

As if reading my thoughts his lip tips up and he winks before finally looking back to his group.

"Come on, Leo, girls can't throw," the opponent jokes, bringing us back to the now.

I spin around and raise a brow. "Bet."

"Bet?"

"I make it, you're my partner's official beer boy for the night."

The guy laughs drunkenly. "You're on."

I look back to Leo. "You, dear Leo, are about to benefit from having me as partner."

He frowns and I turn back around, aim, and throw the Frisbee.

It hits the bottle perfectly, knocking it to the dirt.

They all hoot and holler and I bow, laughing lightly.

"Lucky shot?"

I shrug. "Passed a lot of time perfecting those trashcan paper tosses."

He nods, a light laugh leaving him. "Yeah. Pretty much where I learned to shoot, too."

"You grow up around here?"

"'Bout a mile down the street from the Bray houses. I was lucky though, Pops had a double wide instead of a single." He laughs, but it's bitter. Lucky is the last thing he considers his life to be.

There's a story there, but I don't feel like telling mine tonight so I only nod and pretend to need another drink so I can walk off.

When I glance left, a flash of white catches my eye and I squint to see better, but it's gone.

I look around for the only pair of white shorts I've seen tonight, not finding any. That's when I notice the other two are nowhere to be found.

Curiosity gets the best of me, so I pretend to survey everything around me, and when it's more than clear nobody is watching, I head the way the white shorts disappeared to.

I go around the opposite way so that when I reach the end, I'm coming up the back side of the cabins.

I frown when I realize where I am, a large air hockey table not fifteen feet to my right.

"What the fuck?" I whisper, quickly dropping down behind a parked car when footsteps grow near. Then the voices hit my ears.

"How can you not get it open?"

"They had to have changed the fucking locks. I popped that shit a dozen times last trip. I was fucking ready for it."

"Obviously not."

"Man, fuck you. I tried. Don't see you doing shit to get it."

"I'll bust the fucking window right now."

"Yeah, and then every motherfucker will hear it."

"Both of you, shut the fuck up and let's think."

I shift to the side, seeing it really is just the three of them ... standing not a foot from Collins' cabin door.

Those fuckers. They're trying to break in.

I look to the cabin, scanning the deck and each window.

Bingo.

I pop up and head their way.

"The answer's easy."

Three heads jerk my way, deep frowns taking over.

"Go back to the fucking party," Maddoc orders, suspicion in his eyes.

"What's the point? I already saw you guys trying to break in." I shrug and his jaw clenches.

Royce cuts his eyes from Maddoc back to me. "Got some new fancy lock. Can't crack it."

"You also can't fit any one of your big ass bodies through that shower window. I, however, can." I cross my arms and wait.

They do the whole, 'no way, I don't think so' thing and of course it's Captain who understands I'm the only answer.

Maddoc looks to me. "This is Brayshaw business."

"I'm nothing but a key, I'll go after it's opened." I shrug, looking between the three.

"That's not what I meant—" he growls, but Captain cuts him off.

"We don't have time for this."

They turn for the side of the cabin, so I follow. Maddoc bends down, allowing me to step up on his knee so I can grip the edge of the window. His hands find my ass and he gives me a solid push and with a tiny twist, I'm in.

I flip on the bathroom light quickly and they all start yelling at me, but I leave it until I hit the front door, unlock and yank it open. I go to dart back into the lighted night sky, but Maddoc blocks me and shoves me back inside as Royce runs past to the bathroom and flips the light off.

I tense. "Let me out."

"Hell no. You're not walking back by yourself."

"Then turn on the light."

"And let people come barging in looking to bust us for the fucking game only to bust us for breaking in the damn place? Don't be stupid."

Someone grabs my hand and yanks, dragging me through the dark house. Clearly, they've mapped the place out as not one of them knocks into anything along the way.

I'm shoved forward. A door clicks behind me, followed by a lock.

My heart rate spikes.

Shit.

"Turn on a light."

"No."

More noises echo and I jerk around, but I can't see. Tapping comes from the other corner and I spin that way.

Shit, shit.

I squeeze my eyes shut, but it only makes everything worse.

"Give me your phone," I say to no one in particular.

"Don't have 'em, remember? Couldn't chance one ringing

and us being heard. Your talking isn't helping either," Maddoc snaps at me.

"I can't..." I bound forward, knocking into something, a loud scrape against the hardwood making them all curse quietly. "I need out."

"Raven, chill—"

"I said I need out!" I shout, not caring who hears.

"Fuck, dude. She's gonna get us caught!"

I start breathing hard, wringing my hands at my sides.

Fingers touch my back and I yelp, jerking forward, again bumping into something. A table maybe?

"Fuck."

"Shut her up."

"It's the dark."

"She's afraid of the fucking dark?"

"No way ... really?"

They talk like I'm not here, but I can't focus enough to care let alone respond.

I swallow, trying to calm my nerves but it does nothing.

"Fuck, fuck fuck fuck. I can't. Sorry, but I gotta get out."

"Raven, quiet."

"I said I want out!"

"Bro, shut her up." They start to panic.

"Someone will hear."

"Fuck."

"I swear to fucking—" My words die on my lips when I'm jerked right and heavy lips land on mine.

I tense, but the mouth on mine adds pressure.

A light whimper leaves me and a hand dips into my hair, using the grip to drag me forward and I go willingly, but then the soft sound of a drawer closing in the room has me jumping back.

"Fuck, I need out of here now. I can't." I start breathing heavy and dizziness takes over. "Please."

"It's not enough," says one of them. "She's too tripped out."

"I found it!" Captain whispers urgently.

"Don't matter! We can't fucking go until we get the signal. We're stuck for a minute."

A door slams somewhere and the boys cuss.

"That wasn't you, was it?" I whisper, damn near on the verge of shaking now.

No one answers.

"Was that you, guys?" I say louder, and they shush me.

"Someone's inside."

I let out a small cry when something falls to the floor.

"Dude. Make her relax," Captain hisses.

"I could—" Royce is cut off when Maddoc snaps, "Don't even."

Screw this.

I fight to get past them, but I'm only pushed backward.

"Damn it," Maddoc growls. "Everybody quiet."

"This isn't happening," I whisper to myself.

"Rae—"

"Fuck fuck fuck." Something touches my elbow and a small yelp leaves me.

"Shut her up. Now."

Once again, I'm yanked forward, a warm mouth dropping to meet mine. I try to get lost in the heat of it all, doing my best to draw up images in my mind. The lips are soft and full, perfectly skilled and wanting.

A second set of hands, slightly rougher than the firsts, find my shoulders and slowly inch their way down, causing a shiver to run through me.

The person cradling my face pulls me closer, and I willingly step against the solid body in front of me.

There's a slight shuffle to my left and I pull back a little.

"I—"

"Shh. No talking." I think this gentle command comes from Captain.

Two new hands lift me from my feet, and I'm laid across a soft cushion.

I try to free my lips, but the mouth on mine refuses to let me go and a silky tongue sweeps mine until I relax some more. The kisser skims his heated mouth across my chin to my neck, and then he's gone.

"She'll need more. This isn't enough for her," Royce whispers and the sound of heavy breathing surrounds me.

"We're gonna keep you quiet, RaeRae," he breathes. "You good with that?"

I squeeze my eyes shut, my legs bouncing and all hands on me freeze where they are. I swallow. "Distract me."

There's a pause, and a chill runs over my skin as all connection is lost. I'm ready to shoot from the place they've laid me when finally, one heated hand meets my flesh once again.

Two fingers find my collarbone, tracing over me slowly, not stopping when they reach the top of my swimsuit but dipping in the front to edge along my breast.

My breathing speeds up.

I jerk lightly when a second hand starts at my calf, running up and over my knee, sliding forward when they reach my thigh. They grip me tight, slowly skimming upward.

A moan starts to escape, but a mouth lands on mine again, swallowing any sound before it could be heard.

Warm breath hits my stomach then and hot air is blown across my abdomen, continuing until the heat seeps through the material covering my center.

Two hands glide up, slipping between my suit and skin, moving the suit to the side, and then I'm exposed ... but only to the darkness.

I sense it before it hits, and a breathy whimper makes its way up my chest.

A tongue comes down on me, and I lift my hips, needing all it can give. Reaching out, I latch onto the closest body, finding a solid arm to squeeze.

My chest rises rapidly as a practiced tongue explores me, not letting up until my clit is properly assaulted. When my thighs clench, the lips close over the sweet spot and I start to shake.

My kiss grows hungrier and the mouth on mine growls against me.

I'm right there, so fucking close to losing, I jerk away gasping, and right before I come, a hand hits my hip and feathers south, and my body recharges, unwilling to let go of the feeling just yet. The pleasure starts over, a new fire burning deep in my core. The fingers trace up and over my ribs until I'm a quivering mess. A deep, cry makes its way up my chest and just before it escapes, a hand covers my lips gently, slowly dragging down my neck, forcing my head to tilt back and my back to arch high as those hands slide over my suit covered breast. They pause there, my hard nipples now being squeezed between fingers.

"Fuuuck." I think it's Royce who draws out the word like a song. "She's ... a fucking trooper."

"She's making us work." Captain, I think.

"I knew she would." Maddoc.

Over and over again, from every pleasure point I have, I'm brought to the edge, pushed back and led there again. Until it's too much, until it's everywhere, until they've been everywhere, consuming every inch of my body and mind. My back leaves the cushion one final time, my legs clamping tight against the head between my legs, and my teeth draw blood from the bottom lip teasing mine.

I come hard, the ride even more powerful as I fight for silence when all I want to do is fill the room with my moans, show them what they did to me.

For me.

'Cause that's what this was – the boys keeping me calm in the only way they knew they could.

In the minutes that follow, nothing but the sounds of heavy breathing fill the room.

Right when my body calms enough to realize I'm still in the dark, there are two soft taps against the window, followed by two more.

I jerk, but a hand to my thigh calms me.

"Let's get the fuck outta here," Maddoc rasps and a shiver runs through me.

The hand on my thigh squeezes.

"We sure it's clear?" Royce whispers.

"Leo wouldn't signal if he wasn't sure."

I fix my swimsuit and lace my fingers through the ones that reach for mine, allowing them to lead me out.

When we hit the landing and exit, I see it's Captain who is holding my hand. He lets go the second we reach the door and together, the four of us round the house while I pretend not to see Royce stuff a piece of paper in the front of his trunks.

Leo's eyes widen when he spots me, a mumbled "shit" leaving him.

"Yeah, fucker. What happened to keeping an eye on her?" Maddoc shoves him, but he laughs in good nature.

"Tried. She's slippery."

A scuffled laugh leaves Royce and my jaw drops, my head swiveling his way, but when Maddoc and Captain do the same, we share a laugh.

Pretty sure I might be blushing right now.

Leo's questioning stare bounces between us, but he doesn't ask. He knows his place, they'd talk if they wanted him involved.

He gives a stiff nod, his eyes skating past mine as he turns, walking the opposite way the four of us go.

Royce splits for the house once it's in view, the other two going for the hot tub at the landing of the cabin beside theirs, and I shoot straight for the picnic table turned bar. I pour a quick shot of Captain Morgan's Tattoo and knock it back, letting the too thick, too sweet liquor coat my throat.

Holy shit, I can't believe that just happened.

I toss some ice into the cup and pour some more to sip on.

"Aye, pour me one too, RaeRae." Royce bounds my way, having locked up whatever they stole in the safe, I'm sure.

I do as he asks, holding in my frown when I turn around to hand him his, finding he's slipped into the hot tub as well. The hot tub Chloe and her friend are now in.

She stands in the water, pretending to adjust the tie of her top all so she can push her chest toward Maddoc's face.

Too bad for her his eyes are locked on me over her shoulder.

He likes me watching.

Leo steps up beside me. "Don't let her see you hesitate."

"I'm not hesitating."

"What are you doing then?"

"Laughing at her antics." If she was all she pretends to be, she wouldn't mess with the teasing, she'd go straight for what she wanted.

"I don't hear you laughing. You should just go over there, send her on her way."

"I'm laughing on the inside." I look to Leo, who frowns at the sight and I realize what's happening here. He's jealous. I turn my body to face him, and a splash of water sounds to my right.

The boys are now watching us.

"You want her, and you're trying to use me to help make it happen."

"How would I use you, the way the boys are?" He lifts his chin, but he sure as shit dropped his tone down a bit.

I'm not the one that fears a body, or three, in that hot tub.

"That's right, Leo. Lower your tone so they don't hear you. But if you thought they wouldn't like what you had to say ... why would you still go for the wannabe insult and chance possibly disrespecting your boys like that?"

"What are you trying to say?" He goes for a strong, hard tone, but every inch of him is suddenly laced with tension.

"I'm not trying to say a damn thing. You showed me all I need to know. One comment, one look and I've got you all figured out. You're the odd man out, always. You stay as close as they let you, but you're never invited past the buzzer. And here I come, nothing to offer and uninterested in the game, and I'm staying in that fourth room."

"Don't fool yourself, it's the pussy between your legs they want. They'll throw you out when they're done."

"Like they do Chloe?" I taunt and his features harden. "Yet she still goes back for more, each and every time, leaving you sitting there wondering what they've got that you don't."

"RaeRae!" Royce calls, but he drags my name out more than normal. "I'm thirsty."

Leo's eyes cut their way before coming back to mine. "I can't wait to watch you fall."

"Don't worry, Leo." I smirk, walking backward. "Whores are good on their knees."

I spin on my heels and force the frown to stay away.

It was a joke when I'd say it before, but I did just let all three touch me in some way. Maybe I am more like my mother than I care to admit.

I use my sex appeal against people all the time. I use it to decipher a man's intentions by gauging the look in his eyes, to search for loyalty, to gain advantages. To get out of sticky situations.

My body is my weapon.

But I never take it further.

Laughter has me scanning the hot tub and as I would have suspected, each of the guys' eyes are on me.

But tonight, I did, didn't I?

I don't realize I'm stepping away until Maddoc's hand shoots out, grabbing onto my wrist. He tips his chin ever so slightly, silently demanding I stop with the thoughts he can somehow read.

Fingers brush mine and I look to my other hand where Royce is reaching for his cup, his touch conveying the same.

A palm appears in front of me next and I look to its owner. Captain.

I place my hand in his, looking from Royce, to Maddoc, and back to Captain.

I let him lead me up the steps, even though I don't need the help. Even though I don't know if I want in. Even though all other eyes are on me.

I dip into the water and when Maddoc grips my hips, I let him pull me to his lap.

Chloe shifts her stare to me, rage growing in her eyes.

She slithers back, licking her lips in an attempt to cover her displeasure. She slowly lets the jets push her farther left, closer to Royce, who would probably be all for it, but there's plenty of others willing to play if he says go.

I lock eyes with him to make sure he'd be okay with it, suddenly not wanting to make the wrong move, and he looks from my blue-tipped hair to me.

He gives a curt nod.

I sit up straight and Maddoc's hand slides across my stomach, his chin moving to press against my hair.

And I feel it, the supremacy that is Brayshaw. I shouldn't use it, shouldn't take what he's offering right now with his possessive hold and steady heartbeat.

Yet I do it anyway.

I look to Chloe. "Go."

A laugh spits out of her but when it's only her and the girl she came with who thinks it's funny, her smile slowly fades.

"You can't be serious?"

I lift my cup and take a drink, dismissing her.

"You heard her. Go." Captain stands, looking down at the two.

There's some groaning and unnecessary water slapping, but they do as they're told and step from the hot tub.

Leo watches from where I left him. His face is blank, but his body language says enough. He's not happy.

Fuck him, too.

I call out, loud enough for him to hear, "The entire team is off-limits to you tonight, Chloe. Find another dick to fall on."

She storms off, and he meets my stare a moment, unable to hide the way his lip curls just the slightest.

The twitch of Maddoc's muscles has me thinking he caught it too. But I'm not looking to cause problems between friends. He'll either get his shit straight or cause his own fall.

I don't need Leo's respect ... but I don't want the Brayshaws at the expense of their boy. He was here before me, and he'll be here after.

It's only a matter of time before I'm sent back to my slums, it's how the story always goes.

Girls from the gutter don't belong at privileged cabins in the woods with ruling rich boys and pissy princesses.

I've got enough problems of my own, the last thing I need is to inherit theirs.

Yet here I sit, comfortable on the lap of the king, confident with his palm spread across my abdomen, and strong with his princes at our sides.

This is their world, and it seems I'm in the middle of it.

Chapter 26

Raven

"We just gonna pretend we didn't rock her world last night?"

Oh my God.

"Shut the fuck up, Royce." Captain throws a chip at him and Maddoc shakes his head.

"What?" He shifts in the front seat to look at me.

I lift my hands, peeking at him through my fingers and he grins.

"I'm playing. But I did have to go fluff my ego last night after it took you ten fucking years to—"

"Bro, shut up." Captain shakes his head.

"Fine, but for real, afraid of the dark, RaeRae?" His dark eyes widen. "Never saw that shit coming."

"Anywaaaaay..." I playfully frown at him and he winks, turning back in his seat.

"Right. Yeah, we got what we were looking for, so thanks for that," he says and then ... silence.

He offers no more, none of them do, so I sure as hell don't ask.

I settle in my seat, trying not to let a sour taste take over. It's dumb, because I have no right to feel left out. I'd have to be "in" for that to happen and right now I'm just ... hell, I have no clue what I am.

Fresh? Foreign? A toy? A—

Wait.

I swiftly cut my eyes to Maddoc, who lazily meets my gaze.

"What?" His stare bounces between mine and after a few seconds, his lips smash together.

I scoff, tipping my head back as a bitter laugh leaves me.

Ugh, stupid girl. You should have known.

"Raven—"

"Fuck you, big man."

Royce's head swivels around. I make sure my glare meets his questioning stare, then Captain's in the mirror.

"Fuck all of you."

The distraction.

That's what this was. That's why I was here, why they played friendly lately. The rides to school, the light share of information, a tiny glimpse into their world to make me comfortable.

I always knew comfort was for fools, the man who slipped under my covers after slipping out of my mom's when I was twelve taught me that hard lesson.

They knew I'd roam, it's who I am and what I do. They bet on my stumbling upon the Graven guys at some point. It's why they didn't give me the pre-warning or order or what the fuck ever, to stay away – like they did before.

Because this time, they needed me to be the pawn so they themselves had a reason to survey the setup. Bet they even counted on them moving their party into the designated bullshit Brayshaw zone so they could make their way to the cabin without being seen.

No fucking way could they have gotten in there if they were all partying right outside.

No fucking way would they have gotten in the house if I hadn't made it happen.

"Raven." Maddoc's tone is demanding – a command to look his way.

I close my eyes and tip my head back on the seat.

His light growl and jerky movements have me wanting to scream, but I don't.

I hold it in.

Tonight, when we get back, I'll let it all out.

Maddoc

We don't bother getting our bags out but head right into the house after we drop Raven off.

"She thinks we used her to get to Graven," Royce states the obvious.

I nod, looking from him to Captain.

"Why didn't you tell her that wasn't true?" he barks.

"Why didn't you?" I counter and his eyes narrow.

"Man, cut the shit. We all know she's under your skin. That means you run the Raven show. All we can do is sit back and watch."

"Fuck was I supposed to say?" I throw my arms out and he shakes his head.

"Tell her she was wrong, tell her we like her, tell her to cut the shit and admit she likes us too."

"This won't turn into some fucking four-way, brother," I ease, and he scoffs.

"Not what the fuck I meant, and you know it!"

I sigh, dragging my hands down my face. "Fuck, man. I know. She makes me fucking crazy. She's not gonna believe it just because I say it. She's even more untrusting than we are."

"Yeah well, she won't even get to consider believing it if she doesn't get to fuckin' hear it."

"We really sitting here pretending? We knew having her around would help with the Graven shit," Captain spits. "Just because we started to like having her around don't mean there wasn't purpose behind it in the beginning."

"Yeah, but—"

"There is no 'but' as far as she's concerned. We did what she expected. She's not mad at us. She's mad at herself for thinking we wanted her there instead of needing her there."

"What should we have done then?"

"Ask for her help instead of being sneaky about it."

"She had no reason to say yes."

"No reason to say no either." Captain shrugs. "She'd have done it and you know it."

Fuck if he isn't right.

Royce drops onto the couch. "Go fix it, Madman."

I nod, heading upstairs for a shower, knowing damn well what Royce said a minute ago is true, she's under my fucking skin. Problem is I haven't decided if I'm going to let her stay there or not. Or, if she even belongs. Either way, I wanna play with Raven Carver while I decide.

I take my time showering, then get my shit from the car and put it away. By the time I'm done, it's finally past lights out at the home, so I head down the stairs, deciding to walk down the dirt road to the Bray house.

I'm almost at the edge of the trees when the smell of weed hits my nostrils.

I clench my teeth together, knowing what I'll fucking find when I step past the trees. And sure as fuck, there she is with a dude who must not have gotten his ass lit up good enough, Bass Bishop. They're leaning against the shed at the edge of the guys' home.

He's saying some shit that has her covering her hand to muffle that husky laugh of hers and I'm ready to throat punch him.

I told her ass what would happen if I saw her with him again. I wasn't fucking playing.

A car pulls up at the curb and they head for it, but something has her glancing back.

She scans the trees, so I take the two steps forward into the light.

Her eyes shoot wide and my chin lifts.

That's right. Busted. Now get that ass over here ...

She flips me off, and my muscles lock.

Just when I think she's gonna slide into the seat and take the fuck off, she turns to face me.

Crossing her arms over the top of the door, she leans her chin against them, calling me over with a crook of the finger.

I was already headed for her and she damn well knows it.

Raven smirks when I plant my feet on one side of the door as she stays tucked away on the other.

"What do you say, big man, you want in?"

Now it's me who smirks, and she rolls her eyes playfully.

I pull the door open and step against her.

Her smirk stays in place, but the lungful of air she takes and holds onto, and the more her body pushes against mine gives her away.

She likes when I'm near.

"You were right. You were there to divert. You've been around specifically so we could climb in your head and see what your angle was, so we could use it against you first if needed. But you knew that already," I whisper, and her eyes fly between mine. "Now ask me what's changed since the beginning. Ask me ... what keeps me up at night, Raven."

"I don't wanna know." She tries to hide her swallow.

"Yeah, you do."

Her lips pull between her teeth as I step back.

Like Cap said, she's not mad we used her, but she wishes she was.

She doesn't have that tick inside her to care and she hates that about herself. She doesn't give a damn, because she expects it. It's fucked up, but it's Raven.

She blinks away her thoughts and sassy Raven slides back in place.

"Not coming along, are we?" She jerks her head like she's winning, but then the engine rumbles in the distance and she glances over my shoulder.

She rolls her eyes and steps out so she can close the car door. She dips her head in the window. "We'll follow."

She bumps my shoulder as she passes.

"Not even gonna fight me on it, huh?" I tease, and she scoffs.

"Please."

I catch her by the back belt loop, quickly spinning her around and she yelps, but her fucking smile ... fuck.

I step into her, fire burning in my groin. "You think you've got me all figured out?"

"I know you enough to know how that'd have ended."

"How would it have ended," I rasp, slowly moving to grip her hips.

Her eager eyes darken, and she sways on her feet a bit.

I lean in and her breath hitches.

The light squeal of brakes has her jerking back.

Bad fucking timing.

Captain rolls to a stop beside us and Royce hangs out the

window with a grin. "RaeRae, sneaking off already, are we?" he tsks. "Not sure that'll work for us."

"I'm not sure I care," she gibes back.

I pull open the door and she climbs in.

Royce shifts his smile from her to me then drops back in his seat.

I slide in and she raises a brow when I move to the middle seat.

When I don't take my eyes off of her, she pushes through her edginess with a laugh, turning to look out her side window.

She's got tension rolling off her and I don't like it.

I like her in fuck it mode. That's who she really is. Just ... wild.

I turn, whispering in her ear. "Royce's right. Not sure this arrangement'll work."

"What arrangement is that?" She pulls the sleeves of her hoodie over her hands.

"The one where you're in your bed and I'm in mine."

She drops a grin to her chest before looking to me. "Well, you don't have to worry about a thing like that, big man."

"Yeah, why is that?"

We pull up and park along the long road of cars. She slides forward on the seat, ready to climb out the second the locks click open. She looks back to me. "'Cause I don't have a bed. I'm only borrowing one."

And then she hops out, heading right for Bass and his emo ass friend.

"Dude. Should we be here?" Royce looks from Captain to me. "Half these fools do work for us. We don't hang with them for a reason. Business and pleasure, Madman. Not good."

Cap surveys the scene. "If shit goes down here, cameras could roll."

"They won't. We feed these fuckers."

"Yeah, but you know Graven's been poking around a lot

more than normal lately. Any of them could be waiting for a leg up."

I look back to Raven who stands there, lighting a fucking joint.

"You're right. But I'm not leaving her here." I look to Cap. "Go home. I can't have you getting fucked out here."

He glares. "Fuck you, bro. Like I'd leave."

"I can't ask you to stay."

"To watch Raven?" He unbuckles his seat belt. "Yeah, man. You can. Three for one, brother. That's how it goes."

My chest tightens and I look away.

My brothers, loyal no matter what.

We step out and follow along the orchard line.

Raven tips her head back, blowing smoke into the night, smiling as it disappears. She catches me watching and winks, but when her eyes slide to Royce and she lifts the joint, my head snaps his way.

He quickly glances off, scratching the side of his head.

He's fucking smoking again?

"Hey, Bass, you got more of this?" she asks him, and he looks from her to us.

"Right." She laughs. "Conversation for later."

I don't fucking think so...

She passes what's left to the emo guy and when she does, I swoop in, wrapping my arms around her middle.

She chuckles. "What do you think you're doing, big man?"

"Showing these people what's mine."

"Hmm ..." She muses, spinning in my arms. She looks up, a frisky fire shining at me. She whispers, "Funny ... 'cause you haven't even showed me yet." She pulls away in good nature.

I let her. Any more of that whispered rasp and my dick would be hard.

She walks a few feet ahead, spins to face us, her hands rising above her head as she starts dancing to the music flowing through the trees. "You boys ready to see your first fake campfire?"

"Can we get a real repeat of—"

I shove his ass. "I'll fuck you up you finish that sentence."

Royce shoves me back with a grin and dances toward her. The two make their way to the middle of the crowd.

Me and Captain find a place to chill not far from view.

When Royce gets sidetracked and starts dancing with some random, I wait for Raven to pull back his attention, but she doesn't.

In fact, she doesn't even look his way.

Or ours.

She dances on her own with people surrounding her, hands in the air, hips swaying in perfect rhythm.

Her eyes are closed, her head moving with her body. Sheets of sleek, dark hair fall over her shoulders, the tips brushing the little bit of exposed skin of her stomach. Not a care who's around or hoping anyone is watching. Just doing her because she wants to.

"She seems more relaxed here," Cap voices my thought.

"She's in her element."

We turn to find a blank-faced Bishop behind us, holding up two cans of Keystone. I look from his hand to him. "I'll only offer once. Take it if you want it. It's cheap, but it works."

Cap nods and takes both, and Bishop walks off.

I glance back to Raven.

She opens her eyes but doesn't care to look around to how many she sucked in with the curl of her body, doesn't look to confirm if she's drawn me in. Because she doesn't fucking care.

She splits from the crowd in the next second and I take a step forward, but Captain's hand hits my chest.

"Leave her, brother. Let her breathe a minute."

"Why should I?" I track her every step toward a group set up with a keg.

"Because she let herself get comfortable this weekend, which couldn't have been easy on her, and we left her feeling like shit. If we want her close, we need her to admit to herself she likes being there."

My eyes narrow as they follow her. "Should we be letting her get close?"

"I honestly don't know. We're not supposed to want to. Dad won't approve."

"Dad isn't here."

"Makes no difference and you know it. He always said a woman would make us crazy. We didn't believe him, but Raven, I mean shit."

Raven is proof it could happen. We all feel the shift.

The guy at the keg nods his chin and she pulls out a bill – I can't see how much from here – and hands it over.

He pours her two cups.

I look to my free can of beer.

'Course she wouldn't want one simply handed to her.

Double fisting, she weaves her way through the crowd, injecting herself right between Royce and his partner.

The girl jerks back, ready to fire off, but when Raven steps closer to her, the chick lifts her hands with a nod and walks away.

"What was that?" Captain asks right as I think it.

I look to Bishop who of fucking course has his eyes on her too.

They cut to mine a second before he turns and walks away.

I look around, noticing how everyone near her gives her a few inches of space, unlike the others near who are all smashed against each other.

Son of a bitch. "They respect her," I determine.

Mine and Cap's eyes connect a moment, both our expressions tight.

Raven has gained these people's respect from the few fights she's had here.

She earned it where we demanded it.

"Maddoc ... we need to be careful."

I nod. My thought exactly. But we'll worry about that later. I'm focused on right now.

Royce takes the cup Raven offers him and when he wraps his hand around her middle, laying his palm on her hip, I toss my beer to the ground.

"Yeah." Captain laughs. "Guess that's enough breathing for the night."

Royce sees me coming and chuckles. He whispers something in her ear and spins the other way, grabbing the first girl he can find to grind on.

And I grab mine.

She laughs lightly when I pull her in and without instruction starts dancing against me.

I bend at the knee, pushing mine farther between hers so we fit better.

She looks down, following the movement of my body.

I pull her eyes back to mine, finding the tip of her tongue between her teeth. "Didn't take you for the dancing type, big man."

"If I wanna dance, I dance."

She smiles and swiftly spins in my arms, bringing that ass in, but she doesn't push it on me.

I tug her in until it does.

Her chest inflates and her movements slow. She's getting turned on just leaning on me.

I run my hands up her ribs and hers drops back, lazily laying against my shoulder, so I skim my lips over her arm.

She took off her sweater and it works in my favor.

Her body shivers and she steps away a fraction of an inch, but my grip tightens to keep her from moving farther.

"You should admit it now." I slip my hands in her tight as hell front pockets, right against the curve of her bikini line.

"Admit what?"

"That you want me."

A husky ass laugh leaves her and she turns to meet my eyes over her shoulder. They're glossy and low, probably effects of the weed and the little alcohol she's had, but there's a fire in there too. Defiance laced with desire.

Mine.

"You think I won't admit it, big man?" Her eyes light up, along with the corner of her mouth tipping up. "You're wrong. Do I want you?" Her stare bounces between mine. "When you're pushed up on me like this? Hell yeah, I do."

She makes quick work of pulling away and starts walking backward.

"But when you're a few feet away, the fog wears off and it all goes back to normal."

"Yeah." I meet her every step back with one forward. "And what's normal?"

"Normal is you needing power, and me refusing to give it."

"Trying to pull the old oil and water card, Raven?"

"Nah." She shakes her head. "We're both made of the same things, big man."

"Then what's the problem?"

"Problem is, I want to stay out of sight."

"You think I don't?"

"Oh, I know you do, but it's different. You want to be out of sight, but you're meant to be seen, and me?" She looks left, nothing but dark orchards for miles. "I'm meant to disappear."

I step in front of her and she doesn't jerk away when my fingers grip her chin to pull her attention to me. "Meant to or want to?"

She inhales as my hand slides into her hair. A slow blink. A tight grip on my bicep.

She's ready for me.

"Both," she breathes against my mouth now lined up with hers. Her stare bounces before mine. "You gonna kiss me again, big man? Right here, where all can see?"

"Again?" I raise a dark brow, and hers pull in slightly. "I haven't touched your lips yet, Raven."

She goes to speak but stops when my thumb pulls down on her bottom lip.

My eyes meet hers. "At least, not these ones."

She tenses at first and then, fuck me, a shy-like smile I'd never expect from her spreads and she drops her eyes. That look has my head spinning.

"You ate me out," she whispers.

"Nah." I release her, and she looks up as I'm stepping back with a smirk. "I only licked you a little bit."

Her tongue sweeps over one corner of her mouth to the next, her smile coming right back. Her stimulated eyes track me as I walk backward.

She knows what I'm saying.

That was nothing.

I turn to head for Captain, unable to wipe the smirk off my face.

"Uh, oh." Captain takes one look at me and laughs. He downs what's left in his can and tosses it in the back of the pickup we're standing by. "That look can only mean one thing coming from you, brother."

My smirk deepens.

I think I'll keep her.

Chapter 27

Raven

"Rae."

I ignore Maybell, pretending to be asleep when I heard her walk in the room.

"Come on now, your headphones ain't in, child, so I know you awake."

Despite my best effort, I crack a small smile, and one eye pops open.

She grins and walks over, pulling her shawl closer at the center. She sits down on the vacant bed across from mine.

"Is this about my taking off this past weekend?" Or the journal I stole ... "We didn't exactly talk—"

"I don't know what you're talkin' about. You were here all weekend." She hits me with a stern expression.

I nod against my pillow. "Right."

"You know," she starts. "Lots of girls come on through here. Some stay until eighteen, most take off beforehand, and of course ... some get the boot in their bratty asses."

I laugh lightly, moving to sit up.

She's going somewhere with this.

"They like you."

Neither of us pretends "they" need to be named.

"They hardly know me."

"But they want to, I can see it. You know, never once did those boys pull a girl who came from here into their world."

"No offense, but I don't believe that."

She scoffs. "Oh, Royce may have a few missed curfews here and there. That boy doesn't need to know or like a thing about 'em to, well, you know." She shakes her head, but not in judgment.

"You love them," I observe.

"I raised them."

So that part of the rumor is true.

She tips her head back with a light laugh. "Well, I raised them as much as they let me. Their dad was good to them when he was around, but he was gone more often than not and eventually, they were old enough to be angry over it. The kind of anger a parent can cause never really goes away, it grows like mold from the inside, testing to see if we're strong enough to clean it out. But they still love him despite his faults."

"No offense, Maybell, but why are you telling me this?"

"I can't say." Her face tightens, the truth of her words causing her concern. She stands. "Might have something to do with the person waiting outside for ya. Call it, intuition."

She moves to the door and turns back to me.

"I see something in you, Raven. Something I'm not sure you see yourself. Don't let ... just, trust your gut, child. Trust ... what you know. The rest will come in time."

She doesn't wait for a response but leaves the room, and I'm left really fucking confused as to what she's getting at.

I slip my feet in my boots, taking my time as I lace them up and pull a hoodie over my head.

I'm sure Royce will have a lighter.

I walk out the front door and hop off the side of the porch.

"Well."

Lead fills my veins in an instant and I stop dead in my tracks.

No.

I slowly turn toward the street.

Glacier blue eyes rake over me with pure disdain. "Never seen that smile from you before. Sure faded fast." Her glossy eyes meet mine. "Don't look so happy to see me."

"I'm not."

I glance to the porch when the door opens and Maybell steps out, pretending she needed to pull from the mailbox right then. Her eyes briefly skate past mine before landing on my mother. Her features tighten and she pauses a moment, but then walks back in.

I turn back.

My mom's eyes are stuck on the Bray house, but slowly shift to mine when I move closer to the curb.

She leans against a blue Toyota that must be older than me. I try to glance past to see the driver, but she blocks my view.

I let my eyes travel over her and hate how good the universe was to a piece of shit like her.

Long, perfectly shaped legs, wide hips with a trim waist, and a rack many women pay thousands for, all given to the one who gives it away for a fee.

Her skirt just covers her upper thighs, her underwear string pulled up over her hips and her top is more a thick headband around her chest than a shirt. 'Course, it's white and her bra is a deep silky purple. Her hair, long and dark is curled and piled on her head. Perfectly placed. Her makeup too.

She's ridiculously attractive and she knows it.

Gorgeous on the outside, corroded on the inside.

She's a nasty bitch in a deceiving package.

She wrenches her nose up at my hoodie, sweatpants, and boots.

I don't match, I look like a hobo, and I don't give a damn. I don't live to impress like she does.

Something she could never understand.

"Just because you're staying in a house with a bunch of girls, doesn't mean you need to dress like a lesbian."

"Just because you're a broke, judgmental bitch, doesn't mean you need to dress like a slut." I give a fake laugh. "Oh wait, it does, doesn't it?"

"Watch your mouth, Raven."

"Why you here?"

"Why else?" She looks to her nails, blowing a bubble with her gum.

"Who do you owe?"

"Rol's guys."

I scoff and her eyes fly back to mine. "What, they won't take other means of payment anymore?"

They way her lip curls, it's a clear no. "I need a couple thousand by Sunday night."

I start laughing and she pushes off the car. "Fuck you. Hell no."

"I said watch your mouth." She steps forward with a sneer.

So do I.

"Or what, mother? What are you gonna do, huh? You gonna have your new pimp or whatever he is whoop my ass right here on the street where anyone could see? We both know, you no longer can."

"Don't sound so sure."

"Prove me wrong."

She grips my elbows, her long cokehead nails sinking into my skin, and she yanks me toward her right as I shove off her chest.

The move sends me stumbling back and has her flying against the car.

She pushes off right as I get my footing and we both dart forward, but before I can grab a hold of her and before her swing makes it all the way around, arms wrap around my waist and I'm lifted off my feet and she's blocked, her fist caught mid-air.

"Whoa, whoa, whoa. What the fuck is ..." Royce trails off when Captain steps back and he gets a look at my mom.

My muscles lock, Captain's eyes are on her too.

No. No no, shit no. For so many reasons.

I force myself to glance up at Maddoc. His jaw's locked tight above my head, I can only guess he's staring too.

"Uh..." Royce starts again, his eyes slowly moving to mine.

I jerk in Maddoc's hold and he lets go, but his body stays close.

I look to my mom.

Her eyes flare, in that sickening way they do. Hunger, for both money and more, has her skin flushing. She's one of the sick ones who actually enjoys her "work."

Her tongue comes out, slowly sliding across her lips with purpose and I groan.

"Give me a fucking break."

Her stare snaps back to mine and hardens before she can brush it away, but the boys are perceptive. Not as perceptive as her it seems, because she doesn't notice the half a foot closer they get – to me.

"Raven. Introduce me to your ... friends."

"They're not my friends."

Maddoc's muscles tighten behind me and in my peripheral, I see Royce's head snap my way.

"Introduce me anyway."

"No."

She pries her eyes from Captain. "I come to see you and

you act like this?" Her eyes float left as she deliberately bends her knee, letting her underwear show at the edge of her tiny skirt. "I missed you—"

"You're lying."

Her hand freezes in her hair, eyes snapping to Maddoc.

My stomach twists at the way she studies him, a thought I can't grip flashing through her eyes. Her tightened expression snaps from one to the next and down the line until they lead back to Maddoc and a sardonic laugh escapes her.

She opens her mouth, but Maddoc doesn't let her speak.

"You were ready to put your hands on her before we got here. You're lucky we stopped her when we did, or you'd be in even worse shape."

My mother's eyes widen, and my heart starts pounding in my chest.

And then it happens, worse than her looking for a client in these three, worse than whatever revelation she had just come to a moment ago, she sees this moment for what it is.

These boys, strong and dominant, smooth and valiant, standing with me.

One on each side, the strongest, largest of the trio at my back.

In the world she and I come from, showing protectiveness for something or someone is interpreted one way - to defend is to show your cards, creating a weakness in the place of strength.

Her smirk tells me I'm right, the light laugh confirms it.

If I don't figure this out, she'll find a way to use them too.

I'm not positive they'd care when push comes to shove, but I'll be damned if I become indebted to anyone on her terms.

And besides, they don't need to be sucked into the nightmare that is Ravina Carver. She's my problem to deal with.

Which is why I say, "Fine."

Her eyes cut to mine, suspicion tightening her features. "Fine?"

"Yeah, fine."

She leers, her eyes moving over the three before she reaches for the door handle. "Don't test the timeline, I can't stay in this place too long. I need to get back."

She slides in the front seat, leaning out the window once the door is closed with a disappointed look in her dilated eyes. "You know how fond of you they are; a couple hours of your time could clear—"

"Go."

She smiles, looks to the boys with a wink, and the car takes off.

A normal girl would cry, her mother willing to trade her own daughter's body for powder. But I'm not normal.

I start across the yard.

"Raven."

I ignore them.

"Raven!"

I'm almost to the boys' house when a hand lands in the same spot my mother's did and I yank free, spinning around with a glare. My emotions are boiling, and bad shit happens when they get too high.

"Don't think about telling me what to do," I tell Maddoc.

"I don't want to be told it's not a big deal," I say to Captain.

"And not a single fucking joke," I spit at Royce.

I look between the three. "Back the fuck off."

"We're not gonna say—"

Royce cuts off when I level him with a scowl.

"Okay, fine, we were gonna do ... all that." He laughs. "It's actually kind of freaky how you know how we'd each react."

"Why you trying to get to the boys' house?"

I look back to Maddoc and square my shoulders.

His nostrils flare and he steps into me. "No."

"I said no demands."

"I don't give a shit what you said. I said no."

"You can't stop me."

"Oh, shit RaeRae, don't say that to the man. Damn," Royce huffs.

"Fucking watch me," Maddoc growls.

"Why?" comes from Captain.

"Why what?"

"Why the sudden urge to fight?" He stares.

Because I need to make some quick cash and I'm not about to give her all I have.

I give a half-lie, half-truth. "Did you not just walk up here at the hilt of an adrenaline rush? I need to blow off some steam."

His eyes narrow. All of theirs do. They're not sure if they should believe me or not.

Maddoc licks his lips and looks off. "You're not fighting."

I'm so pissed I'm shaking, and maybe feeling a little on edge and helpless and disgusted in everything.

My mother lets people control her. Lets people run her body and here Maddoc stands, trying to run mine.

It's my fists, so completely different, but it's not his decision nonetheless. This is why I don't make friends or grow close, because disappointing people sucks, but it's in my nature.

So, I don't think. I do what I do and fuck shit up, purposely and out of spite.

He thinks he can govern me? I'll show him how wrong he is and create a situation outside any of our control.

I casually turn back for the house where a few girls have pretended to have a sudden need of vitamin D.

There's no urgency in my steps, so by the time it clicks in the boys' pretty little heads, my fist is already slamming into the cheek of the unsuspecting, probably undeserving, Victoria.

She falls back with a scream, the others gasp, and I go to jump on her, but again, arms wrap around me from behind.

I don't let him hold on. I kick until I'm released.

"You stupid bitch!" Victoria shrieks, but Captain slides in front of her and she clamps her mouth shut.

At that same moment Maybell comes out the door.

I look to Maddoc, then the other two.

All three hold the same expression.

Shock and suspicion. Confusion. I ignore the worry that's also clearly there.

I know what I did – purposely broke the main house rules in front of everyone, so it can't be brushed under the rug.

I'll be kicked out, but I don't care.

I get sent home, and I'll fight there, pay my mom's debt while keeping the guys from being dragged into my mess, and go back to my regular day to day.

Without them.

I ignore the ache the thought causes.

Maybell sighs and turns back inside. "Come on now, girls. Get your things and head for school. Raven, your things will be packed when you get back."

I chance a glance at the boys.

The way their features harden, it's clear they don't understand my decision, not that they could.

How would they know if I didn't clear her, they'd come for me?

Fuck my mom, fuck this place, and fuck them.

Most of all, fuck this life I was cursed into.

Chapter 28

Raven

Vienna catches up with me once I step into the school hallway. "Why'd you do it?"

I ignore her, bypassing my locker on the way to English – no reason to pull out a book for a class I won't be in tomorrow.

"Raven—"

I spin on my heel, leveling her with a bored stare. "Look, I get it. You want in on the gossip so you can spread it around and be the one in the know for once. Well, sorry to break it to you, there's no juice to spread. I felt like fighting, Victoria was within range, and there you have it." I start to spin around but turn back halfway. "Oh, and it's Rae."

"Wow," she calls after me and still, for some ungodly reason, follows. "That was good, I'll give you that. It's all a bold-faced lie, though. Maybe you forgot or didn't care to notice, but my room faces the gap between the houses, Rae."

I turn on my heels and she meets me in the middle, stepping right in front of me. "I don't give a shit what you think you saw or understood. I don't give a shit what you tell these people and I surely don't give a shit what you think, Vienna, so give it up already."

My chest is heaving, and rage is once again building ... and she laughs.

What the hell?

"Man, Raven." She shakes her head, fighting a smile. "You really are more fucked up in the head than I thought."

"What are you doing?"

"I was coming to tell you I was pissed at you for going and getting yourself kicked out. You're the only one – well were the only one – in the house I could stand. Guess it's back to convos with my radio."

"That's pathetic."

She shrugs with a half grin. "It is what it is, right?"

I survey her, finding she really does seem uninterested.

Honest.

I relax some. "Sorry to kill your house vibe."

"Sorry I won't get a chance to use you to get to ride on the Rolls Royce." She wiggles her ass.

I laugh lightly. "Yeah, bet if you asked, he'd let you use him."

"Just like that, huh?" She grins.

I sigh for dramatic effect. "Unfortunately, yes."

The bell rings and she glances down the hall then back to me. "Well, stay real, Raven."

I offer her a half smile then stand there and watch her leave.

Annoyed with myself, I smack the closest locker and lean my head against it.

I hate knowing that I bummed her out. It's one of the exact reasons I don't like people or making friends. I don't want to have to meet other's expectations or consider other people's thoughts or feelings. Shit, I didn't even realize Vienna and I were some sort of, I don't know, not friends but two people who are comfortable around each other, before now.

Not that it matters at this point.

"Raven."

Ugh, shoot me. Why didn't I go to class?

I turn. "Principal Perkins. Hi."

"Everything all right?" He approaches me, his hands slipping from his pockets as he does.

I square my shoulders and rid my face of any feebleness I may have let slip. "Fine. Going to class."

I go to step around him, but he blocks my path, now standing to his full height.

"You sure? You seem a bit ... distracted."

"How the hell would you know?" I go on the offensive.

His jaw sets at my tone, but he fights to stay professional. "I only mean, you seem like you could use someone to talk to. Do you need someone to talk to Raven? Maybe about some of your classmates? Are any of them being overly... authoritative?"

I ignore the question he's pretending to ask and give him the answer to the one he really wants to know. "The Brays and I are far from on the same level, Mr. Perkins. They wouldn't waste time on little old me."

His eyes narrow slightly before he nods. He doesn't believe me.

"I have more eyes around than you realize, Ms. Carver." He looks from my sweatpants I never got to change and my oversized hoodie. "I'd be careful if I were you."

"Are you threatening me?"

"I'm simply letting you know someone, somewhere, is always watching. Even when we least expect it—"

His words die off when a large body steps in front of me.

The screeches of leather against the floor tells me Perkins has moved back a few feet.

"Stay away from her."

"She's my student."

"Let's not do a recap on what belongs to who right now, Perkins." Maddoc steps forward, and I move so I can see the principal's face. "Stay a full ten feet from her. Add that to the list of shit you're not in control of at our hand. Wouldn't wanna go forgetting."

"One day, Brayshaw."

"Damn fucking right, Perkins."

Perkins walks away and the farther he gets, the more Maddoc starts to shake.

I glance from the man leaving to the one in front of me.

"Big man—"

He swiftly turns toward me, a deep frown in place and if I were any weaker of a person – at least on the outside – I'd cower in regret.

When did they get close enough to bring out things inside me no one else has ever seen?

I turn and walk away.

None of the boys are in class all day, but all are sitting at the usual table when lunch rolls around. Too bad not one of us speaks the entire time and when the bell rings, they're quick to take off, so I do the same. But my feet drag a little more than they did this morning.

Chloe talks her shit in PE, but it's petty shit like poor form and a few digs at my baggy gym clothes, so I ignore her, grinning when I remember I won't have to deal with her anymore.

After school, the boys aren't there waiting. It's as bitter as it is relieving.

I hang around a bit so the rest of the house girls and guys are already long gone by the time I make the trudge back.

When I get inside, a few girls look up from their homework tables, but none say a word.

I find Maybell in what just this morning was my assigned room but tomorrow could belong to someone new.

"Look, I'm ..." I trail off with a huff.

Maybell scoffs. "Can't even fake an apology, can you dear?"

I shrug even though she can't see me. "You really want one if it's not real?"

She turns and sits on the edge of my bed, looking up at me. "No. I don't. And I appreciate you not standing here making excuses for what you did. It was stupid. A bad choice. Impulsive. But you know all that already, which is why you did it."

"What kind of place did you grow up in, Maybell?"

"A place where pride was both an honor and a curse. That sound familiar?"

I ignore the question. "Then you know I couldn't allow them to think they had a say."

"I do." She crosses her arms and frowns at me. "But what ticks me off, girl, is you know as well as I do, you'd have figured out a way to do what you wanted anyhow. One way or another, whatever it was they were trying to stop you from, you'd have still done it. So why'd you self-sabotage so quick?"

"Because she's poison."

"And they're strong."

I open my mouth to speak but close it just as quick.

Shit.

"You need to learn how to stop and think before acting. I know, in your life, you're accustomed to new people coming in and out, but maybe this is the first time you found some that you don't completely hate being around. Those boys, they're more than meets the eye. They need someone to care about and you fit more than you want to admit."

"I don't want it to be me."

"Why?"

"Because I had no plan to stay around."

"Had." She nods her head.

"Look, all I want is to get away from everyone who knows what I am."

"And what are you, Raven?"

"I'm the daughter of a whore, dirty by default. Guilty by association."

"And you always will be. Leaving, disappearing when you turn eighteen and never looking back, won't change that." She stands.

"For what it's worth," I tell her after a moment. "I am sorry, but not for what I did or why I did it. Only for disrespecting you when you've done nothing to deserve that from me."

She stares and slowly a smile stretches across her freckled face.

She looks over my shoulder. "Perfect timing, boy."

Maddoc squeezes past me, kisses Maybell on the head then picks up my two lowly bags, leaving my backpack to me, spins on his heels and walks out, not once looking my way.

I look to Maybell who laughs lightly.

"Go on now."

"Thanks for uh…" I look around the room. "For having a safe place like this for girls to be. Even the ones who don't act like it, appreciate this."

Her eyes grow glossy, so I quickly try for an exit, but she stops me with a gentle hand to my arm.

"You, Raven Carver, are more than you let on too, you know. Believe that and share it with them."

"With who?"

"Go, child," she whispers and pushes me out of the room, but I slip into the bathroom, waiting for her to pass and then dart back in.

I quickly pull the binder I stole from its hiding space and stuff it in my backpack then rush back out.

Out front, I find Royce standing with the passenger door open, Maddoc in the driver's seat and Captain hanging out the passenger window.

"Shouldn't you be at practice or something?"

"No practice today, and we had to make sure you were taken care of first. Kind of our fault you went all Ronda Rousey on the blonde."

"It was my own fault."

"Okay, fine," he laughs lightly. "It was your fault. Just get in, RaeRae."

"I'm supposed to be waiting for my social worker."

"We'll drop you."

I glance back at Maybell leaning against the frame.

She nods.

I look back to the three.

Fine.

I make my way over and slide in, Royce moving to sit beside me.

And then Maddoc puts the car in drive when it should be in reverse.

"What ... where are you going?"

They ignore me, the SUV slowly rolling down the little dirt road between the trees.

I don't say anything else, because they won't answer me anyway, so I sit there like an obedient child and wait.

The truck curves around another set of trees then stops ... in front of a house big enough to rival the President's.

Literally.

It's ginormous. Stark white and sitting in the center of a bed of trees, it's a two-tier home that stretches as wide a solid dozen of these SUVs.

"What are we doing?" I finally ask, but I get no response. My words seem to kick the boys into gear, and they climb out, expecting me to follow.

I step out as well because what the hell else would I do?

But when the boys hit the top step of the wrap-around porch, they all seem to hesitate, unease taking over each one in a different way.

Captain frowns at his feet, Royce rubs at the back of his head as he stares down the path we came, and Maddoc's pinched gaze is locked on me, his lips pressed firmly together.

"What?"

"We live here."

"Yeah..." I look between the three, thoroughly confused on this whole situation. "I know."

"You've been back here?" Royce accuses more than asks.

"I said I know, as in I knew you lived back here. One of the girls filled me in, but it's not like it's not obvious once you pay attention."

I look between them again. "What are we doing?"

"Come inside," Maddoc orders, but not one of them moves.

A laugh bubbles out of me. "Is someone gonna unlock it?"

Captain slowly drags his keys from his pocket and moves forward, but I stop him with a hand to his chest.

"Look, if you don't want me to go in, I get it. Just take me back to the house or to the county office already. I really don't care, but stop acting all ... weak and weird. It doesn't suit you guys at all."

"Open the door," comes from Maddoc.

Finally, Captain turns the lock, but I don't go in. I wait for Captain to go first, then Royce slides past.

I step inside and glance around.

The place is wide open, a huge entryway with some shoes lined up in front of a floor to ceiling mirror that spans along the entire wall. To the left looks like a den and maybe a room or something down the short hallway, pool table and dart board and to the right is the living room. It's a giant square that opens into a kitchen I can't quite see other than a couple of bar stools.

There are a couple of black leather couches and a coffee table with nothing on it, a giant TV on the wall and a bookshelf with what looks like school books and binders on it.

Tucked in the far back corner of the living room, opposite of the couches is a set of stairs against the wall. They curve around, disappearing about halfway up to where I'm assuming the bedrooms are.

It's nice, clean for three young guys.

I turn back to the boys, all of whom are staring my way, frowns marring their pretty little faces.

"What?"

Royce looks around then back to me. "Seriously?"

Now I frown.

"Just a nod. Nothing to say about the house?"

"It's ... big." I glance up. "Kinda dark for having so many of those." I point to all the ugly ass, stupidly expensive light fixtures that seem out of place for the sleek look the guys have going on here.

"Big and dark," Royce repeats.

"You don't like it," Captain states.

"What's not to like?" I shrug, sticking my hands in my sweats pockets. "It's huge, expensive. But it's, I don't know ... kinda boring on the inside compared to the out."

I look to the three and they stare a minute before all three start laughing. A deep, good, hearty laugh that has me taking a deep breath.

Royce's smile is huge. "I was waiting for a real girly squeal and a 'this place is amazing, you must be so rich. I always dreamed of such a castle to call home' or something."

I laugh lightly. "I don't squeal and—" I cut myself off. "Wait. What'd you just say?"

"Home sweet home, RaeRae." Royce crosses his arms over his chest.

"Ha! No." I back up a step, glancing between the three. "Hell no."

Maddoc steps closer. "Yes."

"I'm not—"

"Yeah, you are."

"I can't—"

"You can and will."

"They won't just let—"

"It's done."

I growl and step toward Maddoc. "Interrupt me one more time, big man, and you'll be sleeping with an ice pack on your jock."

He gets in my face. "And you'll be right down the hall in case I need you to massage it for me."

"You are out of your ever-loving mind if—"

"Just save it, RaeRae, and come on." Royce grabs my hand and pulls. "So much more to show ya."

My shoes skid across the hardwood, but he yanks, making me fly forward.

With a growl, I let him drag me along like a dog on a leash.

This shit's not happening.

Chapter 29

RAVEN

I drop onto the bed, covering my face with my hands.

This is not okay.

"Why not?"

I sigh and look up. "Spying?"

"No. You're thinking out loud." Maddoc drops in the desk chair across from me.

Yes, there's a desk and a chair and a fucking brand-new computer in here.

Mine, they say.

"I can't live here."

"Why?"

"For one, and it's a big one, I hardly know you guys."

"You've got your knife."

When I scowl his lip twitches.

"Two, I owe no one in my life and I like it that way. Moving me into a big house with new shit and a ridiculously comfortable bed" —he chuckles lightly— "is like a lifetime of payback that I don't have, can't and don't want to give."

"We're not asking you for anything."

"Come on, nobody rides for free." I lift a brow. "Unless they ride for free. Feel me?"

He frowns. "Are you serious?"

"It's normal where I come from."

When his jaw clenches, I chuckle.

"I didn't say I'm guilty of it. I'm just saying ... people don't do shit to be nice in my world."

"You're in our world now."

The way he says it ... so strong, indefinite. It worries me even more, because deep down I like the way it sounds, and because he's wrong.

"I may not fall into the category you tried to force me into, but I'm still the outsider. And to be honest, I have to question your guys' reasoning. A few weeks ago, you wanted everyone to think I was a dirty bird only to put some protective shield around me the next. Now I'm like the shared rag doll."

"Thought you didn't care what they thought?" he snaps.

"I don't," I sass back. "I care what I become. We already had a little freaky Friday fun. I'm not looking for another situation where I turn three shades of Jenna Jameson."

"That won't happen again." He glares.

Right. Not like they wanted it to happen, they just had to shut me up.

And now I sound like I wanted it to happen. Multiples aren't my style.

I shake my head.

"For real, Maddoc, I'm not comfortable with this."

A small grin tips his lips.

"What?"

"Maddoc, huh?" He pushes to a stand and heads for the

door. "Sounds like you're getting more comfortable by the second." With that, he walks out.

I throw myself back on the bed, and when I hit the comforter-covered mattress, I wiggle.

So soft.

With a sigh, I turn my head, my eyes landing on the window. Curiosity gets the best of me and I move toward it. I finger the fancy fabric hanging in front of it, it's not a material I've felt before. Almost silky but still has texture.

I push them aside and glance out, groaning as I do.

The window is wide and looks out over a fresh and green orchard. Nothing but trees and a blue skyline to follow for miles.

It's freeing.

"The back of the property goes on for about three miles."

I turn to find Royce now walking in.

"There's a heated pool, hot tub and basketball court out there you can use at any time." He throws himself on the bed and does the same wiggle move I did.

"Damn, this thing is nice." He looks to me with a grin that quickly morphs into a frown. "What's the problem?"

"I can't stay here."

"Don't start. Look at all this." He waves his hands around the room without bothering to sit up. "It's more than you had at the Bray house."

"It's more than I've had ever." I flick at the curtains. "Never even had these, we had old sheets tacked to our windows to keep the sun out."

"I tried to hang my Spiderman sheets to my window when I was a kid, Maybell 'bout whooped my ass."

I laugh lightly and move to drop on the mattress beside him.

"I don't understand any of this, Royce. Don't get why you

guys go out of your way to have me around. Don't know if I should go with it or fight it. Don't know a damn thing."

There's a nagging in the back of my head telling me I'm missing something.

Royce's hand comes down to grab mine and he lifts it.

I look to him.

"Don't fight us. Stay."

"Come downstairs."

We both look to the doorway to see Maddoc standing there. His face is blank as it shifts from Royce to me and then he turns and walks away.

Royce stands. "I think I'll place a bet."

"What kind of bet?" I step in line with him and head down the stairs.

"On how long it'll take before he jumps your bones."

I scoff, whispering, "Not exactly convincing me to stay, Royce."

"Who you kiddin', RaeRae?" He puts his arm around my shoulder. "We both know you're staying. No reason to not and you got shit to go back for."

"How do you know? Maybe I have a secret love child I'm hiding away."

Royce tenses lightly and a tight chuckle leaves him. "Funny, but a lie."

The other two are sitting on the couch so we make our way over. I go to drop on the coffee table but stop halfway down and straighten again, making them laugh. "My bad."

"You can sit on it, doubt your ninety-pound self could break it," Captain says.

I go ahead and sit. "Far from ninety pounds, but thanks?"

Nobody says anything for a few seconds, and it gets awkward.

"Okay so..." I roll my wrist to get them talking so we can get this over with.

"That was your mom."

"Wow, jumping right into it, huh?"

"Raven."

I square my shoulders and look between the three. "Obviously, yes. That woman who doesn't reflect a day over twenty-five and looks like she stepped straight off the set of Whores-R-Us, is my mother. Every dirty and used, cocaine infused inch of her."

"Don't get defensive. We only want to understand better. With your staying here, we need to know."

"So you set me up to stay in your house in exchange for my life fucking story. Hard pass."

"Look, this is a free fucking place for you to be. Nothing will be expected of you here as far as earning your keep and all that. But there will be a few things you need to agree to."

"I don't need a place to lay my head at night, big man. I lay where I land. Always have. Don't sit there acting like you're doing me a huge favor by sticking me in your tower."

He completely ignores me. "Your mom. Why is she here? Maybell talked to social services, she wasn't given the go-ahead to get you. She wasn't even given your location. How did she find you?"

"I don't know how she found me and even if she was cleared to get me back or not, she wouldn't try to. She never wanted me to begin with. I was a means to a monthly check."

"And that check's gone."

"She's inventive when it comes to money."

"And when she can't?"

"She's a whore, Maddoc. She's always up for a trade."

He eyes me. "What'd she want, Raven?"

"Don't. You want me to stay here? Fine, big man, I'll stay, but only if you stop acting like you make the calls. We're not on the court, I'm not your teammate and you're not my captain. I'll come and go as I please, do what I want and when, and if not, I leave. And if you're thinking 'bullshit' remember ... you guys can't be stuck to my hip at all times. You have practice, you have games, and you have your Brayshaw shit to handle, whatever that includes. If I decide to take off, it'll be easy." I shift to stand, but Maddoc does first.

He glares down at me. This guy has perfected the art of intimidation. Not unlike my mother, he uses his body to get what he wants – fear, fight ... frisky.

It's all written in the way he moves, carved in those cavernous eyes of his.

He's angry, but he doesn't understand the source, so frustration is what lines his forehead in wrinkles, and irritation holds his lips firmly together.

Big man's not used to whatever it is that's going on inside him.

"You won't fight. You won't leave, and you won't go near that woman again if one of us isn't with you, mother or fucking not." He snatches his keys off the side table and slams the front door on his exit.

"Well." Royce smacks a hand down on the couch arm. "That went better than I expected."

"Really?"

"Yeah ... see, he only tipped the iceberg 'cause you got him all hot and heated – yes there's a difference – but there are some more things you'll need to agree to."

"Like?" I snap.

"No drugs in the house – liquor is fine. No breaking shit if you get mad. You can't be bringing people here, dude or chick. You need to fuck, do it at their place or somewhere not here, you could even get it in at the party pad – though, maybe talk to Maddoc on that one, he's prolly got a different rule for yah."

"Fuck off."

He winks. "For real, though. We have another spot for all that, it's our chill pad. We invite people there or to the places we book out for parties, you'll have a room there like us. But we don't like people in our house. This place is ours." His eyes narrow, and just as I'm about to pop up and walk off, his chin lowers in respect, taking me by surprise. "And now yours. Outsiders don't belong."

"We also eat dinner together every night." I look to Captain. "No exceptions."

I force my face to stay blank. "Anything else?"

Neither says anything, both searching for my reaction based decision.

They don't get one.

I stand, bow to be an asshole, and head up the stairs to what is now apparently my new room.

I lock the door and dig my MP3 player and knife from my bag. After kicking off my shoes, I toss my sweater to the floor and climb onto the bed. I put my earbuds in, turning up the volume as loud as it will go.

Closing my eyes, I take a deep breath.

These boys, they think I'll follow their rules.

They're wrong.

Chapter 30

Raven

I drop my fork and lean back in the chair. "I have a rule of my own."

Royce's drink stops halfway to his mouth, Captain stops chewing, and Maddoc slams his silverware down.

"Let's hear it, RaeRae," Royce carefully states.

"Nobody finds out I'm staying here. They can guess and assume all they want, can't stop that, but no confirmations. They ask, you deny, I do the same."

There's a beat of silence to follow, but it's quickly filled with the scrape of Maddoc's chair and the shake of the table as he storms off like a child for the second time today. I glance back to his boys, finding both wearing the same goofy expression.

"What?" I snap.

"Should have expected that, but this is all still new for us too," Royce says.

"I'm not following."

"Can't name a single person who in your position, would ask for something like that. In fact, pretty sure everyone we know would have hit tonight's party already just to spread the word."

I don't know what to say to that so I ask, "And what's the big man's problem?"

"Got an idea." He grins and looks to Captain who chuckles. "But you gotta ask him to know for sure."

With a frown, I spring from my seat and storm after the tantrum-throwing bastard.

Right as I round the corner at the top of the stairs, I'm pushed against the wall, caged in by a growly face Maddoc.

"You don't get to make demands."

"I am not your prisoner, a fact you need to remember." I shove at him, but he doesn't budge, and tension builds inside me under the intensity of his stare.

Mystery swims in his darkened eyes, not sure if it's his collection of thoughts on me or mine on him that has his features tightening.

"Tell me what you're thinking," I tell him.

"No."

"Why not?"

"Because I can't figure it out," he forces past clenched teeth.

"Figure out what?"

"If I hate your rule or not."

"I don't get it."

"You want to hide that you're here with us like you're not proud to be Brayshaw. Like you wouldn't ride with us if we needed you to when we both know you would and have, time and time again."

"It's not ... like that."

"I know," he whispers. "Your choice to hide this cements you here, it tells us you're everything we hoped you'd be.

You're down for us, Raven, even when you try to pretend you're not."

"So why can't you decide if you hate the rule or not?"

"Because, like I said…" His hands move to plant near my head and he lowers his face so it's equal to mine. "Your choice cements you here, with us. With me. And now? I want every motherfucker to know where you are at the end of the night."

Uh ... what?

I swallow, shaking my head lightly. "You've got the wrong idea what's happening here."

He dips his head, letting out a gravelly chuckle.

"Nah," he whispers, his warm breath creating goose bumps across my neck. "You're just slow catching on."

His eyes flick between mine, hardening a little. But the longer he looks, the more they lose their edge.

"What is it about you that drives me insane?"

"My big mouth," I tease, trying to downplay my reaction to him, but his words have my voice layered in a thick coat of desire.

"Haven't even tested that out yet…" He trails off, his heat driven stare burning across my completely covered body. His frown settles back in place.

Right. He's only gone down on me, no big deal.

When a slow smirk appears, it's clear. My body is showing it remembers him.

"Safe to come upstairs now?" Royce shouts from the first floor and Maddoc steps away.

"Yeah!" Maddoc shouts when he reaches his room, closing himself inside.

"You coming to the party?" Royce asks when he hits the landing.

"No. I'm tired."

He grins and whispers, "Liar. Don't forget, we got eyes everywhere, RaeRae."

Ignoring him, I head into the room and change into a T-shirt and sweats. I lie on my bed giving the illusion I'm going to sleep so I don't get too much shit from them for not going out.

It doesn't work.

They come in, all fucking three and laugh.

"We're not dumb, but you should know that there are dogs in the orchards. You try to walk out of here at night, you might just get a chunk taken out of your calf," Royce joyfully informs me with a wink before they disappear from the doorway.

And I'm stuck with no escape.

With a groan, I flip over on the mattress. Of course it's the most comfortable bed on earth.

I sigh.

Shit's gonna get interesting.

I HEAR THEM WHEN THEY COME IN.

Their laughter is loud as they joke with each other, talking about different events of the night.

I find myself smiling.

These boys, there's no competition between the three other than good fun and time spent on the courts, but not the kind that grows jealousy and hate.

It's a rare bond, one I hope they never lose.

They start up the stairs, laughing as they attempt to get Royce to the top without him falling over.

"We should have left his ass on the couch," Captain laughs.

"No way, man. I don't like waking up down there by myself," Royce admits, and I chuckle quietly.

He's such a little boy under all that, well, horniness.

"Be quiet, Raven's sleeping."

"If she's even still here." Royce snorts. "Doubt she believed the shit about the dogs. I mean, dogs would bark, right? That'd be obvious."

My jaw drops, and I punch at the mattress.

Son of a bitch.

Of course dogs would fucking bark! Damn it!

"Shut up, Royce," Maddoc hisses.

Oh, too late, big man. I heard.

A few shuffles sound, the faucet turns on and off a couple times and then three doors quietly close.

And then mine pushes open and Maddoc slips inside in nothing but a pair of tight ass boxers that fit his strong thighs like a second skin. He closes and locks my door, steps up to my mattress, and waits.

With a deep breath and an ease I should try harder to fight, I pull the comforter down and with a frown, he slips in.

Maddoc wastes no time pulling me to his side. His left arm slides under my pillow, his right gripping me behind the knee. He pulls my leg over his, then lifts the covers to my shoulders.

When I shift, he jerks, and gently removes the earbud from my ear.

"Metal's cold. Move the knife, Raven."

Can I? Better question, should I?

I pull the knife from my shorts and set it behind me.

He moves us back to the exact same position.

"I knew you were awake," he whispers, his chin sliding across my hair. "But you won't be long. Close your eyes."

His hands shift, now locked behind my back.

After a few tense minutes, my mind shuts off and my body takes over allowing me to completely melt against his.

A sigh escapes, but I don't care.

Sleep is finally coming.

Chapter 31

Raven

"Bacon," I whisper, my eyes still closed, but the chuckle beside me has them flying open.

"Captain rises with the sun."

Good God, I'll never get used to his morning voice. So scratchy and deep, it belongs on a dirty hotline.

His eyes wander across my face before settling on mine. His instant frown has me laughing.

"What?" he asks.

"Nothing."

"Just say it."

"Fine. Every time you look me in the eye, you glare."

He shifts his stare to the ceiling, not denying but not bothering to explain either.

I change the subject. "Your brothers know you're in here?"

"Don't know. Didn't announce it, didn't try to hide it."

"Maddoc."

He looks at me.

"Why did you come in here?"

"Because I wanted to."

Because he wanted to.

Just like that. Well, okay then.

"I'm hungry."

He grins, standing to stretch. And damn if my greedy eyes don't follow along.

A private, erotic dance is the only way to explain the way his muscles move during this simple act. His back tightens, sides bulge and the definition to his biceps prove carved to perfection – not that it wasn't obvious before.

When his hands come down, I follow, squeezing my legs together when he mindlessly grips his morning wood to adjust. He's standing half sideways, so I can only see his knuckles, but the width at which they're bent does wonders for my imagination. It was too dark to actually see his dick when it was hanging in the wind at the cabin, but I've got a good read on what's under that satin now.

His eyes dart to mine and I realize a small sound made its way up my throat.

He pops a cocky eyebrow and I shrug. Can't deny what he so clearly heard.

But the longer he stares, the hungrier I get – not for bacon.

I slip from my bed and walk past him for the door, but he grips me by the wrist and pulls me back.

"Where you goin'?"

"Food."

"Put some clothes on," he orders.

"I will." He lets go slowly and I run out the door, shouting, "Later when I need to!"

I grin to myself when he growls from the hall.

I go into the kitchen to find a huge spread already set out across the kitchen island.

"Raven."

"Packman." I steal a piece of bacon. "So, you the house cook when you're not hungover?"

"We all cook."

"Really?" I scrunch my nose, and I leap up on the stool. "Even Royce?"

"Hey!" A groggy voice comes from behind me then two arms are around me. "Heard that. And yes, even me. I happen to make a mean ass lasagna."

I spin lightly, and he grins. "I'll believe it when I see it."

"How's tonight? Just gotta ask Cap for permission to use the kitchen. He likes cooking on the weekends." Royce kisses my hair and pulls away.

I spin back around. "Let's make it happen, Captain."

He scoffs. "Cute. Because I never heard that one before."

"Where's Maddoc?" Royce pours a glass of chocolate milk.

Right then, Maddoc enters, having slipped on some sweatpants. How the sweats look better than the boxers, no fucking clue.

He moves for the coffeepot, a regular ass Mr. Coffee one, not some fancy espresso machine or one of those one cup contraptions.

"Only one scoop today, huh?" Captain observes, and I lean against the counter to watch them move around.

But I can't help and notice how Maddoc grows tense at his brother's words. "Yeah."

I look to Royce, tipping my chin at the two across the kitchen, he leans over.

"Cap leaves the coffee making to Maddoc, so he can decide how strong he wants it."

When I make a face that screams as if that explains it, he chuckles and leans over again.

Maddoc's eyes meet mine right as Royce whispers, "Maddoc don't sleep." He laughs lightly like it's a silly superpower.

It's not, but you can't fault Royce for thinking so.

People who can lay their heads down and fall asleep with ease don't understand the struggle or how bad those of us who can't wish we could.

They don't know what it's like to lay awake at night and replay minutes of your life, wondering what you could or should have done differently. Or how you could be better at something or fearing what comes next. Sometimes it's even as simple as playing a movie back in your head, anything to fill the hours.

Time is not your friend when your mind is at the point of exhaustion.

Maddoc's eyes bounce between mine.

So, big man doesn't normally sleep well, yet I know for a fact he did each time I've shared sheets with him. Something unwelcome settles in my chest so I look away.

"What's up for today?" Royce asks and Maddoc breaks our stare.

"Shooting hoops with Richards at noon, he needs to clean up his free throws," Maddoc tells him.

"I'm there." Royce nods.

"I'll come by after if you're still out," Captain adds.

Maddoc nods, but nobody says what "after" is referring to.

I don't ask.

"You're coming with us, Raven."

I fill a plate and move for the table. "Can't wait." I roll my eyes.

There's no way I'll be able to get out alone to talk to Bass today and be able to slip out for a fight this weekend. I have no fucking choice but to give my mom the money I saved from my last two fights, which will leave me low but not completely dry. I'll already have to pull some shit just to meet her and hand it over.

After breakfast, everyone disappears into their rooms to change and we meet back at the door a few minutes later.

Royce and Maddoc are donned in basketball shorts and tank tops – hot. As. Fuck. But Captain, he's got a gym bag over his shoulder, yes, but he's wearing nice jeans and a fresh white shirt. He's sporting a fresh shave and his hair is on point, a nice little sideswipe, but the swaggy kind. Not revenge of the nerds.

"You look good." I let my eyes trail over him before meeting his. "Hot date?"

A small grin finds his lips. "See you later, Raven."

I nod, not at all sure that's a yes or a no.

When I turn to the others, I find Maddoc frowning.

"What?"

"Change."

"Change…" I trail off and then I get it and I cross my arms. "Funny. Are we going or not?"

"We're going." His eyes narrow. "After you change."

"Say it."

"Say what?" he forces out through clenched teeth.

"Tell me what's wrong with what I have on if you want me to change. Learn to use your words instead of that mean mug you've perfected, big man."

"Fine. Your tights are outlining every inch of your calves, thighs, ass, and pussy. I don't want my teammates, or anyone else on the courts, to know the shape of your cunt."

Caught off guard at his bluntness, a laugh escapes me. "I…" I laugh harder and Royce joins in. "I got nothing to say back to that. They're leggings, not tights by the way, but yeah okay. Since you did as I asked, I'll entertain your bossiness. This time."

I run upstairs and pull some baggy sweats over my leggings and run back down.

"Man, RaeRae." Royce shakes his head and Maddoc

curses, throwing the front door open harder than necessary as he steps out.

I raise my arms as to ask 'what.'

"Maddoc is trippin'. It's not what you wear, it's how you wear it."

He holds the door open for me to slip through. "And how do I wear it?"

"With a plump ass and a 'fuck you too.'"

I laugh and move for the SUV calling, "Shotgun," with a wink.

And the boy actually pouts as he climbs in.

I put my seat belt on but spin in the seat to look back at him. "Come on, Royce, don't be a baby about it. Consider this game on for an epic battle of the throne that is, a heated leather seat in Maddoc's ride."

He says nothing, still seeming put out, so I face forward again.

Maddoc keeps side glancing me, but I pretend not to notice.

He wants to know what I'm thinking, to confirm if I'm as perceptive as he assumes. I am, and now the front seat doesn't feel so good.

Maddoc climbs out right away and heads straight for the guys waiting – something tells me it was purposeful.

I unbuckle and climb over the center console, dropping next to Royce as he ties his shoe.

He glances at me quickly. "What's up, RaeRae, ready to watch us drive on these fools?"

"Royce."

"Hmm?" He drops his foot and looks up, and when he does his features tighten a bit.

"You don't like being alone."

He opens his mouth, but clamps it shut and looks out the front windshield. "I like it 'bout as much as you do."

My head draws back. "I don't mind it."

He scoffs and glares my way. "Come on, Raven. You're used to it, sure, you don't mind it, fine. But do you like it?" He climbs out, looking back at me quickly. "No. You don't. And it's a lie if you tell yourself different." And then the door slams.

With a sigh, I lay across the back seat 'cause fuck this shit now.

He's half wrong. I never minded being alone, but that was before I knew what having someone there looked like. And stupid me, I'm accidentally starting to like it.

A couple hours pass before Captain's SUV pulls up beside this one.

I quickly shove open my door and knock on his passenger one before he can even shut off the engine.

The lock pops and I climb inside.

"What's up, Raven?" He rubs his hand over his eyebrow, and I note the defeated look in his eyes.

While I do want to know what happened, I have to be selfish right now.

"I need a ride."

His posture stiffens, and he eyes me a moment before it hits him. "Raven ..." He starts to shake his head, but I shift toward him.

"Look, it's either one of you takes me or I blow this bitch and things go down a helluva lot differently. Say no all you want, but that'll only be your words. Not my actions."

"Why you doin' this?"

"I have to."

He shakes his head. "I'm not talking about where you're wanting to go or why. I mean, why you doing this, coming to me when you know you should be talking to Maddoc right now."

"What difference does it make?" I grow defensive and he frowns.

"Raven, you need to stop acting like the two of you aren't happening."

Unease stirs in my stomach and I glare. I ignore his direct comment and fire back with a different truth. "You think I want any of you, let alone Maddoc, anywhere near my mother? She's fucking cancer, Captain, a damn contagious kind if such a thing exists. She's literally toxic. Maddoc will ask questions, demand answers and likely hand her her own ass. I need someone who will let me handle her."

His eyes narrow and just when I think I've got him ... he honks the fucking horn and in an instant, one becomes three.

"We don't make decisions alone, Raven," Captain tells me quickly before the other two slide in the back.

"She wants a ride."

"No," Maddoc says quick and calm.

"Hell no," comes from Royce.

"For fuck's sake." I shake my head, then spin in my seat. "I get it, you guys need to be the boss. You even think you are the boss, but guess what, fuckers, you're not my boss. So, for you to sit there and think you can bring the hammer down, you've got another thing coming. I'm not asking 'cause I have to, I'm asking to make my life easier, so I don't have to figure out another way, and I'll admit, hoping it keeps you off my case a bit."

"You're not going to meet your mother, Raven."

Damn it. This isn't working.

I drag my hands down my face in frustration.

Okay, second approach.

"You seem to want to shadow me, so doesn't it make more sense for one of you to take me there?"

"She's got a point." Royce shrugs.

Maddoc studies me. "Why do you need to see her?"

"To give her back the money I stole from her before I left." Lie.

"You're lying," Maddoc states but I shrug.

"I'll take her," Captain offers but of course, Maddoc disagrees and it ends with him as my driver, but oh well. At least I can get her gone.

The longer she's here, the more trouble she'll bring.

Chapter 32

RAVEN

"How do you know she'll be there?"

"Common ground. It's her one consistency."

"How do you mean?" Maddoc asks.

I take a deep breath. "Well, when she takes off for days at a time and can't come straight home when she decides she's ready, she comes to me."

"Why would she not be able to come home?"

"Usually it's the person she was with, she doesn't want them to track her down. Likely she did them dirty or plans to. Or if she gets into trouble and is running from a warrant but wants to avoid jail a few days longer - usually that's when she's got clients lined up and wants to go in with money on her books. There are a dozen different scenarios, but my role is always the same."

He glances my way. "And what role is that?"

"I'm the clean up."

"You pay her way out."

I nod. "Pay my way or fight my way, depends on who we're dealing with. People who know of me want the free fight – more money in their pocket that way – the others want what I won't give, and I'm left to figure it out another way. And if it's not them demanding, it's her."

Maddoc's grip on the wheel tightens.

"She's uninventive though, always goes after guys in my schools, so I'm ridiculed and forced to listen to the stories of the tricks up her skirt." I look out the window. "Seems she is good at what she does, if word of mouth is worth a damn."

I hate her.

"That why you'd fight at school? To get yourself kicked out when she fucks it up for you?"

"I fight to defend who I am and what I'm not. To show I'm stronger than they believe. I may come from a weak woman, but I will never be one." I roll my head against the seat, looking to Maddoc.

When he stops at a stoplight, I grin and shift the mood back to bearable. "Besides, I didn't get kicked out of all the schools for fighting."

He doesn't let me brush it off though. His hand lifts and I swear my heart stops beating when his fingers slip into my hair, a gentleness I'd have never believed he was capable of. He doesn't move for me, doesn't say a word, but I can tell he wants to.

For someone who walks around owning the ground, he holds back a lot.

The light turns green, and his focus is forced to the road.

I close my eyes and fight to erase the sense of security swimming inside me. My mother has a nose for good and a knack for spoiling it.

"She's already here."

My eyes pop open as we pull in the school parking lot.

She's laying across the hood of the car with her feet

planted on the bumper, knees open and in the air – in a fucking skirt.

She's alone.

"Any chance you'll stay in the car?"

"No."

"Fine but stay back. My mother, my business. If she starts talking crazy just ... ignore her. She's a bitch. I can handle it."

He makes no move at first, then with a soft curse he unbuckles and rolls his window down to listen, staying in his seat.

With a tight smile, I step from the vehicle and round the hood.

"Mother."

She blows smoke in the air, not bothering to look at me, not even opening her eyes. "You're late."

"No, I'm not, but nice try, I'm not adding in a bogus ass late fee."

"Put it on the seat."

My teeth clench and I bend to toss the sandwich bag of cash inside. My muscles lock when I spot the lid to a retractable needle on the floorboard. The methadone clinic by our trailer park started giving those out last year to help keep the parks clean – the needle disappears inside the syringe after use.

My mother's a snorter, though. Fucking with a needle is a lot messier, not to mention dangerous on a new level.

Maybe it's the guy who owns the cars method of choice.

"Don't get in my business, Raven. Go away."

"You're a piece of shit."

This time she sits up, a cigarette hanging from her lips as she slides off the car. She keeps her eyes on me as she makes her way to the driver's seat. She takes a long hit of her smoke, slowly blowing it out as her eyes float to Maddoc. "Yeah, and you will be too. It's only a matter of time."

She hesitates a moment, her eyes still glued on him.

I tighten my fists to keep from raging on her and shift my body, effectively blocking Maddoc from view.

Her eyes snap to mine, narrowing in the same second. She tries to read me, but she never has been able to understand me. "Raven, don't be a fool. Don't fall at their feet."

"Keep your eyes off him, don't speak. Go. You're the one not welcome."

Her head pulls back slightly, and an unbelieving laugh escapes her.

Silence stretches between us, and anxiousness grows, but then a wide chest hits my back, and everything settles.

I hadn't even heard him step out.

"This is Brayshaw and you don't belong. Leave."

"Bravo, Brayshaw," my mother laughs lightly, and I frown.

She shakes her head, gets in the car and takes off.

Anger swims in my stomach to the point my muscles actually start to ache, and my chest tightens.

With a lick of my lips, I slip back into the SUV.

After a few moments, we're headed back to yet another home that isn't mine but holds my things.

One day I'll understand why I exist in a world I'm not needed in.

One day.

I FLIP MY KNIFE OPEN OVER AND OVER, EVERY FEW MINUTES stopping to read the inscription on the side: family runs deeper than blood.

I click it back in place, and right when I flick my wrist, sending the blade flying forward again, my door quietly opens.

Maddoc looks from it to me, then locks the door behind him.

He makes his way over and when he reaches the edge, he holds out his hand, asking me to give him my safety net.

I close the knife and slip it behind me instead.

He eyes me a moment before pulling his shirt over his head. He looks to the spot he laid in last night, waiting for me to make room and I breathe a sigh of relief I shouldn't. He pulls me against him, just as he did before, and I close my eyes, welcoming his warmed skin.

"Don't say it," I tell him, knowing damn well he planned to. "I don't want to hear what you think but don't know. She could be right, but only time will tell."

"I don't need time to know you're nothing like her."

"You hardly know me, Maddoc."

"I need time to figure you out. Give it to me."

"You don't want to know me," I whisper. "You want to understand me so you can decide if I'm a threat to you or not."

He doesn't deny it, and I'm almost glad for that.

Almost.

Chapter 33

Raven

"She lives with us now."

My jaw drops as I spin to Royce.

"What?"

"What the hell?!" I hiss. One look around confirms it's useless to try to cover it. There may only be a handful in ear's distance, but phones are already out and I'm officially a sister wife. Or maybe they're brother husbands. Wait. No.

Not the point here.

Fuck this shit.

I storm off, but only get five whole feet before Captain falls in line with me.

"You on babysitting duty for Mondays?"

"You didn't come down last night, and we were running late this morning. Didn't get to ask how it went with your mom."

"Don't play like you didn't get the rundown from your brother." I pull my locker open, cursing to myself when I remember I didn't do any classwork or homework Friday because I didn't expect to be back here.

"'Course I did, but I wanna know how you felt about it."

"Warm and fucking fuzzy, Captain."

He drops a shoulder against the locker beside mine. "Do you always get this defensive when someone asks you about your feelings?"

"I don't know, Cap, do you always have to be the fucking meddler just to make yourself feel needed?" I slam my locker closed, gaining attention around me. "Not everyone is fixable or wants to be taken care of. Back off."

I purposely hit his shoulder as I pass by. I know how fucked up my words were. The fact that I'm bothered by what I said only irritates me more.

"I'm going to the bathroom," I snap and round the corner.

It works to get him off my ass and I move for first period.

It's still early so there's only a student or two inside and both have their faces buried in a book.

Captain's voice floats through the door in the same moment and I pause there to listen.

"What do you want, Tisha?"

"Just wondering what's going on with you and Raven?"

I snort quietly.

"Nothing that concerns you."

"She doesn't concern me. What I'm really asking is if you want to get together later?"

"Can't." His dismiss is instant.

A beat of silence follows and then, "Why not?"

"Busy."

"Well maybe—"

She's cut off when Royce interjects himself into their conversation. "Do you not know how to take a hint, Tisha? Pretty sure he said no, and yet here you are, making a fool of yourself and looking desperate. See, I'd have told ya I don't waste time on loose goose, but Cap is more subtle. Clearly subtle don't work on you, so lemme help him out. None of us want you, nor will we ever."

"Whatever, keep wasting your time on trash like her."

"Like ... who?" he baits her.

"Who else?"

The menacing laugh that leaves Royce has me standing taller against the door. "Let me tell you something, Tisha, Raven is more than you'll ever be. She's with us and she didn't even try to use what's between her legs to get there, but you just did, didn't you? Got dissed and still tried. No conversation, no lead-up, just an open-legged offer for a ticket to the top." He laughs again. "You're the only trash I've seen today, and I've been with Raven all morning. Consider this? You running your mouth, your marker. You're done. Find a fucking normal and stay twenty feet from us. Always."

Confusion draws my brows together and I drag myself to my seat.

He just defended me. Having no idea I was listening, Royce had my back.

Why did he do that?

I don't like this, they're confusing me now and I don't know who or how to trust. I never wanted to be a part of a team.

And then I met them.

I'd be lying if I said I didn't feel the shift, but to hear him with my own ears hold me up instead of throwing me down makes it more real. More genuine and ... possible. I don't know what to do with that.

My mind is trying to deny the risk, so why do my shoulders lift higher as if weight's been removed?

Perhaps some now sits on three new sets of shoulders ...

No.

No.

Royce pops in, all smiles and smirks, bobbing his head to

whatever it is that's blaring in his earbuds. He drops in the seat beside me.

I wait for him to tell me all about how he told off that girl and put some stupid order on her, but he doesn't say anything. Doesn't gloat or make it funny liked I'd expect from him. He only winks at me and pulls out his school shit.

Halfway through class, he passes me a note and I roll my eyes but grab it.

Are you mad at me for telling everyone you're staying with us? Say yes, if you never wanna taste my lasagna. Say NO, if you want to taste it tonight. I'll even take you for ice cream after.

I can't help but smile a little. I peek at him, but his eyes are on the legs of the brunette a seat forward and to the left of him.

I write "no" in bold letters, underlining his offer of ice cream.

"Ms. Carver, you're wanted in the principal's office."

My head jerks forward and Royce sits to attention.

"For what?" I ask the teacher who only narrows her pointy eyes.

"Guess you'll find out when you get there, won't you?"

I offer a bitchy grin and snag my backpack off the floor. When I stand, Royce stands with me.

"Sit down, Mr. Brayshaw. He called for Raven only."

"Heard you. Don't care, and while we're talking ... let me remind you to watch your tongue, teach. Don't get comfortable behind that mahogany desk."

I look from Royce to the teacher.

Her face is beet red as she steps back pretending she's okay by moving on with her lecture – she knows who writes her checks so to speak.

We walk out and down the hall ... where we're flanked by the other two.

"Do we know what he wants?" Captain asks Royce and my eyes bounce between them, each holding their phones in their hands.

Royce.

Change my mind, I am mad at him.

"Uh, hi." They turn to me. "What's going on here?"

Silence.

Right. An insider's only issue I'm not privy too.

Well, fuck them too then.

I pretend to be swaying on my feet and then dart off, down the hall and slip into the office before they reach it.

Probably a horrible idea, but I lock it behind me.

His head jerks up right as there's one solid pound on the other side of the door.

He sits back slowly.

"Ms. Carver."

"Mr. Perkins."

"Sit."

"I'd rather stand, thanks."

"I got a call a little while ago informing me of your move."

Fucking Royce.

"Yeah, the other location didn't really work out. You need a new address form or something?"

He levels me with a stern look. He's about to spew some fake shit, so I drop into the chair, forcing him to look me in the eye as he lies through his perfect teeth.

"Listen, Raven. I understand being new somewhere isn't always easy, and sometimes the stress of it all is too much. I was thinking, maybe you'd like to transfer to another local school here? I could put in a good word, get your transfer processed for you. I think you'd really thrive at a place where students are free to be who they wish, not to mention the great programs they have for someone in your position."

"What position would that be?"

"I know your plan is to simply graduate and move on, find a job somewhere and get settled – I read your English paper. You want a new life. I can help you get it." There's a sick gleam in his eye. He feels he has insight into me.

Bastard.

I remain quiet.

"See, here at Brayshaw, we're limited on opportunity since half of our district supports the youth program you're currently in. While we do have many wealthy families who support us, their focus is on the sports and dance here. If you switch schools, you can join a real work program. They have several to choose from – legal aids, mechanics, carpentry, bookkeeping, and a few more. The school trains you, free, and when you graduate, you hold a certificate in the chosen field you can take with you anywhere. Get a good job right out the gate."

Wow. He knows what he's doing. Dangle a slab of meat in front of a starving wolf and wait for it to jump.

My silence has his stare shining in victory.

He wants me out.

"Sounds like a great opportunity."

"It is."

I tilt my head. "You offer this to all the students at the Bray houses? I bet they'd be all over it."

"Unfortunately, no. Only ... select students are given the chance."

Right.

"What school?"

"Graven Prep."

A laugh bubbles out of me before I can stop it and anger lines his eyes.

"Is something funny, Ms. Carver?"

"I was raised by a liar and a con, Mr. Perkins, so let's cut the student teacher 'I want what's best for my students' bullshit, shall we?" I lean forward, and he meets my move. "You don't care what I do or where I go, hell you'd probably send me straight back if you could. You want me out because, in your mind, it's the clear way to keep me from them. You don't want me to get too close to them because then I'll see what's really going on, am I right?"

"I'm not sure what you mean." He forces a steady tone.

"I'm perceptive, as are you. That's how you see the threat. Three men already outnumber you, but add a female and a pack is born."

"You think I'm afraid of three punk kids?" he growls through clenched teeth.

"I think you're terrified." I stand, and his cunning eyes follow.

"Don't be a fool, Raven. Take the offer. Leave the school and build a better life for yourself. Unless you want to end up like your mother."

When my eyes narrow, a sinister smirk tips his lips.

"She was a little cheaper than I'd expect. Body like hers, she could have asked for more and gotten it, especially since I was able to role play. Gotta say…" He tries to grin, but his lip curls instead. "She wasn't too happy when I asked if I could call her Raven instead."

I bite into my tongue to keep myself calm when really, I want to yank his tie off and choke him with it.

He fucked my mom, which means he fished for information – not that she knows a damn thing about me.

I hate her.

I force myself to speak, not acknowledging his attempt to play the big bad man. "I'll pass. I can make a life on my own."

I turn and reach for the handle.

"Did I mention," he's quick to add. "After graduation, the program puts you in an apartment and sets you up with a five-thousand-dollar bank account to get you on your feet."

I tense.

"You turn eighteen a few months before school's end. You'll age out, be on the streets or back in your trailer park. Graven can change all that. I can change all that."

"You can let the attendance office know I'm going home sick."

I swallow and yank the door open, colliding into Maddoc on my break from the room.

Perkins slams the door after my exit.

Each one of their faces holds a blank stare, no emotion to be found, but the longer they stare, the more the tension grows, and the worry they try to hide comes forward to cloud their eyes. But Perkins fucked me up and I'm not in the mood for talking, so I spin on my heels and head for the front.

That kicks them into gear and suddenly I'm crowded.

"That's it?" Royce spits. "You cut us out when we try to be there for you, then take off without a word?!"

I skid to a stop by the exit. "I need to go."

Captain hangs his head, hands on his hips and Royce's jaw clenches in defeat.

I look to Maddoc, who simply frowns at me.

My head pulls back. "What is happening right now?"

Nobody says a word.

"Look, I gotta get out of here for a bit, I'll see you guys later."

"Wait—" Royce starts, and Captain's head shoots up. "So, what, you're just … you're going home? Our home?"

Our home.

Shit.

My eyes bounce between the three. "Yeah, I … fuck. I didn't … think. I'll just hang around 'til school gets out and—"

Royce laughs, cutting me off. He moves in, squeezes me then jogs off down the hall.

Captain scans my face but gives nothing with his expression, and a heavier foot carries him back to class. And then there's Maddoc.

His features are tight, his lips in a thin line.

"What?"

"You really going back to the house?"

I start to say yes then shrug my shoulders. "I think I need some air."

He licks his lips.

"Wanna come?"

He studies me a moment before a sexy ass grin takes over. He pushes me out the door.

I have to laugh. Seems all the big man wanted was an invite.

Chapter 34

Raven

"Okay, it's been fifteen minutes of staring at nothing. What are we doing, Raven?"

"Almost."

"Almost wha—"

The ringing of the crossing guards echoes down the track and I look up at Maddoc with a grin.

"Here it comes."

His eyes follow the sound.

I rush from the SUV, quickly pulling my hair up.

The first part of the train blows by and Maddoc gives me a look that says 'no fucking way are you doing what I think you're doing' but then it starts to slow, the blurry images becoming clearer as the speed lessens, and his shoulders relax a bit.

"Get ready, big man."

"Raven..." he warns. "I don't fucking think so—"

"Now!"

I take off, running parallel with the train, moving closer every few feet. I grin when Maddoc catches up to me.

I glance back, then cut a quick nod at Maddoc. I turn in, gripping the front railing of an open cart and yank myself up. Maddoc does the same on the back handle.

He quickly tosses himself inside, but I stand at the open edge for a moment longer.

When he shouts, I pull myself inside and lean against the wall.

I take a second to catch my breath then look to him, laughing at his pissy expression.

"Not fucking funny," he growls.

I wave him off, my hand hitting my stomach as I take a deep breath, settling my heart rate from the short sprint.

I push off the side and Maddoc's stare grows panicked. He darts forward, but before he can step past the side wall, I run across to him.

"Goddamn it, Raven."

I drop onto my ass and lean against the metal, close enough to the door where I can feel the force of air as it flies past my shoes.

"Chill, big man." I meet his stare. "Sit."

He considers standing just to prove a point but drops against the opposite side.

After a few minutes of silence, he says, "I take it you do this a lot?"

"All the time. Or I used to do it all the time." I look out the car. "I've been wanting to come ride here though."

"You've been out here?"

I nod. "Few times, yeah. I spent a couple hours watchin', trying to get the timing down for when they slowed enough to jump." I take a deep breath.

"So, what now?"

I tilt my head so I can see the rusted iron containers as the train makes a wide curve down the tracks. Some are blank, some telling other people's stories in the form of bright paints.

"Now you chill, let the outside world fly behind you. Pretend wherever the driver has to stop somehow lines up with right where you're supposed to take the leap but jumping off is the easy part. After, when you have to decide if you get back on or step away and never look back? That's when shit gets real.

"That's when you find out if you're as weak as everyone thinks, or as strong as you always hoped." I chance a look at Maddoc and when I do, my skin grows warm.

His stare is forward for him, completely unconcealed. Curiosity and realization, a need to know more sitting at the edge of his lips. So many questions. So many misconceptions.

But I know him by now. His words won't match his wonder.

"Conductor," he rasps.

I pinch my lips together, but a soft laugh still escapes. "What?"

He licks his lips and looks off, moving to prop his elbows up on his knees, his back against the gold metal. "The driver, the term is conductor."

"Right." I drop my grin to my feet, then look out the car again.

I close my eyes and smile at the wind. "Tell me something, big man."

"Like what?"

I pop a shoulder. "I don't care. Anything."

He's quiet a few minutes and I think he won't play along, then he surprises me. "I hate going to the movies."

I laugh, my eyes still closed. "Not surprising."

"How so?"

"You're extremely aware. You read every situation, spot things others don't, it's why you're so good at basketball. It's like a natural sixth sense. A dark theater would make that impossible, and if you can't read what's happening around you, you're constantly on edge, not in control." I open my eyes to meet his. "And control is something you need to feel like you."

He glares.

"I'm not being a bitch, I swear, I'm just saying it's a part of who you are. Nothing wrong with it if you believe in yourself."

He looks like he wants to argue, but instead jerks his chin.

"Your turn." He drops his head against the cart. "Tell me something. Something I wouldn't be able to guess."

"What, like I sleep with a nightlight?" I joke, but he doesn't laugh, just stares.

After a quiet moment, he says, "Yeah, like that."

"Um..." I pull my sleeves over my hands. "I hate milk by itself, but I love it in cereal."

"I hate chocolate."

"What?" I shout with a laugh. "Nobody hates chocolate."

"I do."

"Wow," I explain with exaggerated awe. "Weird."

His lips tip into a small grin. "Your turn."

"I hate my mother."

He doesn't say anything, so I look his way again. "But that's no surprise, right?"

His brows lower.

"She's always been a piece of shit, my whole life, as far as I can remember anyway. But there was one time where everything sucked the teeniest bit less. Wanna know why?" A wry grin slips. "A client stuck."

"Since he knew about her job of choice, she didn't have to lie about who she was and what she did. Used and abused and all, he accepted her. Me too. He even claimed to have kids, but I never met them." I focus on the sky.

"She got better with him, wasn't clean, but functioned like

a human instead of a toy with dying batteries – still turned tricks, but he never seemed to mind.

"For the first time ever, I had a dinnertime. Every night, when the sensor lights on the trailers started popping on – there were no streetlamps in my neighborhood – I'd run back. Excited for a stupid dinner that was never anything more than macaroni and cheese with hotdogs or rice and sauce. Dumb shit, but it was the first time she'd ever seemed to care if I ate since I was big enough to make my own cereal, so I thought it was cool. Lasted about a year."

"What happened?"

"I ruined it."

"How?"

With a deep inhale, I look to Maddoc. "Puberty."

His features morph in an instant, flashing with incomprehensible anger. "Raven."

"He started paying more attention to me, 'neglecting her,' she'd say. She beat my ass, told me I wasn't allowed around him if I couldn't keep my mouth shut." I remember how angry she'd get. "Kinda hard when my room was the two feet between the table and the couch, that was also my bed."

Silence stretches between us for several minutes before Maddoc speaks, his voice a deep raspy mumble.

"I like cheese on popcorn."

My stare flies to Maddoc and I grin earning a dismal one in return.

"We should probably get off, we'll need to catch one back before dark."

Maddoc stands, eyes locked on mine as he holds his hand out.

I stare at it a moment before slipping mine into his and allowing him to pull me to the other side.

I move to grab the handle, but he spins, tucking me away into the safety of the car corner, his big ole body caging me in, shielding me from the wind and anything else that may come close. His green eyes bore into mine as waves of strength flow from him, fighting for a way inside me.

But my armor is strong, my mind and body built on defense alone, and self-preservation allows for no safe passage.

Salvation can be a bitch, taking away our own choices before we even decide what's right versus smart.

I reach out planting my hands on his chest, to keep him back, I think, and he drops his gaze to the contact.

"If someone tries to hurt you, I need you to tell me."

"I can't do that."

He pushes closer, his expression angrier. "Why not?"

"Because I'm not your problem."

"Be my problem."

My stomach about bottoms out at his words, but before I can even consider a response, the train jolts and the brakes screech.

"Time to jump." I push him back and he lets me.

We wait another minute, letting the speed decrease a little more, then swing outside the doors and push off.

Maddoc, of course, lands on his feet, but I stumble a little, catching myself before both knees hit the ground.

I laugh lightly, taking a deep breath as I look around.

Instead of dead grass surrounding the tracks like where we hopped on, there's rock. And not fifteen feet forward is a line of food trucks and what looks to be a bus station.

We walk over to an old electrical box to sit and wait, watching the sun go down as we do.

"Thanks for coming with me, big man." I exhale deeply. "I needed today. This basic day-to-day, get up, go to school, go to bed, shit isn't me."

"Yeah, and what is 'you,' Raven?"

"Think of it like this - you guys like order. It's like you need your normal so you don't go crazy, but me? I need crazy to feel normal."

"There's no such thing as normal. Normal is an opinion."

"So is drug free the way to be, but it's still right, isn't it?"

"That's not the same thing."

"Still true."

He shakes his head and hops down. "Come on."

"We—"

A horn starts blaring right then, gathering the attention of all the homeless people against the wall of an abandoned building.

I turn to find a black SUV jammin' down the road.

With a laugh, I shake my head. "'Course." I step ahead of Maddoc and spin to face him as I walk backward. "Where one goes, the others follow."

"Nothing wrong with having people in your corner, Raven."

"Sure there is."

"Why's that?"

"If your corner's already empty, no chance of losing anything along the way."

His shoulders straighten a bit. "Fear's not your style."

I don't respond because he's as right as he is wrong with that one. Fear isn't my style. I don't show it, fight not to feel it, but at the end of the day, fear is the very thing that keeps me up at night.

I slide in the SUV where the guys are jamming out to Lynyrd Skynyrd, so I lean across the seats and crank it up more.

Maddoc slides in beside me but doesn't move any closer.

We all bob to the music the entire way home.

That night, sleep never comes.

And neither does Maddoc.

Chapter 35

Raven

"Rumor's true?"

I prop against the fence, looking over the empty field. "Depends which one you're referring to."

Bass scoffs. "You ain't lyin'. There's at least a couple dozen floating around now."

"At least."

He looks to me, blowing his smoke right in my face. "You really staying with them?"

"I am." I eye him. "But you know that already, don't you? Bet they made you aware right away, even asked you to keep me off the cards?"

"They didn't ask me shit, Carver." His stare hardens and I sigh.

Right, they didn't ask. They demanded.

"What'd they say?"

"Come on now, you know how this shit works."

I nod. "No singers."

"No fucking singers, Rae."

Fuck.

I snag his cigarette from his hand and take a drag, dropping my head back. I blow the smoke into the sky, then look to him. "Guess there's no chance you'll add me on then, huh?"

He snags his cigarette back and takes the last drag before smooshing it under his foot. He walks off.

"See you around, Carver."

I follow his form and just when he curves around the corner, I lock eyes with Maddoc in the distance. He stares this way with his sunglasses in place.

I walk to him.

"What'd he want?"

"Nothing." I lean my shoulder against the wall. "I approached him."

"Why?"

"Don't play dumb, big man."

"You have no need to fight."

"You have no idea what I need."

He crowds my space and my body turns against the wall. "Wrong." His fingers slide inside my open jacket and skim down my side.

When my body shivers, he pushes closer, whispering, "I know exactly what you need, and I guarantee you won't find it with some G-Eazy wannabe."

"I happen to love me some G-Eazy," I tease. "And Bass' lip ring does something for me."

"Yeah?" he growls. "Well then a dick ring will really set you off." When my lips part he steps back, licking his. "Stay away from him, Snow."

And then he's gone, but I barely register his retreat, because I'm too busy replaying the sight of him in his boxers, trying to figure out if he's kidding about dick jewelry or not. I know I didn't feel it on me when we laid together in bed.

When the bell rings I jolt, shaking myself from my Maddick fog and make my way back into the cafeteria.

The rest of the day passes with a blur and then it's time for the boys to practice.

I post up on the bleachers as they move to the courts.

Royce runs over and tosses me his hoodie and glasses. "Put that under your head."

"Thanks. Hey!" I shout and he turns back, nodding his chin. "Why this old court, why not the fancy gym or at the house?"

"It's real out here." He shrugs. "This is home."

When I grin, he winks and runs off.

I'm betting Maybell has a lot to do with this side of these guys, the home-grown side. I know they have money, but they don't live like they do as far as their person. They don't eat at steakhouses or yacht clubs like I assume ritzy people do but make dinners in their own kitchens instead. They use an old beat up court because it's more comfortable than a half a million dollar one built just for them – I saw the plaque on the wall. I know their dad had it built it in the Brayshaw name just in time for their freshman year. They don't walk around with their noses in the air, but their shoulders are wide, and heads still held high. If I saw them walking down my streets with the athletic gear they've got on right now, I'd swear they belonged.

I stuff the hoodie over my head and slip his shades on, so I can comfortably enjoy Maddoc commanding the show.

Basketball is like a fast pace dance, one that Maddoc has perfected.

With each swift move of his feet, no matter if he cuts left or right or simply drops back, he makes every basket effortlessly – not a single brick shot. But he's not trying to eat up all the play-time. He works as a captain should, makes sure the ball is sent where it needs to go, but like a magnet seeks its metal home, the ball finds its way back to the big man's hands.

He runs down the court, and one of the guys comes up to block, so he spins and tosses the ball backward over his head. Captain runs out of nowhere to catch it and dunks the ball before anyone can even attempt to stop him.

"Ooh, dropping dimes, boy!" Royce laughs and the rest of the team shout out their excitement.

I don't miss the way Maddoc slyly cuts his eyes to me as he looks down to wipe his hands on his shirt.

I laugh to myself.

I saw, big man.

They high five then continue. After a few minutes, they break up into smaller groups and start working position-based drills, so I close my eyes and pretend this is my life.

"Hey."

Fuck.

I pull myself into a sitting position. "Hey."

"So ... you're still here." Vienna eyes me.

I push the glasses on top of my head. "Still here."

"You really staying with the guys?"

I ignore her question and she nods.

We sit and watch the guys together, turning to each other with grins when a few shirts come off.

"Hot damn. And I thought football made you ripped."

"Right?" I look around, counting abs and comparing builds.

"Madman, let's go!" Royce shouts and I pull my eyes from a fine specimen to look over. When I do, my stare meets a deep glare.

"Oh, girl..." Vienna teases through closed lips. "Somebody doesn't like your eyes roaming."

"Maybe if he took his off, they wouldn't." I pop a brow at Maddoc even though he can't hear me.

Vienna laughs at my side.

And then he does. His hands find the hem at the back of

his neck and he pulls, and fuck me if that slight bend doesn't set him up real fucking nice.

Sweat shines against his tanned skin, rolling over every curve of packed muscle. I have the sudden need to know how his body feels when covered in hard work like it is.

"Damn," Vienna breathes in awe and I nod along, my eyes locked on his small dark patch at the edge of his shorts.

"Think he'd hook up with me?" she whispers, and I frown.

"I don't know. Maybe." It's the truth. I turn to her. "Think I could kick your ass?"

"I don't know." She finally looks to me with a grin. "Maybe," she mocks.

It's a lie. We both know I could, which is why when she starts laughing, I do too. But when I turn back to gawk at big man some more and find him staring, yet again, I realize what just happened.

He knew Vienna would say something and I'd react.

He baited me, the conceited shithead, and it worked like a damn charm.

"So he's off the books ... but what about the other two?"

I look to Royce, then Captain. With a sigh, I turn back to her. "Yeah," I sigh, "They're mine too. You want one? Earn him."

She starts laughing good-heartedly, and I grin, leaning back on my elbows.

"All right, fellas," the coach calls out. "Twenty suicides then you're good to go. Tonight's assignment: one hour of game film. As always, wear your jerseys to class tomorrow with pride."

All the players call out "yes coach" then do as they're told.

"I should go." Vienna hitches her backpack over her shoulder. "It's cool you're still here. Wish I could knock the shit out of Victoria and stay." She grins.

"Trust me," I laugh. "It was the last thing I expected."

"Look, if you find yourself between a rock and a hard place, needing to throw blows or something, find me. Don't ruin what might be a good thing."

"What makes you think I would?"

"That punch had nothing to do with Victoria. You self-sabotaged." Her eyes bounce between mine before shifting the three heads our way. She looks back to me. "I do it too. It's natural for girls like us."

Girls like us.

Royce throws himself beside me and looks between me and Vienna.

Captain glances my way but drops his frown to his gym bag when he sees me looking and Maddoc glares over his water bottle.

"See you later, Rae."

She turns and walks off, but I call out, "Wait!"

Maddoc's eyes flick between mine.

"We'll take you home."

The corner of his eyes tighten, but before he looks away, I spot the slight grin he tries to hide.

I step in front of him, slipping my hand in his gym pocket as he looks down his nose at me. I slowly pull out the keys he just stuffed inside.

"We'll be in the car."

I catch up to Vienna, ignoring the laughter behind me.

A few minutes of us bullshitting in the back seat pass before the three slide in, Royce, of course in the back with us.

"I think I should sit in the middle."

"Stay where you're at." Maddoc glares in his mirror at his brother, who sits beside Vienna.

Vienna, who says not a word the entire drive – not even sure she breathes – and only waves when she gets out at the house.

Maddoc continues down the dirt road, parking right in front of the porch as we pull up.

Together, the four of us head inside.

"One of you mind doing dinner tonight?" Captain asks, already headed for the stairs.

"I got it." Maddoc nods then looks to us. "Lemme shower then I'll start."

Royce and I shrug, and I follow him into the kitchen, watching him wash his hands and start pulling out shit for Maddoc to cook with.

"What's up with Captain?"

"What makes you think anything is?"

"He seems off."

Royce turns to me with a scowl that quickly grows into a grin. "You're starting to see through our masks, RaeRae. Careful, you might actually be forced to admit you like it."

"Whatever." I push off the counter and start walking away.

"Raven."

I look back to Royce.

"Go ask him." It's almost a plea, like he knows what it is and thinks I can fix it.

Unsure why, I head upstairs and knock on Captain's door.

He doesn't say anything, so I walk inside anyway finding him sitting at the edge of his bed, looking out the window.

"What's up, Raven?"

"How'd you know it was me?"

"You're the only one who'd knock in this house."

We both laugh lightly, but my chest feels tight at how hollow his is.

I move around the room and climb on to the bed, sitting against the headboard. "What's wrong?"

He hesitates a minute before speaking. "If I ask you something, will you tell me the truth without needing to know why I need to know?"

"Honestly?" I ask, my face scrunching. "Probably not but try me."

He chuckles and looks my way. With a deep sigh, he shifts on the bed to face me.

"Why did Perkins call you into his office?"

"That's what you wanna know?"

"Come on ..."

"Easy." I shrug. "He wants me to leave Brayshaw."

"He say that?"

"Painted a real pretty picture for me."

Captain nods with a frown, but it's not for me. "Yet here you are."

"I've got my own crayons, Packman."

He studies me. "You don't trust him."

"You don't trust him. Neither does Royce, Maddoc. How am I supposed to?"

His eyes soften the longer he stares and then he looks away. But something's plaguing him.

"Pretty sure he thinks the longer I'm here, the tighter we'll get, and he doesn't want that," I tell him.

"He thinks you'll make us stronger." His eyes bounce between mine. "He's right. You will. You are."

I look away. "I'm just ... the girl living across the hall, Cap. And who knows how long that'll last."

He scoots closer. "That's not true and you know it. You fit. And Maddoc—"

"Is like a puzzle missing key pieces."

"Yeah." He nods. "Think there's a perfect five six, hourglass cut out that needs filling."

"Ha! Funny guy."

Cap laughs lightly, dropping back on his bed, so I move to lay my head near his.

"You want the exact details, Cap?"

He's quiet a moment and then his head shakes against his comforter. "Is it a one-time offer?"

"No. When you're ready, we'll talk."

"And you'll still be here?"

I nod for his sake, knowing it could be a lie.

"Why aren't you asking me questions, Raven? Why you willing to tell me what I wanna know without answers?"

"I don't play eye for an eye."

He takes a deep breath, and his hand finds mine on the comforter. He gives me a light squeeze before pulling away and sadness fills me.

For him and whatever he's going through.

These boys are ... more than I was ready for.

We both look to the door when the rattle of a doorknob catches our attention, but it is open, so we stifle our laughter as we watch Maddoc at mine. When he opens it and walks in to find it empty, he frowns and glances off ... right inside Cap's room.

He freezes when he spots us, and we start cracking up.

He gets a look at his brother. "You good, man?"

Cap nods and Maddoc looks to me, concern lining his brow.

I glance at Cap and he winks. He'll tell him all about it later if he doesn't already know, so I smooth it over for the time being. "We ... decided to watch a movie and veg tonight. Anything we can maybe pop in the microwave?"

Maddoc runs a hand over his mouth, nodding. "Lemme figure something out. We'll meet you guys in the media room." He looks to his brother again before walking off.

Maddoc ends up frying some burgers quickly and we pair it with chips and salsa, also homemade – another thing to thank Maybell for, I'm sure.

Once everyone's done, I offer to collect the plates and run

downstairs for snacks to give the three a few minutes to talk in case they need to.

With everyone's shit in hand, I snag the blanket off my bed on the way back.

I pass everyone their stuff, then drop beside Maddoc.

"Ew, get your nasty ass feet off me," I laugh, shoving Royce away.

"I have socks on!" he defends.

"So, feet are nasty."

"Not mine, look at these babies?" He wiggles his toes and I cringe.

"You've got some big ass feet."

"And a big ass dick."

I laugh, rolling my eyes and Maddoc throws a pillow at him.

He reaches in his bowl, then cuts a glance my way.

I wink, turning back to the screen. I sneak my hand into his bowl and stuff my mouth.

Cheese on popcorn isn't half bad.

Chapter 36

RAVEN

Everyone is standing, biting at their fingernails as the final seconds on the clock tick by. The boys are up by one, but the other team has the ball and there's still seven seconds on the clock – seven seconds is a lifetime in basketball.

The play gets down the court and Maddoc goes on the attack, but the one with the ball throws an elbow and he's jarred to the side, an angry growl leaving him, but he starts running after the guy in the next second.

The guy rounds the court, hopping up to attempt a shot, but Royce flies up behind him, his vertical jump a little better, his reach a little longer, and he smacks the ball away. The final buzzer sounds and the crowd grows wild, celebrating yet another win for the Wolves.

But I keep my eyes locked on Maddoc who shoves his face in the guy who fouled him and didn't get called on it. Their foreheads are touching and Maddoc drives him back with his.

The guy doesn't want none. He takes it.

Maddoc gives him a hard shove and he flies back into his teammates. They don't dare step closer.

In fact, they hold their hands out to shake his in apology, but he gives them his back.

Some might call it bad sportsmanship, but they did him dirty first.

They don't deserve his hand.

With a grin, I make my way out of the gym to wait for them to get cleaned up.

Fifteen minutes or so pass and almost all the cars are out of the lot when a blue Jeep pulls up in front of me. The window rolls down revealing Collins and a few of his Graven buddies.

"Rae. How you doin'?"

"What are you doing here?"

"Like that now, huh?" He attempts a grin, but his tone is laced with malice.

I scoff. "What, you thought different?"

"Still mad about that little incident?" He smirks like a dick.

I ignore him.

"That's a damn shame, Raven. Damn shame." The window rolls up slowly and they take off.

Not a minute later Royce's loud ass is yelling behind me.

I spin around with a grin.

Running full speed at me, he swiftly dips down and lifts me up. "How'd you like that ending, RaeRae?" He drops me to my feet just as quick, planting a sweaty kiss to my cheek.

I laugh and look to Captain who has his phone to his ear, he smiles my way then goes back to his conversation.

Maddoc steps right in front of me.

"Good game." When he doesn't say anything, I tease, "You waiting for a reward for all your hard work, big man?"

He pushes against me now, so my head has to fall back on the hood in order to look him in the eye. His hands find my hips and slowly slide up the curve of my waist to my ribs –

something he seems to love doing. Those full lips of his tip up in satisfaction when a shiver runs through me. He knew it was coming. He was waiting for it. "That all it takes to get those lips on mine, a good game on the court?"

"Hmm." I try to grin, but my body's so heated it only holds for a few seconds. He knows it, senses it, and his tongue runs along his bottom lip. "Only one way to find out."

"That's exactly what you want, isn't it?" he whispers, his thumbs moving to skim beneath my chest. "Me to take what I want. Me to bite into that lip you keep sucking between your teeth. Me pullin' on this hair." He slides his fingertips into my hair at the base of my neck and my core muscles clench. He tugs too gently on purpose, and a harsh breath leaves me. "Me all over you." He leans forward and my eyes close when he blows against the hollow of my ear. "Me in you."

I'd swear my eyes rolled back if they weren't already squeezed shut.

"It would be so good," he breathes and fuck, my toes curl in my boots. But in the next second the warmth of his body slips some and my eyes peel open. "But not until you stop trying to convince yourself it ain't you and me."

His bottom half is still locking me in, but his torso has lifted a bit, so my lungs are able to capture more than just his scent and some of the fog clears as his words register. I swallow.

"I don't know what you're talking about," I croak out, turning my head, but he pulls my eyes right back with a grip to my chin.

His eyes slice between mine. He's almost unhinged, thoroughly horny and pissed off about it. "Yeah, you do. And you'll pull the trigger."

"If I don't?"

"Someone else will."

My eyebrows involuntarily snap to the center and a deep

chuckle makes its way up his chest, causing his body to vibrate against mine.

"Imma let you sit on that." He leans forward. "And maybe later," – he moves my hand, sliding the back of it against his hard-on – "you'll be sitting on this."

My eyes must have closed again at some point because when a gust of wind hits me and they pop open, I see nothing but a dark parking lot.

I jump when the horn blares.

I glare at the dark windshield. I can't see shit, but they see me, saw all that. Their laughter floating out the sunroof confirms it.

Maddoc is in the passenger seat, so when I reach his door as I walk around, I lift up on the sidebar and stick my upper body inside. I quickly bring my lips to his, right fucking against him, but I pause there. I lick my lips, and I'm so close my tongue touches his lips.

He growls and I grin, slip out, and into the back seat.

Royce gives high fives, Captain shakes his head with a grin, and Maddoc? Well, he adjusts himself where he sits, slamming his poor head against the seat.

Checkmate, big man.

I GRAB TWO BEERS FROM THE FRIDGE AND MOVE TO THE couch, dropping beside Maddoc. We ran home for them to change, then came over to the West Main house they use as their kickback zone – the place people are allowed. Well, their people.

"Yo, Raven!" Royce calls from the other side of the room.

Maddoc said when they started using it as a party pad, they had two walls knocked out so the den, living room, and kitchen area all become one wide open space. He said they wanted to be able to see every corner so they were always aware of what was happening around them.

Royce lifts his hand, three darts slid across his palm, he nods. "Bet I can whoop that ass in darts?"

"You won't be whooping her ass at anything."

I turn to Maddoc. "Neither will you, big man."

He turns to me with a brow raised making me laugh.

"All right, I'll rephrase, let me metaphorically spank that fat ass 'til it leaves a perfect imprint of this big ass hand so everyone knows who laid it on you…in darts…metaphorically." Royce crosses his arms proud, but can't hold it in and starts laughing and I join in.

Maddoc throws a bottle cap at his brother who dodges it.

"I'm gifted in the art of a target. I'd embarrass you."

"Get out—"

"For real, man, Raven's got some serious aim."

All eyes jerk to Leo.

"Oh yeah…" Royce drags out, slow and looming.

Leo stares at me and I force myself not to narrow my eyes.

I know what he's doing. He's testing the situation, looking to see who, if any, I've got wrapped up like he assumes – his motive is still in the air.

I said I'd let him run this show.

We'll see if he buries himself.

"Hell yeah." The bastard licks his lips, holding his eyes on me a moment longer before looking to Royce. "At the cabins, she …" He trails off, wiping at his mouth with a grin. "She put on a good ass show. Proved she could hang."

"The fuck?" Maddoc questions, sitting forward with his elbows on his knees, but he glares over his shoulder at me.

In my peripheral, Royce's glare hits me just the same, but I don't look away from Leo.

His lip twitches just the slightest.

This bitch.

"So, this the route you wanna go?" I ask him and he lifts his head, but I don't miss the shift of his feet.

"No hard feelings, I expected it."

Funny thing, words, and the many ways one can interpret the meaning behind a sentence. I didn't want this for him, hoped he'd come to his senses. Clearly that's not happening today.

"You think you know me, Leo. That was your first mistake. You think I'll take your words as a threat, that I'll laugh it off and keep my mouth shut because the seed's already planted now, right?" The room grows silent. "Well, I'm not a little bitch like you seem to be. So, you can sit here and make it seem like I was on your jock at the cabins when we both know that's far from the truth." His eyes harden as I lean forward. "But let me ask you, why exactly, do you want the Boys of Brayshaw to think I fucked with you when I never even attempted?" I raise a brow slowly.

He pauses a second, making his decision – it's the right one, but a few too late.

Leo laughs, but it's nervous and before he can attempt to dig his way back, I stand, dismissing him.

He just showed them he purposely tried to get under their skin – the shovel is officially in his hands. No going back now.

"I'm a boss at darts, Royce. Sure you want your ass kicked?" I go to step forward, but Maddoc's hand shoots out, gripping my jeans by the pocket.

I glance back, tipping my chin lightly as I slide my fingers over his, and his hand starts shaking. I squeeze, giving an almost unnoticeable shake of my head.

I'd never, big man.

His eyes cut between mine, and as if he understands, he lets go.

I head over to Leo and Royce. Royce, who hasn't stopped glaring at the side of Leo's head.

I stop in front of Leo and in my peripheral, Maddoc stands as Royce steps closer. Leo's jaw locks tight and when I hold my hand out, he drops the darts inside.

"I gave you a choice," I whisper for only him to hear.

"Fuck you," he hisses, and I grin.

"Not even with the tip, Leo."

He steps back, laughing again like we shared some joke and grabs his keys off the stool. "I'm taking off. See you guys tomorrow."

He doesn't say a word or make eye contact with anyone on his way out the door. The second it shuts, I'm practically run into the corner by Royce and Maddoc.

"What the fuck was that?" Maddoc speaks through his clenched teeth.

"Your friend is a dick.

"What'd he do?"

"Nothing."

"Cut the shit, Raven. What the fuck was that?"

I pull myself up on the stool. "He's been your boy for years and I'm the newcomer. You guys were driving me to school, had me staying in your cabin, and now I'm at your place."

"What's the fucking point here?" Royce asks.

"He's probably sleeping with roaches running across the shoes at the edge of his bed, if he even has one, and you've known him for years."

"So, we're supposed to just give all our fucking friends a place to stay?"

I shrug. "I wasn't even your friend yet when you gave me one."

"Yet?" Royce grins.

I laugh tilting my head back and forth. "I kinda like you."

"Back on fucking track." Maddoc glares at us both, settling his stare on me. "Why would he act like that?"

I survey him and curse to myself.

He trusts too little in his life, and in his mind, he needs to trust Leo.

"Look, it's not a big deal. He don't like me, oh well, welcome him to the club. I can deal with that. If he's being protective of you guys, then I can respect that."

"You didn't say anything." A deep crease takes over his forehead. "Why?"

A snort leaves me. "I wasn't about to cause unnecessary problems between you guys and your friends. If he ends up being a little bitch, then he'll be the one to make you see that, not me. We'll have to wait and see how it plays out."

They both stare, and I grow anxious, looking between the two.

"What?"

Maddoc steps closer.

"Damn," leaves Royce in a whisper and he steps back.

I look to Royce over Maddoc's shoulder and he winks, but it's not a cheesy, teasing wink. It's softer. Different.

"Party's over, people," Royce calls out as he steps away and the few teammates and their chicks grab their stuff and head out.

When Maddoc's body steps between my legs, I look up.

He studies me, a bemused expression etched across his perfect face.

"What?" I breathe.

Before he can answer, Captain bounds around the corner, a deep frown in place.

Something's wrong.

When Maddoc moves, I do too.

"Cap, what is it?" I ask him cautiously.

He looks between the three of us. "We gotta fight. Don't ask me why."

"I'll get the car." Maddoc disappears.

"I'll lock up." Royce disappears.

Just like that, no questions asked, no answers needed, three becomes one.

A small grin starts to form on my lips when my name is called from the doorway.

Maddoc stands there, his green eyes zoned in on me. He tips his chin and when his hand reaches out my heart stops.

I look to Captain.

There's no scowl, no annoyance, and no demand. He won't be hurt if I stay back, doesn't expect me to take on his trouble, but he hopes I want to.

I grab my jacket from the edge of the couch and slide past him, patting his chest as I do.

I step in front of Maddoc, keeping my eyes locked on him as I slip my fingers into his. The corners of his eyes dip when I squeeze, then we're out the door.

Everything happens quickly from there. The boys leap in, we skirt off and game faces slip over their eyes – masks without the mask.

We pull up at a house I've never seen on a street I've never been down and jump out.

Music blares from the inside and several cars line the street.

The boys don't wait but charge for the door. The two fall back slightly, letting Captain take the lead on this one.

Maddoc leans toward me as we approach the door. "Stay close to me."

I shoot him a wink, embracing the adrenaline that forms in the pit of my stomach as it always does before a fight, and rush in after Royce, leaving Maddoc as the last to step past the entryway.

And big man doesn't do subtle or sneaky. He loves a good and loud entrance.

I smile when he slams the door, making a show of locking it behind him.

All eyes shift our way and a few girls shriek.

And all hell breaks loose.

Captain charges forward, rushing a guy who tries to stand against him. He tosses his ass and keeps going for a taller, more built guy a few steps behind him.

I jump when Royce rams a guy into the entertainment center right in front of me and shift back.

Maddoc lands a blow to another guy's ribs, making him fall to the floor before spinning to wrap another in a headlock.

I look back to Captain in time to see him lift the big guy off the ground and slam him into the kitchen table, making the wooden legs beneath it give out.

He hops on top and concern has me running forward.

A drunk bitch shoves me from the side as I pass and I hit the wall.

I spin on my heels and grip her under her armpits, driving her against the wall. I don't even have to hit her because she's so sloppy her head smacks hard enough to take her vision. I let go and she crashes to the floor.

A guy tries to block my advance, but I rip the bottle from his hand and before he can stop me, I crash it into his head, nailing him in the nuts with my knee in the same second.

I step over him, tripping on my face when he grips my ankle.

I plant my hands on the floor and kick, but he yanks me back. His hand reaches my waistband, and he jerks but then a deep grunt leaves him and I scramble away, glancing back to find Maddoc's fist in his face.

I look to Captain who is still beating the shit out of the guy on the ground who is quickly losing his ability to block the blows.

I glance back at Maddoc and his head pops up, motioning for me to go.

I pop up and dart forward.

Captain's knuckles are split open, blood from his hand and the guy's face making for a nasty scene.

A guy tries to pull Captain off and he flings his head back, head-butting the dude who flies back, tripping over a tossed chair. He goes forward again, but I pick up a piece of split wood and hit him behind the knee, knocking his feet from beneath him.

I turn, finding Royce standing with a ripped shirt, glaring at a guy on the floor.

"Royce!" I shout and both his and Maddoc's heads snap up.

I move so they see Captain and they rush forward.

This time, nobody tries to stop them.

They yank their brother off the guy who lays limp.

He jerks from their hold and together we rush back toward the door, but when Maddoc yanks it open, something has me pausing.

I glance back, finding a girl I didn't notice before hiding off to the side, tears running down her face. She glances at Captain, who spits blood on the floor as he continues toward us.

I stop and look to Cap. He just whooped some serious ass, yet his chin hangs to his chest.

Defeat. Regret.

I look to the girl who does the same.

Fuck. That.

I move forward and when Captain grabs my elbow on my way past, I jerk free, not meeting his eyes, not taking mine off hers. "Just one."

The girl's eyes stay on Captain, but when I'm a foot in front of her, they flick to mine. She doesn't flinch, doesn't fret or look away. She knows it's coming and for whatever reason has decided she deserves it.

Good.

I swing, hitting her right in the jaw and she stumbles back. Her friends shriek and rush to her side.

I turn around, walk past the boys and lead us out the door and into the vehicle.

Once we pull in front of their house, Captain sighs and drops his head against the seat.

Royce lifts a hand, smacking it down on his brother's shoulder. He squeezes.

I sit forward and lean my head against the side of the seat, inspecting Cap's bloody hands. "Come on, Packman. We need to ice those babies."

His head jerks and he curses like he just saw the damage done.

He steps out slowly and so does Royce.

When Maddoc holds back, I turn to him.

With a frown on his face, he inspects his own knuckles.

He glances at me.

"What?"

He licks his lips, reaching for his door handle. "Nothing."

I meet Captain in the upstairs bathroom. He tries to push me off, but I smack him, and he chuckles, finally propping himself against the counter so I sit on the toilet and play doctor to his wounds.

He hisses when I pour the hydrogen peroxide on it.

"Don't be a baby," I tease, earning a half smile.

After the right is done, I move to the left.

"You really not gonna ask?"

I look up confused. "Ask?"

His brows lift. "Seriously? You don't wanna know why we went there, who they were. You ... the girl..."

I shrug and go back to work, tilting his hand to see how far the cut goes. "It's not my place, Packman. Besides, you told us not to ask so why would I?"

"Because you don't listen to shit," he laughs, and I join in.

"Yeah, but this is different. This isn't about me, this was personal. I'm betting there isn't much in your guys' lives that you get to keep just for you." I pat the final bandage and he flexes his hand.

I sit back.

"You'd be right, there isn't." He eyes me, crossing his arms over his chest. "If you wanna ask, I'll tell you a little bit."

I laugh and stand, tossing the wrappings in the garbage. "Sorry, Packman. I'm not gonna make this easier for you by doing what you pretend you don't want." When his frown drops to his chest, I keep going. "When you're ready to talk, you will on your own. You gotta be strong enough to make that choice by yourself."

He glares at me and I lift my shoulders.

I go to walk past, but he grabs hold of me, pulling me in. He squeezes me tight against him, and I let him, wrapping my hands around his lower back.

A shuddered breath leaves him and unease grows in my stomach.

My eyes lift, connecting with Maddoc's in the hallway.

"Don't fuck this up for us, Raven," Captain whispers. "We need this. He needs you."

Maddoc's eyes search mine and I drop mine to the floor.

I slip from his hold, past Maddoc, and into my room.

The room. Not my room.

Shit.

I start pacing, running my hands down my hair, I lift the ends, inspecting the blue I touched up this morning.

I move to the window, pulling it open. I take a deep breath of fresh air, spinning to sit on the sill.

I close my eyes.

These boys, they're making me feel what they feel. I can't stop it.

I shouldn't be here.

I shouldn't feel the need to protect them.

I shouldn't want to.

I shouldn't—

My door is thrown open and Maddoc charges in.

He stops right in front of me, a wild glare making his green eyes appear darker.

I shouldn't...

I reach up, grip the inside front collar of his shirt and yank his lips to mine.

I kiss him, hard, punishing and fucking reckless, and he meets my demand with anger of his own.

His tongue sweeps mine and I push back, fighting for control he won't give.

I bite his lip until he growls and yanks away.

He glares and so do I.

I stalk past him, rushing into the bathroom, closing and locking it behind me.

I turn on the shower and start stripping.

I'm an idiot.

I kissed him.

And I'm pretty sure I'll do it again.

The lock jiggles for a half second and then the door is thrown open and slammed shut in the same second.

Maddoc holds up a bobby pin, tossing it to the floor. He stalks over to me, so I hop in the water with my top still on and slink back against the wall.

He steps in, clothes and all and presses himself against me, the rough material of his jeans rubbing against my clit.

I drop my head back and his eyes trail my chin and neck. He doesn't move back to look over me but grips my jaw instead.

His eyes bounce between mine, and then his mouth crashes against mine.

I moan, growing limp and he presses close to hold me up,

his own groan escaping. His hands move to my waist and slide down my wet ass. He grips my ass cheeks tight, spreading them slightly as he pushes harder against me.

My entire body shakes and he grins against my mouth.

And then he's gone, and I'm left panting in the shower with nothing but my fingers to get the job done.

Chapter 37

Raven

"You're sick," I laughed at Royce as he dips his pizza in his soda then stuffs the entire thing in his mouth. I bump his shoulder. "Move, I'll wait outside."

He grins with his mouth full and I roll my eyes, sliding from the booth.

"I gotta take a piss, here." He hands me the keys and disappears.

I walk out front and toward the car, but stop when Collins plants his feet in front of me.

"Hello again, Rae."

"Collins, we really need to stop meeting like this." I give him a blank stare.

"We could..." He steps closer and my spine straightens. "Meet at my house or a hotel room."

I scoff and glance off.

"I've got five grand with your name on it."

"Five grand, huh?" I pop a brow. "That what I'm worth to

you?"

He smirks, showing off his movie star veneers. "Ten if you help me out."

Ten thousand dollars – chump change to this asshole.

"Sorry, Collins." I shrug. "I don't have the cure for erectile dysfunction. Not really sure what I'd be able to do for you."

I push past him.

Royce walks out then, Captain behind him and they both stop when they see Collins on the sidewalk.

He looks from them to me. "Think about it, Carver. That's a game changer for you."

I keep my face blank – the bastard was serious.

"Get the fuck out of here, Collins. Graven ain't nowhere near here, pretty boy," Royce tells him and Collins jerks a chin, turning to walk off.

"What was that about?" Royce waits to ask when Collins can't hear.

"Rich boy doing what rich boys do. Trying to throw money around to get his way."

Both frown but neither says another word.

"Where's Maddoc at today?"

"He went to see our dad."

Uh ... what?

"He do that often?"

"Nope," Royce replies and looks to Cap.

Captain clears his throat, but nobody says a word. Really, I shouldn't have asked.

The three of us climb in – I let Captain have shotgun – and head back for the house.

"I've got a hot date with a freshly waxed vagina, so I'll slow to a roll, but you guys gotta jump."

"You're an idiot." Captain shakes his head. "We're in my truck. Park the damn thing and get your ass out."

Royce hops out grinning and runs to his own vehicle as

Captain steps out the passenger door and when it's clear he's rounding the hood and making his way back to the driver's seat, I leap over the middle console and into the passenger seat.

Captain yanks his door open, his eyes snapping to mine. "What are you doing?"

"I'm bored."

"I can't help you, I gotta go."

I pull the seat belt over me and he frowns.

"Raven, out."

When I sit back against the seat, he steps back and charges around the hood.

I swiftly lock the doors then jump over the seat to close his.

He bangs on my window and I grin.

"Open the fucking door."

I turn up the radio, pretending I can't hear.

He turns to Royce, who is backing out past us and throws his hands up. "A little help here."

"Can't. Fresh. Waxed. Vagina, Cap." Royce slides on his sunglasses and peels away.

Captain runs his hands down his face before glaring at me. "Raven, I need to leave. Now. I cannot be late."

"Get in then."

He hesitates a minute, then curses and heads around again.

I unlock the door and he jumps inside.

He doesn't look at me as he pulls out and on to the road. The first twenty minutes we're on the road, I take in my surroundings – nothing but orchards and corn and boring shit. But when I'm over it and ready to complain about where we're headed and cry about how much longer, I look to Cap, who glares at the road.

His leg is bouncing, his fingers keep flexing against the wheel, and he keeps taking deep breaths. He's anxious.

The vehicle slows and he turns down a small side road. He starts bouncing his shoulders as if he's trying to shake loose, and slips into the first spot he finds, facing an open field that dips down. If all the families shuffling in and out of the cars around means anything, I'd guess there's a park at the end.

He looks at his watch, then his phone, then his watch again.

"Cap ..."

"Just ... quiet, Raven. Please."

I pull back, shocked and a little unsure what this is about, so I attempt to lighten the mood.

"Wow, Captain," I feign annoyance and he drops his head back, not at all wanting to deal with, well, me. "I had no idea you were aware 'please' was a thing."

He scoffs, a small laugh in there somewhere and drops his eyes to me. After a minute he says, "You shouldn't be here."

I shrug, because too late now, right?

I look away, sinking back only to lean forward when I spot someone. I squint to see better. "Is that ... that's my social worker."

Captain's head snaps forward and he curses. He blows out a deep breath and climbs out. Before his door slams, he turns back, leveling me with a hard look I've yet to see from him. "Stay in here, Raven. I mean it."

His words are strong, but there's something deeper than anger in his eyes.

"Okay." I nod and he pauses a second, before walking away.

I sit back in my seat, crossing my legs Indian style as I trail his every step across the grass. He stops a few feet from Ms. Vega. A few words are exchanged, and then she turns and walks away. I look back to Captain, but he doesn't move, his eyes follow her.

Just as I look back, a streak of blonde catches my eye.

"What the..."

Captain bends at the knee and a teeny tiny little thing, with a little blonde, bouncy ponytail, and chubby cheeks runs straight into his open arms.

My jaw drops.

Captain buries the little one against his chest and her baby hand sneaks over his shoulder and pats. He pulls back to look at her, only to hug her close again.

He stands, lifting her with him.

And then he carries her down the hill as she giggles in his arm, patting his cheeks playfully.

I'm not sure how long I stare after the two, but when I snap out of it, I lay flat in the front seat, staring up at the roof forcing myself to think of any and everything other than that fact that I just forced him to share something he wasn't ready to.

Captain was right, I shouldn't have come.

The door opens and closes with a soft thud.

I wait for the engine to start but nothing happens, so I don't move.

After about five minutes, his low sigh has my chest growing tight.

"You can stop pretending to be asleep now, Carver."

"I don't wanna look at you, Cap. I'm a bitch."

"That's not news to me."

My eyes pop open and I slowly sit up when a hint of a smile hits his lips.

"I shouldn't have forced you to bring me," I tell him.

"Nope, you shouldn't have," he agrees. "But you did and now here we are."

"Cap... I..." I throw my hands up and shrug.

"You can't tell anyone."

"I don't have anyone to tell."

"I'm not playing." His tone is sterner this time.

I shrug again. "Neither am I, Cap. I have no one to tell, but even if I did, I wouldn't."

He eyes me a minute before nodding back and then we're back on the road.

I try not to stare as he drives, but it's impossible.

He's smiling so bright, probably replaying the last hour in his head, but it's short-lived and the closer we get to the house, the more his shoulders sag, and his face morphs back into the blank stare he shares with the world.

"Do they know?" I ask him quietly.

"They're my brothers. They know everything..." He trails off.

"But?"

He swallows. "But they haven't met her yet."

"Well," I whisper. "She's beautiful, Packman."

He smiles wide, a light laugh leaving him.

I bet he's picturing her little curls and the sound of her voice.

"Tell me her name?"

His features tighten along with his grip on the wheel. "Not today."

"Fine." I bounce in my seat, knowing neither of us needs to go back like this. "Take me to get ice cream then."

Captain throws a grin my way. "All right. Ice cream I can do."

Maddoc

I jog down the stairs, moving to check the garage, finding nobody. I pull out my cell.

"Yo?" Royce answers on the first ring.

"Where the fuck you guys at?"

I look over when the front door opens and Royce holds his hands out, the phone still to his ear.

I roll my eyes and toss mine to the couch. "Where'd you guys go?"

"I went to Rumi Grey's house for some solid cardio."

I look past him, but he shuts the door.

His frown meets mine. "What's up?"

"Where's Raven?"

"With Cap, I think."

"Nah, man, it's the second Sunday of the month."

"Fuck." He winces. "I forgot. It was my turn to make a plan for tonight this time."

"It's cool. I'll message the team, tell them to gather some people and meet at the party pad. But where the fuck is Raven?"

"No idea, but chill. She's probably hiding in the trees smoking or something." He grabs a water from the fridge and we both drop on the couch.

I turn on the TV, but when a half hour passes, I turn it off and sit back.

When Royce sits forward instantly, I know I'm not the only one on edge here.

"Think she's fighting?"

I frown. "No. Told Bishop if he so much as invited her to watch a fucking fight, he'd get his ass beat and lose his gig."

Royce nods. "She wouldn't leave would—"

The front door flies open, banging against the security screen as it does. Raven stumbles in as Captain tries to keep her steady and carry a bag of shit at the same time. She trips, catching herself with her palms against the wall, and starts laughing, dropping her head lazily.

Captain laughs and moves to help her, but she only trips over his shoe and smacks her ass on the hardwood.

She laughs harder, her dark hair falling all in her face.

Royce and I glance at each other and slowly stand.

Raven drops onto her back, spotting us from upside down.

"Oh." She smiles. "Hey."

I look to Captain. "She drunk?"

"Yeah, actually." He laughs, setting the bag down that he was holding so he can help her to her feet. "We stopped for ice cream and she had the bright idea to make vodka floats."

She clings to him and my eyes shift to his.

Royce walks over then and lifts her over his head.

"Hey!" she playfully scolds him but laughs as he carries her up the stairs.

When I look back, Captain's eyes pinch at the sides. "Don't, brother," he speaks low.

"You took her with you. To see Zoey."

"She wouldn't get out, couldn't be late." He shrugs like it's no fucking big deal.

I narrow my eyes and he looks away.

"Guess I didn't fight her on it too much."

Holy shit.

My eyes widen. "You trust her."

He looks down a moment, and when he looks back, it's clear. "Guess I do. How 'bout you?"

"I don't know," I answer honestly. "Does Royce?"

"Maybe not all the way yet but it's happening slowly. He wants to trust her."

Fuck.

"Should we?" I ask him and he gives a small smile.

"I don't know, my man. Guess we'll find out." Captain pats my shoulder as he walks past and into the kitchen. "So, what'd the old man have to say?"

"Wild guess." I drop onto the stool, running my hands through my hair.

"Heard we were at the warehouse."

"Yup."

"Fuck." Cap spreads his hands out on the counter, his chin dropping to his chest.

"What's going on?" Royce walks in and I motion for him to sit beside me.

He frowns but sits.

"It was what we thought. Dad got word we were at the warehouses that night."

"And Raven." Royce scans my face. "If he heard we were there, he knows damn well she was."

"He's right," Cap says, pushing off the countertop.

"He didn't mention her, so neither did I." I look from Royce to Captain. "That shit Collins said that day was true. He told me tonight. He's up for parole in a few months."

Captain's hands instantly go to his hair and he runs them down his face while Royce throws himself from the stool and starts pacing.

"Maddoc..." Captain shakes his head, dread all over his face. "I..."

"I know." I shoot to stand and both Royce and I make our way to Cap. I grip both their shoulders and they do the same. "We won't let him come in and ruin shit. Getting Zoey is priority."

"I'm not ready to tell him about her." Captain's features tighten.

"I know." I nod. "I doubt he'll get it. They're not just gonna take his word on being a changed man or fucking whatever the first go. We'll deal with it as it comes."

"Yeah, all right."

Royce nods too and then we hear a bang and laughter up the stairs.

Royce grins despite the shittiness we all feel when our brother comes home helpless like tonight.

"Forgot. She asked me to help her get in the shower."

My frown is instant, and he laughs, holding his hands up.

"I told her to wait a minute and I'd be back." He grins. "Thought we'd play a game of sending you up there and see if she was too drunk to notice."

I scoff and Captain laughs lightly.

"She's not that drunk. Just feeling good."

"How 'bout you, Cap?" I ask him.

He sighs. "I'm good, man. Zoey's getting bigger every time I see her. I just ... hate driving away without her. She cried when she got put in the car today. That shit fucked me up." He looks between us, then glances past us. "Raven." He swallows. "She's intuitive. That's what the ice cream fun was about. Doubt she'd admit it, but she understands us. I'd say she cares, boys. We need to be careful with her."

Unsure of what to say I head for the stairs.

Chapter 38

Raven

I yank at my socks, falling against the wall with a loud thud.

"Whoops," I laugh, tossing one to the floor and move to start on the other.

"What the hell are you doing?"

My head jerks toward the door, but my hair falls in my face, blocking my view. "Trying to get this shit off but my arms aren't working."

His deep chuckle has me shaking my head in an attempt to see him better, but more hair sticks to my face from the steam that's overtaken the bathroom.

His fingers touch my forehead and he pushes it away.

He's so close, bent in front of me like he would be if he were tossing my legs over his shoulders so he could bury his face between my legs.

My tongue slides between my teeth.

"Stop."

"Stop what?" I ask, but my eyes continue to travel the curve of his shoulders and down his arm.

"Letting your horny show."

"Can't help it." I throw my hand forward, weakly squeezing the packed muscles of his biceps. "You try sitting a foot from a beast in the flesh with crazy eyes and a dirty smirk and let's see if your thong stays dry."

The bounce of his shoulders has my eyes lifting.

"There's that smirk I'm talking about."

"Your shower's getting cold."

"Yeah. But I need food."

"Can you stand?"

"I'm too lazy."

He sighs but moves his hands beneath my arms and yanks me off the floor, and right into him.

I laugh and turn, planting my hands on the wall behind him. His brows lift just the slightest. "You ever let a girl run the show, big man?"

"No."

"Never let her push you into a wall and pin you there?" I run a finger along the collar of his shirt. "Never let her do as she pleases, tease until you can't hang and beg for her to wrap her lips around your dick?"

He drops his head back. "I wouldn't need to beg. I'd push her to her knees, and she'd be lucky to put me in her mouth."

A small hum leaves me, and I rest my weight against him, his hand coming around to keep me still. "I wasn't talking about those lips, big man. I'm talking her pussy lips. You never begged to slide in a girl's heat, never 'bout died to feel her suck you in and squeeze to try to keep you there?"

He groans, and I'm quickly spun around, so my back is now to the wall.

"Like I said. No. Now you want me to take your clothes off for you or not?"

"No."

His forehead pinches. "No?"

"No."

"Royce said you needed help undressing."

"I lied."

"Why?"

"To get him to go away. He was giving me the look."

Maddoc's stare shifts between mine and he steps back. "What look?"

"You know, the open-eyed, flat-lipped look you guys got going on lately. Like you're trying to figure me out. I don't like it."

"Maybe we just wanna know you."

"Maybe I don't want you to."

"Maybe you should get over that." Maddoc frowns and moves into the hall. "Starting dinner in an hour."

He gets a few feet away when I call his name.

He pops his head back in.

"Is Cap ... I don't wanna come down if he's got that beaten look on his face again."

Maddoc licks his lips as he searches my eyes. He nods his head. "He's good, Raven."

When he walks away, I peel my clothes off my body and by the time I get into the shower, Maddoc was right. It's cold as hell, so I quickly wash and get out, wrapping the towel around me as I run into my room.

I drop back on my mattress and stare at the ceiling a minute before grabbing a water bottle off the nightstand. I down it then pull myself up again.

I pull on a pair of black sweatpants, socks, and a random shirt and head for the kitchen, running my fingers through my hair as I do.

"Whatcha makin'?" I slink beside Maddoc and he scoots over for me to see the veggies he's cut up.

He smacks my hand when I try to snag a piece of broccoli, so I snag a piece of bread instead – it'll help with the alcohol better.

"Quick beef and broccoli." He glances my way as he shifts for the sink to rinse his hands. "Wanna start the rice?"

My nose scrunches. "Uhh ... sure?"

He eyes me. "You don't know how."

"I mean, you got instant rice? I can pop it in the microwave like a champ."

He leans back crossing his arms. "You know how to cook at all?"

I lift a shoulder, leaning back on the opposite side of the kitchen. "I'm sure I could if I read instructions, but can I slide in here and make magic? No."

He nods and pulls a pot from under the counter. He hands me a measuring cup and tells me what to do. We get the rice rinsed, the water measured and I look back to him.

"So how do you know when it's hot enough?"

"What?"

"The stove."

He frowns at me. "Have you never cooked before?"

"Made pancakes at the Bray house, but Victoria helped me out, reluctantly. What I did isn't really considered cooking, but I have made spaghetti a bunch of times."

"And you don't know how a stove works?"

"Never had one."

His forehead pinches. "How'd you cook the meat?"

"We didn't use meat. Cost too much. We could go to the ninety-nine- cents store and get a pack of noodles and a can of sauce for two bucks. That was like three meals for us if it was only us two. Four or five if I was home alone."

He drops his stare to the counter and turns back to the food.

"We had a hot plate for a while. My mom would make

things if she got a hair up her ass, which was maybe once a month if that. She usually ate out with her clients, though, so I'd heat up a hot dog or soup or something."

"She'd go out to a restaurant and leave you there with nothing?"

"It's not a big deal. It was normal where I lived, other kids were running around late, scrounging just like me."

He frowns. "Have you lived in the same place all your life?"

I jump up on the counter. "Yep. Same trailer since I was born. Out of all my mother's fuck ups, she at least did that right. We didn't always have food or hot water, electricity was off a lot, but she never did lose the place." I scoff as I think about it. "Probably 'cause then she'd have to spend some of her payment on a hotel room like most the other girls she ran tricks with, but no, she liked to pocket as much as she could."

Maddoc drops the knife in the sink with force, spinning to glare at me. "She'd fuck around with you there?"

Almost every single night.

I lift a shoulder.

"Raven."

I shake my head and look over at him, finding he has a death grip on the counter. "It's life, big man."

He gets in my face, misplaced anger staring back at me. "That's not life. That's a piece of shit person putting her daughter in danger."

I eye him and the longer I do, the more his worry seeps through.

He jerks away when my hand lifts and goes back to the job at hand.

"Check your rice, Raven."

I roll my eyes and jump down.

Like I know what that means.

"Yo." The other two walk in, beers in hand.

Cap laughs at me. "He put you to work?"

"He's trying to teach me." I lift a fork of white mush. My shoulders fall. "But I'm a shit student in all areas, it seems."

"You still feelin' the vodka floats?"

"Nope. Now I'm feeling the pounding on my temples."

He and Royce laugh and start pulling out the dishes and shit for dinner.

We all move to the table like we've done every night since they pulled me into their little world.

Little world...

I look to Cap and right as I do, his eyes lift to mine and he gives a small, sad smile.

I drop mine to my plate.

"Her name is Zoey."

My head snaps up and all movement around the table pauses. Dead fucking silence surrounds us, no one even dares chew.

"She's two," he continues. "Be three in June."

My ribs start to ache. "What color are her eyes?" My question comes out quieter than I planned.

His mouth twitches. "Sometimes green, sometimes blue."

"Like yours."

He laughs lightly while nodding. He drops his eyes to his food. "Just like mine."

"Captain..." I breathe, glancing from Royce to Maddoc, both who stare at me.

I don't want to ask, but I want to know everything. So I wait.

"She's with a foster family."

I frown, sitting back in my chair.

"Zoey's mom hid the pregnancy from me. I had no clue I was going to be a dad until after I already was."

"What the fuck?"

"She was there, all was good, then Perkins called her from class that afternoon."

Fuuuck. Now it makes sense why they freaked after my meeting with him.

He got in her head.

"She was gone after that. Took off, hid away, and came back in the summer. When school started, she was suddenly going to Graven," he continued.

"I didn't care. I wanted nothing to do with her when she showed back up, wrote her off completely. But someone wanted me to know." He looks to his brothers who offer small nods of encouragements. "Found delivery records in my gym bag two weeks into school. Confronted her, finally got the truth from her. Then I found out she signed over her rights, gave my little girl up."

"She can't just do that. How did she just ... do that?"

"She lied to the right people. Said she didn't know who the father was, so there was no one to fight her on it."

"Captain..."

He drops back in his chair. "I went straight to Maybell. She helped me get everything ready so I could bring her home, but Perkins showed up the night before the hearing."

"Here?"

"Here. He had been collecting shit on us, did some digging, found out some things. Said I'd lose her for good if I tried. Said no court would let her go to a home where we lived with no adults and had a few dozen troubled fuckers on our property. Technically we can't live how we do, but Maybell makes sure we're covered there. It was too risky. So I went, took what the court offered when I should have fought harder. They gave me visitation twice a month, fucking supervised until they decide I'm fit to parent." His laugh is hollow, and I want to cry. "My daughter can't even meet her uncles."

I shoot from my seat and move to the other side of the table. I drop onto his lap, aware the other two are watching, aware Maddoc is watching, and run my hand through his hair, until he looks up at me. I don't care that it seems intimate. He needs this. "You did what you thought you had to be a part of her life. There's nothing wrong with that," I whisper.

His hand slides up my leg and I move mine to cover his, squeezing lightly. Deep creases frame his eyes and his nostrils flare. His grip on me tightens.

I slide my hand down the back of his hair, bringing my forehead to his.

"Captain," I breathe and his shuddered exhale fans across my mouth. When he swallows, I tip his head back slightly so I can softy press my lips to his temple. It's not much, but something tells me he needs it.

I pull back, my hands sliding down until I'm cupping his cheeks. "Don't ever feel like you've failed her. You didn't. You made an impossible decision because it guaranteed you a place in her life. It's what a good man would do."

He blows out a ragged breath, drops his forehead to my shoulder, nodding against me.

I move back to my seat.

When I glance at Royce, I find him watching me. He winks and cuts his eyes to Maddoc.

I look to my left, but Maddoc's gaze isn't on me. He's frowning at his plate, so I grip his chin and force his stare to mine.

I drop my hand to squeeze his knee, and his shoulders relax a bit.

When I go to finally take a bite, a flash of blonde clicks in my mind. I gasp, my head snapping up to meet Captain's eyes. "Oh my God!"

"What?" he asks wearily, looking from the boys to me.

"Raven," Maddoc rumbles unsure.

With a groan, I run my hands down my face. "That was her, wasn't it?"

First, he frowns and then a grin splits his lips.

"I punched your baby mama, didn't I?"

The wretched look in his eye disappears, and he starts cracking up, Royce too. But Maddoc's lip only twitches.

"Aye, yeah." Royce leans forward. "What made you do that?"

"I saw her look at you guys, saw the guilt in her eyes, watched her watch Captain." I shrug. "I could tell she deserved it."

If I'd have known what I do now then, I'd probably be in jail. Taking away a child from a loving parent like that is sick. I don't care who the person is.

Captain looks down a moment, and when he lifts his head, a fierce glaze comes over his eyes. "She's mine when I turn eighteen."

I nod, having expected him to say that next.

"Why did Perkins step in at all, what was the point?"

Captain looks to Royce then Maddoc, who tips his chin. "We're still trying to figure that one out."

When Captain glances at Maddoc before dropping his gaze to the floor, I turn to look at him.

"What?"

His eyes shift between mine, tension clouding his features.

"Look." I pull my legs up on the chair. "You guys started talking first, so naturally I have questions, but that doesn't mean you have to tell me shit. We can keep talking, or we can clean this shit up and go to your little party. It's whatever."

"We found old yearbooks in a couple boxes in the rafters out back," Royce throws out before anyone else has a chance to speak. "There's a picture of our dads with Perkins and another guy. His arms around his shoulder and they're smiling. Prom or some shit."

"Okay... so they knew each other. You think something happened?" I ask and they nod.

"We don't know anything else. We've searched through everything over the last fucking year and found nothing."

I lick my lips, hesitation pulling at my brows. "When you say you looked through everything. What do you mean?"

"Old files and records, random shit our dad saved."

I take a deep breath and stand.

Fuck it.

"Where you going?" Maddoc asks, low and cautious.

"I have something that might help."

"The fuck does that mean?" Maddoc leaps to his feet. "Have what?"

I don't answer but run up the stairs, ignoring all their chatter as I do. I dig the binder I stole from Maybell's out of the back of the closet where I stuffed it when I got here and head back down the stairs.

They jump to their feet when I appear on the stairs, heading back down.

I lift it higher and Maddoc charges for me.

He glares at the item. "What is this?"

"I stole it from Maybell." I hand it over, but he only stares. "I think it belongs in your guys' hands anyway. Take it, Maddoc."

His face turns hard and he locks his eyes on me as he snatches it from my fingers. He lifts it over his shoulder and Royce appears, pulling it from his hand.

Maddoc steps back, and all three stare my way, anxious and angry. Maybe a little unsure.

"What's in it?" he asks.

"Look for yourself."

"I asked you a question, Raven."

I gesture toward the binder. "Bunch of shit, I don't know."

"Did you read them?"

"Flipped it open, saw the letter in the front but didn't read it or anything else in there."

His jaw locks. "Why should we believe you?"

I look between the three. "You shouldn't."

"Raven," he growls, and it has my spine vibrating as a small slice of fear hits me.

"Look, I know some things I've heard from the girls at the house, but I didn't read anything in there to know if any of it is true."

"What is it you think you know?" His voice is clipped. "Just say it."

"Rumor at the house is your parents ran in the same circle, but only your biological dad made it out of a deal gone wrong. He became a father to all of you, but got locked up a few years later." I tell them the rest of what Victoria told me, about the moms and Maybell caring for them.

"You were just waiting to use this as ammo?"

"Ammo for what, Maddoc?"

Royce flips open the top and starts rummaging, brows furrowed.

"Everything is in here, Maddoc. Birth certificates, hospital records, staffing reports." He looks to me, but the anger is gone and something I can't read covers his eyes instead.

Captain and Royce rush from the room with the binder, but Maddoc only stares.

When I start to walk away, he darts to the side to block me.

His eyes burn with an intensity I've never seen. I take a few steps back.

"You have had that this entire time and didn't say anything."

"I wasn't sure I should."

"No." He creeps closer, shaking his head. "You've had that, all our fucked-up secrets, our fucked-up pasts and problems in your hands and you didn't say anything."

I can't argue, it's true. I should have given it to them the day I got it, yet here we are.

"You didn't blackmail. You didn't expose." His chest is touching mine now. He tilts my head back with a knuckle under my chin. "You held on to it. Why?"

"Nothing in there is anyone else's business." My eyes shift between his when he pulls his lips between his teeth. "It's your lives."

He tilts his head, his thumb lifting to brush across my bottom lip. His voice is so low I almost don't hear it.

"Why you always protecting us?" he breathes.

I inhale a choppy breath, shaking my head lightly. I whisper back, "I don't know."

He drops his hand and steps back. "I believe you."

With that, he goes to meet his brothers.

And I stand there, wondering what the hell I'm doing here.

I head for my room.

Pulling the blanket from the bed, I grab my stash from the drawer and drop in the recliner in front of the window. I unlock it and push it open.

I put the joint to my lips and light the tip, puffing lightly as I spin it in my fingers to get a good burn going.

I run over to my door and flip off the light, the moon giving me more than enough light to be comfortable. I plop into the chair again and close my eyes, letting the early December breeze wash over my face as I take a hit.

The joint's half gone when my door swings open and Royce steps inside.

"Told you no drugs in the house."

"It's an herb. And technically it's legal so, not necessarily a drug."

He scoffs and moves to sit across from me.

He stares at me a moment too long so I pass the goods and after a second of hesitation, he grabs it and takes a hit.

We sit like that, in the semi-dark, smoking weed, without saying another word.

When it's too small to grip with our fingers, he puts it out in the soda can we've been ashing in.

He steps in front of me and I offer a small smile.

He nods his head, drops down to kiss my hair and walks out.

I watch him go and the second his feet pass the door frame, Captain steps into the doorway. He looks the way Royce disappeared and then back to me.

He stares just the same.

"Night, Cap," I call out, giving him the okay to not say a word. It's not necessary.

When Cap looks behind him, I know who is coming next.

Captain steps into his room but leaves his door open and Maddoc steps toward mine. He stops to lean on the frame.

He glares at the soda can.

"Come here," I tell him, and his eyes snap up. "Shut the door."

He's slow to move but does as he was told, even doing one better when he bends to scoop me from the chair and deposits me on the bed.

He climbs up, nudging my legs apart so he can rest his between mine, his hands planted near my head to hold him above me.

His eyes are more forest green than jade as he stares down at me.

"Talk," he demands softly.

"I don't want to talk, big man." I run my hands up his biceps, over his shoulders, and into his hair. "I want your mouth on mine. Now."

A deep rumble makes its way up his throat and his hips lower to meet mine.

When I take a deep breath, the corner of his eyes tighten, and his elbows bend, bringing him closer. He runs his lips across my jaw until he reaches my ear.

"Ask nicely, Raven."

A chuckle escapes me.

I yank his hair making him growl, bringing his scowl to me. "You've got a lot to learn." I plant my feet flat on the mattress and grind my hips up into him, loving the way his eyes darkened by the second. "There's nothing nice and sweet about me. If you won't give it..." I whisper, forcing my eyes not to roll back when I swirl my hips against him. I lift my chin. "I'll just take it."

With that, I lift to meet his mouth.

He pretends to deny me for a moment, but big man snaps, his need to be in control taking over and in the next second, my hands are removed from his hair and locked beside me.

He pushes into me, rubbing the zipper of his jeans against my thin sweatpants.

My legs fall open wide, hoping more of him will fill the gap.

His mouth moves to my neck where he sucks and nips as he travels down until the fabric of my T-shirt blocks him.

His mouth comes back to mine.

Fucking finally he releases my hands, his need to touch me overtaking his want to keep me still.

His hands push my shirt up slightly, his grip on my ribs almost too much to stand.

I slide my hands over his shoulders, squeezing at his muscles there, before helping guide his mouth over mine.

He bites my lip when I try to turn his head, making me laugh.

Okay, he's not ready to give me a say.

When his fingertips dig into my back, my legs wrap around his hips, pushing him into me more.

One of his hands curves around me, skimming down my back until he can slip into my bottoms. His fingers spread across my ass cheek and he grips me.

I swallow his groan.

My hands move down to push his shirt up and he lifts for a split second so I can yank it over his head.

When he drops back down a shiver runs through me as his heated skin hits the exposed skin of my stomach and he smirks, his hand moving to slide down the underside of my thigh, adjusting me just the way he wants.

This time, when he grinds into me, my eyes close, my head pushing against the pillow.

"Maddoc," I pant and he growls, grinding into me, and then the bastard pulls away.

He throws himself beside me and my hands slap against the sheets.

I jerk my head to the side to glare at him, but he's covering his face with his arm.

"Are you serious right now?" I complain, and he lifts his arm slightly to glare at me before dropping it back down.

I growl and shoot from the bed.

I pull out another joint I pre-rolled and throw myself into the chair.

When the lighter sparks he jerks upright.

"We said no drugs."

"Yeah, well..." I inhale, turning toward him to blow it out. I glare. "Oops."

He scoots to the edge of the mattress and I scoff when he shifts to adjust his hard-on in his pants.

I look out the window and after a few minutes of silence my shoulders sag and I drop my head back.

"Raven." Where before, his demand was imbued with carefulness, this time it's firm.

Fucking whatever.

I exhale, watching the smoke rise above me before floating out into the night. "How is it, a royal piece of shit like my mother, who hates her daughter, gets to keep me for seventeen years before someone steps in, but someone like Captain, who wants nothing more than to love his child, to hold her every day and show her what she means to him, can't have his for even a night? How does that happen? How is that acceptable?"

"It's not."

I shake my head, unable to forget the way the little girl smiled at her daddy. I blink hard. "The system sucks."

"Raven."

"Stop." I close my eyes, a deep crease taking over my forehead before I can stop it. "Don't say it."

"What you did today..."

"I said don't."

"For us, for Captain. Your need to ease him in a way we can't."

I roll my neck to the side, to meet his stare.

While unease lines his eyes, gratefulness shapes his features.

"It's not a big deal."

"You're wrong." He frowns. "It is a big deal. Real fucking big deal."

I look away.

"We're not sure how to handle you."

I frown at the cherry of my joint. "That's how I like it, big man."

"I don't care what you like. This is our fucking future and you just became a problem."

"Became a problem. Right." I give him a blank stare. "I didn't become anything. I've been the problem and you know it. Now I'm just more dangerous to you because in your world blackmail is a way of life. Well in mine, we don't rat. We don't share detail. When we learn, hear, or see things we turn the other way."

"That's a fool's way of thinking."

"That's a smart man's way of surviving," I bite back. "Life isn't this simple outside your comfort covered issues. You may not have answers to everything, but you have way more than most, Maddoc, and more than the house and the cars and the money, you have Royce and Captain, and they have you. Your side and your back are covered. People like me? We have to sleep with one eye open. I don't need enemies, so why would I make one out of you three?"

"Money."

"Please." I roll my eyes at his attempt to reach for straws. "I can make money at the snap of a finger if I needed to and you know it." It's disgusting but true.

He glares.

I lean toward him.

"Don't let this mixed up sexual tension we've got going make you forget. My being here? That was all you three. You owe me nothing, if you need me to go, tell me and I will."

He leans forward this time, his teeth bared as he growls more than talks. "You still don't get it, do you?"

"What's there to get?"

"We want you here more than we should. All fucking three of us. Maybe even enough to force you to stay if you try to leave."

When my eyes widen, he stomps to the door, but pauses and turns back to me before exiting.

Anger now acts as his shield and his eyes bore into mine. "Touch me again when you're fighting to forget something, and you'll regret it." He leaves.

I drop back against the chair and shake my head.

His words are delivered as a threat, but I know better.

Seems big man wants my all and my not laughing over it proves what a dumb girl I've become.

I need to break away, distance myself and get my head straight.

Even thinking it I know it's a bad idea, but most of mine are so ... fuck it.

Chapter 39

Raven

Since tonight was an away game, more people than last time linger, waiting to see what the boys have planned, no doubt. We played a rare Friday night game, so everyone's extra hyped to get the after-party rolling.

"'Sup, Rae."

I turn to find Bass coming down the bleachers. He drops beside me and raises a brow.

"Watch out Bass, you keep popping up at these kinds of things, I'll start thinking you actually enjoy it."

He nods, spinning his lip ring with his tongue as he eyes me.

"What?"

Laughter fills the room and his gaze flicks over my shoulder.

"Nothing." He stands, making his way down the bleachers. "See ya."

I frown at his back. "Later."

I spin back around right as the team starts to shuffle from the locker rooms, freshly showered and ready to get the night started.

Maddoc steps from the back, looking all dressed to make 'em spread in simple jeans and a T-shirt. That hair perfectly mussed on top. Lazy but sexy. Fresh fade.

He glances my way, doing a double take when he meets my eyes.

The corner of his mouth lifts.

Yeah, he knows he looks good.

In the next second, his attention is captured by a cheerleader for the opposing team. She slides up – literally, slides her foot across the squeaky, freshly polished hardwood – planting her little body in front of him.

My eyes jump to his, following along as his trail over the wide curve of her hips and thick thighs in her short skirt. She's packing way more sex appeal than I ever could.

He smirks and her pretty painted nails plant themselves on his shoulders so she can pull herself up to whisper in his fucking ear.

Acid fills my mouth when his arm wraps around her middle to hold her there and then they stumble back a half step, laughing as he rights them.

"I see things have escalated, huh?"

My eyes snap to Vienna's a moment. "What are you talking about?"

She rolls her eyes. "Please. You're two seconds from shredding a pair of pom-poms."

Both our attention turns back to the boys, all three plus a few extras now standing there with a pack of fucking sharks with pink lips circling, ready to attack their prey.

Maddoc's arm leaves the girl right as his eyes hit mine only to dip back down and whisper in her ear this time.

Are we playing this game, big man?

"He yours, Rae?" Vienna asks.

Apparently not.

My brows snap together at the thought. I don't answer.

"You his?"

His eyes narrow as if he can hear what we're talking about and he takes a half step forward, but another brunette plants herself in front of him.

I look at her.

She doesn't push, but instead asks, "Feel like getting out of here?"

I glance back at the boys, finding each one's focus elsewhere and stand. "Let's go."

"Wait, really?" She smiles wide, then a light squeal leaves her. "Hell yes! Let's bounce!"

I don't turn around again as we exit the gym and make our way to the parking lot to catch up with her other people.

I spot Victoria among them right away.

She scowls, crossing her arms as she waits for me to grow closer.

I shrug. "It wasn't personal, even though it probably felt like it."

Her glare hardens a moment before she rolls her eyes. "Whatever. Wasn't the first time a girl with a chip on her shoulder punched me in the face."

My mouth turns into a grin and hers follows.

"Okay, so since we're all good now, can we get outta here?"

The three of us pile in the rear of the Tahoe while a handful of other girls fill the middle seats and front.

"We're going to hit my house, get sexed up and go dancing!" the driver announces before spinning to face me. "I'm Mello by the way."

I wave, glancing to Vienna who nods lightly, meaning she's cool.

Mello's house is only a few blocks from the school, so we're piling into her room – a pool house built a solid hundred yards away from the main house.

One of the girls starts pouring shots for us while Mello begins tossing random dresses onto the couch.

And just like that, the other girls, Victoria and Vienna included, start stripping and trying on things my mother would die for.

Me? Not so much.

"Here."

I turn and take a plastic shot glass full of something from a redheaded girl.

"I'm Bre."

"Rae."

She giggles, pointing to the side of the cup where she wrote my name in Sharpie. "I know."

She doesn't stand there long enough to see me frown, disappearing to pass shots to the rest of the girls.

I down the contents then set the cup on the coffee table. Glancing around, I'm instantly aware I'm out of my comfort zone.

I should have stayed at the game, waited for the guys.

Watched the girls flock Maddoc.

Wait, no. I don't care.

I roll my eyes at my own damn self.

"Rae, come back here!" Mello calls from around the corner, which is really just a solid wall that separates the bedroom from the living room area.

She smiles, pulling a tiny skirt over her hips. "I thought you might want to pick something else out. You don't strike me as the dress type."

"Not at all."

"That's a shame." She looks me over. "You're fit, bet you'd kill in one."

I don't say anything, and she shrugs, turning to her closet.

"I have tons of jeans in here, some tanks or more dressy shirts." She glances over her shoulder, frowning when she sees mine.

She walks over.

"Look, this might not be your usual thing, dressing up and all, but there's nothing wrong with that. Nobody will think you're being a poser or whatever if you get dolled up with us, not that that's your concern but still. And you can even do it as you. Give me ten minutes and if you hate it, we scratch it and you can wear what you have on." She gestures to my hoodie, jeans and used Hirachis. "The club isn't strict on dress code, it's whatever really, so either way you're fine."

I'm trying to figure out her angle here. Why, would a pretty girl like her, wanna help me "sex up" as she called it. My mind screams set up, but my senses tell me this is just how friends – not that she's mine – do things in a normal high school world. I mean a world where high schoolers have fancy cars and closets the size of my trailer and clubs they can get into.

"No glittery shit," I tell her.

She squeals, moving back to the closet. "I have the perfect outfit in mind."

The shot girl makes her way back, handing me a refilled cup.

"All right." I pull my hoodie over my head and kick my shoes off. "Hit me with it."

"Okay girls!" Mello turns around in the front passenger seat. "If you leave with someone, make sure at least one of us knows so we aren't searching at the end of the night. We can swap clothes back Sunday. We'll have brunch."

She kisses the cheek of the dude she had drive us and we

all climb out, making our way to the door of a place called The Tower.

"Don't say a word, girls, and they'll open the gate," Mello tells us.

Vienna links her arm through mine, pulling on the hem of her dress.

"This thing rides up with each step."

"Exhibit A, why I don't do dresses."

She laughs. "Yeah, well. We can't all pull off a pair of skinny jeans like you."

"Okay, quiet," Mello whispers and we step in front of the bouncers, bypassing the line completely.

"Mello, baby. Missed you last week." The guy unclips the little rope blocking his side of the door.

"Me too, Buck." She leans over, kissing his cheek on her way past and we follow behind her.

The guy's eyes narrow when they hit me, and he glances at his buddy quickly.

I keep quiet through the door but peek behind after I'm down the hall a little, and wouldn't you know both are staring this way.

"Catch you later!" Mello calls out and heads for the left side of the club with two of the other girls.

Me, Victoria, and Vienna, head right as the rest jump straight to the center to dance.

We get a few feet from the bar when Victoria spins around. "Okay, they won't card us now that we're inside, so bar's ours if we want it. I have some cash but not enough for all of us to get drunk on."

Vienna shrugs and glances around, smiling when she spots a guy staring at the end of the bar. "Don't worry about me," she says and walks off.

"Okay then." Victoria snorts and turns back to me.

I pull two twenties from my back pocket, letting her know I'm covered.

We step up to the bar and give our order, but when the dude comes back with our drinks, he doesn't take the money, only points to a group of guys at the nearby table.

The guy at the end leans back in his chair, and blond hair appears.

"Oh hell no."

Collins waves two fingers and I yank Victoria's drink from her hand.

"Hey!" she shouts and follows after me.

When I stop in front of their table, she yanks it back, glaring.

"Raven Carver." Collins leans back with a grin. "Surprised to see you." He glances around.

What he really means is he's surprised to see me without the guys.

"We can pay for our own drinks."

He looks to my cup. "Came straight from the bartender, it's safe. And if you leave it, it'll be wasted. No point in that."

I look around seeing they're all drinking beers like pussies.

I snag Victoria's back, lift both our Jack on the rocks and fling the alcohol across their table.

"What the fuck?!" they shout.

I slam the glass tumblers on the tabletop and move back for the bar, signaling for two new drinks.

"What the hell, Raven?" Victoria complains, sliding up beside me. "That was free!"

"I'll buy you another one. We're not taking shit from him."

She scoffs. "Look who's feeding into all the Brayshaw and Graven shit now."

I spin, getting in her face. "Brayshaw problems or not, Collins is a piece of shit. You want something from someone who will put hands on you without permission, be my fucking guest."

I grab our fresh drinks and turn to hand her hers.

She eyes me warily. "Did he ... I mean, were you ..."

I shake my head. "He'd only got brave a split second before my boys showed up."

She fights a grin and I frown.

"Your boys, huh?"

I drop my eyes to the floor, a light laugh leaving me. "I don't even know. Feels like it sometimes but ... anyway they're for sure flippin' their shit right now."

"Well ..." She trails off and I look up. "Gotta keep them on their toes, right?"

I scrunch my nose and she laughs.

She's not half bad.

"Come on, let's dance." She pulls me along and Vienna meets us halfway, drink in hand.

"You two kiss and make up?" she jokes, but we shrug it off.

We're quick to finish off our drinks and after a second trip to the bar, I'm feeling good. The lights die down, the music shifts, and my body starts to roll on its own.

With Vienna dancing in front of me, Victoria and her new dance partner to my right, Mello and the redhead on my left, I relax a bit without my newfound shadows and let loose, pushing all thoughts from my head for the first time in weeks.

Maddoc

I toss my water bottle in the trash, glancing around the store parking lot.

We came here after the school officials kicked us off the grounds so they could lock up.

"Dude, where the fuck would she go?" Royce complains. "You sure she wasn't in the bathroom?"

"I told you, I checked myself." Captain shrugs. "She wasn't there."

"Think she left with Bishop?" he asks me.

I shake my head. "Bishop was gone before she was. She was talking with that chick from the home."

Leo turns to us then. "Vienna?" he asks, and I glare, waiting for him to talk since it seems he knows who she is. "She was with that Mello chick from West Wood earlier."

"If she's with West Wood girls, they're—"

My phone beeps in my pocket right then and they look at me.

"It's Buck." I look to my brothers. "She's at The Tower."

"Fuck." Royce shakes his head and we slide in the vehicle, Leo and our boy Mac with us.

We head south on the highway and ten minutes later, we're walking toward Buck and the other guard dog.

"You sure she's in there?" We give props and he nods.

"Girl, you sent me that picture of a few weeks ago and told me to tell you if I ever saw her coming in? Yeah, man, I'm sure." He waves a few girls in and they slip past us, dragging their nails across our shirts as they do.

I shrug the last one off and look back to Buck.

"I'd have called you earlier, but got caught up. Dickheads in line started brawling."

I glare. "How long she been here?"

He shrugs. "Hour or so."

Royce shoves past and into the club. We follow.

Leo and Mac make a move for the bar while Cap, Royce and I scan the room.

I tilt my head, peeking through bodies when the ones in the front shift left.

My eyes zone in on shiny black hair.

But the girl in front of me doesn't quite fit my Raven.

"Is she—"

"Did she—"

She sure as fuck did.

Her body continues to sway, more and more until her front is facing us and goddamn, a lax Raven in sweats and T-shirt is sexy, but this Raven is ... fuck me.

She's got on white jeans so tight I might have to cut them off with a tiny ass black top that has half her stomach out and ties around her neck. Her eyes are closed, and framed in jet black color like her hair, and those lips, a little parted and a lot pink.

I hold in my groan.

One of the girls from the home steps up, wedging herself between Raven's legs, and draping her arms over her shoulder.

Raven's quick to grab the chick's hips.

I look to Captain and Royce.

Captain shrugs with a side grin. "I say we let her have some fun."

Raven laughs at the girl in front of her, and then her head lifts.

She spots me instantly and those eyes pop wide open, an obvious "oh fuck" making its way past her painted lips.

Her movements slow as she gauges me, but when I stay planted where I stand a small smirk appears and she winks.

I look to Cap, just about to agree with him, when I get a drug out, "Oh, shit," from Royce, and our eyes cut back to Raven.

A hand reaches between Raven and the girl and they separate. Right as the girl steps back, the hand drops to Raven's waist and she tenses.

And then his head slowly lifts and my blood boils, a fog taking over my eyes.

"Fuck," Cap spits and starts forward, but I stop both him and Royce with a palm raised.

Collins.

Raven attempts to shift, to look over her shoulder, but he holds her head in place.

"Maddoc ..." Royce draws out.

She yanks herself away and spins to face him, getting in his face, arms flailing around like a wild woman.

And he steps closer to her.

I grind my teeth to keep my feet rooted.

"Maddoc," Royce begins to panic.

"Wait."

"You really fucking testing her right now?" he snaps, but I ignore him.

I'm not testing her. I'm giving her what she thinks she wants.

I'm letting her handle shit on her own, like she keeps asking.

She says something that has his chin dropping an inch and fire flares in my muscles.

He might just try and grab her again.

She sees it and moves backward a few steps, and then it happens, like I fucking knew it would.

Her eyes seek mine and a hammering begins in my chest as uncertainty clouds her features.

It's okay to need me, baby...

She's strong, we all know it, but she's afraid to let go, even a little.

Independence and defiance make up a large part of her, but loyalty and hidden longing are in there just the same.

Raven wants what we give her. What she knows damn well

I could give her. She might have been sent here and was never meant to stay, but things have changed. She feels it too.

The longer she stares, the faster her chest rises and falls.

I widen my stance, lifting my chin just a little to encourage, and she takes a step toward me.

But the piece of shit behind her makes a foolish move, desperate to show dominance when he has none, and darts forward, grabbing her elbow hard enough to make her eyes wince. But she doesn't whip around to flash on him, her eyes stay on mine, a fierce expression taking over. She gives a curt nod.

"Now?" Royce growls beside me.

"Now."

My brothers rush forward, and she's released right before Collins is shoved back. He stumbles into the crowded dance floor.

Fists fly, people scream, but Raven doesn't turn around.

She knows they've got it handled, knows where she belongs in this moment and who has her back.

She steps in front of me, her shoes bringing her body more level with mine, but still not equal. She starts chewing on her bottom lip, so I push into her, my thumb coming up to free it, and her mouth follows, holding onto the feeling a second longer.

She doesn't lift her head but watches me through her lashes.

Royce and Captain step up in the next second, and her fingers find mine, lacing ours together.

My eyes hit hers again and she shrugs.

The four of us exit the club.

I release her hand to give a couple twenties to Buck and Raven scoffs.

"Rat bastard," she mumbles, making him grin.

"Name's Buck for a reason, girl!"

She rolls her eyes, and steps ahead of us, her ass bouncing around, hips swaying like fucking crazy in those damn shoes.

"Damn, brother," Royce grunts and I cut a glare his way. "You better wrap that shit up quick before someone else does."

When I shove his ass, he laughs, shoving me back. "Not me, fucker. But hips like that are meant for a good gripping."

Yeah, no shit.

Soon as she hits my ride, she spins on her heels.

Now out in the fresh air, her mind has cleared and she's fired up again, but I'm not having it.

"I don't care what you're about to say." She looks between the three of us. "I can and will come and go as I please. If that's a problem—"

"Stop talking." All eyes swing to me. "It is a problem and you know it. You're also okay with it, and you do care. It's why you left in the first place. You thought we were making plans that wouldn't include you, so you bailed before we could."

"Please," she snaps, but there's no power behind it.

"It's why you were glad when we arrived." I get in her face and she doesn't cower but cuts her eyes left. "It's why, when Collins grabbed you for the second time, your eyes wanted mine."

"I don't know what you're talking about." She licks her lips and damn, if I don't wanna do the same.

I step even closer. "You know, if I were with you, I never would have allowed him close enough to touch you."

She stands tall, ready to sass me when I run my fingertips up her side and her thought dies on her tongue.

"Tell me I'm wrong."

She drops her face into her palms, and I glance at my brothers.

Then she starts laughing.

"Ugh." She pretends to be annoyed, hitting my chest but leaving her palms to rest there. "You guys are impossible!" She laughs, glancing from my brothers to me. "Fine, you're right. There, I said it. Happy?"

"No," I tell her and her eyes slice to mine. "I'm not happy because all this was avoidable. We should have come out together, but you're stubborn as shit and keep fighting yourself when you should have done what you really wanted back at the school."

She fights a grin, want rising in those stormy eyes. "And what'd I really want to do, big man?"

"To put West Wood's cheer captain in check." When she drops her frown to the ground, I force it back up with a knuckle under her chin. "You really think I was up for that?

She shrugs, unapologetic. "Wouldn't blame you if you were."

"You should."

Her features tighten, her eyes shifting to where my brothers stand, staring before coming back.

Leo and Mac step up before anything else can be said.

"Hey." Mac nods. "What do you guys wanna do now?"

Royce shrugs, looks to the club, then back with a grin. "Wouldn't mind some dancing."

Raven scoffs. "Yeah, well, go on ahead then. I'm not going back in tonight after that."

"Thought you didn't care what people thought of you?" Leo asks and my head jerks his way. I don't like the way his eyes narrow on her.

She steps out of my shadow. "I don't. But I also don't feel like spending half the night answering questions and telling girls to fuck off when they beg for introductions."

"Why not introduce them?"

My brows snap together, and I look to Captain, who frowns at the two the same.

"Do you even know your friends, Leo? You think they'd ever entertain the idea of a girl who doesn't have the balls to approach them on her own if she wanted to get friendly? I'll help you out." Her gaze flicks over his form. "The answer is no."

He looks ready to say something, but she doesn't give him the chance.

"We're going home," she lays down the law, then slips into the back seat without even sparing anyone another damn glance.

Royce laughs, salutes Mac and Leo and climbs in.

"You guys want a ride back?" Captain asks them.

"That's what Uber's for, man." Mac steps forward to give props.

"Later." Leo nods and they head back for the club.

Captain turns to me before we get in the truck. "She said home."

I nod, I caught it too.

With a small grin, he pats my shoulder and makes his way to the driver's seat.

Once all four of us are in, we head home.

Chapter 40

Raven

I nearly spit all over myself when Royce stands up and starts gyrating.

Captain laughs, leaning forward to smack him and he falls back into his seat, pouring another.

"I told you, I dated a stripper once. She taught me some shit." He winks at me, then gets punched in the arm by Maddoc.

"Okay, I'm done." I lift my feet into my lap and yank off the black, closed toe wedges Mello lent me tonight. "I'm going to bed. You fuckers do you." I wave at Captain and Royce then plant my feet in front of the big man who sits on a bar stool. I lean forward, looking up at him, my hands planted on his thighs. "You help me upstairs."

His eyes move between mine and he nods. He stands and turns around, motioning for me to grab on. I lock my hands around his neck, and he lifts me from behind the knee.

We both ignore the light laughs from the shitheads downstairs as we make our way up.

When he reaches my bed, he spins releasing my legs so I can land on my feet.

I lean forward, whispering in his ear, "Thanks, big man."

His shoulders tense beneath my touch and I grin.

He can't escape quick enough and I laugh at his retreating body, knowing as well as he does when he makes his way back in here tonight, our hands won't keep to themselves.

I make quick work of putting on some sleep shorts and a tank, then throw myself back on my mattress. I lay there listening as the other two make their way to bed maybe a half hour later.

I pull my knife from under my pillow and spin it around, careful not to flip open the switchblade when I'm still a little tipsy. I read the engraving again, understanding the notion a little more than I should for the very first time: family runs deeper than blood.

As if written specifically for them, it defines what the boys have with each other, a bond so deep they are brothers, even though they share none of the same genes.

Family runs deeper than blood, such a powerful statement when true.

I drop the knife beside me and plug in my earbuds, bobbing around to the girl song about revenge and redemption, but then the music shuffles and Ariana Grande comes on, singing to me about how dangerous her man makes her feel and my body grows hot again.

I kick off my blankets, flipping my pillow to the cool side, but it doesn't work, and the look in Maddoc's eye from earlier tonight flashes in my mind.

The unhinged look in his eyes, wild and wanting.

I half expected him to bend me over his knee so he could smack my ass in punishment and play, but that's not his style.

No, he's a words man, an observant bastard with a fighter's instinct. He digs in deep and forces you to face yourself, demands strength and craves fearlessness.

Pretty sure he craves me.

The possibility has my body tingling.

My eyes open and I sit up in bed considering my options.

Two perfectly good hands or a brooding boy with jade eyes and a six-pack. Not to mention, the serious girth he teases me with when wearing basketball shorts.

Yeah ... easy decision.

His door is cracked when I reach it, so I sneak inside, quietly closing it behind me.

"What do you want?"

I jump and look around but don't spot him, so I push off the frame and walk farther into the room.

He's got his forearm leaning against the wall, staring out his window at the empty night like I had been the other day.

Only he's ... I follow his other arm, finding his hand hiding behind the thin layer of fabric at his waist.

My eyes snap to his and he turns, leaning his shoulders against the wall.

His hand stays where it's at.

"What are you doing?" I breathe and he arches a brow.

"What are you doing?"

Fuck the scratchiness in his voice has my toes curling into the carpet.

"Whatever I want."

His tongue slides out to lick his lips, his teeth scraping across the bottom one as it disappears back into his mouth. "Imma need you to break it down for me."

I lower my gaze, making sure my eyes touch every inch of his chest and stomach on their way down.

If I was standing against him and looked down, I might get a glimpse of what he's holding onto.

"Raven."

My eyes dart up.

Right.

I push forward until I'm a foot in front of him. "If there's ever a night where I get to do something that might be real stupid, it's tonight."

"How do you figure?"

"'Cause tomorrow, I can pretend I was too drunk to remember ... if I wanna forget."

"What'd I tell you about using me to forget?"

"This is so different and you know it."

The muscles in his bicep, the one leading to the hand on his junk, flexes and my core tightens.

"What are you trying to say, Raven?" he rasps, lazily tipping his head to the side, he stares and a chill runs over me.

Which makes no sense because I'm hot all over.

His hand starts moving, up down, up down, the only sound heard in the room the silk of his boxers as it scratches against the roughness of his knuckles.

My hands find my thighs and plant there.

"You wanna forget whatever it is you came in here for?"

"I don't know yet," I breathe, pushing up on my toes, trying to get a better look.

He groans lightly, squeezing himself in his palm. "Not good enough."

"It's all I got. It's honest." I pull my shirt over my head and drop my bottoms to my ankles, kicking them somewhere on the carpet. Stepping into him, I place my naked chest against his.

Instantly, his free hand shoots around me and slides down the curve of my ass.

"All you got," he rasps, leaning down to speak against my neck. He blows hot breath across my collarbone and my nipples harden against his skin. His tongue comes out, sliding across my neck. "So, this, us in my room tonight, would be you giving me ... all you have to give?" He's slow to bring his head back and locks his eager eyes on mine.

His gaze is penetrating, fighting to slip past the surface I've polished in cement over the years.

I tense, but only for a moment before I nod my head in response.

My fingertips slide inside the elastic of his boxers, skating to the center, ready to relieve his hand of its work and take over. But then he pulls it back, and it finds my ass like the other. I'm jerked forward.

He grips my ass in both hands and pulls, demanding I jump and wrap my legs around him.

His mouth meets mine and holds. "Then I'll take it."

Finally, his lips press against mine, right as my back hits his mattress, my legs falling open for him to settle between.

They're hard and greedy, needy. Just how I want him.

He groans and slides his mouth across my jaw before running his lips down my neck. He kisses right where my breasts dip, then runs his tongue to my right nipple, swirling it around, before pulling it between his lips.

My back lifts a few inches, my head diving deeper into the pillow.

When he pinches my left nipple, I gasp, my knees coming up to rest against his ribs, heels touching his ass.

That sets him off.

With a deep growl, his mouth rips from my chest and crashes against mine, his dick slamming into me at the same moment.

I cry out and he jerks inside me and holds there.

"I've been waiting to slide inside you, Raven," he whispers against the hollow of my neck and I shiver beneath him. "So fucking soft. So damn wet."

A whimper leaves me when he flexes inside me.

His hips do all the work. With each thrust timed just right, perfectly deep with a slight grind when he's at his deepest, it doesn't take long for pressure to build.

I scrape my nails down his back as incentive and he responds like I knew he would. Wild. Crazed.

He jerks back, quickly making his way to his knees. He grips my hips hard and yanks me down. He holds me steady, my ass off the mattress completely, and slams his hips against me.

I'm frantic, gasping, and I try to reach for him but in this position, I can't, so I grip my own breasts and squeeze.

He growls, using one of his hands to slide up my pussy and stomach until his rough fingers can wrap around my neck gently.

It sets me off more and my hands shoot up to grip his wrists.

His thumb brushes along my skin as his eyes command mine. "Come for me," he rasps, and with one more thrust I am, my toes curling into the mattress, and he's right there with me.

He lets his knees slide back so he can fall on me, pushing in as deep as he can and holds. His forehead against my breastbone.

After a minute or two, his tongue flicks across my nipple and I jerk, making him chuckle.

I hit his shoulder and he rolls off but doesn't move.

Me either.

Chapter 41

Maddoc

My eyes peel open and I groan, bringing my hands up to run over my face when I freeze and look beside me.

I sit up, blinking into focus.

Empty bed, no panties on the carpet.

I frown, shaking my head.

I knew when she came in here last night what we were about to do, so did she. To be real, I'm surprised it took so damn long, but I knew her stubborn ass would cave and accept her body was mine to play with.

Clearly, her head still doesn't agree.

Irritated, I stand and pull on some clothes and head downstairs.

Captain is sitting on the couch, holding his head. He looks up. "Hey, man."

"'Sup." I walk around, adding an extra scoop to the coffee today, and lean back to wait for it to brew.

Grumbles come from the stairs and both me and Cap grin as Royce walks in, his eyes hardly even open.

He throws himself back on the couch beside Captain, dropping his head back. "Excedrin me. Fucking please."

I grab the bottle of pills and a water and drop beside them.

Cap turns on the TV and we sit like zombies a minute when a door opens upstairs, then bare feet hit the stairs. My eyes lift when her legs come into view, then more of her with each step taken.

She bends to meet my eyes, leans her forearms on the railing, and pops a dark brow. Hair a fucking mess, last night's makeup smeared all around her eyes, shirt wrinkled and ... mine?

I slowly sit forward.

"Is she..." Royce trails off.

"Yup," Captain finishes for him.

"Sneak out of your own room, did you?" She tilts her head.

My forehead creases and she grins, leaning over the edge.

Oh hell yes.

"Nothing to sneak out on."

Her eyes bounce between mine. "I had to pee, brush my teeth. Now I'm ready to go back to bed."

"Are you now?"

Royce and Captain chuckle quietly.

"Yeah. I am." She grins. "Which bed should I go to, big man?"

No, no ... we're not playing this game.

I lick my lips and her eyes dart to follow. My smirk is slow. "You tell me."

A throaty laugh leaves her, and she smiles. "Don't make me wait." She winks, and heads back up the stairs, shouting out once she's out of sight, "Mornin', boys!"

"Mornin', Raven," they tease back at the same time, then hit me with their grins.

"Good luck, brother." Captain stands.

"With what?"

Royce laughs. "She's got us by the balls, and she's not even ours. Can't imagine what she'll do with yours."

Captain grins. "We'll go get a table for breakfast. We'll wait thirty minutes then order."

I nod and the second the door closes I take the steps two at a time.

I give her no warning, no notice other than my footsteps then I'm on her, crawling over her body, loving how her legs are already lying open for me.

She laughs and scoots back on the pillow, sliding her hands up my bare chest until she can grip my shoulders.

She brings her feet up and slides them inside the back of my sweats to try and push them down. "You lied to me."

"'Bout?"

"Being a metal head." She grins.

"Metal head."

She laughs lightly. "Your dick's not pierced."

"You pissed me off, I had to come back at you with something," I admit, annoyed at the memory and she smacks me.

"Hmm ... shame," she whispers playfully.

"We didn't use a condom last night," I point out, and she nods, licking her lips. "If you tell me to, I'll go grab one." I drop my hips so I'm pushing against her and she moans lightly. "But if I had it my way, you'd let me slide in bare." I skim my lips across hers and she gasps. "Heat to fucking heat."

She pushes against me, chasing for friction, begging for more pressure against her clit. Her eyes hit mine. "Heat to fucking heat," she whispers with a sinful ass grin.

I groan, rolling my hips against her.

Her hands slide down, her nails scratching against my skin creating a fire trail to my dick. "Make me feel good," she demands, and I smirk.

I dip, running my lips across the hollow of her throat, and whisper, "Patience."

She chuckles huskily, then is gripping my hair to pull my head back.

Fiery eyes meet mine and my dick twitches. "When you're on me, in me, or about to be, patience is the last thing you'll get."

I groan, pushing my hard-on against her, loving how her eyes darken before me. "You eager for me?"

She licks her lips, nodding against the pillow, her knees sliding up the comforter, showing flexibility I didn't see from her last night.

Her hands run down my ribs, a dark brow lifting with satisfaction when my muscles lock under her touch. She pushes my boxers down so my skin can touch hers.

"Tell me," I whisper, against her, sliding the tip of my dick across her slickness, growling as it's coated with her excitement.

"Tell you what?" She lifts her hips, trying to get the tip inside of her. "How bad I want to fuck you?"

"How bad you want me to fuck you."

She grins and lifts her head off the pillow until she can catch my bottom lip between her teeth. She doesn't let up, forcing my face down with her.

She quickly lets go, flicking her tongue across my lips. "I want you inside me, big man. Now. Deep. And I want to come quick. We can test your stamina later." She grins, but it disappears when I shove inside her.

"Yes," she whispers, pulling her own knees back, begging me to hit the spot that'll set her off.

I tilt my hips sideways a little and grind into her, not pulling out an inch and her hips start to roll against me. She starts shaking instantly, her clit rubbing with every move.

I dip my head, scraping my stubble across her sensitive nipples and she twitches.

"Oh, fuck," she cries out. "Do that again. Now."

I grin against her skin, pulling out some so I can rock back inside slowly. It's the grinding she likes, she wants her clit worked right along with this pussy. Double the pleasure points. I give her what she wants, scraping across her other nipple and her shaky hands grab my face, pulling it back to hers.

She kisses me like a starved fucking animal, and I growl against her, quickening my pace. She slides her hand under both our legs and cups my balls, squeezing lightly, and I jerk inside her.

That fucking raspy laugh floats right into my ear and I'm ready to come.

I pull back to look at her and she nods, her tongue between her teeth.

I slam into her, over and over and over, her legs flying out, her knees sticking straight into the air.

Her pussy convulses around me and I'm fucking gone.

We both come, loud and fucking untamed.

Raven

"Hello sister," Royce jokes as I slide into the booth beside him.

"Get punched, Royce." I steal Captain's coffee and he frowns, but only for a half second before he motions for the waitress to bring another.

"So..." Royce grins, looking from me to Maddoc. "How'd it go?"

"Shut the fuck up." Maddoc drops next to Captain, picks up a sugar packet and tosses it at him.

"Hey, I just wanna know if it was as hot as I imagine it was."

"You imagine your brother fuckin' often, Royce?" I tease, flipping through the menu.

Royce leans over. "So there was fuckin'?" He grins, making me laugh. "And he's not my brother, 'member? Cabin .... hotness ..."

I shake my head with a grin, catching Maddoc's eyes on me a minute before he looks to his menu too.

"We ready to order?" Our waitress comes over with waters.

Everyone nods, gives their food choices and she's gone as quick as she came.

The boys start talking basketball strategy, so I slip from the booth and head for the bathrooms.

I'm just flushing when I hear the door open and a male voice telling the girl washing her hands to get out.

I hesitate a moment before unlatching the stall and walking out. I pause at the sight of Collins.

I keep a steady pace and loose shoulders as I walk to the sink. "Lost?"

"Nope. Saw you come in here."

I nod, turning off the water and reaching for a paper towel, a way to lean against the farthest corner from where he stands near the door. "So, what's up?"

He laughs lightly. "Checking on you is all. Seems the Brays get more protective of you by the day."

"Seems so."

"Wonder why?"

I keep my face blank, not answering him. Clearly, he has something he wants to say. Best way to hear it is to let him do all the talking.

"But so do you, don't you?" He steps closer. "I could tell you, if you want. Because there is a reason."

Pressure hits my chest, but I ignore it.

"And what is it that you want, Collins?"

"Just you."

A laugh bubbles out of me. "Liar."

When he scowls, I stand taller.

"You want to feel like you've won something of theirs, gain an upper hand somehow. For whatever reason, you've decided that thing should be me. But you're wasting your time, Collins. I'm as disposable as the next to come along." I run my tongue along my teeth as acid fills my mouth at my own words.

"If that's the case, why don't you come home with me tonight, Rae?"

"Disposable or not, I'm not stupid."

"You sure, not even for quick cash? You get down like your mom, right?" He tilts his head. "Tell me you can't use the ten grand I promised."

"You know, you're not as smart as I thought you'd be, it's no wonder you're forced to be overly aggressive in your efforts."

"What the fuck does that mean?"

"You're getting braver, Collins. Cornering me in here like this, alone, with all three of them sitting just a few feet away. This means you're more desperate, and you're showing your cards. You want me away from the Brays and bad. Makes me wonder why you'd go through all the trouble just to take me off their hands. You and I both know, nothing good ever comes of a curious female."

He blanches before he can stop himself, but it's quickly replaced with anger. "You seem to think I give a fuck what trash like you thinks. You know nothing about this world you were dropped into. Your eyes aren't as open as they should be. You're a fucking fool, Rae. Take the money."

This bitch.

"The fact that you'd waste ten grand on paid pussy tells me

how pathetic and underperforming you must be." I step around him.

"You don't belong with them, Raven."

When I pause a moment, a dark chuckle leaves him.

"You'll see."

I exit the restroom and for a second, worry he won't let me, but he doesn't even attempt to keep me back. And that tells me all I need to know.

Collins has or does know something, or at least he thinks he does and he's waging on my confronting the boys about it, trying to force fouls between us, but I keep my mouth shut.

Whatever it is doesn't matter because, at the end of the day, I know where I stand, if not by their doing then by mine.

I knew from day one this was only temporary. It has to be.

I glance at Maddoc, right as he looks to me and unexpected dread fills me.

All of it.

Chapter 42

Raven

"So what's the deal with you guys versus them?"

"What?" he teases. "You didn't read it in the files?"

I roll my eyes while dropping onto my back beside him. "Told you I didn't read them."

"I know." He pauses staring at me a moment before he continues. "The Gravens and the Brayshaws used to run this town together. They were the most powerful families, stronger as two than one. Nothing happened here without their permission, down to nomads, families not tied to theirs, even moving in. They were all screened and had to be given the green light to live here and raise kids. Jobs were earned based on loyalty. It was like their own little royal world."

"Until..."

"Until a Brayshaw son decided he wanted to be a black-tie gangster instead. Brayshaws and Gravens were given respect because of who they were and the control they had here, but that wasn't enough for old-day Brayshaw. They wanted respect, but they also wanted fear. Eventually, they had both."

"How'd they get it?"

"Blood and money. Power in numbers. That's when our families were brought in. The Brayshaws were top tier, but the Malcaris - my born last name - were their second hand. It wasn't until my great grandfather that Royce and Captain's families were brought in. Four families became one. It didn't take long before it was all about the Brayshaw empire, leaving the Gravens out completely."

"So, the Brayshaws were in charge and your families worked under them?"

"Basically, yeah, but for the core members, they saw each other as family. To them, they were all Brayshaw, like we are all Brayshaw now."

"What did they actually do?"

"They all held power positions, still do. Judges, lawyers, engineers. Help keep the town in check. Watch the crime, control the gangs, shit like that. But we evolved when my dad took over."

"How."

"We find things out, then make sure people pay for it. Clean, if we can."

Wait ... "The teacher. That was you guys?"

He nods. "He moved in with her mother last year. Has sexually assaulted her every day on the way to school since."

My stomach turns. Jesus. "How'd you find out?"

"We don't know. Another clue left lying there, just like the delivery papers left for Cap when Zoey was born. Or the email sent from Captain's email to Royce's warning us that chick you choked out with the hose had a video that needed destroyed."

"The girl had said it would ruin your season. How?"

He considers lying, I can tell by the way his eyes tighten at the corners. But he doesn't.

"Our coach is a good man, he just loves someone he shouldn't."

"So, the video..."

"Was him doing something he shouldn't have been, especially with a wife at home."

I push away slightly. "Why would you hide that? Let the wife find out, he's a piece of shit for it and deserves to be busted."

Maddoc's eyes slide to mine. "She blackmailed him, Raven. Trapped him and his money in a marriage he never wanted a year ago." His eyes bounce between mine. "He doesn't love his wife, but he loves the girl in the video. Who would be fucked if that got out?" He shakes his head. "Not the wife."

"You're Saints," I joke, honestly a little in awe of all this, and he laughs.

"So, what about the Gravens, Collins?"

He groans, fake complaining and turns me onto my side. He pushes up behind me.

"Collins is Graven. Like we're the last of our families, other than my dad, he's the last Graven other than his mother and grandfather. Where we know we're a fucked-up bunch and own up to it, the Gravens are dangerous because they pretend to be noble when they're not. You saw the officer who searched us on the courts the day we found you smoking there? He's their runner, so to speak. His badge gets him access to shit other Gravens blackmail our people for. He's not Graven blood or brought in, but he's on their payroll. Collins is the gutsiest Graven they've seen in decades. He challenges us, but we're stronger."

He buries his face in my neck.

"You guys fell into a war between men." I push against him when his tongue slips out, sliding across the vein in my neck.

"We were born to be their army." He lifts my knee, running

his fingertips down my thigh until he can slip past the bottom of my shorts.

"Wait—" I gasp when his finger slips inside me.

I turn my head to meet his lips.

"No more questions," he whispers, and I take his mouth with mine.

He's slow in his movement, taking his time as he drives me wild. When I clench my pussy muscles over his finger, he shifts onto his elbow, his tongue sweeping so deep into my mouth I hold my breath.

He adds a second finger, curving his knuckles into a hook and he increases his speed, his thumb coming up to push against my clit as hard as his grip will allow.

When I start to push into his hand, he pulls his thumb back and scrapes my clit with the tiny nail of his thumb, making me moan into his mouth.

My hand finds his dick in his pants and I start to stroke him as quickly as I can, taking the time to run my fingertips over his head every few pumps.

Finally, he growls, rips his mouth from mine and jumps on top of me.

His pants are down, my shorts are moved over and he's inside me in the next second.

He pulls my legs back, bringing my knees to meet his ribs as he thrusts in and out in manic motions.

My hands shoot up to push on the headboard to keep my body as steady as can be so I can feel every hit against my clit.

My pussy starts to convulse around him, and he slips his hands under me, gripping me behind my shoulders. He increases his speed.

It's hard and loud and so are we.

"Oh God..." I moan, my head falling back as every muscle in me tightens, and then I come, hard and pulsing. My body shakes against him, but he doesn't let up, doesn't slow his pace. He fucks me harder and my walls clench again.

He pulls out and I whimper.

Maddoc bends, kissing my stomach before pulling my clit into his teeth. He bites, then sucks while rolling his tongue against me and I start to shake, my knees clamping over his ears, my feet locking over his head, but right before I come again, he yanks back and flips me over, pulls my ass up and pushes back in.

Three deep thrusts and he grunts, running a hand down my spine as I wobble on my knees. He pulls out, spreads my ass cheeks apart and then his hot cum is coating my asshole, running down my slit to blend with mine as it's forced from me.

He slides his dick against me, rubbing through our cum a minute before he smacks my ass and falls beside me.

I face-plant into my pillow, making him chuckle with the little breath he has control of.

A minute passes and then there's a bang on my door.

"If you guys are done, we need to talk."

I groan against my pillow and look to Maddoc with a raised brow. "Any chance you could go again real quick?"

He grins in amusement and covers my back with his body, pushing his dick against my ass. "I could go and go and go, Snow, but I like knowing you're sitting around waiting to feel my dick stretching you again."

My core heats and he laughs lightly like he knows it.

"And you thought you could pretend to forget this," he says smugly and my jaw drops, a laugh escaping.

He smirks and walks out, shoving Royce back when he attempts to slip past him and closes my door.

I laugh, grab some fresh clothes and head for the shower.

By the time I get downstairs, I figured the boys would be

done with their little powwow, but I find them sitting on the couch, eyes on me.

I slow my pace. "What?"

"Did Collins corner you in the bathroom yesterday?" Maddoc asks, his face blank.

"Yeah," I admit. No point in lying if they already know.

"And you didn't fucking tell me?"

"No ..." I eye him, suddenly wondering if I made the wrong move. "I didn't purposely not mention it, I just didn't think about it."

"Are you for real?" Royce snaps, shooting to stand. "You didn't fucking think about it? You didn't think we'd want to know if the one piece of shit who constantly tries to fuck us, was fucking with you?"

I eye them and my mother's pitiful words spread inside me like the disease she is, wrapping around and squeezing my ribs and dare I say the organ that beats beneath them.

Foolish, worthless, unworthy of more than she gave.

I pick up my backpack from behind the couch and head for the door. "I'm not gonna be your little rat, so if that's what you were hoping for ... find another piece to play with." I push out the door and lean against the SUV to wait for the assholes inside.

Captain is outside just as quick as me.

He stares at me over the hood and when I widen my eyes like a bitch, he glances off. "Don't push us away because you're feeling things you never had."

"I don't know what you're talking about."

"Well, I know what I'm talking about. And just so you know, that was about you. And not because we need to know everything but because we care. If someone is bothering you, threatening you, or hurts you. We want to know."

The front door opens, and Captain finally unlocks the car, so I slip inside.

Nobody says a word on the drive to the donut store, nor on the way to school.

Lost in our own heads, the four of us exit the vehicle and head inside.

When I spot Bass leaning against my locker down the hall, I cut from the group, but Maddoc grabs my arm and yanks me back.

Captain and Royce step back but keep close.

Everyone around slows their steps and dozens of eyes land on his grip on my arm and my glare on his face.

Then he pulls me in, wraps his hand around my waist and leans forward while I lean back.

He speaks low, intensity he's never shown me making up his every word. "I have every fucking intention of getting to that point." Maddoc's eyes harden.

"What point?"

"Knowing where you are, who with, and what was said. And it has nothing to do with wanting to piss you off and everything to do with keeping me sane."

"Careful, big man," I whisper, a sudden pounding now hitting against my temple. "That sounds a lot like a king falling. The ground isn't very soft at my feet."

He leans even closer, his mouth damn near touching mine and I bite my tongue to keep from doing or saying something stupid. "I can handle it."

"Maybe I don't want you to."

"Liar," he hisses, and I'm released and dismissed in the next second. "Two fucking minutes, Snow. Don't push me."

I flip him off, ignoring all the side stares and make my way to Bass, fighting to get my pulse under control when all it wants to do is scratch to the surface.

Bass looks from where Maddoc stands to me.

"Don't," I warn him, opening my locker to grab the books

for my first few classes, putting the ones in my backpack in their place. "Thought I was on your ban list?"

"I don't have a ban list."

"No, but you have an 'avoid to keep the peace' list. Same shit." I lean against the metal, facing him. "What's up?"

Bass frowns at his badass combat boots before lifting it to me.

"People been asking for you. They want you to fight. They're talking big numbers."

Big money. I could use it after my mom practically drained me, but...

Can't.

I shake my head with a tight-lipped frown. "I'll pass on this one."

"Not sure there'll be a next time."

Bass and I both look down the hall where Maddoc leans against the wall ignoring the others who talk around him as he focuses on the two of us.

"Thanks for the offer, but I'm good."

He nods, pushes off the locker and walks away.

I don't watch him go but keep my stare on Maddoc as he heads for me in the same second.

He steps in and I lean back against the cool metal.

"What'd he want?"

"Don't worry, big man. It was a chat that didn't go his way." I look to Royce as he and Captain step up, and nod in the direction of our first class. "Ready?"

I don't wait for an answer but start toward it and after a minute, Royce falls in line beside me. He doesn't pester with an arm on my shoulder like normal, doesn't make a scene as we walk in together. In fact, he doesn't say a word.

I drop into my seat and wonder when I started making decisions that are bad for me but follow the line three bossy boys drew for me.

Not good.

Chapter 43

Raven

"You got dicked."

I glare at Vienna when she plants her ass on the top of the picnic table where I'm waiting for the boys' practice to end.

"Hello to you too."

"Oh you totally got dicked and now your moral compass is broken."

I drop my hands into my lap. "What are you talking about?"

"You're stressed, almost sulking, and in my experience, those things are linked to a penis." When I stare blankly, she pulls back slightly. "Vagina?"

I laugh rolling my eyes. "Not gay, and dick has nothing to do with my problems right now."

Her eyes light up and she moves to straddle the bench so she's level with me. "But you did get some?"

"Why you so interested?" I grow defensive and she holds up her hands.

"Sorry. Forgot. You suck at having friends." She laughs, pulling out a bag of chips from her backpack. "Heard Maddoc took you to trade back Mello's shit?"

"Yeah, I wasn't sure how to find her, but turned out Royce knew exactly where she lived." I laugh and Vienna grins.

"'Course he did."

"How's everything at the house?"

She shrugs. "Same as always. Routine and boring but ... safe."

I nod.

"Seems trash sticks together."

We both look left finding Chloe standing there with her followers.

Neither of us says anything and she rolls her eyes.

"Word on campus is you and Collins Graven were seen kissing at The Tower last weekend."

With my elbow on the table, I drop my chin in my palm, not impressed with her lame attempt to get a rise from me.

"Then you heard how the boys showed up later, went caveman, and stole Cinderella away after kicking his ass." Vienna smiles brightly.

Chloe's minions' eyes round and she licks her lips a slight frown forming on her forehead.

She hadn't heard that part.

Her little mole only gave her half the juice.

"You better watch yourself, Rae. I can make you go away with one phone call if I really wanted." She lifts a brow and my eyes narrow.

"Just give it up, Chloe," Vienna snaps. "Or maybe, you know, don't and you wouldn't get so attached to guys who don't care for more."

But Chloe ignores her and sashays away with her smirk still intact.

"That was—" I'm cut off when my name is called. I look

left to find one of the guys from Maddoc's team. Think his name is Jason.

Seems practice must have just ended.

"Hey."

"I'll ... catch you later, Rae." V wiggles her eyebrows and bounces off, so I turn to face the guy fully.

"You going to the party tonight?"

"I am."

"What color will you be wearing?" When my head pulls back, he chuckles.

"I don't know what you're talking about."

"It's a traffic light party." He explains, "Red means you're taken, Yellow means you're unsure, Green means you're available."

"How about black for not interested?"

He gives an easy smile, looks over my shoulder then back down at me. "See you tonight."

Maddoc steps up beside me, his stare following the Jason guy away. He looks down at me. "Ready to go?"

"Ready to go."

She laughs again, shoving his shoulder when he leans over to speak to her. Yeah, it's loud as fuck in here and to be heard you have to shout, but I'm over this motherfucker and his obsession with her. I told his ass to watch himself around her. He must have decided I was playin' and it's pissing me off.

In fact, all these assholes are pissing me off, comin' at her like they can, as if she's free game when she's not. To make it worse, she somehow ended up wearing green, when I told her ass to wear red – I didn't tell her why but who the fuck cares.

I thought it was obvious she's not just the girl in our group, protected by us but open for others. Guess I haven't been clear enough.

It's time these people learn.

It's time she admits it.

I stand and head straight for her.

She's got her back to me, but Bishop sees me coming and his grin slowly falls as he looks off. That prompts her to look over her shoulder, right at me.

"Catch you later, Rae," Bishop tells her before stepping away, as he fucking should.

And she doesn't bother looking after him.

Nah, her stormy eyes stay locked on me as she slowly spins her body to face mine.

I slide my hand behind her, slipping my fingers halfway into the back of her jeans as I pull her against me.

Her tongue pushes between her teeth and she bites down, eyelids lowering in a silent demand.

I lean closer and her chest inflates, but still, so much fucking sass laces her features.

She's a stubborn one, unwilling to give in completely but unable to hold back just the same.

I start dancing and she follows, her hips rolling perfectly with mine, our bodies now acquainted with each other's.

Finally, her hands land on me, her grip on my neck just as possessive as mine on her back.

Show them, baby. Make them see.

Her fingers fan out across my collarbone and slowly slide up, brushing through my hair in deep, massage-like movements.

Her features smooth as her fingertips dig into my skin – she's getting horny for me.

But when the song changes it jolts her and she snaps out of it, sliding her hands down to rest on my chest.

I lean forward, ready to whisper in her ear but she uses her position to nudge me back, unintentionally making me lose my footing, but I catch myself quick, as well as the attention of the rest of the room.

I'm slow to walk into her and I don't stop until she hits the entertainment center with a soft thud.

"Sorry, big man," she whispers. "But your public show was looking a little too much like purpose."

"Say you're mine," I demand and her brows jump. "Show you're mine. Quit fucking letting them think you might not be."

She frowns. "I'm ... not."

"Yeah, you are. Say it."

She scoffs, hissing in a whisper, "Then what, huh? I 'belong' to you? You 'own' me?"

"You wanna be juvenile about it, yeah." I stand tall. "Both those things."

"What do you expect to get from me?" she forces out.

"Whatever I want."

She sets her jaw, turning away. "I'm not up for that."

"Bullshit." I run my hand down her ribs, curve them around to cup her ass, and her tits involuntarily push into my chest, and she swallows a moan making its way up her throat. "You don't want no one else, so just give me what I want." I squeeze her and she flexes in my grip. "That way I can keep giving you what you need."

She swallows and swings her glare back to me. "I don't need you."

"Prove it."

A chuckle makes its way up her throat and she stands taller. Her smirk slowly morphs into a warning, and before I can issue one of my own, she slips right, gripping my boy Mac by his neck.

My brows snap together when I realize what she's about to do.

I dart toward her, but he's already spun around, and her mouth hits his.

His hands are instantly sinking into her hair as he tries to swallow her fucking whole.

But I'm right there, yanking him back in the same second.

He rips his shoulder from my hold and spins to see who's grabbing on him, but when he sees it's me his hands lift, but so does mine. He catches one to the fucking jaw.

The music cuts off and complete silence takes over. That is, until my pain in the ass opens her pretty little mouth.

"Maddoc! What the hell!" she shrieks, looking from Mac to me.

"I said you're mine!" I shout and her mouth clamps shut.

She fights to keep herself in check, but she's ready to tear into me. She doesn't like being the center of attention.

Too fucking bad.

I spin, holding my arms out wide. "Everybody hear that?" I look around the room. "Raven Fucking Carver belongs to me. Touch her and I'll break your jaw." I cut my eyes to Mac, he's my boy ... but she's my girl. "Let her get close enough to touch you? I break your nose. Either way, you lose and she's still mine."

I turn to Raven, who is practically shaking in anger, and I dare her ass to say a word before leaving the room.

She'll follow.

RAVEN

THIS MOTHERFUCKER.

He takes off like I won't fucking follow.

He cuts left and heads down the hall and I'm not far behind.

"Un-oh, RaeRae's maaad," Royce teases.

"Someone's getting a spanking," Cap joins in on the fun.

"Bets on which one?" Both bastards laugh so I stop where they are, snag their drinks from their hands and pour them over their heads, quickly tossing the cups at their faces.

They both growl as I keep walking down the hall, but I hear the assholes laugh after.

I find him in the last room on the left with his palms against the wall, back to me. I slip inside and turn to shut the door, but Royce's body blocks me.

He grins like a fool, looking from me to Maddoc.

"Go away," I tell him.

"But this'll be fun."

When I glare he sighs and spins, walking away. "Buzz kill."

Such a child.

The second I've got the door locked, I'm shoved against it, Maddoc at my back.

He grinds his hard-on against me punishingly. "Your lips," he whispers into my neck. "Your hands, maybe not even your eyes, should ever touch another man's skin." He bites at my collarbone and my head falls back, hitting his shoulder. "You ... are with me. Period."

"You've got problems," I pant, and he shifts his hips, making my thighs squeeze together.

"I'm aware. Changes nothing," he growls angrily, but his warm breath fanning across my neck is featherlight and his hands slide from my hips to frame the curve of my thighs until he's got his long fingers wrapped around my panty line over my jeans. "Do I need to remind you why you wanna be mine, Snow? 'Cause I can, all night if you can hang."

A moan leaves me, and I turn my head, trying to catch his lips, but he moves them to my shoulder.

"This won't play out how you want," I warn him. "If you want anything other than now."

"Why is that?"

"I told you. I'm a fuck up."

His hand lowers, officially cupping my pussy so he can push my ass into him more and my skin starts burning for his.

"So am I."

"I don't trust."

"Me either." His other hand comes up to flip open my button on my jeans and my feet widen, begging his fingers to slip inside.

"You're not hearing me," I pant, so fucking ready to feel him. "I know I can be fun to play with, but don't dig deeper. You won't find anything there to hold on to. Fuck me today, sure, but don't fall, 'cause it'll likely be me fucking you tomorrow."

"So today, say it and mean it. And I'll worry about the tomorrow bit."

"I'm- mmm," a moan shoots up my throat when his free hand grips my breast, and my palms slap against the door. "I'm not joking."

He grips my chin, pulling my face to his. His eyes are clear, his features tight. "Me either. Say it, Raven. You belong to me. Not Brayshaw, not the three of us." His dark eyes bounce between mine and I'd swear there's uncertainty in his stare, but it's hidden behind determination. "Only me."

His hold loosens as I push and he lets me spin into him.

I lick my lips, dropping my shoulders against the door and he steps into me, his hand sliding up my chest and neck until he can hold my head at the perfect angle, my lips inches from his, our eyes glued to each other's.

I put my hands on his chest, and I have to admit, there's a voice screaming in the back of my head, telling me to push, but I silence it, and do what I want, as always.

I pull.

He's flush against me now, his lips, his forehead, his nose, all touching mine.

His hands skim over my body until he can cup my ass, and I jump with his tug, wrapping myself around him.

"Okay, big man," I whisper, licking his lips before kissing them lightly. "Have it your way."

He growls and bruises my lips with his.

He kisses me hard and long until I'm full on grinding against him, fighting for friction I can't get, but he senses it and suddenly he's sitting in a La-Z-Boy.

He pushes me to stand as he remains sitting. His shirt's the first to go, then he unzips his jeans and lifts his hips, sliding them down with his boxers and his dick springs free, pointing at me accusingly, begging me to ease it.

And I will.

I kick off my shoes and he leans forward, pushing my pants and underwear down as I massage his head with my fingertips.

I step on my jeans to pull them off the rest of the way and Maddoc sits back, staring up at me, completely fucking naked.

His eyes trail over me from head to toe, and he grips himself, his tongue coming out to wet his lips. Hooded eyes slowly lift and lock with mine.

"Sit on me, baby."

I swear to God, I grow ten times hotter.

His head is tilted back, his chin tipped back.

He moves his knees together to make room for me, but I turn around instead, my hands planted on his strong thighs as I lower myself onto him.

He sucks in a breath, before growling and sitting up to pull my shirt off, my bra next.

One arm comes around to wrap across my chest, cupping my breast as the other slips between my legs.

I push down farther and we both moan.

And I start riding him, reverse cowgirl style, following the beat of the music seeping from under the door. It's slow and sultry and sets the perfect fucking mood for an erotic ride.

And with the way he's touching my body, it's perfect.

He's got a tight grip on my nipple, as his palm massages my breast, the other smashed tight under his forearm.

The hand between my legs slaps against my inner thigh and I jolt, widening my legs for him, just as he requested without a word. His fingers slide down the crease of my sex until they're gliding around himself and me, before sliding back up to my clit. My body starts to shake. He does it again, and again and then pushes on my clit, pulling both of us back until his back hits the support of the chair, mine against him. My pussy is in the air, his hand covering it and together we roll and grind and fuck, deep and bare and son of a bitch.

My legs start to quiver, my moans getting louder and louder.

He lets it happen, doesn't fight to keep me quiet and soon his match mine.

We're loud and carnal and covered in sweat.

His dick starts throbbing inside me, so I flex around him and he growls in my ear, biting it as he does.

My toes curl against his feet and his thighs lock under me and together, we come, hard and long and satisfying.

It's not until our breathing slows that I realize I gave Maddoc exactly what he wanted tonight.

If I'm not careful, he might take more.

I squash the little voice that tells me he already has.

Chapter 44

Raven

A raspy ass groan has my eyes peeling open. I push my hair from my face to find Maddoc burying his head in the pillow. When he looks up, he tosses the blankets over his head.

"You need to start remembering to close the fucking curtains. It's too damn bright in here every morning."

"That's easily fixed."

"Yeah, by closing your curtains."

"Or ... by sleeping in your own bed," I joke.

He jerks the blanket from his face, frowning.

I laugh lightly, looking to my window.

I never had a window that faced the sun. I mean, the first window I really had was the one at the Bray house, but it faced the opposite side, so the sun didn't shine through it like this one.

"Hey." Maddoc's unexpected gentle tone has me jerking to look at him. His features match his voice and my stomach starts to turn. "You like the sun?"

I shrug, and he gives me a pointed look that has me grinning.

"Yes, big man, I do." I look away and continue. "Our trailer had a couple windows, but I wasn't allowed to move the sheets to let light in." I frown thinking about it. "Not even when the electric was out."

"Why not?"

"Plenty of reasons. She didn't want people to see inside, didn't like the sun in her face when she was coming down, slept through the day to work through the night. The list goes on and on."

"So you were locked inside a small, dark space most of the time. How's that work for someone scared of the dark?"

I lick my lips. "It doesn't. I spent as minimal time home as possible. Once I got older, I tried to only be home when she was gone, but she was so unpredictable I never knew for sure. She'd work from home for a couple weeks then take off for one, come home and sleep for days at a time, then start over. But I mean, it was all normal to me, so it didn't seem as fucked up as it sounds now."

He stays quiet.

"I know nothing about her life before me other than her dad died from hepatitis from using dirty needles – it's why she's always stayed away from injecting."

"And her mom?"

"A different type of lethal drug combination."

"Damn."

"Sounds crazy, but" – I think about the younger kids in my trailer park and the things they see, parents they live with and the vices they can't escape – "others have it worse."

"And you punched that girl, ready to go right back. You can't prefer that over this place."

"I know that place. I ran through those streets at night. Not without danger, but at least I know my role. I don't have to think to function there, everything is second nature. I'm not saying it's where I belong, but ... at least I know what to expect if I decide to go back."

I look over at Maddoc.

He stares for a few seconds and I know he wants to argue, maybe even say I belong thinking I need soothing or something when I don't, but he accepts it for what it is and nods instead.

I stretch against the mattress and flip over on my stomach, facing him.

I change the subject.

"Were you ever gonna admit you sleep better in this bed than yours?"

He groans and pulls me half on top of him, my torso laying sideways across his naked chest. "No. I wasn't. My brothers have big mouths."

"And big dicks!" Royce shouts from the hall.

Maddoc reaches over, picking up his water bottle from the nightstand and chucks it at the door. "Quit fucking listening by the door!"

"I was doing no such thing!" Royce shouts from the other side. "I was simply walking by and heard you talking."

"Keep walking, Royce!" I shout and I hear his feet carry him away.

Maddoc shifts his frown to me. "Why's he listen to you?"

"'Cause." I grin, running my fingertip across his pec lines. "He likes an authoritative woman."

Maddoc glares, making me laugh.

"We need to get up. You have practice and I need to go to the store."

He lets me go, but I feel his questioning eyes on me as I stand and pull out a pair of jeans from the drawer, slipping them on. I pull a hoodie over my tank top and put my hair up into a ponytail, smoothing the top with my hands before dropping onto the mattress to put shoes on.

I stand and turn to Maddoc, finding him still staring. "What?"

His eyes travel over me with unnerving thoroughness, and a small smile pulls at his lips. "Just like that, huh?"

When I tilt my head in question, he makes his way to me. Slipping his hands up the back of my shirt, he pulls me to him.

"You just stand, throw some shit on, run your fingers through your hair and come out looking like a fucking wet dream?"

I pop a brow. "Thanks?"

His eyes bounce between mine before he takes his time leaning down and catches my lips between his. He nips, then kisses me with a slow, obsessive rhythm.

"Let's go, fuckers!" Royce shouts from down the hall and Maddoc pulls back.

"I'll meet you downstairs." He goes to walk out but pauses in the doorway. "Why can't you wait until we're done at practice and we'll take you to the store?"

"That question sounds a lot like suspicion."

He shrugs a shoulder, unapologetic at his inability to trust.

I appreciate it. It lets me know we're still in safe territory when it's starting to feel a little more than risky.

"Come to practice. We'll stop after."

"I guess I can wait." I meet him in the doorway.

He grabs the ends of my hair, running his fingers through the colored tips of my ponytail.

And like a real dumb girl, I smile when he smirks and walks away.

Stupid.

I'M NOT SURE I'LL EVER GET USED TO WATCHING THESE BOYS play.

It's pure heart and natural ability. They're born athletes, but it's their dedication to the sport that makes them shine above the others.

Every shift of their feet counts, every twist of their body is purposeful.

Everyone feels it, the passion behind the grind seeping from each of them.

It's the end of practice and the last few shots are being taken in the mock game the key players have going, and the others around stop mid drills to watch Maddoc fly down the court like he's running freely, as if he doesn't even have to focus on the ball that's effortlessly and consistently bouncing against the old gravel. One of his teammates attempt to guard, but Maddoc spins and overheads the ball to Captain who wastes not a second to shoot, purposely a little to the left as the defender pushes off from the right, and Royce hops up for the assist.

Swish.

Everyone claps and the team starts doing their little wolf calls as they form a tight circle to call break.

I grin and push to my feet, heading back for the parking lot to wait while they have their end of practice pep talk.

I lean against the bumper and close my eyes for a minute, letting the sun beat down on my face. It's cold, being December, but the sun is out and soon it'll be gone. I can't help but feel like all this will be too.

A car door slams and my eyes pop open to find Leo standing there, glaring my way.

"I won't let you cause problems for them."

"For them, or for you?" I tilt my head considering him. "I honestly can't tell what your angle is, Leo. I'm not even sure you're a bad guy, to be honest. But let me tell you what I do know. You're attempting to manipulate your 'friends,' and they won't be thanking you for it in the end. If you have legit concerns about me, go straight to the guys and make them listen to what you have to say. Be honest. Don't be sneaky. You know as well as I do, they won't put up with that."

He grins with his teeth together. "Fuck you."

"You're trying, but in the end the only one you'll be fucking is yourself."

He glares hard before dropping his stare to the ground and moving for the driver's seat, and imagine that, Maddoc steps up in the next second.

He looks from where the car Leo's sitting in, to me expectantly.

"He's got a problem with me."

"It's called blue balls, RaeRae," Royce teases, stepping around Maddoc and ushers me out of the way so he can lift the hatch and put his shit inside. "Trust me, I know how they feel at the hands of you."

"Shut the fuck up, man," Maddoc snaps and shoves his laughing brother away, refocusing on me. "What'd he say?"

I roll my eyes. "Not that it's a big deal, but he said he won't let me fuck shit up for you guys."

"The fuck's he think he can do about it if you did?"

"Guess you'll have to ask him."

I step around Maddoc and climb inside the SUV and close my eyes.

Leo's trippin' if he thinks I'm more than the girl giving these boys the female presence they so desperately crave.

Someone for Captain to care for, someone for Royce to worry about, someone for Maddoc to protect.

Eventually, maybe this week, maybe next year, one of them will meet a person who matters, and she'll come in to take over for me, not that I'll be here that long. But either way, she'll belong like I never could.

The fact of the matter is if I never went home, my mother

would be fine. If I left tomorrow, the boys would be fine. If I never came back, Maddoc ... he'd be fine.

A nasty little ache forms in my chest as I'm slammed with realization, it climbs up my throat, trying to choke me with my own self-honesty.

They'd all be fine ... but I wouldn't.

Chapter 45

RAVEN

"Hurry up," Maddoc tells me as Captain puts the SUV in park.

Once in the department store and grabbing my necessities, I take a couple minutes to go through the five-dollar bin of DVDs. I find one I've heard of but never seen and head for the munchies aisle, spotting Bass.

"Hey." I walk toward him, checking out his stash of snacks he's got in his hands, choosing Bottle Caps and caramel corn for me.

He does a double take and then focuses back on the candy boxes stacked in front of him. The way his features go rigid has me squaring my shoulders.

"Something on your mind, Bishop?"

With a low curse, he turns toward me. The reserved look in his eye has me masking my unease.

"Look, I decided not to say shit since you were shacking up with the Brays, but I still think you should know."

"Know what?"

He opens his mouth, but promptly closes it and dips his head to whisper, "Come to the warehouses tonight. Don't put it off."

"What—"

An arm snakes around my middle and I'm jolted back.

I don't have to look to know who it belongs to.

Maddoc's body starts vibrating against me the longer we stand there, so I lift my hand and cup the back of his neck, forcing his eyes to mine.

His jaw clenches, his features tightening even more as he glares. I push up while pulling his face down and skim my lips over his. His hold though only grows tighter, more possessive.

"Move on, Bishop," Maddoc tells Bass, his voice jarringly calm.

"Later, Raven." Bass walks away without acknowledging Maddoc.

I snag a second box of Bottle Caps and make a move for the registers, but Maddoc spins me around to face him.

"You really gonna stand there and make me ask, Raven?" He frowns. "Why is he always near you? Why do you always have to fucking stop and talk to him?"

I take a deep breath, eyeing him, agitation taking over impulse. "Careful, big man. That sounds a lot like jealousy."

"I don't need to be jealous, you're already mine."

"Yet here you are, working yourself up over nothing."

"You better hope so or I'll make sure shit's fucked for him. No more fight money, no more Bray house. I'll even make sure no small-time bookies around here will take his sorry ass in if he so much as taps you on the shoulder." He steps back.

I don't say anything, but slide past him and head for the line, his shadow taking over mine.

If I address what he said it'll lead to me telling him to fuck off and then I'll really have no chance of getting to Bass to hear what he has to say.

Maddoc told me not to fight, but he never said anything about going to watch other people fight.

I slip through the cut-out part of the metal fence at the farthest end of the rusted buildings and slowly make my way around, following the sound of music and shouting.

A few people recognize me from my couple fights out here and as I squeeze through the crowd, I get a few waves, couple head nods – respect, self-earned.

I find Bass toward the back, where the fighters drop their shit and collect payment at the end of their fights. He's cashing someone out when his eyes lift and he spots me.

He motions for me to wait, so I hop up on the crate closest to me and turn to watch the next two on tonight's card getting ready.

Looking from one to the next, the common eye leads you to believe the pick for winner is a no-brainer, but to anyone who knows a damn thing about fighting beyond a good swing would know, these two are more equal than they appear at first glance.

The ignorant choice would be the six-foot monster with roadmaps for arms, not the one warming up across from him with a lean torso and tight muscles, not to mention a good four inches shorter.

But the giant one, he's bouncing his shoulders, ducking his head, and swinging at the air, showing me he's betting on a solid hit to take the other guy down, while his opponent shifts on his feet, practicing bobbing and weaving around, working on combo punches.

He's quicker, more likely has better cardio than his opponent. He's focused, sees and hears nothing around him, while the guy he's bound to beat the shit out of tonight is laughing and high fiving the people who are starting to form the large circle as it grows closer to go time.

Bass hops up beside me.

"Bets still open?" I keep my eyes on the fighters.

He looks at his watch. "Two minutes."

"Put me down for five." I glance his way and he tilts his head.

"I don't—" He starts to deny me, but I cut him off.

"Is my money not good, here?"

He glares a minute, then asks, "On the big guy?"

I level him with a blank stare, and he laughs, bumping my shoulder, taking the money I hand over.

"Bunch of fools out tonight." He shakes his head, looking around. "More than half these fuckers bet against your guy."

I laugh lightly. "Figured so."

The crowd is told to shut the fuck up by the new dude on the megaphone and the rules are laid out, but I tune him out and turn toward Bass.

"So, what's up, what was with the secret shit earlier?"

He eyes me. "You with Maddoc?"

I rub my lips together at his question, considering what answer to give him, not that I owe him one at all. I go with the easiest answer.

"Yeah."

He nods, having no choice but to accept my response. "All right, I can't say for sure, because it hasn't hit my boys' hands yet, but word is there's a video of you coming. And not just in the it's almost here way, Rae."

Confusion has my forehead wrinkling in thought. The sound of the crowd going wild pulls my attention and I glance to the center of the makeshift ring. My guy's dominating.

"Rae."

I shake my head and look up at Bass. "A sex tape?"

"Yup."

"How do you know it's me?"

"Said it was my new girl, long black hair, fucked shit up out here and disappeared." He lifts his hands as if to say, 'who the fuck else could they mean?'

Fuck.

A video of me is coming ... as in almost here and ... coming.

"Okay..." I trail off. "If there was one, why would anyone care to wait to show it off?"

"You're not the only one in the video. This isn't some random fucking scene of you handling yourself. I asked if you were with Maddoc. Supposedly, this video tells a different story. It's you with the Brayshaws, all three of them."

Fuuuuck.

I bury my face in my hands and Bass lets out a low whistle.

"So it could exist?"

"It's not what it sounds like ... exactly." That's when it hits.

Shit!

I rush down and right when I do the crowd freaks out, my bet's hand is raised as he's announced winner.

I turn back to Bishop and hold out my hand.

Concern lines his brows as he slaps a grand in my palm.

"Look," I start. "If the video's real, it's more than what you're hearing. It can't be seen."

"Why not?" He narrows his eyes, way too fucking smart to even consider this is about embarrassment.

"There's more to it than the obvious."

Bass doesn't like that answer, but he knows it's as good as he'll get.

"I gotta get people paid, but I'll talk to my boy some more tonight, find out what all he knows. You gonna tell them?"

"Tell them what, Bass?" I pocket my money. "That I heard a rumor?"

"They don't need your protection, Rae." He eyes me a minute, and I'm surprised he's in favor of me telling them. "If anything, maybe you need theirs."

I brush his words off. "Thanks for telling me about this. Talk to you at school."

He nods and walks off while I go back the way I came, stressing out on what to do.

So, there's a video of me and the guys that night at the cabins. Which means we were caught on tape breaking and entering into the fucking Graven cabin. If this gets out, it'll cause major problems for the boys. This could ruin everything.

They'd get arrested and their dad would flip his shit. The Graven cop could maybe fuck with them in there. Captain's visitation with Zoey will be taken away and they'll lose their fucking season, Maddoc won't be picked up to play in college like I have a feeling he wants to.

"Raven Carver."

I jolt at the call of my name, spinning around to find a fist already flying.

My face hits the dirt in the next second, then a boot connects with my ribs, but it's the blow to my head that has my eyes rolling back and darkness taking over.

There's shouting coming from somewhere, but I can't focus, my head's fucking spinning.

Footsteps hit the ground in the distance, growing closer and closer as the screaming gets louder, but before they reach me, a rushed hiss hits my ear, "You don't belong with them."

And then they're gone.

I'm lifted into someone's arms in the next second.

"Shit, do we take her to the hospital?" a male asks.

"No! She's in the system, we have to keep her off the books." I recognize the female voice.

"Well, what do we do with her?" the guy asks, and my eyes fight to open as I'm lowered onto the seat of a car.

"I know where to take her. Just ... drive before those dudes come back."

I squeeze my eyes closed a few times, and finally, they open a bit, but everything is a little blurry.

"Stop trying to open your eyes, Raven. You probably have a concussion."

My forehead wrinkles. "Victoria?" I rasp and she scoffs.

"Yeah. I know, not sure why I'm helping you either."

A laugh fights its way out, but I hiss from the pain, my head or ribs, not sure what's worse. "Where we going?"

"You know."

I start shaking my head, but her hands grab the sides of my face to hold me still.

"Stop fucking moving. And as if I would take you anywhere else and deal with the aftermath of that. No thanks."

"Fuck," I groan, and it has nothing to do with the pain of my body.

A few minutes pass, and I'm jolted when the car is thrown into park.

"We're here—" She starts but cuts herself off and yells, "Shit, they're running!"

I blink several times to see all three guys flying down the porch, each going to a different door. Mine's thrown open, while the others are yanked out of the car.

"What the fuck!" Maddoc growls loudly, his eyes horrified as they travel over my face. He goes to grab the hem of my shirt, where a huge muddy shoe mark sits, but I smack his hand away and he starts shaking in rage. His nostrils flare and he reaches for me, but I force myself to sit and push against his chest so I can slowly stand from the car. I use the door as support to steady myself when everything blurs. That earns me another glare from Maddoc.

"Someone better start fucking talking, right now!" My eyes snap wide when that comes from Captain.

I look his way to see he has a glaring Victoria pinned against her door while Royce has the driver by the collar against his.

"Let them go," I rasp, fighting to swallow past the dirt in my throat. "They just gave me a ride is all."

"Don't fucking lie for them," Royce warns, and I wave him off, hitting the hood.

"Let them go."

Victoria shoves Captain away and flips him off, while the driver keeps his hands up like there's a fucking gun on him.

"Thanks for the ride, but you can get out of here, Mike. I'll walk to the house," Victoria tells him when she sees how nervous he is.

He doesn't make eye contact when I thank him but slides behind the wheel and backs away.

The boys crowd me in the next second.

"What the fuck happened?"

"Nothing." I shrug, struggling not to wince as I do.

"Nothing?" Maddoc gets in my face. "Nothing. Your face is busted, and I'd bet your ribs are fucked too. You trying to tell me you fell?"

Forcing a hardness I don't feel, I glance between the three. "I fought tonight."

"Raven—" Victoria goes to step forward, but I snap my head to her, my hand shooting to my temple as I do to dull the ache.

Don't say anything...

She swallows and looks to the ground, but the guys aren't dumb.

"You're lying," Maddoc accuses, but when I pull the money from my pocket and throw it in his face, he's not so sure.

He frowns at the cash as it blows across the dirt.

Royce starts picking it up, then hits it against his hand. "We told you no fighting. If you needed money, you should have asked!"

"Don't act surprised." I lift my chin in challenge, lying through my teeth, and fight not to feel two feet tall when each one looks at me with absolute disappointment.

I don't want to disappoint, not them.

The realization has me swallowing past the lump growing in my throat.

"And I'd never ask you for money. You all knew—" I'm cut off when a tiny rice rocket peels through the trees, kicking up dirt behind it.

The boys square up and move to block me, but when I see who jumps out of the car, I let my head hang.

Fuck.

Bass runs forward, his eyes wide in panic as he tries to take in my injuries, but of fucking course, Maddoc rushes him and knocks him back against the hood, his hands wrapped tight around his throat. Bass is a scrapper by nature though, so he slips his arms over Maddoc's hold and drops his weight in his elbow, allowing enough space for him to knock Maddoc across his jaw, forcing his hands to loosen enough for Bass to shove him back an inch.

"You're fucking done!" Maddoc yells in his face and Bass clenches his jaw. "I told your bitch ass if she set foot in that fucking ring again, you were out!"

"The fuck are you talking about?!" Bass screams, getting in Maddoc's face now.

The boys take a half step forward and I grow anxious.

"Her busted up fucking face!" Maddoc shoves him, but Bass stays on his feet. "And ribs, and if any other part of her is wronged, I'll fuck you up!"

"Why the fuck you think I'm here?" Bass shouts back, not

fighting back when Maddoc shoves him once more. "I heard what happened and came to check on her!"

"You weren't there?"

"Yeah, I was fucking there! Running the damn ring like you pay me to do!" Bass shouts then flings a hand my way. "She was ju—"

"Bass!" I shout, cutting him off.

He freezes a second then, a low laugh leaves him as he drops his head back to look at the sky. He shakes his head.

"What the fuck is going on here?" Maddoc booms.

Captain pushes against Victoria who glares up at him. "What happened tonight?" he demands, and she scoffs, turning the other way.

"Please, buddy. I know this game."

Captain glares at her then me.

I look back to Bass.

"Come on, girl. Don't do this shit." He shakes his head, his eyes solemn. He won't rat on me, but this is his livelihood. I can't fuck him over for personal gain.

I sigh and go to lick my lips but hiss when it stings.

I look to Maddoc openly.

"You were jumped." He figures it out, his tone full of complete and total shock.

I nod, running my tongue over my teeth, the taste of copper from my bleeding gums has me frowning.

"Wait, seriously?" Royce shouts.

"You know who it was?" Maddoc demands.

"I have an idea." I glance at Bass.

He frowns but then his wheels start spinning, his eyes widen.

"Did your boy know I was coming to talk to you tonight?" I ask him and he curses.

"I told him you might." Bass looks to the three angry guys at my sides. "Honestly, I didn't think you'd show."

I snatch the money Royce has of mine in his hands and hold it out to Victoria.

She frowns looking from it to me.

I sigh. "Just take it, and please don't say anything."

"I don't need your fucking money to keep my mouth shut."

I grin. "I know. But I want to give it to you. This is me thanking you for tonight. You didn't have to run over and scare them off, but you did, and you brought me here. Thanks."

She eyes the hundreds and I can see the need in her stare, but her pride is keeping her from taking it, especially with them watching.

I wink and stuff it in my pocket, and she nods before heading down the dirt road. I'll give it to her tomorrow when no other eyes are on us.

I blink a few times, grabbing my head and Maddoc steps closer. I look up and his forehead creases, his fingers moving to trail across my cheek making me wince.

His face falls. "Baby, who did this?" he whispers and something inside me thaws. I lean into his touch.

I try to clear my throat but fail. I look to Bass who frowns at the two of us.

"Come back in the morning. You'll come in and we'll talk."

"Breaking all the fucking rules, huh, RaeRae?" Royce glares at Bass.

I don't say anything as I walk away and head upstairs, and what do you know, three sets of feet follow me all the way to my room.

I ignore them as I move around slowly, grabbing fresh clothes.

"Raven."

"Just stop. It's nothing."

"It's not nothing!" Maddoc booms and I jolt, the sound making my head pound more. "You—"

I spin around. "I got jumped! Big. Fucking. Deal. It happens. Often where I'm from actually."

"It doesn't happen here," he growls, his chest heaving. "And it will not happen to you."

"My mom's done worse, big man. I can handle it."

"You shouldn't have to!"

"I don't live in a world like yours. I come from a different fucking place. There is no such thing as enough precautions where I live. You're never fully prepared. There are possibilities and then there's reality. Reality is always worse. This." I point to my face. "Is what happens in my world. Just because you say you put some sort of protective shield around me doesn't mean it fits. Stop trying to pretend I blend. I don't! Your world or mine, it means nothing! I'm still me!"

"None of this would have happened if you wouldn't have taken off tonight!"

"Maybe not today, but probably the next!" I shout back. "When someone wants you jumped, they catch you anywhere."

"That's not the fucking point!"

"Then what is?!" I scream.

"They could have hurt you for real!"

"Who cares!"

"I do," Maddoc shouts right as the other two say, "We do."

"I..." I trail off, having no clue what to say.

My chest constricts, the pain in my ribs and the pain coming from somewhere completely different making it hard to breathe.

Maddoc creeps closer to me, the veins in his neck throbbing against his skin. "Next time you pull—"

A bitter laugh escapes me, and he clamps his mouth shut.

For a second there I thought maybe there was more going on here, but he just needed a minute to get to the threat.

There's always a threat to follow.

"You'll what, huh? Ruin me. Break me. Because been

there, done that. The worst you could do is kill me, and even that will be a cakewalk compared to the shit I've lived. You wanna be pissed, fine. Wanna act out for things not going your way. Cool. But don't pretend to give a shit about what happens to me when the real concern is your pretty little plan and the kinks I'll cause in it. You fucking brought me here. Don't forget that."

Maddoc's murderous glare burns through my skin, but I don't falter. I stand like I'm strong when really I need to hit the warm shower to wash away self-hate.

He looks over his shoulder at his brothers, both standing nice and quiet like good fucking boys – too bad I know their silence is worse than words.

He doesn't say anything yet still both leave the room.

Maddoc slowly makes his way toward me and I steel my spine, but he sees it, feels it even, the fight leaving me. My need for him that I refuse to voice right now but want just the same. Somehow he knows it, though.

He grabs my fingers gently, like he's afraid they may be hurt too and pulls me toward the shower in his room. He closes and locks the door, moving to get the water going.

He undresses then helps me do the same. Dropping to his knees, he kisses my stomach lightly as he unbuttons my jeans and slides them down until I can step out.

He stands, running the back of his fingers over my cheek. He nods his head, motioning for me to go first, so I do.

I step into the shower, wincing as the warm water first hits the cuts on my face. I still haven't looked in the mirror, but I never do until after the dirt is gone. I don't like to see who I am staring back.

At least the cuts and bruises feel like part of the process, a few steps closer to freedom. It's the steps before them I like to pretend don't exist. The fighting, the attacks, the abuse.

One way or another, my skin is marked negatively at the

hands of others. The saddest part is nine times out of ten it's my own doing. A snide remark to my mom or decision I know she'll rage from. A fight I took or a shortcut home through claimed territory.

A solo trip to the warehouse...

Truth is, my world is a little more like the boys' than I admit.

They have separate schools, separate social systems and family standings that need to be followed, and I have a town divided into sides – North Side and South Side. You're born into one, loyal to no others.

Unless you're me, born to the whore in Gateway Trailer Park, the only area on the outside of the clearly drawn lines – who doesn't play by the rules and services both sides, knowing her problems roll over into mine.

She fucks someone over, they come looking for me, knowing I'll deliver. They probably think I do it for her, but I don't. I do it to keep peace for me so that I'm still alive when I finally get to run.

I stopped caring what happened to her years ago. My main goal in life is to be somewhere she won't be able to find me, and not in some fucking system where a paper trail will lead her sorry ass my way should she try.

The door opens and Maddoc slips inside, and it's not until his hand slowly and gently finds my hips that I take a deep breath. Not until he steps against me, molding my back to his chest, that my muscles relax.

Not until his lips meet my neck that it hits. His touch, it's soothing in the worst way.

The needy way.

The stupid girl way.

The kind that makes me want to keep his hands on me, and not just tonight.

His grip to my chin is a soft demand as he directs my eyes

up so I can meet his over my shoulder. His gaze roams my face, his fingers following the trail they take.

I close mine, allowing him to inspect the damage, somehow knowing it's something he needs to do to calm himself.

"Raven..." My name leaves him as a distressed whisper and I open my eyes, locking onto his.

I should kick him out, cut the cord quick. Nothing good could come of this.

Instead, I slide my fingers into his hair and pull his lips to mine.

His fingers glide down my hip bone until he's cupping me.

When his fingers start to swirl, I drop my head against his shoulder, and his lips move to skim over my skin. "I need to make you feel good," he whispers against my throat. "Let me."

A shiver runs through me despite the warm water running over my body.

He glides the palm of his hand over my chest and just like he wanted, my nipples rise to attention, begging for his mouth to close around them, and he doesn't disappoint.

Still half behind me, he bends forward, flicking his tongue across the sensitive flesh until I'm panting against him, then his mouth comes down, his tongue swirling around before he sucks and moves to do the same to the next.

The hand on my pussy slides lower, and right when his middle finger slips inside me, his free hand comes up to pinch my nipple.

I clench around him as he works me from the inside, adding a second finger as he does. He pulls on my nipple, his grip creating a vibrating motion until my body starts to quake.

A deep moan makes its way up my throat and he captures it with his mouth. When he tries to pull back, I don't let him. I grip his hair and force him to let my tongue in, fucking his while I ride his palm.

He feels when I'm close and yanks away, moving to nip at

my left nipple while still twisting and pulling on my right. The speed of his fingers increases to where all I can do is fight not to fall over as I come apart.

I come for him and he hums his approval against me.

We stand there, his fingers still inside me, my body slouched against his until the water runs cold.

Chapter 46

RAVEN

Bass is hanging up his phone when I finally make my way down the next evening. I stayed in bed all day nursing some killer ass aches. Cap meets me at the landing with some more Ibuprofen and a bottle of water while Royce holds out two shot glasses.

"She needs painkillers, not that shit right now."

I take the pills Captain gives and pat him on the shoulder before taking the shots from Royce's hands. I hold them up. "I kinda need both right now."

I quickly down both shots back to back. I take the open seat next to Bass, while Maddoc stands and Royce and Captain drop on to the couch.

Bass nods, looking me over. I spent an hour in the bathroom, working with what I had to cover up most of the mess – another trick I learned from my mom. "You good?"

"Fine." I eye him and he frowns. "You told me to come out last night and this happened. Who else knew?"

"Just my guy."

"What fucking guy?" Maddoc growls.

I consider my words carefully. If I mention the video, they'll go all out-revenge mode and get screwed in the end.

"Bass said someone called him talking about causing trouble for me."

Bass's features tighten, but he doesn't throw me under the bus.

Maddoc's eyes narrow, searching for a lie.

He won't see it. I can hide the truth behind omission like a champ, especially when I have no choice. Especially if it means protecting them.

"Who is he?" Royce demands, leaning forward in his seat.

"Name's Benny." Bass looks from me to the guys, like he's trying to decide what he can and can't say in my presence.

But if I hadn't already put two and two together, he threw it out last night anyway when he said Maddoc pays him.

The guys are behind the fighting at the warehouses. It's why they want me to stay away and why they can't be seen doing business there. It's illegal as shit and they can't afford that right now.

Which is also why the video can't see the light of day.

"He's a nomad, gets in where he fits in."

"Meaning he's loyal to no one but himself," Maddoc adds.

I shrug and his stare slices to me. "It's natural for people who don't belong. Self-preservation."

Maddoc's glare shifts back to Bass and they start talking who he is and what he's about, but I tune them out. I got their conversation going, purposefully so. But I already figured out who's running the playbook.

Once I woke up and the fog of last night disappeared, the answer was obvious.

I heard what that last asshole said to me before he ran off, and it's no damn coincidence the same exact words were just spoken to me by another.

Collins Graven is a real piece of work.

He laid down his little bread crumbs, whispered to the right people in order to get the information to Bass. All he had to do from there was have him tailed and wait for me to come around. I bet he's real proud he got me on Brayshaw ground, too.

He hinted he had something on me when he cornered me in the bathroom the other day, but I didn't think he'd go and have me jumped to force my attention.

I know Captain's eyes are on me, but I don't dare look. He's too perceptive in his nurturing nature.

I pull the joint from my hoodie pocket and wave it around so nobody freaks out when I stand and exit the room.

They keep talking and I slip onto the porch, letting my legs dangle over the side as I stare at nothing in the dark trees.

Just as I'm blowing out my first hit, Captain drops beside me.

"What are you up to?"

When I don't say anything, he sighs. "Don't fuck this up, Raven." I go to shake my head, but he keeps talking. "You don't understand what you being here is doing for us."

"Cap ..." I close my eyes, wishing he'd stop talking.

"Please," he begs, not even knowing what he himself is asking for.

He has no clue something is being held over their heads by the very same person who had me jumped. The truth is I have no damn idea if the video Collins has is enough to take down a Brayshaw, let alone three.

It could have little or immense consequences for my boys. The fact of the matter is I'm not willing to leave it to chance. Not when I know how I can fix it.

It's why when he says, "We'll figure it out. Together," I play dumb.

My leg starts bouncing, and a sickness swims inside me, making me queasy. Tears prick the back of my eyes. "I don't know what you're talking about, Cap."

He hesitates before standing and pulling me to my feet so he can gently wrap me in a hug. "This is where you're meant to be. You're a part of us, that means we handle our problems as a team."

He slowly steps inside, and the first tear falls without permission.

I warned them I'd cause trouble. I didn't even have to try, and it fell at my feet anyway, as always.

I wish I didn't run on impulse. I wish I could stop and think a little longer, but my brain doesn't work that way. I can't be controlled or convinced.

Warnings and threats go right over my head and every action taken is for one reason and one reason only.

Because I want to, consequences be damned.

They'll be angry, but I can't worry about that.

I have to stop this, and I know exactly how to do it.

I knock on the door, turning to look over my shoulder as I do.

I know the second I split through the trees, they came looking. Three engines fired up and screams filled the orchard as they called my name over and over, curse after curse until finally, they sped off down the street. But I ran through the alleyways until I hit the neighborhood across the bridge.

My lungs feel like they're caving in and my head is pounding, but this can't wait.

It's the last place they'd come searching, at least tonight.

I'm not new to this shit, so I know this, what I'm about to do, is only the beginning, which is strange since it also seems a lot like the end.

The thought shouldn't leave such a void in my chest. Yet here I stand, appearing strong and tall and so damn sure of my next move when for the first time, there's a shrieking cry in the back of my head, begging me with all its got to turn back, to go to them.

To trust Maddoc could fix this and believe he'd want to.

But again, I'm not new to this and I know how this goes. I know I have to stay standing where I am until the threat is gone.

I already know it won't be cat and mouse, it'll be the snake and the savage, a game of street smarts versus dollar signs.

The thing about the streets though, no price is too high, no bid too low.

We make it happen, get what we want no matter the cost. And I'm not talking money.

The door opens slowly, a weary look on his face as he scans the area behind me.

"Only me."

He relaxes when he's satisfied with my answer and leans against the doorway. "Then what can I do for you, Brayshaw?"

Pressure hits my chest, but I fight to hide it.

"I want the video and every backup copy you've made gone."

He pretends not to know what I'm talking about for a moment, then nods slowly. "What'll you give me for it?"

His arrogance tells me he knows he's locked me in, yet still, I'm the one that holds the key. Fact is, I could walk away right now and the upper hand he's counting on would be as good as gone, but even if I did, he'd still come out on top. The video would still be his to do with as he pleases, and I can't accept that.

I swallow the bile in my throat and say a silent prayer if such a thing exists that I can stomach what comes next. "The only thing you're willing to take in exchange."

His frown is instant. "Just like that."

"Just like that." For them.

His slow, malicious smirk appears as he opens the door farther and steps back. "Come on in, Rae. Let's have a chat."

I step through the entryway, knowing when I step out, I'll have given up everything I didn't know I wanted until recently while becoming the one thing I knew I never thought I'd be.

My mother's daughter.

They'll think I'm disloyal, a con or a liar, and that's almost enough for me to turn around and run. But that would be selfish when I can help them, easy. And the only thing they have to lose in the process … is me.

Moisture fights for a place in my eyes, but I blink it away with a final thought.

I'm sorry, boys.

Quick note from the author

O.M.G!!!!! I can't BELIEVE this baby is in your hands!!! This book has been screamed at me for sooo long and the fact that it's out in the world for you to enjoy (hopefully LOL) I can't even! And you guys ... there is sooo much more to come!!! Consider this the jump start to an EPIC journey of WTF!

Now, are you ready to read book 2???!!!

READ BOOK TWO,
TROUBLE AT BRAYSHAW HIGH,
RIGHT NOW!

Find book on Amazon today!

Want to be notified about future books releases of mine?

Sign up for my Newsletter today @ www.meaganbrandy.com

Quick note from the author

Be the FIRST in the know and meet new book friends in my Facebook readers group. This is a PRIVATE group. Only those in the group can see posts, comments, and the like!!

Facebook Readers Group @ Meagan Brandy's Reader Group

Stay Connected

Head over to www.meaganbrandy.com or search Meagan Brandy on any of the platforms listed:

Amazon
Instagram
Facebook
Twitter
Pinterest
Bookbub
Goodreads

More from Meagan Brandy

Boys of Brayshaw High
Trouble at Brayshaw High
Reign of Brayshaw
Be My Brayshaw
Break Me

FAKE IT 'TIL YOU BREAK IT

Fake.

That's what we are.

That's what we agreed to be.

So why does it feel so real?

I thought it would have been harder, convincing everyone our school's star receiver was mine and mine alone, but I was wrong.

We played our parts so well that the lines between us began to blur until they disappeared completely.

The thing about pretending, though, someone's always better at it, and by the time I realized my mistake, there was no going back.

I fell for our lie.

And then everything fell apart.

It turned out he and I were never playing the same game.

He didn't have to break me to win.

But he did it anyway.

FUMBLED HEARTS:

He's the persistent playboy who refuses to walk away. I'm the impassive new girl with nothing left to give.

Things are about to get complicated...

After months of refusing, I finally agreed to make the move to Alrick Falls. My family thought it was best - that a new scene would be good for me—and I was sick of having the same conversation.

So here I am, and the plan is simple. Smile through each day and avoid her at all costs.

It's perfect.

Until the cocky quarterback comes into play.

The last thing I want is his crooked grin and dark brown eyes focused on me.

Yet here he is, constantly in my space, pushing me, daring me to care. Telling me what I think and feel, as if he knows.

He doesn't know anything. And I plan to keep it that way.

More from Meagan Brandy

DEFENSELESS HEARTS:

After months of silence, here she stands on my front porch, waiting to be let in again. But it's the same play every time, and I know how this ends - I give her all I have and she carries it with her on the way back to him.

I should turn her away, but I won't. Couldn't do it if I tried.

Because no matter how many times she pops back up, pulls me in and drags me under, it will never be enough. I'll always want more.
    More of her.
    More for us.

And she'll always choose him.

WRONG FOR ME:

They say to keep your enemies close, but 'they' never had to deal with the likes of Alec Daniels, the broody bad boy next door who loved to make my life a living nightmare...up until the day he disappeared.

See, Alec was a thief.

He stole my happy.
    My sanity.
    My first kiss.

I told myself I was glad the day he went away, and I'm reminded of why not five minutes after his sudden and unexpected return.

More from Meagan Brandy

Now he stands before me with a heavy glare and hard body.

But those greedy green eyes, they're darker than I remember, and brimming with a secret...

A secret I didn't discover until it was far too late.

Because this time, he didn't steal a simple kiss.

This time... Alec Daniels stole my all.

Find these titles on Amazon!

Playlist

Amen – Halestorm
Sorry Not Sorry – Demo Lovato
F*ck With U – Pia Mia, G-Eazy
Ghetto – August Alsina
Bad Intentions – Niykee Heaton
Fuck Apologies – JoJo
Bad Bitch – Bebe Rexha
Bad Things – Machine Gun Kelly
Some Kind of Drug – G-Eazy
I Fall Apart – Post Malone

Acknowledgments

I have never been more terrified for a release!! No joke!!

Down to the very last second of now or never, I was making changes and the end game ... good GOD! Every frustrated moment. Every deleted and rewritten word was SO worth it! The book is a thousand times more than what it was at the start. And I have so many to thank for it!

First, as always, to the man of my house, thank you! This book took so much, especially in the end when the polishing time came. All my late nights in, you were amazing! Thank you for being the best dad ever and making sure our bambinos didn't feel my extra hours in front of the screen! As always ... they call it chaos, we call it family.

Thank you to my editor, Ellie, for cleaning out up my mess of words at a moment's notice! Thank you so much for being flexible and sorry I was a pain in the ass, but I hear most get used to it! lol

Virginia, you're awesome! Thank you so much for putting the final gloss on my baby! Look forward to working together again!

My irreplaceable alphas, Stefanie Pace and Kelli Mummert! Girls. You never fail me (Stef, you're cringing at that *italicized* word, aren't you? LOL). Thank you both so much for being my safe place. I always know I can drop my raw AF words in your lab and fear no judgment. Thank you for being a part of my forever team!

Lisa S., who is still my Cali twin, I very much enjoy your constant badgering for more. Keep it up, girl. It motivates me more than you realize!

Next, my BISH, Melissa Fucking Teo. Thank you for being you and consistently going out of your way to back me up! Without your excitement, my fear would run deeper! Thank you for taking that load for me. I have to say it again because it's forever true ... you are THE reader every author would love to have, and I am beyond honored to have you as a friend. You my Bish.

Now, to thank a person who transformed this book without even realizing it. One day, she saw a post about BOBH and started stalking me relentlessly. Every post, she commented first. Every time our boys were mentioned, she was right there to get in on it. So, I mean, I HAD to ask her to BETA, right? LOL. I didn't know what to expect from her as far as feedback, and let me tell you, it was quite honestly the best decision I have ever made as an author. She is one in a million and I already begged to keep her. I heard every single word she said, because they were valid and constructive. She loved it at 102k and it now sits at 113k. She challenged me to challenge myself and the end result ... I am so blown away at what even I was able to accomplish with her hand. So, thank you, Sarah Grim Sentz, for your honesty and support of BOBH. It truly wouldn't be what it is without you! #braygirlforlife

To my review team and everyone who has helped spread the word, THANK YOU! I'm so honored you want to be a part of this crazy journey!

And to my readers, you taking the time to read Boys of Brayshaw High is appreciated more than you will ever know. I hope you enjoy this new world as there is so much more to come from it!

About the Author

Meagan Brandy is USA Today and Wall Street Journal best-selling author of New Adult romance books. She is a candy crazed, jukebox junkie who tends to speak in lyrics. Born and raised in California, she is a married mother of three crazy boys who keep her bouncing from one sports field to another, depending on the season, and she wouldn't have it any other way. Starbucks is her best friend and words are her sanity.

Printed in Great Britain
by Amazon